W9-BYK-353

Feels Like Falling

Feels Like Falling

Kristy Woodson Harvey

THORNDIKE PRESS
A part of Gale, a Cengage Company

This book is a work of fiction. Any references to historical events, real people, or real places are used fictitiously. Other names, characters, places, and events are products of the author's imagination, and any resemblance to actual events or places or persons, living or dead, is entirely coincidental.

Thorndike Press® Large Print Core.
The text of this Large Print edition is unabridged.
Other aspects of the book may vary from the original edition.
Set in 16 pt. Plantin.

LIBRARY OF CONGRESS CIP DATA ON FILE.
CATALOGUING IN PUBLICATION FOR THIS BOOK
IS AVAILABLE FROM THE LIBRARY OF CONGRESS

ISBN-13: 978-1-4328-7846-7 (hardcover alk. paper)

Published in 2020 by arrangement with Gallery Books, an imprint of Simon & Schuster, Inc.

Printed in Mexico
Print Number: 01 Print Year: 2020

To my forever friend and partner in crime,
Kate McCanless McDermott,
who introduced herself by cutting my hair
the first day of kindergarten.
The rest is history.

Chapter 1

Gray: Perfect Island Blonde

I had always been a planner. My calendar was filled a year in advance, vacations chosen from a well-curated spreadsheet of bucket list destinations ranked in order of interest, and my son's potential summer camp options were mapped out for the rest of his childhood, categorized by activity and color-coded by region. My company's succession plan should I (a) die, (b) retire, or (c) never return from one of the aforementioned bucket list vacations had been detailed since the day I filed for my first LLC.

Needless to say, when my startup took off, and I got married, had my son, and bought my dream house all in very short order, I thought my hard work had been worth it. The hours spent goal setting, evaluating, strategizing, and visualizing had come to fruition, bloomed into the beautiful garden that I had been seeding, sowing, and watering for the past several years. I thought I had this adulting thing in the bag. I thought I was set.

Life had other plans.

I put the car in park, took a deep breath, and stepped out. The heat rose from the asphalt of the parking lot as I hoisted my rattan beach bag onto my shoulder. Cicadas sang in the tall sea oats, and the dunes in front of the beach club rolled like hills, their valleys revealing a spectacular view of the ocean. The hazy sky went pink, yellow, or orange depending on where I looked, blending to a seamless blue over the ocean at the horizon line.

I gave my outfit a final once-over in the car's reflection. Large floppy hat, huge Jackie O sunglasses, vintage pareo tied around my neck, and plain but chic flip-flops. I stood up straighter and cleared my throat. It was going to be okay. On a day as spectacular as this, it couldn't help but be. I had gone over the plan at least a hundred times in my head: Park car on the far side of the lot, directly opposite the pool. Exit car and veer left of the octagonal patch of grass visible from the terrace and outdoor dining area. Walk briskly but nonchalantly straight into the protective watch of my best friend, Marcy, who would be waiting for me poolside.

My flip-flops traveled in measured steps across the concrete pavers as *Step on a line, and you'll break your mama's spine* came to mind, reminding me that, always and forever, we are children at heart.

No matter our age, first days back are never easy. I was a grown-up now. I could have avoided this first day. But I refused to hide out in the shadows as though I had something to be ashamed of; I refused to sacrifice a summer at one of my favorite places in the world because of a little scandal. On this opening day at the beach club, members from near and far who called Cape Carolina — this little slice of sandy paradise — home each summer would gather together again for three glorious months by the shore. They would be chattering excitedly, catching up on everything that had happened over the past nine months while they were apart. Suffice it to say, I would be a hot topic.

As I turned the corner, I gave my friendliest wave to the brunchers on the terrace who called out greetings. But I passed by quickly. For every person who would give me a hug in true concern, there were four who would try to gather dirt and then whisper about it behind my back later.

My plan didn't account for the fact that the teak lounge chairs between the terrace and the pool deck were teeming with sunbathers, mimosa sippers, and bridge players.

I had almost passed through unnoticed when Mrs. Jenkins, a remarkably agile octogenarian whom I hadn't seen since the previous summer, jumped up from her chair and stopped me in my tracks. "Gray, darling," she said dramatically, her bright abstract-print caftan blowing in the breeze. "I am so sorry . . ."

Here it was. I nodded in polite recognition and braced myself for the blow. I knew it was inevitable, but I wasn't ready to hear how sorry everyone was about my impending divorce. I knew they were, in their way, even the ones who weren't as charitable about their delivery. But they were also relishing a new scandal to discuss this summer.

But then she continued, "I am so sorry I didn't make it to your mother's funeral, sweetheart. Burl was in the hospital, and I simply could not leave him." She took my hand, making the bangles on my wrist jingle, and I was grateful for my huge, tear-concealing sunglasses. I gave her jeweled left hand an understanding squeeze, my ring finger conspicuously empty in comparison to hers. This was how it was when we came back together, as though the past few months had never happened, were suspended in time. I usually loved that. But this year it meant rehashing things that had happened almost nine months earlier, including my mother's funeral.

"It was a beautiful service," I said. It had been. I had enlisted my favorite florist to make the arrangements nothing short of spectacular. Mom had specifically told me not to waste money on flowers. They weren't a waste, though. They were glorious, the backdrop of the church's stained-glass windows making them even more so. Those flowers brightened one of the darkest days of my life. No one in the church except for Marcy realized that I was grieving the loss of three people. My mother, of course. My husband, who was next to me in the pew but no longer next to me at night. And my sister, whose brand-new husband, Elijah — who, to put it mildly, I believed was a cult leader — had brainwashed her out of our family. To add insult to injury, he had performed the service, per my mother's request. I hadn't had the heart to tell her in her final days that the man she thought had saved her wild child, Quinn, and brought her to Jesus was nothing like he seemed — much less that Greg had left me.

Mom had died in September barely seven months after her February diagnosis, after a swift but valiant battle with a cancer that seemed determined to take her from here, from me, from all of these earthly problems. It was a blessing; I knew that. But it still hurt like hell. She had left when I needed her the very most. I needed her today, to help me face this firing squad head-on.

"It was magnificent," Mrs. Stoddard added, standing up to join us.

I was trapped. The plan had failed. I quickly scanned the property for Marcy, but she was nowhere to be found.

"And congratulations on your sister's wedding," Mrs. Stoddard added, raising her wrinkled hand to shield her face. "I only wish we had been invited," she said lightly.

Wow. I felt like I was getting away with murder. The first dig of the day didn't have to do with Greg. Even still, I couldn't help but imagine everyone around me whispering about my marriage. *If she hadn't worked so much. . . . If she had cared a little more about the man being the man. . . . Did you* see *her travel schedule? . . . Poor little Wagner. . . .* It is the worries that plague us the most that cut the deepest when other people call them to the surface. Because this year had been difficult for my son. He had adjusted remarkably well to his new circumstances, but that didn't keep my shame and guilt from being very real.

If only Greg would agree to the very generous settlement I had offered him, this could all be over, and I would feel so much less self-conscious. Once it was over, it was over. No one would have anything left to talk about. But Greg was turning a simple divorce into a now sixteen-month soap opera by demanding half of my affiliate marketing company, ClickMarket. *My* company, the one I had been building since I was twenty years old. Just thinking about his greed made anger rise in me. He didn't want me, as he had made abundantly clear on our "second honeymoon" last February, three days after I found out my mother had cancer. But he wouldn't let me go either. So I was stuck here, in legal and emotional purgatory, waiting for a bunch of strangers to decide my fate to the tune of $500 an hour.

Deep breath. I reeled myself in and replied to Mrs. Stoddard: "It was such a small wedding. I'm sorry we weren't able to have all our friends there, but Quinn was insistent that our mother see her walk down the aisle, so time was of the essence."

She looked contrite now. "Of course it was, sweetheart. Of course."

They meant well, these ladies. I knew they did. They had seen me through good times and bad, were the first to bring meals when Wagner was born, to throw parties when a celebration was in order. Maybe now they'd want to throw a party for my divorce. Or my thirty-fifth birthday, which was looming large.

Just when I felt myself start to relax, I saw her. *Her.* The twentysomething blonde with the MBA I had hired to be my husband's executive assistant when I had somewhat begrudgingly promoted him to CFO of my company and given him a corner office. It wasn't that I didn't want my husband on my playing field. Greg just wasn't a very hard worker, and everyone except him could see that he didn't deserve to be a part of my C-suite. There were positives to Greg's aversion to work, especially when it came to raising our son, but I'd always had serious qualms about his being a part of my business.

Ironically, his executive assistant was not one of them.

Suddenly I was thankful that these ladies had taken post along my route to the pool.

Though we hadn't specifically addressed the Greg and Brooke situation — thank God — I knew they were abreast of the drama. *Everyone* was abreast of the drama. So I nodded my head slyly toward Brooke as she approached and said, "Mrs. Jenkins, Mrs. Stoddard, would you do me the very large favor of keeping her occupied for a few minutes?"

They laughed delightedly, always glad to be caught up in a scheme.

Brooke was in full makeup, a sundress, and five-inch wedges that seriously slowed her pace. As she called "Gray!" I pretended not to hear her and crossed the final few yards of concrete pavers to the pool gate. Before she could catch me, Mrs. Jenkins and Mrs. Stoddard descended on her with small talk. They were so good; it didn't even seem suspicious. But just when I thought the worst was over, I heard a muffled "how humiliating" from a "friend" as I walked by. I'm sure she thought I couldn't hear her, but I have ears that rival a bat's. So I turned, shot her my most genuine smile, and said, "You have absolutely no idea."

"Oh, no," she stammered. "I wasn't talking about you."

But I was already gone, lifting the safety latch on the iron gate and walking past the elaborate hut with its Bermuda shutters that served as the pool bar. There were a dozen or so sunbathers lounging around the perimeter of the pool, some in full sun and others under the club's black-and-white-striped umbrellas. Children splashed and played in the water. Even in my state, I couldn't help but smile at their joy.

Palm trees swayed above the white wooden cabanas. The trees weren't native to this area, but the club kept them alive by wrapping them through the winter. The view across the pool of the otherworldly blue ocean was transportive, and it made this little oasis in Cape Carolina feel like a tropical mini-vacation. Not that I was eager to return to the tropics after last time.

"Gray," I heard Brooke calling again from behind me, louder than before. *Good Lord, leave me alone,* I thought. I was being immature, I knew. Still unable to locate Marcy, I quickly and calmly removed my sunglasses, hat, flip-flops, and pareo and set them in a pile by the edge of the pool. There was one place I knew Brooke wouldn't follow me. She would never ruin a perfectly good blowout, which, to be fair, I respected.

I had been mature when Greg told me, on our trip to the British Virgin Islands, as we were sipping mimosas on the stern of our boat — still sex-sticky, no less — that he was leaving me. I had been mature when he moved out of my house and straight into Brooke's the day after we buried my mother. I had been mature when they asked to take my only child on a three-week vacation to Europe, which they were leaving for tonight. I was done being mature.

As I heard Brooke's footsteps behind me, I flashed back to the BVIs, to Greg looking me in the eyes and saying, "Gray, you are the mother of my child, and I will always love you. But I think it's time for us to go our separate ways."

Ten years of holding his hand and smelling his particular brand of morning breath and feeling his cold feet underneath our sheets. Ten years of his bad jokes at my office and even worse show tunes in the shower. My husband — the man I had made love to less than thirty minutes earlier, the man who had held my leg in the delivery room, who had stood at the other end of the aisle when I was in a white dress — was out.

Trapped on that boat with Greg, I panicked. I had just found out my mother was sick a few days earlier, and now this? All I wanted to do was flee. Before I could gather my thoughts to respond, before Greg could try to stop me, I climbed onto the side of the boat and dove off into the clearest aqua water. I held my breath, ears roaring from the pressure of my descent. I could feel my hair, which I'd had tinted that perfect island blond for this trip, for this husband, streaming out in a sleek V behind me.

Now, feeling the same primal urge to escape the clutches of Brooke, I raised my arms above my head, bent my knees ever so slightly, and dove gracefully into the deep end. No splash, no fanfare, just a simple, swift motion that united me with the water. I had known that day in the islands that that dive, like it or not, was the beginning of something for me, the start of a new life. Now, as the water covered my streamlined body, it washed away all the things those people on the terrace and the pool deck were saying about me, all those judgments, all the hurt and fear that losing my mother and my husband and, for all intents and purposes, my sister in such short order had caused.

Safe from the noisy world above the surface, I told myself things would get better. I was strong, I was smart, I was proud, and I was worthy of being loved, even if I had forgotten those things during the past few months. My dive, that tiny snapshot of fearlessness, of freedom, did more than set me a pool's length apart from Brooke; it offered a moment of meditation that would propel me forward into a summer of change. There is nothing like the deep, immersive water to cleanse us of even our darkest demons, to wash us whole and set us free, until we can emerge, as I did that day, gasping, reborn into the light.

Diana: Royalty

My brothers and sister and me, we're all named after royalty. Diana, Charles, Elizabeth, and Phillip. But my momma was wrong when she said naming people after royalty would make them grow up to be like royalty. My boyfriend was a case in point.

"Harry, I don't give a damn where you were all night," I said. "All I care about is that you get out of my sight." I threw one more wrinkled shirt into my duffel and put my hand up to my throbbing jaw.

Harry was behind me, his breath stale from the night before, pleading, "But, babe, I'm gonna win it all back. Don't you know your man well enough to know that he's an ace at poker?"

I turned around, so pissed I could hardly speak. "Are you freaking kidding me? An ace? You blew all my money on that poker tournament. You got any damn idea how long it takes to save a thousand bucks? You got any damn idea how I'm going to fix this toothache, now that you spent all my money?"

"Babe, you gotta understand. I can win all that money back like that." He snapped his fingers. "All I need is another hundred to put in down at the bar tonight. I'm feeling lucky."

I hoisted an overstuffed bag over each shoulder and marched to the car. "You're nothing but a drunk and a gambler, Harry, and you can bet your sorry ass I won't be back this time. Good luck finding your hundred dollars."

He was lumbering behind, trying to keep up, trying to get between me and the door of the creaky old Impala that I could've traded in if he didn't keep spending all my money. I shoved him away from the door, slammed it shut, and lit a cigarette.

I shivered at the stained pits of his old T-shirt and the beer belly rolling over the band of his cargo shorts as he leaned against the car, fogging up my window. His hairline had receded since I met him, revealing an oddly red scalp. Harry wasn't ever magazine handsome, but in his day he'd been all right. Some days, when I could get him into a collared shirt, he was even something to look at. Let's just say, Harry hadn't aged gracefully.

Maybe I wasn't some prize pony at the fair either, but I'd kept myself up pretty good. And I figured I'd rather be alone than deal with his crap for the rest of my life. Thank the good Lord I'd had the sense not to marry the bastard. I took a long, slow drag of my Marlboro, feeling it calm my nerves even though the smoke made my throbbing tooth hurt worse. Where was I going to go? I didn't have any family nearby. My girlfriends would take me in in a hot minute, but they'd warned me sideways and backward about Harry from the beginning, given me down the country about dating him. He was worthless. He was no good. I was too proud to admit they had been right.

I sighed and resolved to head to the shelter if I had to. Wouldn't be the first night I'd spent there. Probably wouldn't be the last. "One of us has to go to work!" I shouted through the glass, sounding less intimidating than I would've if my busted window had rolled down. But that ship had sailed around January. "Get out of my way, you moron. I swear to God, I'll run over you. Don't make me do it."

I shifted the car into reverse, ignoring

Harry's muffled whines. The Impala was rattling and shaking, the air-conditioning blasting and the radio up. It seemed right fitting that "Goodbye to You" was playing as I backed out of the short dirt driveway of the tiny house Harry had inherited from his mother, where we'd been living for eight years. People were always asking why Harry and me didn't make it official. Well, this was why.

He was all right. I mean, he was a nice guy deep down, the kind of guy who makes them weepy speeches about how beautiful you are and how he's so lucky he's got you and all that bull. But then you turn around and he's lost his job again, and he got ahold of your savings and blew it at some blackjack table at some casino his friend swears he got rich at. The man just didn't have any sense and that's the God's honest truth of it.

I was forty years old and starting over again. I briefly thought that maybe I should stick with Harry, that the devil I knew was better, that at least I wasn't alone.

But then the tooth pain shot all the way through my ear and reminded me that it wasn't me that should be feeling bad. If it weren't for Harry, I'd be on my way to the dentist right now. If it weren't for Harry, I wouldn't be in all this pain because I wouldn't be flat broke with nowhere to go, praying I could make it through the day at work.

"Morning, Mr. Joe," I said as I walked through the back door of the fluorescent-lit local pharmacy for another long day on my feet in the photo lab. The job at Meds and More made me a living, yeah, but it sure wasn't what I'd dreamed of back when I was a kid and my momma said that anybody named Diana'd grow up to be a princess.

"You all right there, D?" Mr. Joe asked. He was about the nicest manager you could ever hope to have. He was an inch shorter than me, kind of round, with a nice head of hair even though he was in his early fifties. The thing I liked best about him was that the blue shirts he wore tucked into his khaki pants were always pressed. Either he was good at ironing or he had some kind of generous girlfriend because I knew his wife had died a while back.

I nodded and tried to smile but ended up wincing instead. "My tooth is hurting something fierce again. I'd saved up all the money to get a root canal and whatnot, but that damn Harry found my stash and blew all my money in a poker tournament."

Mr. Joe looked real nervous, and I said, "Now, don't you worry. I'll get me something back in the pharmacy to numb it up enough to get through the day." *And I'll get a bottle from the ABC store to get me through the night,* I thought.

"Now, Diana, I'm not gonna have any of my girls running around in pain all day. You get on to the dentist. I'll cover photo until you get back."

I shook my head. "I can't pay for it anyhow. I'll be all right."

"Look here. Let's you and me go on up to the bank in a few minutes, and I'll see if I've got enough to help you out."

I wanted to refuse, but there wasn't any denying pain like this. I wanted to save that tooth like the dentist said, but at this point there wasn't any choice but to pull it. Even that'd be a couple hundred bucks. I nodded and pulled Mr. Joe into me. "I can't stand it anymore. You know I'm good for it."

He smiled proudly and said, "I got your back." Then he added, "Hey, D. Don't you know a good girl like you could do a whole hell of a lot better than somebody like that Harry?" Then he looked down at his feet. "I know people aren't supposed to say things like that, but I've sat around here and watched him hurt you about long enough now. I'd say it's time to move on."

I nodded, suddenly feeling sick to my stomach from being in so much pain for so long. I took a deep breath, put my hand on my jaw again, and said, "Mr. Joe, think we might be able to go right now? I can't make it much longer."

Mr. Joe led me to the car, and I swear I don't much remember the rest of it. Next thing I knew, I was crying I was so happy because that tooth was numb. I couldn't bear to put my tongue there, on that big hole in my mouth. I'd sworn up and down that I wouldn't be like my momma, I wouldn't just get my teeth pulled and get some dentures later on. But I'd sworn a lot of things that didn't really pan out these last forty years.

"I'm real sorry, Doc," I said. "I wanted to save that tooth like you said, but I don't have any insurance."

He had a mask over his mouth, but you could tell by the way his green eyes were sparkling that he was smiling. "It's okay, Miss Diana. I have this new machine I'm testing out that makes crowns, so this one is on the house."

"Crowns . . . Wait . . ." I thrust my tongue back on my molar. My tooth was there! With a crown. Maybe I was a princess after all. My eyes filled up again. "Oh, Doc. You didn't take my tooth out? I promise I'll pay you every last penny and —"

"Diana, you've been a really good patient all these years, and besides, sometimes we all need a little help. You just help somebody else out when you can, and we'll call it even."

I leaned up and hugged him tight. He laughed and said, "You should be as good as new."

I wasn't all that used to somebody really helping me out. I mean, I was always kind of scraping by and whatnot, more used to somebody pushing me down than pulling me up, so this was a nice treat.

He turned back to me and said, "Oh, and Diana?"

"Yeah, Doc."

"This would be as good a time as any to quit smoking."

I groaned. Tomorrow, maybe. Tomorrow I'd quit.

Mr. Joe was in the waiting room, and he jumped to his feet when he saw me. "You okay?"

I smiled as best I could with my cheek all numb. "Good as new. Let's get to it."

My job at the photo lab wasn't a real natural fit for me because I'd never been any good at computers. But it was the only job I could find after the plant I'd been working at closed down a couple years ago, so I took it. I'd probably have looked for a new job if I had time, but, even still, I liked it pretty good. When somebody came to pick up their pictures, it was like I knew them already. We weren't just meeting over the counter. I'd seen their kid's school play and them posing with their momma at her seventy-fifth birthday party. I'd seen some other stuff too, but I'm lady enough to look away and not talk about it to anyone. Well, maybe Harry. I felt a pang in my stomach for Harry. He wasn't a bad guy when you got right down to it. He simply wasn't made of sturdy stock like me.

I looked up from where I was alphabetizing the photos and saw Mr. Marcus, the owner, walking in. He was tall and slender, and you could tell all the suits he wore were expensive. It almost made you laugh to see him and Mr. Joe walking beside each other, like he was a Great Dane and Mr. Joe was a little Chihuahua running alongside to keep up. I sighed under my breath. He was real nice about it, but I was always getting in trouble with Mr. Marcus for doing something or another wrong. Today was no exception.

"Hi, Diana." He smiled.

"Hi, Mr. Marcus," I said, getting up and wiping my hands on my pants. I tried to smile and lisped, "Sorry about my swollen face."

"You're a real hard worker, Diana," he said. "I admire that. Most people would have laid out after having their tooth worked on."

I nodded and said, "Thanks," knowing that my loyalty to the job was the only reason Mr. Marcus kept me around. Well, that and the fact that I'd half raised his kids that year his wife got the harebrained idea to run for Senate.

"Look," he said, "this probably isn't the best time, but you should know that I've had a couple of complaints lately about photo cropping and, you know, people's heads being chopped off."

"I'm real sorry," I said. "The machine just wasn't —"

He put his hand up. "It's all right. Just consider it a warning."

I got back to my alphabetizing but looked up when a pretty girl in a short skirt came in, looking like she just got out of a tennis racket ad with her long skinny legs and blond hair. I wondered what it would be like to be one of those girls, all tan and pretty and lying around by the pool all summer. Probably not too bad. But I'd never know.

"May I help you?"

"Sure. I need to pick up some photos for Howard."

"Got them right here," I said. I knew from the photos that she had a little boy. Blond like her. She had some professional shots of her and the boy on the beach.

I handed her an envelope, and she pulled out the pictures right away. "Oh, they look great," she said, her blue eyes sparkling like she'd looked at the water so long they near turned into water themselves. I guessed it was easy to be sparkly when you didn't have a care in the world.

I nodded, wondering if a picture of her had ever not looked great. "I just need to get a copy of your release for the professional ones," I said.

She bit her lip, perfectly plump and pink without even a hint of lip gloss. "Oh, I have it, I promise. The photographer is a really good friend of mine, and she gave me the thumb drive with all the pictures and a written release."

I didn't mind fighting with Harry, but otherwise I'd never been good at confrontation. And I felt like one was brewing here.

"Okay," I said hesitantly. "Well, in order to let you leave with the photos, I either need a copy of the release or this form signed by the photographer." I handed her a paper from under the counter.

"Look," she said. "I'm having kind of a rough day. Maybe I could bring the release back later? I promise you that I have it."

I wanted to say she didn't know what a rough day was, but I didn't. Mr. Marcus was real particular about those releases, saying we could get sued and all kinds of mess if we didn't have them. My cheek was starting to get some feeling back in it again, and I thought about what the dentist had said: *You just help somebody else out when you can.*

I sighed, the butterflies I always got when I was doing something I wasn't supposed to do fluttering around in my belly, and whispered, "You make sure you bring it back before we close today, okay? Because I could get in real deep trouble for this."

She nodded and smiled. "Thank you so much."

But when she pulled out the professional photos, she frowned.

"Everything good?" I asked hesitantly.

"The color is all wrong on these." She pulled out her phone, opened an e-mail with the photos attached, and held one up to the prints. "The blues of the ocean look black, and Wagner's shirt looks almost green."

"Something the matter, Gray?" I'd had no idea that Mr. Marcus was standing only a few feet behind me.

"These pictures are not right," she said, sounding more than a little testy.

Mr. Marcus's response was soothing, but I could tell he was frustrated and even a little embarrassed. "Don't you worry a bit about that. We'll get that all straight." He paused. "Take the ones you're happy with. On the house. I'll personally drop the others by this afternoon."

Before he even said anything, I knew that soon I'd have all the time I needed to look for a new job.

CHAPTER 2

Gray: Seven-Year Itch

After my impromptu solo diving competition, Marcy, my favorite partner in crime, still hadn't shown up. I pulled out my laptop and tried to get some work done, but I couldn't keep my mind off how miserable I was going to be without Wagner. We had said our pre-trip good-byes that morning because Greg and Brooke were taking him to their house straight from tennis. But I needed one more hug and kiss — maybe two.

I smiled when I saw him talking to his friends in front of the tennis hut — and I realized right away that I had made the right choice stopping by. I mean, sure, the tennis pro was just a kid, but it did my battered self-esteem some good that he did a double take when I walked up.

There's some universal rule that tennis pros must be delicious. I don't mean good-looking. I mean *delicious.* And Wagner's tennis teacher for the summer was no exception.

"Hi," he said as he conspicuously took in the long expanse of leg peeking out from my pareo.

He winked at me underneath his Straits Club sun visor. "So, you here for my class?"

I smirked; his class was the twelve and under clinic.

Before I had a chance to respond, Brooke said, "Excuse me." I struggled to keep from rolling my eyes.

I eyed the tennis pro to see if he thought she was as hot as my husband apparently did, but he barely glanced her way as he told her, "Moms can watch if they want, but don't feel like you have to hang around."

Wagner ran up to me excitedly and said, "Mom?" and then looked over his shoulder, making sure that nobody had seen. "What are you doing here?"

I ran my hand through his shaggy hair, controlling my impulse to lean over and kiss him. "I missed you already."

Much to my surprise, Wagner squeezed me tight and kissed me on the cheek. He must have needed one last hug and kiss too.

The tanned, racket-wielding man-child to my left looked from Brooke to me and said,

"Wait, you mean you're his *mother*?" Then he laughed. "No way. What, did you have him when you were twelve?"

It was the absolute best-case scenario. I mean, he would be getting a tip so large at the end of the summer that he could retire.

"I'm Wagner's soon-to-be stepmom," Brooke announced, wiggling the fingers on her left hand. I couldn't help but notice that my engagement ring had been much bigger, which was ironic since Greg had so much more money now. He probably didn't want to invest as much in this one in case he decided to trade her in for a newer model too.

Andrew looked at Brooke blankly and said, "Great. I can already tell he's an awesome kid."

"Hey, Mom, I'm going to go warm up," Wagner said.

"I'll be watching!"

"Me too," Brooke called behind, before turning her attention back to the pro. "Andrew, when should I come back to pick up Wagner?" She shot me a look. "I was trying to ask you this morning, *Gray,* but I couldn't get your attention."

"What? I didn't even see you," I lied.

She raised one eyebrow. "You're a beautiful swimmer," she said pertly, as if she didn't want to compliment me but couldn't help it.

When your big brother drowns when you're a baby, your parents' life mission is to make sure you and your sister are expert swimmers. I almost said that just to see her reaction, but it felt like overkill. I wondered if she already knew about Steven. I wondered what else she knew about me, what secrets I had shared with Greg that this total stranger was now privy to.

This afternoon Brooke and Greg were taking Wagner to Raleigh, where we lived the rest of the year, and then off to France, Italy, and Spain for three weeks on their first "family" trip. As if trying to take my company from me weren't enough, he had to take my child away for nearly a month too.

"Brooke," I said, "we need to go over a few last-minute details before the trip."

Her smile was so self-satisfied that this time I couldn't control my eye roll. "I sent you all the travel details this morning. Did you not see them? And I got the bags you packed and the lists you sent." She paused and put a hand on my shoulder. "Gray, I promise you. I will take the best care of him in the world. I won't let him out of my sight."

I fought the urge to shrug her hand off my shoulder, but I had to admit her assurances did make me feel better. I mean, I still thought she was the devil. Even so, I knew she would take care of Wagner.

The tennis pro, witnessing the whole awkward exchange, looked from Brooke to me again and said, "So, wait. If she's the soon-to-be stepmom, does that mean that you aren't married . . . ?"

He paused, and I said, "Gray. My name is Gray. And I am very, very close to being not married, God willing."

Andrew laughed, and Brooke pursed her lips. It was obvious that she knew she should walk away but wanted to see what would happen next. "In that case," he said, "can I take you out sometime?"

I nearly doubled over with laughter, and Brooke, clearly unable to help herself, said, "You can't be serious."

He looked to her again and said, "You can pick Wagner up at noon."

She flushed and finally turned to walk away.

When Brooke was out of earshot, I smoothed my wet hair down my back and said, "Okay, okay. I see what's happening here, and I appreciate it more than you know. I'll see you around." I turned to walk away, but Andrew grabbed my hand.

"I don't have a clue what you're talking about." For a second the twinkle in his dark-brown eyes mesmerized me, but then I snapped back to reality.

"Asking me out so my replacement could get a taste of her own medicine? That was chivalrous of you."

He looked down shyly and let go of my hand. "Um. No. I mean, I am chivalrous. But I really just want to take you out to dinner."

I eyed him skeptically.

He grinned. "If you don't want to commit to dinner, what about a drink?"

"What are you, twenty? Twenty-two?"

I could see the blush rising up his cheeks. "Twenty-six," he said, clearing his throat. "But, I mean, a couple years' age difference is no big deal."

I burst out laughing again. I guess I was hyperaware of age gaps because of Brooke and the whole divorce thing, but it was a fact that in a matter of months I would hit a large birthday milestone. There was a vast difference between twenty-six and thirty-four.

He shrugged.

Brooke called, "Andrew, the kids are getting antsy. Are we planning to start anytime soon?"

I shook my head and said, "Listen. Thanks. Take care of my kid."

I wanted to yell bye to Wagner, but I knew better. I would embarrass him in front of his cool summer friends, and I had spent too much money on tall socks (the short ones were out), New Balances (the only good shoe brand this summer), and Under Armour everything else (extra points for a smaller, understated logo) to risk mortifying him now.

As I started across the street toward the clubhouse and pool, Andrew called, "I'm serious. I'm going to track you down later today." I glanced back to see him say, more quietly, "I'm impossible to resist."

I laughed and shook my head — but I had a feeling he was right.

Marcy was standing on the sidewalk waiting for me in a linen cover-up with a deep V, the sleeves casually rolled. I could just make out the outline of a teeny bikini underneath.

I threw my hands up as if to say, *So now you decide to show up?*

"What?" She looked truly mystified.

"I felt like I was very specific about meeting here at nine a.m.," I teased.

"You said ten," Marcy said. Then she paused. "Or maybe you said nine, but I knew I would never be up that early so I decided to hear ten. . . ."

I laughed and wondered what it would be like to be that carefree. Marcy was thirty-one, only three years younger than I was, but our lives were so different. She had never been married, had no children, and lived footloose and fancy-free year-round in the waterfront home beside mine that her parents, who lived in Maine, had bought for investment purposes and visited only once a year.

I had been married for nine years, had an eight-year-old son, and had bought my second home in Cape Carolina when I landed the largest client of my career at ClickMarket. *My* company. I was mad all over again.

Marcy pointed toward the tennis courts. "What the hell was that all about?" she asked.

I rolled my eyes, and we made our way toward the beach for one of the long walks that comprised our summer exercise routine. There was nothing I looked forward to more than the sand under my feet, the surf splashing around my ankles. "Wagner's tennis pro asked me out for a drink, but I think he must have been kidding. You know, doing it for effect because Brooke was standing there being Brooke."

Marcy stopped, her hand frozen to the top of the pool gate. "Wait. Brooke was standing there?"

I smiled. "Yeah. It was kind of awesome."

"Gray, the hot tennis pro wants to date you. When God gives, you take. You take and you run and you don't look back."

I smiled. I knew logically that my thirty-fifth birthday wouldn't magically make me old. But I think everyone has a scary age, an age by which they think they are supposed to have it all figured out. For me, it was always thirty-five. And it wasn't scary for a long, long time because I had it all together. And now, only months before my scary age, my perfectly choreographed life had fallen apart. I was back at square one. Barring a miracle, it didn't seem like I was going to have it all back together by October.

We walked through the pool deck exchanging waves with the women already lounging there, watching their kids train for swim team. As our feet hit the warm sand, she said, "But don't you remember it?"

"Remember what?"

"Dating a twenty-five-year-old," Marcy

said wistfully.

I raised my eyebrows at her.

"Oh, right," she said. "You haven't been on a date in a hundred years. How do I always forget that?"

I smirked.

"Seedy bars and karaoke, beer pong tournaments and sleeping on the beach just because you can. Meeting new people, kissing without the expectation of anything more, your stomach flip-flopping over whether he'll text you the next day. . . ."

"So, not nice dinners followed by *20/20*? No neatly hanging your clothes up in the closet and lining your shoes up by the bed before slipping between the pressed sheets trying not to get them wrinkled?"

We both laughed.

To be honest, I had kind of enjoyed the nice dinners and the *20/20*. I thought my seventh year of marriage was amazing, blissful even. Wagner was old enough that having a child wasn't super stressful anymore. Greg was making money, which made him feel like I wasn't the sole breadwinner. ClickMarket was up 20 percent in the first quarter, and I felt like my meticulously edited staff was the dream team. Our friends were fun. The living was easy.

And then the storm broke. Seven years

and eight months into the marriage, and he didn't love me anymore. They call it the seven-year itch for a reason.

I looked down at my pedicured but unpolished toes, nauseated at the mere thought of dipping them back into the dating pool. I sighed. The cellulite-blasting exercises in my Self.com e-mail that morning ran through my mind. "It has only been sixteen months. That's not that long."

"Sixteen months?" Marcy put her finger in her ear and wiggled it around as though she couldn't possibly be hearing this properly. "Sixteen *months*? I've heard after a year you go into spontaneous menopause. Your reproductive organs give up and you get chin hair and it's over."

I couldn't help but laugh, which was something Marcy had been good for since the day we met. The day my now almost ex-husband, Greg, and I closed on our beach house five years ago, Marcy came by with a measuring cup in her hand.

"You need sugar?" I'd asked.

"No," she replied. "Vodka."

I knew right then and there that this girl and I were going to get along just fine.

"Weird that I've decided to get married the year you've decided to get unmarried," Marcy said. "You'd probably have way more time for me now."

I nearly choked. "What? You didn't tell me you met someone!"

She waved her hand as if that was a small detail. "Oh, I haven't. But I've decided I need to get married this year so I can have two kids before I'm thirty-six."

"Why thirty-six?"

She shrugged. "Just what has always been in my head."

I was getting ready to say how impractical that seemed. But Marcy, with legs up to her neck, her perky strawberry-blond ponytail, and not even a sign that a wrinkle was planning to visit her face, would probably find a husband in record time. Plus she was smart and fun and cool. Perfect wife material. If she weren't my best friend, I might have been jealous of her.

"One problem," I said. "Haven't you kind of dated everyone around here who's even an option?"

There were only so many men in Cape Carolina.

"Yeah," she said. "But I figure every eligible bachelor from Raleigh east will be here at some point this summer. So my plan is basically to work even less than normal and spend every spare moment man hunting." She ran her hand through her ponytail.

"I'll need a sidekick."

I laughed, even though my brain had moved on to my to-do list for the day: *Check with marketing to see if the banners are ready for the Design Influencers Conference. Schedule a lunch with the CFO of Glitter. Whittle my unread e-mails to below 250. Sign Wagner up for basketball camp. Send last month's profit-and-loss statements to my attorney.* I lifted my stainless water bottle and clinked it with Marcy's. "To husband hunting," I said. "But just so you know," I added, "husband hunting for me is the last thing I ever want to do again."

We turned as we reached the row of brightly colored houses that was our halfway point.

I had heard — especially from my sister, Quinn — that I should stick my marriage out so Wagner could have as normal a life as possible. The problem is, when your husband walks out that door, there's not one thing you can do about it. Greg was fully immersed in the pleasure zone that was Brooke. I probably should have paid more attention earlier, but when you're growing a media empire and trying to be supermom, it's easy to become caught up in your path to success.

"It's a good thing you've stayed hot,"

Marcy said, getting me out of my thoughts.

I looked at her doubtfully.

As we reached the pool deck again, Marcy refilled our water bottles from one of the large coolers all around the pool while I spread towels on a pair of matching teak loungers for us, folding my cover-up neatly at the bottom of mine. Returning from the cooler, Marcy raised her eyebrows and pointed toward my bathing suit bottoms. "What is that?"

I shrugged. "What do you mean?"

"What's with the high-waisted bikini bottom? You hate those."

"Yeah . . . but they're in, right?" She looked at me skeptically, and I laughed. "Okay. You caught me." I looked around and then whispered, "It covers my ringworm."

Marcy's mouth hung open. "Ew. Ew. And again, ew."

"Wagner found a stray puppy that ended up belonging to one of our neighbors. We gave him back, but not before he gave Wagner ringworm. And Wagner gave it to me."

"Oh my word. I'm rethinking having kids."

I nodded. "Yup. They're vile little beings. He's lucky he's cute." I felt a lump forming in my throat. I cleared it to keep myself from crying. How was I possibly going to make it three weeks without him?

"Are you sure that's what it is?"

I smiled. "I was certain I had some late-onset STD from Greg, so I ran directly to the doctor. He was pretty amused by the whole thing."

"I guess that would have been worse," Marcy said. "But just barely," she added under her breath.

I couldn't help but smile as I caught a glimpse of Andrew, who was opening the gate, out of the corner of my eye. He was even cuter than he'd been earlier, if that was possible, with a line of sweat around his slightly wavy brown hair. I tried to ignore my racing heart as he approached.

"It's just a drink," he said, shrugging. "That's all I'm asking."

I adjusted my ponytail. "You're sweet, Andrew, but I'm really trying not to be that stereotypical divorcée."

He grinned. "So you won't go out with me because of your reputation, but you still think I'm a fox?" He flashed that dimple at me. "Okay, how about this? I promise I won't tell anyone."

"Yeah, Gray," Marcy chimed in, clearly amused. "Just give him a chance."

I shot her a warning look.

"Fine. One drink. Next week. But you

may not take me anywhere even decently nice where I would know a single person."

He laughed. "Oh, believe me, I know just the place."

When he was out of earshot, Marcy clapped approvingly. "Why would you throw all that hotness at some eighteen-year-old who's too drunk to even appreciate those sexy diagonal ab lines peeking over his shorts?"

"He had his shirt on, Marcy."

She leaned her head back and closed her eyes. "Yeah, but you know they're there." She sighed. "Just think, Gray. You two can date for a couple of years, get married, have another baby with those dimples and your eyes. It's all so dreamy."

"I'm having one drink with him and that's it," I said unconvincingly. Weren't you practically required to have a few inappropriate flings in the midst of a divorce? "But get serious. It's not like I'm going to marry the guy, Marce."

She pulled her sunglasses down the bridge of her nose and peered at me from underneath her hat. "Famous. Last. Words."

Diana: Some Kind of Home

I've had the same nightmare since I was eleven years old. It doesn't matter that I'm forty now. Every time I'm too stressed or worried, that nightmare sneaks up on me. And the worst part is that, yeah, it's a dream. But it also happened. I had to live that mess.

The nightmare always starts with Charles talking. Charles, he's the oldest, bless his sweet soul. Charles, then Elizabeth, then me, then Phillip. He was only fourteen when it happened. Elizabeth was thirteen. I was eleven. Phillip was ten. Irish twins. That's what they called Phillip and me.

We were used to being alone. Damn used to it.

Momma had had Charles when she was sixteen. Her parents had thrown her out on the street when they found out she was pregnant, and, as you could probably guess, she didn't make real good choices after that either. Not a one of us knew who our daddy was. Poor Charles, when she was out gallivanting around town doing God only knows what with God only knows who, he'd be trying to figure out something to feed us for dinner, usually cereal. He was just a kid, so young, so handsome, living in the projects and trying to take care of his brother and sisters.

Now, Elizabeth, tiny little thing, she didn't look a day over ten even though she was thirteen, but, thank the good Lord, she couldn't stand a mess. She was always trying to get the house straight when Momma was gone or laid up on the couch. Even once Momma left, she washed up all our clothes every day and made me take a bath so we'd look clean for school.

"That's the most important thing," Charles would say. "None of our teachers can know that Momma's gone."

Pretending didn't seem real hard to me since it'd taken us a good week to figure that Momma was *gone* gone. She was in the habit of disappearing now and then, leaving us alone for a couple days.

"Should we call the police or something?" Elizabeth had asked.

Now, Phillip, he was just sitting over in the corner, real quiet and scrunched up, while me and Elizabeth and Charles got this stuff straight. We knew Phillip wasn't quite like the rest of us, but we didn't have a name for it yet.

"Yeah," I'd said. I missed my momma so bad. Oh, I'll never forget that emptiness way down deep in my soul. She was kind of crazy and she had a habit of running off, but she loved us kids. When she was around she took the best care of us in the whole world. She'd pile us all up in her bed and read library books. She'd try to pull together some sort of dinner for us to all sit around the table together and eat. She always told us how much she loved us. She really was a good momma — except the leaving us, that is. I was trying hard not to cry, but I couldn't help it. I needed my momma. I needed her to brush my hair and hug me and tell me it would be okay.

So I nuzzled up to Elizabeth instead. Some days she would've been real annoyed by that, but not that day. That day she hugged me tight to her side like she would take care of me now.

"No," Charles said, "because if we call the police and they know Momma is gone, they'll take us away and put us in some kind of home or something."

I looked over in the corner. Phillip was rocking back and forth now. It was hard to tell how much he understood, but he knew something was wrong. It made you want to hug him, but you couldn't hug him on account of he'd get real mad and start hitting you.

"Yeah," Elizabeth chimed in, changing her tune on a dime. "And don't say nothing at school. If anybody asks about Momma, you say, 'Oh, she fixed us the best supper last night,' or something like that."

Charles nodded. "Yeah."

Looking back, this was obviously a plan made by a bunch of kids. We had some cans and some cereal in the house, but that was about it. We scrounged up all our money, and Charles walked down to the 7-Eleven to buy some food. Even though it seemed like all the money in the world at the time, it couldn't have been more than ten bucks.

It seemed like we lived that way forever without Momma. We'd get up and Elizabeth made sure we looked tidy and our clothes were clean, and Charles would put Momma's signature on our papers and everything since he had pretty good cursive. Then we'd get on the bus, and we'd come home and we'd lock the door and, when somebody knocked, we wouldn't answer it.

Phillip cried a lot, and Elizabeth and I would try to calm him down. Sometimes we'd put him in front of the TV, but then the TV quit working. And then one day, it must have been a week or two later, we got home and a couple of grown-up ladies were sitting on our couch.

At first I was real excited when I saw people because I figured one of them was Momma. Maybe she'd come back and it'd all be all right.

But it wasn't Momma. Charles tried to

run when he realized what was going on, but the police got him right down the street.

"We only want to help you," one lady had said. She'd seemed nice to me, but Charles had screamed at her, "No, you don't! You want to take us away from each other!"

I remember crying and saying, "Where's my momma?"

Phillip, he'd got real quiet and done that rocking-in-the-corner thing again. Elizabeth, she'd put her arm around me and stroked my hair. She said, "Diana, you just remember that no matter what happens, I love you."

She was so young. Charles too. All of us. So young. She just left us there like a bunch of stray kittens that nobody wanted. If your own momma doesn't want you, who could? To this day, I don't know what happened to my momma. Part of me hopes she's been dead all this time; that's the only explanation that lets me sleep at night. I'm sure I could look into it and find out. I could probably find out who my daddy is too.

But why should I? If Momma got killed in some awful way, it's only going to make me feel bad. And if my daddy didn't want me back then when I was cute and little, he sure as hell doesn't want me now that I'm all grown-up.

After those ladies showed up, I didn't get to see Charles and Elizabeth and Phillip anymore. Foster families, they were all right with taking on one kid, sometimes maybe even two. But nobody was going to take on four, especially with one like Phillip. They'd put him in a facility instead. It took me more than twenty years to find him, just up the road. It was my thirty-second birthday. Finding Phillip was the best gift I've ever gotten, even better than the sparkly shoes the Salvation Army brought over one year at Christmas.

I remember how excited I was, going to see him that first time. I knew he'd be grown-up, but I also expected him to be that same Phillip. I imagined that he'd smile and say he was glad to see me even if he wouldn't look me straight in the eye or anything.

But then I got there, and, oh my Lord, it almost brought me to my knees to see my sweet brother just sitting in that chair and staring into space. I'd tried to talk to him, but he'd just looked at me kind of blank and turned back to the window. You didn't have to be real smart to figure out what was going on.

"What in the hell do you have him on?" I asked the first woman in scrubs I saw.

"He has to be sedated, ma'am. He gets violent."

"Gets violent?" I felt like *I* was about to get violent. "He's the sweetest thing in the world as long as you don't come at him too quick or try to hug him."

"Ma'am," she said like I was an idiot, "I'm not equipped to fend off an unpredictable grown man."

I was mad as hell — but I did have to put myself in her shoes. I really didn't know what Phillip was like, much as it pained me to admit it. But I was determined to prove her wrong. From then on, I'd drive there every week on my day off. I'd hold that docile hand, and I'd talk to Phillip. I mostly told him stories about when we were kids.

Sometimes I'd tell him about Harry's latest stunt or some funny photos at work. He didn't smile or respond, and maybe I'm crazy, but I swear something about him changed when I got there. He seemed almost happy.

Now that I was showing up regularly, things had gotten a lot better. When we were kids in the '80s, no one knew a whole lot about autism, so they kind of wrote him off as never being able to do anything. But once I found him, I worked so hard to get him moved. It took three years and a lot of paperwork, but I did. And a really nice doctor at the new home started working with me. We got him on some good medicines to help him control himself, so maybe he wouldn't get so angry, so maybe he didn't have to rock so much or flap his hands. We even worked on words, and he was back to talking some. Sometimes it was scary, and sometimes it was hard, but Phillip was my family, and I had to step up. I had to be his voice.

And that morning, with my tooth waking up and my job lost and Harry gone and everything in the world feeling like it was falling apart, I needed to see my baby brother. I drove to Cape Nursing just like I did every week and parked my car in the parking lot. The first time, the nursing home smell and fluorescent lights and cracks in the floor had bothered me. But now I was used to it.

Karen was at the reception window just like every day, her brown hair in a knot on the top of her head that I never could quite replicate on my own, dressed in navy-blue scrubs like always.

"Well, hi there, Miss Diana." Karen handed me a clipboard so I could sign in and said, "Mr. Phillip's in the solarium." She smiled at me conspiratorially. "He's doing so good now, isn't he?"

I nodded. My head was too full of everything that was going wrong to even pretend that it could be right again. Even so, that made me smile. I'd been seeing Phillip every week for eight years now, and let me tell you, those first three, when I couldn't do anything for him, I was about to pull my hair out. But when I finally got him transferred here five years ago, it had made all the difference in the world. I saw progress at least every few months.

"He really is doing good, Karen." It brought tears to my eyes. She came around from behind the counter and hugged me tight. "I love y'all so much for helping him," I said, wiping my eyes. I shook my head. "You can't imagine how bad it used to be."

Karen said, "That's what we're here for." She squeezed my arms, the fabric of my Sam's Pub and Grub T-shirt wrapping tight around them. I actually kind of liked Sam. He was a decent guy. Smart. Hardworking. But there hadn't been much of a spark there. Although maybe things would be different now. Maybe I'd look him up, at least to see if I could get my old waitressing job back.

As I walked down the hall to see my brother, I felt lighter somehow. Things were bad, but they weren't the worst they had ever been.

Solarium was a pretty grand word for a place that was nothing more than a small room with some fake ficus trees in the corner, a row of windows looking at the parking lot, and a skylight. But whatever. I saw Phillip right off in his wheelchair at one of the windows. He was wearing gray drawstring pants and a sweatshirt, and they weren't much to look at but they were clean. Even though I wasn't able to take care of my brother, I was grateful somebody was.

I knelt in front of Phillip's wheelchair with my hands on his knees. "Hey, buddy," I said. "It's me. It's your sister, Diana." And with no warning whatsoever, hot tears started rolling down my cheeks. Not just because I was alone again. Not just because I was broke again. But because I had always dreamed that I would save up and get Phillip out of here. I checked out books on autism at the library, read articles on the computers there about his medicines, techniques to help him control his anger, exercises to help with his dexterity and his emotional responses. I knew he was in there. I had always known it. I would get him out one day. I would give him the life he deserved.

But, damn, how was I going to take care of him now?

Me and Charles, we'd talked about getting him out a couple of years ago. But Elizabeth, she'd come down from Indiana and said, "How are y'all possibly going to take care of him? We can barely take care of ourselves."

Except, well, Elizabeth could. She was real lucky. Her very first foster family was a nice, rich one. They had one kid they'd adopted when he was a baby, and they hadn't planned on having any more, but Elizabeth, sweet and smart and pretty and helpful as she was, she'd won them over right off.

They put her through private school and college. She'd married a guy who's a lawyer, thank God, because, good as Charles grew up and nice as his wife and kids are, the boys — well, you can't escape genetics. They're always getting a drinking ticket or smoking a little pot in the park. Nothing dangerous, but they seem to need a lawyer more often than not, so it's a good thing we've got one in the family.

I'll always love Charles because, as soon as he turned eighteen, he got himself a job, and he went to court and tried to get me back, out of my latest foster home, bless his heart. He didn't win, but I'll tell you what,

I'll never forget that.

Phillip turned his head to look down at me, as he said slowly, "Hi, Diana." Then the best thing in the world happened: he moved his hand on top of mine. Some days he wouldn't look at me, wouldn't talk to me, would back away if I tried to lay a finger on him. But not today. Today he put his hand, pale from years without the sun, on my tanned one, and I squeezed it quickly as he put it back in his lap. I looked up into his green eyes, just the same as mine. Irish twins. Irish eyes too. When I looked in his, I was looking into my own. I think that's what got me most. But while my face was starting to line around the eyes and mouth from smoking and stress and too little sunscreen, his was as smooth and unlined as a child's.

I cleared my throat and stood up and said, "Buddy, that hair looks like a squirrel tail on a windy day." I got a comb out of my purse and fixed his thick chestnut hair for a few minutes longer than it took to get it straight because I thought it must feel good to have somebody take care of you. I knew it'd feel good if somebody'd take care of me. He didn't try to stop me. Just like me, he had a few grays at the roots, but nothing to speak of, nothing noticeable enough to give away his real age.

I sat down in the chair beside my brother. "I'm never going to leave you, Phillip," I said. "Not ever." And then I said the thing I said every time I visited, the one I wondered if he knew, the one I wondered if he believed: "I'm going to get you out of here one day. And me and you, we're going to be a family again. The way we were supposed to be."

The promise made me happy, but it made me sad too. Because I'd had dreams, big ones. I'd known real love and had high hopes for a family of my own. But now, broke and alone and past my fortieth birthday, I had to face the fact that my brothers and sister were all the family I was ever going to have.

I can't tell you why I drove from Cape Nursing to Gray Howard's house. It's not like me. I'm the kind of girl who stands real still in the background and doesn't make too much noise so nobody'll notice she's there. But when I saw Gray's address on the outside of that envelope at Meds and More, I'd realized that I used to clean that house way back before she lived there — way back when I cleaned houses. It made fire burn in me. I'd done nothing but work my tail off my entire life. I would bet my last dollar that she'd never had to work for anything.

I didn't have a plan, really. I didn't have any money, anyplace to stay, and now I didn't have anything to do. So I guess I thought I'd just drive by, maybe get a nice look at her big house on the water, its cedar shakes and perfect painted shutters and pretty flower boxes filled with yellow and white blooms. And I could think how ironic it was that she had everything, I had nothing, and she'd managed to take away the one thing I had.

I lit a cigarette. My last one. I guessed it'd be easier to quit now that I didn't have cigarette money anyway. On the bright side, my tooth felt better.

I sat on her front steps, feeling beads of sweat forming on my back. I hoped they wouldn't show through my T-shirt. There was a nice breeze over here on the water, but, sitting in the full sun like I was, it was still hotter than the hinges of hell. But I needed vitamin D and fresh air. They were good for me and the right price: free. Still smoking away, I started thinking about what I would say when Gray got home. *You walk around here in your big, rich house with the million-dollar view, and you don't even think about the people you're hurting. You don't give a damn about anybody but yourself and what you want and how you feel. You just sit over here on your high horse and don't even think about the little people like me.*

She'd probably call the police. *Then at least I'll have a cell to spend the night in,* I thought. Oh Lord. I really was spiraling now.

This is why people have kids. Then they have somewhere to stay the night when they leave their boyfriend. Although my kids probably would've been no good and wouldn't have jobs or anyplace to stay because they'd be half Harry's DNA. Then I'd be struggling to look after them too. Sometimes, on your own isn't the worst way to be. I got a familiar pain way down in my belly, knowing that I couldn't have had a baby even if I wanted to.

Gray's white convertible, top down, pulled into the concrete driveway, and I rolled my eyes. She was yammering away on her phone. "I know, Dad, and I'm so sorry, but I have so much work to do today. I promise we'll do it next week." She sighed loudly. "Dad, I know. I get it. But he's my kid, not a chess piece. . . ." Pause. "He's taking the kid to Europe, not enrolling him in Al Qaeda training." Sigh. "I know I'm his mother, but Greg's his father, and while I think he is the scum of the earth as a human, he's a decent dad. I think it's only fair to Wagner. . . ." She got out of the car, paused, and leaned over the door, looking like she was stretching out her hamstrings. "Yes, Dad, I know. My attorney has informed me of that." She laughed ironically. "And you think *I* don't want to save my company? I put myself through grad school with that company. I bought our houses and our cars with that company. That company was my first baby. Trust me, if anyone wants to save it, it's me." She paused one more time, then said, "Hello, hello, I can't hear you. I think I'm losing —" Then she ended the call with an exaggerated click.

Still standing in the driveway, Gray let out a tight-lipped, low, frustrated groan.

It was kind of funny because I'd pictured her having this perfect life. Knowing that she really didn't, I sort of felt less mad. "That yell there for your husband or your daddy?"

She let out an actual scream that time.

I looked at her, glued to my spot, and crossed my arms. So she had some problems, but I had *problems.* As in, I was getting hungry for a dinner that might never come.

She looked confused at first and then, putting two and two together, said, "Oh my gosh. Are you here for the release? I can go get it right now —"

"That ship has sailed, sweetie pie," I said as I crushed the butt of my cigarette with my flip-flop.

"What do you mean?"

Gray walked toward me, her bare feet leaving prints in the grass. Her toenails were perfectly shaped and shiny with no polish. I curled my own toes to hide them. My red polish was chipped and fading, and you couldn't see it much, but underneath it my nails were yellow in places with some white spots. I could never have let them be bare like that. It was one more way she was better.

"Mr. Marcus fired me for not getting that release." So, no. That wasn't technically true. He'd fired me because all the photos I developed sucked, and we both knew that wasn't changing anytime soon. But making him look bad in front of a woman who anyone with eyes could see he had the hots for had been the final straw. No matter how you sliced it, Gray Howard was the reason I no longer had a job.

She caught her breath and put her hand up to her mouth. "No. You're kidding me. Oh my gosh." She sat down beside me on the brick step — not too close — putting her elbows on her knees like a kid. "Well, listen, I know Bill really well, so I'll go down and talk to him and get him to give you your job back."

"I don't think that's going to work."

"I'll just take him the release and explain that I didn't give you a choice."

I nodded, but I knew that the chances of him giving me my job back were slim to none. But now that I had Gray on the hook, now that she felt responsible for all this, I knew I could squeeze something out of her guilt. I looked back at her big house again. If she couldn't get me my job back, well, she could at least get me another one.

I'm not proud of it. But I'm a girl who grew up with nothing. I know how to manipulate people. I know how to work the system. It's the only way to survive sometimes. I said, making my voice shake the slightest bit, "I had to move out of my boyfriend's house this morning because he —"

She gasped. "Oh my God. Is that what's wrong with your face? Did he hit you?"

I put my hand up to my swollen jaw. I put on my best sad face and looked nervously down at the ground. "I don't want to talk about it." There. I hadn't lied, per se.

She gasped again, and I could see her eyes

softening. I knew I had to make a connection with her now to seal the deal. "Having a hard time with your daddy?"

She shook her head. "I love him to death, but ever since my mom died, it's like he doesn't know how to talk to me. Sometimes he's way too distant, and other times the man needs to butt out." She rolled her eyes. "I mean, I'm not five years old. It's *my* divorce. *My* kid." She laughed. "I'm so sorry," she said. "I have no idea why I'm telling you all this. Why don't you give me your number, and I'll go talk to Bill and see what we can do about making this right."

I had her right where I wanted her.

We exchanged information, and she said, "Again, I really am so terribly sorry. I never would have gotten you in trouble on purpose."

"Oh, I know you'll make it right," I said, starting to feel a little guilty myself. It wasn't really Gray's fault. But, again, survival of the fittest — or the sneakiest. When you grew up like me, you had to be both. "That job was all I had," I added. "It was my pride and my independence and my self-worth all rolled into one. It was my never having to depend on anybody else to take care of me."

Her face changed as I said that. She looked at me. I mean, really looked at me.

Something flashed in her blue eyes as they met mine, and a powerful understanding zapped between us. I knew then that maybe I had been all wrong about how easy this girl had it. I knew she was going to help. And I realized that I wasn't just saying that job was all I had. I might have been manipulating her, sure. But it startled me to learn that I meant it.

Chapter 3

Gray: Decent Human Being Stuff

"Yeah, it really was not what I needed," I was saying to my assistant, Trey, as I drove through town toward the pharmacy, his voice blaring over the Bluetooth. "But, I mean, good Lord, I got the woman fired."

I thought of Diana sitting on my front steps saying that her job was part of her identity. I knew how that felt, because my job was a huge part of mine. And *he* was trying to take it.

Diana had lines around her mouth, probably from years of smoking, but that was the only thing that betrayed that she was aging. Thick, wavy chestnut hair, bright green eyes, tanned skin that didn't need a speck of makeup. Toned, shapely legs under her jean shorts. Her oversize T-shirt wasn't doing her trim figure any favors, but she was a very attractive woman. I wondered how old she was. Probably in her late thirties, if I had to guess. Although, admittedly, I was bad at telling ages. I thought of Andrew and smiled.

"All I'm saying is that this is one of the biggest accounts of your career," Trey said. "I need you to focus right now, not save the world."

"Trying to get Bill to give Diana her job back when I got her fired isn't necessarily an act of great love or anything. It's more like decent human being stuff."

He sighed. "Whatever. I know you insist on working from the beach in the summers, but I feel like we need to be face-to-face to tackle everything we have going on right now."

I laughed. "Yeah. Okay. I'm not buying that, but come on down."

"Yes!" he said. "I'll be there. Also, Miraval just sent a case of rosé as a thank-you, so I'll see if I can sneak that down too."

"Uh-huh," I said. Trey could play me like no other. And he was working his magic now to get a free summer at the beach. But, truth be told, I would be happy to have him. He was the perfect antidote to Wagner's being gone.

"Okay," I said. "Type, please."

"Typing!"

"Dear Heather, I understand that you

believe your affiliate marketing needs are being met by ConsumerMart. But I have gathered four of our top influencers — all of whom sell more than five hundred thousand dollars per year of merchandise for their top five affiliates — to let you know why they use ClickMarket instead of a competitor. Because, you see, our increased functionality doesn't just help you on the corporate end. It also helps influencers find you and sell your products more easily, and incentivizes them to sell your brand over all the others."

"That's perfect," Trey said. "Now insert one of your signature emotional response pleas and this one is good to go."

"What did I say to Eliza from Home-Goods last week?"

I turned left into the parking lot and felt the sun on my face. Part of me thought I must be crazy for trying to work from the beach for the summer — especially now that I wouldn't be able to spend much of it with Wagner — but another part of me knew that if I didn't get a break from the eighty-hour weeks and constant connectedness, I would totally burn out. Even though I was still working like a dog, I felt infinitely more centered with a daily dose of sun and sand.

Trey interrupted my introspection, rattling

off: " 'At ClickMarket, we don't just specialize in top-tier affiliate marketing. We specialize in relationships, in putting brands and influencers into partnerships that don't just make sales. They change the story. Let us help you change the HomeGoods story.' "

Not bad. "Don't forget to change HomeGoods to Glitter," I said.

Trey sighed dramatically. "Is this my first day, Miss Priss? I think not."

God, I loved him. Sometimes I had nightmares about his quitting, and without fail I'd wake up in a cold sweat.

"I just arrived at the pharmacy," I said. "Got to go save a woman's job. Kiss kiss." This, unfortunately, wasn't something Trey could handle for me.

"I'll be there tonight!"

"Oh, yay," I said with feigned sarcasm. We liked to give each other a hard time, but really, I couldn't have been more relieved.

When I walked into Meds and More, an arctic blast of air-conditioning gave me goose bumps.

"Is Bill here?" I asked the girl behind the counter.

She nodded. "I'll page him."

A few minutes later, while I was absentmindedly reading yet another headline about Jennifer Aniston — couldn't they leave the poor woman alone? — Bill appeared, and I wondered, as always, if he colored his hair that particular shade of brassy blond. I had known Bill and his wife, Sharon, for at least ten years. We made a point of going out to dinner together at least once a summer. They were a good bit older than Greg and me, but down here, everyone was friends with people of all ages. It made things so much more interesting.

As Bill's face came into view, it almost took my breath away. I mean, literally. My chest constricted, and I felt like I couldn't breathe. Our couples' dinners with Bill and Sharon were over. My marriage was over. Oh my God. *I* was over. For nine years I had been Greg's wife; we had been part of a pair. We had been a family. What would become of me now? It hit me so hard sometimes, in unexpected moments like these. Everything was normal; everything was fine. Until it wasn't. I bit my lip and looked away as tears came to my eyes, mortified at the quiet scene I was making. I had been on the verge of tears all day over Wagner's leaving, and this put me over the edge.

Bill winked at me and, as if reading my mind, said, "Don't think you can get out of dinner just because you had the good sense to drop that deadweight." He put his arm around me and squeezed me to him sideways. "I promise you, Gray, you're better off."

People said this kind of stuff all the time, and sometimes I could even say it to myself. But it didn't take away the shame. I had failed. Our marriage hadn't been perfect. Hell, even I knew it wasn't all Greg's fault. Yeah, he had cheated and he had been jealous of my success, but I had been too wrapped up in work and Wagner. I had been overly stressed. I had let my marriage fail. It was a hard pill to swallow, and the realization furthered that deep, dark, scary thought that I didn't deserve to be with anyone else. I didn't deserve to be happy.

I nodded, a little teary from Bill's kindness. "Thanks, Bill. I'll look forward to it."

The older man squeezed my shoulder. "What can I do for you, Ms. Gray?"

I was so glad he didn't say, "Ms. Howard." Because I wasn't. Or maybe I was, but only in name. In my heart, Howard didn't belong to me anymore.

I shook my head. "I feel horrible."

"Why?"

"I got Diana Harrington fired."

He chuckled. "Oh, honey, no way. She was terrible at her job, just terrible. She was always getting orders mixed up and pictures cropped wrong and jamming the machine. You were my scapegoat."

I was relieved, but also a little miffed that I'd come out here to do the right thing only to find that Diana had the story all wrong. I would call and tell her that I tried to set things straight, but it wasn't my fault she got fired after all. "You promise?"

"Oh yeah. She had a file as thick as my forearm of infractions and complaints. It's a shame, though." He looked down at the floor and shook his head.

"Why's that?"

"Oh, we go way back with Diana. She cleaned our house for ten years before she went to work at the factory. Kept our kids. Hell, half raised them. Then when the factory shut down, I hired her to work for me. But she's always been tough. She'll figure it out." He shrugged.

I nodded, feeling another tug of guilt. Whether it was my fault or not, here was a good, decent woman out of work. It put my ClickMarket woes in perspective. Whether I got to keep all my company or not, I wasn't in danger of being hungry or out on the street. I thought of my parents, of how hard they had worked to make ends meet, of how many years they had lived paycheck to paycheck when my mom had been too depressed to go to work after my brother died, when the anxiety that, if she wasn't the one taking care of Quinn and me, we would die too had kept her tethered to home and to us. I never wanted to live like that. I'd promised myself that I wouldn't. I had thought, very naïvely, that money could protect me. It had taken me until now to realize that it couldn't.

My phone buzzed in my hand, and I looked down to find a text from Andrew. Can't wait for next Friday. I promise, I'm taking you somewhere no hoity-toity blue-blooded woman in her right mind would go.

I smiled and looked back up at Bill. "Well, thanks. You've eased my mind. Glad I'm not responsible for putting some poor woman with a bunch of mouths to feed out of work."

"No. And Diana doesn't have any kids anyway, so you don't have to worry about that."

I nodded. "I guess I'll see you around the club then."

"See you around."

I got back in my car and, determined not to let the memory of Greg ruin another day, penned a sassy reply to Andrew: Where? Your house?

Before I could even get out of the parking lot, he texted back: No way. All the ladies want to come to my house.

I laughed and raised my arm out of the top of my midlife-crisis convertible to feel the warm wind as it rushed by, the gems in my bangles sparkling as the sun hit them, my chest opening back up, my panic from only minutes earlier dissipating out the roof as my hair blew behind me. I had, like, five errands to run. Trey was right. I really did kind of need him down here. I thought about calling Diana, but when I thought about having to tell her that I wasn't the reason she got fired I felt sick to my stomach. I could always call her tomorrow. Or have Trey call her. . . . No. This was something I had to take care of on my own.

Diana: Spilt Milk and Spoilt Men

Life is all about patterns. I do the same thing over and over, which is why I keep getting to the same places. I don't mean that in some figurative way. I mean, literally, the same places.

So I guess that's the best explanation as to why I found myself steering the Impala back in the direction of that sorry excuse for a house I'd shared with Harry for eight years. Hell, I didn't have anywhere else to go. Plus it was getting to be suppertime, and I was starting to worry that neither of us would have anything to eat. Maybe it's because I never had any kids, but I sure treated Harry like one. Lord knows, he needed taking care of. But maybe he could get a job for a little bit to tide us over, and I wouldn't have to worry quite so much about finding my next one. That sounded nice.

As I turned into the driveway, it was like all my insides were annoyed as the devil at me coming back to this place, but I was feeling kind of happy too about seeing Harry and him apologizing and giving me one of those big, warm hugs that you sink into on account of him being all squishy and soft like a water balloon. It would feel right nice after the day I'd had.

I opened the door and yelled, "Honey?"

I didn't get far because, standing in my kitchen at six in the evening, wearing nothing but one of Harry's shirts, pouring batter from a ready-made Bisquick container into a skillet, was a redheaded woman. She was a big girl, probably Harry's size, and at least five years older than me, just standing there barefoot with crooked toenails and thick ankles, looking at me like *I* was catching *her* off guard.

Harry came out of the bedroom, whistling,

wearing his boxers with that pale, hairy belly jiggling all over the place. He stopped short, looking shocked, and said, "Baby, you're home! I thought you'd left for good this time."

I didn't know what to say. He was standing there, red and puffing, a fish flopped on the shore. It took my breath away how hard it hurt my heart to see Harry with another woman. I guess when you've been with somebody such a long time you start to take them for granted. You forget how much you love those big hugs and hearing how beautiful you are and that somebody, anybody on the planet, loves you so much that they want to be better for you. It had taken me until right then, seeing Harry with this *creature,* flipping pancakes in what used to be my kitchen like she owned the damn place, to realize how much I needed him, how much he looked after me in ways that, yeah, weren't quite like the ways I looked after him, but that still meant something. He soothed those inside parts of me, the parts that were made hard with not ever marrying or having any babies. He made them soft again, like pork fat in the crowder peas.

Big Red, well, you could tell right off she wasn't too bright. She said, "You want some pancakes? I can make more."

I wanted to be mad, but, hell, it wasn't her fault. Not really Harry's fault either, I guess. I mean, I walked out and that was that. And looking around my dingy kitchen, it still seemed like walking out was for the best.

I finally got my wits back about me and said, "I thought I forgot some stuff, but I can come back later. It's no big deal."

I turned, but Harry grabbed my arm. "Babe, wait. Please don't go."

I started to pull away.

"I know this looks real bad, but I love you. You're the only woman for me. Please come back. We can get married. I'll get a job and quit drinking and quit gambling. Hell, I'll even try to get us a baby if you want. Just stay. Please."

His eyes were all teary and glossy, which I guess should've been sweet. But instead it made me see him as the sniveling little boy he'd always been. I'd loved him for eight years, but in that moment I knew it was time to move on for good. I needed a man.

Big Red piped up, "Oh yeah, I wasn't trying to come between nothin'. It was just kinda hot this afternoon, and I didn't have nothin' better to do. But I got to get home now anyhow on account of my husband'll be out here with his shotgun looking for me if I don't get back soon. He gets all suspicious when I say I'm going to the store and don't come back for a while."

Harry looked startled, and I could tell he was realizing that his afternoon fling wasn't a good idea. "Di, look, babe. Come on. You got to forgive me. Please. There ain't no man on the planet who's been as faithful and true to a woman as I have to you. This here was just me thinking you was gone for good and just trying to feel better, is all. It wasn't nothing to do with me and you. You and me are perfect."

That made me laugh. "Honey," I said, patting Harry on his freckly shoulder, "you and me, we're a lot of things. But perfect is not one of them." I shook my head, wondering why I had come back here at all. "I was making sure that you had some dinner. That was all. And it looks like Big Red's got you all taken care of." I raised my eyebrows.

She padded over from the kitchen, chewing on a pancake, offering me the plate. "Name's Ronda," she said, "and I'm real sorry if I caused problems here. But I think there ain't nothin' can't be solved with pancakes between friends."

With that, I turned before Harry could grab me again and was out the door before I lost my nerve. And where a minute ago, seeing the man I thought I loved with another woman had made me feel jealous, angry, and pained, now it made me see how pathetic Harry was all over again. Still parked in the yard, I opened my wallet to evaluate my options. I had sixty bucks, and I needed gas. I shut off the air and rolled down the three windows that still worked.

I could always pay Charles a visit. Could I make it the seven hours to Asheville on sixty bucks' worth of gas? Probably not.

But Charles would help. I knew he would. So I called him, feeling grateful that I'd just paid my phone bill the day before. That meant they wouldn't turn it off for at least a month and a half. I had become a master at juggling bills. Paying the electric enough to keep it on the day before it was turned off; learning that quite often they'd keep the cable on even if you canceled it; paying a dollar a month on medical bills. I wasn't proud of it. But I was proud that I'd figured out how to survive.

"Hey, Di," he answered the phone, real friendly. Charles said that after what he'd seen growing up in foster care, he felt real happy to just be alive. And it showed. He always sounded like he didn't have a care in the world, even though I knew he did.

I needed to tell him what was going on,

that I needed help. But the words wouldn't come out. "I had that dream again," I said instead, groaning.

"Oh no," he said. "The one where the social workers are there to pick us up?"

"Yeah, and Phillip's rocking in the corner."

"Oh no."

He got quiet, and I felt bad for even bringing it up. I wished I hadn't said anything, so I changed the subject. "How's Lanna doing?"

"Oh, she's real good," he said. "She just got promoted from assistant manager to manager of Kohl's, and she's real excited about it. And the boys had good grades this quarter, and Rusty's enrolling in community college in the fall."

It made me happy how proud Charles was of his kids. When they were coming up, I got to play with them a lot because Charles and Lanna were still living down here at the beach. It took away some of that sting of not being able to have any kids of my own.

"I'm real proud of him," I said. "And, hey, I wanted to tell you I'll have a new address soon."

111 My Car in Some Parking Lot.

"Oh no," he said. "No Harry?"

"No Harry."

"Well," he said, "he's a nice guy but, you

know, kind of a train wreck."

"Yeah. So, when you coming up here for a visit? I miss you."

"Soon," he said. "Hey, Di?"

"Yeah."

"I've got a better question for you."

I laughed. "What's that?"

"When are you going to open up Carolina Di's Boils?"

I smiled. Opening a tiny restaurant had been my dream since I was a little girl. I knew I wanted to cook Carolina Boils. Some people called them Steamer Pots. As you can imagine, there are any number of slightly disgusting sounding names a big brother can figure out to call a restaurant incorporating either "boil" or "steamer."

I'd always loved to cook, and taking care of people was what made me happiest. I had visions of this stand on the beach where people would wait in line for baskets of my simple fresh seafood. Phillip would be in a chef's hat lining the red-and-white-checked cardboard baskets with paper and dishing my boils into them, filling up cups with ice. He wouldn't like serving the customers, but I could do that part. He would have a job and a paycheck all his own. I thought he'd like that.

Charles believed in me, even when the

chips were down. And I knew then that I couldn't tell him. I just couldn't. I'd never asked him for anything, and I didn't want to start now. I'd had to borrow $1,000 from Elizabeth a few years back to keep from starving and being on the street, and I still felt ashamed about it every day. She didn't give me a hard time about it or anything, but still. Sometimes pride is all a girl's got left. "Damn, Charles. Why'd you have to move all the way to Asheville? Why not just Raleigh or something?" I asked, changing the subject. It broke my heart how far away that dream of my own place seemed.

He chuckled. "You know as well as I do that if it ain't the beach or the mountains, it ain't worth living in."

I laughed in agreement, though I would've been happy to have anywhere to live right now.

I couldn't face the idea of going to the shelter, so for tonight I settled on setting up camp in the Impala, which had a big enough backseat. I could get some fast food for dinner, take a walk on the beach, and then, when it got good and dark, park at the beach access down the street from Gray's house where I'd been earlier and take me a little snooze. And I'd do the same thing I'd always done: I'd worry about tomorrow tomorrow.

I wiped away the tears staining my cheeks. No use crying over spilt milk or spoilt men or the rest of this mess. I knew as good as my own backside in the mirror that tomorrow the sun was going to come out just like always. And a new day can change everything.

I checked my phone again, just to make sure Gray Howard hadn't called about the job. I didn't expect her to work miracles or anything, but I figured if anyone could pull strings down at Meds and More, it was someone like her. The silence made me think that maybe she hadn't gone and talked to Bill after all. I drove slowly down the street, past Mr. Marcus's house, past the water, down to Gray's house. I was planning to pull all the way to the end of the street, where there weren't any houses, and scope out whether I could park and sleep there. Cops didn't patrol the nice areas a whole lot because nothing much happened in them anyway. But when I turned my head, I did a double take.

There in Gray's driveway was a man lying on the ground, on his stomach, a huge box beside him. There's something that happens to a body when it seems like somebody else is in trouble. And that's what happened to me. I threw the car in park, jumped out, and ran to him. "Should I call nine-one-one?" I screamed.

He scrambled to his feet. He was a nice-looking boy, probably around his early twenties, in jeans and a sports coat, with this big, goofy smile.

"Oh, sorry," he said in an accent that meant he wasn't from around here. "I didn't mean to scare you." He held up his arm. "One of my cuff links fell under the car and I was just looking for it."

I put my hand up to my heart trying to slow its beating.

"I'm Trey," he said, reaching out his hand to shake mine. "Gray's assistant."

I nodded. "I'm Diana." I smirked. "The woman she got fired."

I didn't expect him to know what I was talking about, so I was taken aback when he said, "Ohhhh. She felt awful about that. I was on the phone with her when she was going to the store to try to get your job back."

So, she *had* gone down to the drugstore. And she hadn't called me. That couldn't mean good news.

He picked up the box with some effort and, handing me a key, said, "Hey, do you think you could open the back door for me?"

There was something unsettling about that. "Oh, um . . . I don't think it would be right."

He smiled, his eyes gleaming. "What wouldn't be right is for me to drop an entire case of decadent rosé."

I looked around to see if anyone was watching, then followed him to the back door, put the key in, and turned the knob. I didn't walk inside, but I could see towels strewn about on the pair of matching sofas on either end of the fireplace. There were cups on the side table, dishes on the coffee table.

"Good Lord," I said.

Trey nodded. "Oh, I know. Gray is brilliant, but she's a total slob."

I've always been real picky about having everything in its place and all that, and it killed me to see this house I used to clean in such a state of disarray. I couldn't stop myself from walking into the kitchen, where it just kept getting worse. There were dishes all stacked up in the sink, mail scattered around, some kind of fake milk still on the counter from the morning — surely spoilt now.

She was a grown woman, but she wasn't

living like it. I didn't owe her anything. Hell, she owed *me.* But I can't stand a mess. Just like my sister, Elizabeth, when I see it, I clean it. I planned just to get a handle on the dishes in the sink, but I couldn't leave the counters like that. And then those damp towels on those white linen sofas . . . And Trey was coming in and out, in and out, carrying groceries and papers and saying things like, "Gray never has any food in the house," and, "I'll pay you a hundred bucks to clean this place so I don't have to."

And I needed the money, and it was kind of like when I saw Trey lying in the driveway. My body just took over, and here we were. Before I knew it, I was vacuuming and humming, totally lost in my own world. Well, lost until I looked up and saw Gray standing there with her jaw hanging open like a fish on a hook.

My face got hot. I turned the vacuum off and could hear the Van Morrison Trey had playing. He walked in, saying, "Diana, I'm trying to do the guac like you told me, but —" And then he saw Gray and stopped in his tracks too, and we were all standing there, staring like trapped animals. Almost like me, Harry, and Big Red a few hours earlier.

"I'm having a hard time deciding where

to start," Gray said. She turned to Trey. "But I guess, first, how the hell are you here so quickly?"

He smiled disarmingly at her. "I was in the Dunkin' Donuts parking lot across the street when you were dictating that e-mail."

Gray sighed and rolled her eyes. "Good Lord."

Now she turned to me. "I have no words."

All I had done was clean the woman's house. But, then again, I was a near-total stranger who'd showed up unannounced on her front steps that morning and appeared uninvited a few hours later in her living room.

I looked at Trey. "I'll take my hundred bucks and then I'm out of here." Then I did what I do best when I'm on the defensive: I turned it around on her. I gave Gray a good once-over and prepared to deliver a zinger. "No wonder your husband left you. Making a mess, no groceries in the house." *Note to self: When you have money again, get Nicorette.*

But instead of getting upset, she laughed. "Well, Maria did most of the shopping and cleaning and cooking."

"So what did you do?"

Gray looked up toward the ceiling. "Well, I grew an affiliate-marketing empire out of a little blog I started in college and made sure I was at every school party and baseball game and bought the house and paid the bills and planned the vacations and the nights out and the playdates." She smiled pointedly. "That's what I did."

"So where's this Maria?"

"Greg got her in the divorce. He got Maria and Brooke and half of Wagner and the vast majority of my self-worth. I got my world turned upside down and our fine china."

"Yikes," Trey said. "Bitter divorcée at the party. We need to back that up, sister."

I waved my hand. "Oh, honey, it'll pass. It's just one of them stages. When my girl Robin got divorced the first time, we thought we were going to have to have an intervention for her. All she could do was bash her husband. I mean, you'd say, 'Oh, damn. I'm out of bananas.' And then she'd be like, 'Cal never remembered to get bananas.' But she got over it. Well, I mean, they got married again. . . ." I paused, realizing maybe this story wasn't as relevant as I had hoped.

She just looked at me like she was still confused, and that's when I remembered that I had not been invited, and here I was holding her vacuum cleaner.

"I promise I'm not stalking you. I was in the neighborhood, and I thought Trey was hurt in the driveway. . . ."

Gray looked skeptical. She turned to Trey. "You were hurt in the driveway?"

He held up his arm. "My cuff link was hurt. I was on the ground, so I guess it looked that way."

"And then he needed help carrying this stuff in, and then there was all this mess and I just . . ." I continued, feeling the need to defend myself.

Gray looked around, as if she had just noticed her surroundings. "It's really clean in here," she said.

"Well, I cleaned it up," I said. I couldn't tell if she was happy it was clean or mad it was clean. "I don't know what came over me —"

Gray nodded knowingly. "Ohhhhh. Now I see. You've been Treyed."

He smiled victoriously, and I was confused. "I'm sorry. I've been what?"

"Treyed," she said. "It's when you plan on doing one thing and then you're doing a million others, and you don't even know how that happened."

I snapped my fingers. "Yup! That's it." I wagged my finger at him. "You're sneaky."

Then another girl came walking in the

back door. And now she looked confused too.

"Marcy, meet Trey," Gray said. She paused. "And Diana, I guess. And, Trey, meet Marcy."

Marcy squealed. "Oh my God! It's you! It's the famous Trey. I have heard so much about you, and I am just the most excited person in the world." She took his hands and started jumping up and down, and there was his goofy grin again.

"I have heard so much about you too," he said calmly.

This Marcy lady stopped her jumping and looked at Gray, frowning. "He isn't gay," she said accusatorily.

"Um, yeah. I know."

"Well, why didn't you tell me he wasn't gay?"

I didn't know who these rich people were, but they didn't seem like the sharpest knives in the drawer.

Gray crossed her arms. "I mean, I don't know, Marce. Did it ever come up?"

Marcy studied Trey. "I just assumed that an assistant who worked at ClickMarket and called you Miss Priss was gay."

Again, none of my business, but I couldn't help but jump in. "She has a point. You wear cuff links on weekdays. And say things like 'decadent rosé.' "

Trey shrugged. "Sorry to disappoint."

Marcy raised her eyebrows at Gray. "This is even better."

She gasped. "It is not better. It absolutely is not." She pointed her finger at Marcy. "You stay away from my assistant. He is the single most important person in my life."

"More important than me?" Marcy protested.

They all laughed, and I was tempted to sneak out the door before Marcy started asking questions about me too. But Trey owed me money, and Gray might have information I needed, so I said, "Um, sorry to disrupt the party, but, Gray, did you have a chance to talk to Mr. Marcus?"

Gray bit her lip. "Let's just say, it didn't go well."

I crossed my arms and raised my eyebrows at her, and she shrugged.

"So do you have any suggestions of what I should do now?" I asked. I put my hand up to my swollen jaw for effect.

"Oh, oh!" Trey chirped. "I know. She should be your housekeeper. Lord knows you need one."

Marcy looked at me. "She can't cook either."

That's what piqued my interest. Because I

could clean, yeah. But I could really cook.

"That is untrue," Gray interjected. "It's not that I *can't* cook. It's that I don't have time. Those are different things."

This wasn't exactly what I was expecting. I guess I thought that she'd get me some new job with all her connections. I mean, working the picture counter at Meds and More wasn't a glamorous job or nothing, but it beat some others out there.

I'd sworn up and down and around that I wasn't ever going back to being anybody's maid. I mean, it's not a pie job, to say the least. Washing up underwear and cleaning up dishes. But ever since I was little, cleaning has been something that calms me down. And Lord knew I could use a little therapy, not to mention a little cash.

Gray hadn't asked me herself, so I didn't know if the offer was real. Hell, I didn't know if I'd even accept.

She just shrugged. "I think it's a little weird that you showed up here twice today, but I got you fired, and this feels like a way to make it right. You can balance my karma." She paused. "What do you think?"

I let out a pained sigh even though I was probably more relieved than I had ever been. "I think we've both been Treyed."

Gray smiled and shook my hand. "Welcome to the crew, Diana."

CHAPTER 4

Gray: Innate Goddesshood

Two days later, as Diana was making me a smoothie that tasted like heaven in a glass, I was returning morning e-mails at the kitchen island. Normally I would have been doing that in my office upstairs. But I didn't mind being around Diana, and I had to admit that, despite Bill Marcus's endorsement, I was still a little wary of letting a virtual stranger roam around my house unsupervised.

As I took the first sip of her apple-pie smoothie, though, I realized nothing else mattered as long as she could feed me like this.

Diana's head was lost in the fridge, and she started pulling things out and setting them on the counter.

"What are you doing?" I finally asked, after sending off an e-mail.

She pulled her head out, wiped her brow,

and said, "I'm cleaning out your fridge."

I didn't want to tell her, but I couldn't even guess when that had last been done. She turned back to the fridge and pulled out a hunk of what had perhaps once been cheese that was now black, brown, and green. So, yeah, she knew it had been a while since the fridge had been cleaned.

"What did this used to be?" she asked.

I made a face. "Camembert, maybe?"

She tossed it in the trash and said under her breath, "Looks more like cam-ouflage."

We both laughed. Then she held up a bottle of ketchup with the lid crusted shut. "This expired in 2016. Were you doing a science project or can I toss it?"

This was the best thing about Diana. I never had to tell her what to do. She showed up at my house at seven, got everything straight, made me a smoothie, made the bed, did the laundry, wiped stuff down that I didn't know had to be wiped down, went to the store, made food that should have been at the finest bistro in the world appear on my counter, and left it hot for me so I could eat or have guests or whatever. I made her eat too. Breakfast, lunch, and dinner. What in the world would I do with all that food with just Trey and me to eat it if she didn't?

I told Diana she didn't have to stay all day. I told her she didn't have to work so many hours. But I guessed she had a lot to catch up on around my house because she had stayed until five both days. We had agreed that one day a week she would come in around ten so she could go see her brother. That made me happy, and a little jealous. Family was so important. I knew that. I wished my sister did.

Diana sprayed the inside of the now empty fridge and said, "Do you know that crisper drawers are for produce, not wine?"

"Ohhhh," I said as if that were brand-new information. "I thought they were for keeping summer wines crisp."

She laughed. "Are you and Trey eating here or at your club today?"

I groaned. Diana turned and shut the fridge, leaning against it. "What's that about? Bad sushi up there or something?" she asked sarcastically.

"It's silly," I said, taking a sip of smoothie.

She raised her eyebrows.

"It's just that I feel like everyone is talking about me." I paused. "No, I know for sure that everyone is talking about me."

Diana nodded knowingly as she began to throw expired items into the trash can. "That's a bad feeling. I know all about that." She picked up a jar of jelly, read the label, and tossed. Then she said, "When I was little, kids used to talk about me and pick on me all the time. When we were in foster care, there were some years I didn't have more than two or three changes of clothes, and at this one house no one would brush my hair, so it was a rat's nest, and I always had holes in my off-brand shoes." She paused and took a breath. "But worst of all, we got free lunch — and breakfast — which might as well have been a target on my back. . . ." She trailed off, and I felt like my heart had stopped beating. I couldn't bear the thought of that happening to any child. "I got picked on real bad, but it made me strong too, you know?"

"Jesus, Diana. That is *not* the same thing."

She shrugged and turned toward the sink, rinsing a bottle and setting it back on the counter. "Well, no. I guess it isn't, because that was a long time ago and it was really more about material things, and this is more about your life —"

I interrupted her, feeling sick. I couldn't believe what she had been through, what she had endured. I'd had no idea. "No, I mean, that is real, true trauma. I'm just being a brat, and I'm old enough that I shouldn't care."

Diana leaned over the counter toward me. "You know, hon, everybody's got their own problems. I've got mine, you've got yours, the mailman's got his."

"Davy?" I gasped in mock horror. "Not Davy!"

We both laughed.

"For real," I said. "I am so sorry you had to go through that." I could feel tears coming to my eyes. I was so grateful that I could take care of Wagner. "Gosh," I added, "I think it has been hard not having my mom this past year, and I'm a grown-up. I can't imagine doing it as a child."

I was giving her a subtle opening. I didn't want to say, *So, what happened to your mom?* But I was so curious. Diana was spraying the counters now, wiping them with rags I had made from Wagner's old, threadbare T-shirts during my brief, post-split Martha Stewart phase. I had a feeling Diana had a hard time standing still. She wasn't taking the bait. But then she stopped dead in her tracks and looked me straight in the eye. "There comes a point when we all have to learn to survive on our own, Gray. Mine just came early."

I bit my lip. There was so much truth in that. This was my moment, I guessed. I was learning to survive on my own. No husband.

No mother. Not even Wagner here to bring joy to the hard days. Just me on my own two feet.

She turned and started spraying again. "We got smart, though, one of my foster brothers and me. I got picked on because of my hair not being brushed, and he got picked on for smelling bad. We were too young to get jobs, so we spent weeks collecting cans. We got on the free bus and took all those cans down to the recycling center in our backpacks and some old grocery bags we'd found around the house, and we got up enough money to buy a hairbrush for me and some deodorant for him."

"Damn, Diana." I felt sick to my stomach again. I hadn't been getting a Porsche for my sixteenth birthday or anything, but I had had two parents who loved me, who made sure I always had what I needed even if it meant they had to sacrifice something for themselves.

"Just having my hair brushed didn't fix anything. It didn't keep the kids from picking on me. But it gave me the confidence to face the bullies." She turned and smiled at me.

I guessed that was what I needed too. I needed to find what would give me the confidence to face the bullies. "My mom always used to say people picked on people they were jealous of, but it isn't true, is it?"

Diana shrugged.

"I mean, when they were making snide remarks about my being a bad wife and mom when I was building my company, I could write it off as jealousy, but now . . ."

"I was lucky," Diana said, "because I found my best girlfriends right around that bad time in foster care. We took care of each other. We still do."

"Your ride or die," I said, smiling.

Trey came bounding into the kitchen in a pair of Lululemon gym shorts and a T-shirt. "I heard you call?" he said. "Oh, yum, a Diana smoothie."

"I didn't call you."

"You said 'ride or die,' " he said. "That's me!" I patted his arm. He was my ride or die. I didn't know what I would do without him. Trey looked over my shoulder. "Why are you reading those e-mails? Those e-mails are in my inbox."

"Well, I was up and you weren't."

He looked at me like I was crazy. "It's seven-thirty. It's okay not to return e-mails at seven-thirty." He slammed my laptop, poured some smoothie for himself, and said to Diana, "I don't know what to do with this one. I think she would work herself completely to death if it weren't for me."

"Hey! I was about to log how many hours I slept in my chart," I protested.

"What are we talking about?" Trey asked, as if I'd said nothing. He thought my spreadsheets were a little overzealous.

Diana and I shared a glance. "Nothing, really," I said, though that couldn't have been further from the truth.

"Have you filled her in on what a loser Greg is?" Trey asked.

I groaned. "No Greg talk. I don't want to think about him or even hear his name today." The only side benefit to Wagner's being gone for three weeks was that I didn't have to deal with Greg.

"It takes a certain kind of man to be married to a successful woman," Diana said. I didn't take it as an insult, but Trey evidently did. He rushed to my defense.

"Are you kidding me?" Trey countered. "It's 2020. Who cares who's most successful? It's about being partners."

"Honey, you're a whole different generation," Diana said.

"I don't even know if that was it, though. I mean, yeah, I was more successful, and I know it bugged him, but he benefited from my success more than anyone."

"It's an ego thing," Trey chimed in.

"Yes!" Diana agreed. "Maybe *that's* why Harry stole my savings and gambled it all away. He inherited his momma's house, but I was paying the bills. If I had more money than he did, I had more power. I could leave. I didn't have to depend on him."

I nodded, realizing how vastly different our lives were and how, even still, the themes were kind of the same. "Yes!" I said. "That's so true."

Trey shook his head. "So what you two need is to find men who aren't threatened by your innate goddesshood." He paused, putting his finger to his lips. "Like maybe someone a little younger . . . maybe someone who isn't scared of a strong woman."

I cut my eyes at him. "What do you know?"

He shrugged innocently.

Marcy burst in practically singing, "Girls' night tonight! Oh, hey, Diana."

I gasped. "Oh my gosh! I totally forgot I have girls' night tonight." I looked at Diana pleadingly. "Um, do you think you could throw together a few appetizers?"

Diana nodded. "Sure. Of course. What do you want?"

These were the kinds of decisions I could no longer handle. I made decisions all day, every day. I told people what to do and how to do it. Today I just wanted someone else to deal with it. I shrugged. "Just make what you would make if you were having girls' night."

Diana nodded. "Perfect. Easy enough."

With that, I grabbed my laptop — and my Trey — and headed up to the office to get some work done, leaving Diana and Marcy to work out the particulars.

When you get divorced, you have to choose one of a few well-established personas. Well, maybe some people don't *choose* per se. Maybe they just *are*. There's the bitter divorcée who blames her ex-husband for every single thing that's wrong on the entire planet. The one who wallows in her self-pity forever, refusing to reclaim her life. There's the divorcée who immediately jumps into another serious relationship like nothing ever happened. And there's the one who goes through a wild phase, dating every inappropriate man (or woman) she can get her hands on. I had to choose which kind I was going to be before the kind I didn't want to be chose me. So I settled on the free-spirited divorcée and practiced saying in my mirror, "It was a beautiful period of my life and now it's over."

That was my external persona. Outwardly,

I was fine. Fine, fine, fine. I was grateful for our years together, for Wagner, for what Greg and I had shared, and now I was happy we could both move forward. Inside, I was anything but happy. I was sad to have lost someone I had shared so much of my life with. I was scared that I would never find anyone else and would be alone forever. I was embarrassed that I had to walk around, the woman scorned, with every Southerner and her mother doing the thing I hated the very most: pitying me. And, most of all, I was furious. Furious at Greg for not being able to keep it in his pants. Furious at Brooke for being such an opportunistic hussy. Furious at myself for being the kind of woman who calls another woman an opportunistic hussy and, worst of all, for falling for a man who I knew deep down, even from the beginning, could never give me the kind of partnership I wanted in this life.

And now, speaking of lifelong relationships, I was wishing that I hadn't checked my e-mail one last time before my friends arrived. But I had. And the note at the top of my inbox was a charming one from my sister. Trey must have been busy, because he was pretty adamant about immediately transferring any e-mail from Quinn into its own secret folder in hopes that I would never see it. It wasn't his worst idea, but the inevitable moment of reckoning had arrived. The subject line: My Previous E-mails.

I hadn't read her previous e-mails because I knew what they said and, well, I didn't want to hear it. But now I couldn't help myself. I fell on the sword.

Dear Gray,

I know you don't want to hear what I have to say, but I promise you it comes from a place of love. God doesn't like divorce, and I am only thinking of you when I urge you to reconcile with Greg, to save your marriage. Think of Wagner. Think of your family. And, most of all, think of your immortal soul.

Love,
Quinn

I know everyone handles grief in a different way, and I guessed this was how Quinn was handling our mother's death. But to go from being the ultimate party girl — and the ultimate devoted sister — to being solely focused on Elijah Taylor and his church was so extreme.

People almost always know when they are about to cry. There are warning signs: the tears welling up, a lump in the throat. Reading Quinn's e-mail didn't give me any of that. In fact, I only noticed the tears after they'd already started. Which made me realize that, despite my cool exterior, I fell into the divorcée category of total and complete mess.

I heard Diana's voice saying, "Gray," and she was beside me before I could pretend I wasn't crying. The natural reaction to another person's tears is to ask them what's wrong. Diana didn't ask. She sat down in the chair on the other side of my desk, looking right at me, and said, "Honey, I know it feels like your life is falling apart. Hell, your life *is* falling apart. But my life falls apart all the time, and what I've realized is that when your life falls apart, the universe is just teaching you how to trust."

This time I felt an ironic laugh coming. "Oh yeah," I said sarcastically. "My divorce is doing wonders for my ability to *trust.*" (Bitter divorcée had arrived for another visit.)

She rolled her eyes at me. "Not other people, honey. *You.* When the shit hits the fan, you're the woman left standing; you're the one left holding the bag. And you learn how strong you are. You figure out real quick that nobody's going to fix your life but you. Nobody else is in charge of your happiness."

That sounded plain lonely to me, and I braced myself for more tears.

Diana looked at me sideways. Again, no hug, no sympathy. But she was kind enough not to compare our situations. She easily could've pulled the *You think you have problems?* card, but that would've gotten us nowhere.

"Are you going to sit in your room and cry? Or are you going to get your ass up and take on the world?"

I'll be honest. I wanted to sit in my room and cry. But then Diana got up to leave and said, "The only person who gets to pick how you feel is you."

Was that true? Was I choosing this? And if I was, could I stop?

When I heard Diana's footsteps again, I thought she had decided she was going to have to come extract me from my chair of pity. But then she appeared with a plate. It contained a Ritz cracker with a blob of something that I thought I remembered from my childhood as being Easy Cheese, pigs in a blanket, saltines with what appeared to be melted marshmallows on top, and those jalapeño poppers from the freezer that Wagner and his friends liked that I only let them eat when I needed cool mom points.

When I looked up, her face mirrored my confusion. "For your girls' night," she said. "Thought a taste test could get you out of here a little quicker."

I couldn't help it. I started laughing. I mean, uncontrollably, tears running down my cheeks in the best possible way, laughing at the idea of prissy, perfect party-planner-to-the-rich Mary Ellen walking into my house and, instead of being greeted by prosciutto-wrapped asparagus, grabbing a whing-ding, which is what my mom called saltines with cheese and a marshmallow on top.

Girls' nights at Mary Ellen's were always the most extravagant and over-the-top — and the most shared on social media. Every seemingly random get-together was a self-promotion opportunity. 9:08 a.m: "Arranging the flowers for #girlsnight with @grayhoward!" 10:42 a.m.: "Cupcakes for #girlsnight arrived from @spouterinnbakery. Aren't they gorgeous?" 12:01 p.m.: "Putting the final touches on the bar for #girlsnight. Don't you love paper straws? #partyon." 12:14 p.m.: Block further notifications from @maryellenentertains.

I had two choices. I could run to Friendly

Market and throw together a fancy cheese plate and try to salvage my friends' opinions of my party skills. Or I could stick with Diana's version of appetizers and not hurt her feelings. And her apps were kind of campy. There was a theme.

"Are you having some sort of fit?" Diana asked.

I think that was when I realized how much I'd made the past several months about everyone else. Walking into the club that first day had felt like getting a bad report card — and having it read over the PA system for the entire school to hear. I was Gray Howard. I was successful. I was self-made. My ultimate idea of success as a child had been being able to go to the Dollar Tree and pick out something I didn't expressly need. But I had made it big. I was happy. I was proud. And I was acutely aware that there were more than a few people out there who couldn't wait to revel in what was, to date, my largest failure.

When you are in a marriage — or a divorce — sometimes it's impossible to see outside of it. When you're in your house sitting across the kitchen table from the man who used to be your world trying to reconcile how he became a stranger in such short order, all you can think about is your intensely private anger and your very personal pain. You forget that you are going to be subject to the merciless scrutiny of the outside world, that the comments and questions and snide remarks being hurled at you from all directions can be almost as bad as your husband's unfaithfulness. I knew I shouldn't let other people's opinions affect me. I shouldn't care.

But I was a human being. So of course I did.

But I was tired of caring about other people's opinions. I popped one of Diana's pigs in a blanket in my mouth. It was delicious. And I figured, why not? My friends should love me even if I served them Cheez Whiz crackers.

Diana was still looking at me expectantly. Then a light bulb went on. "Oh," she said. "When you said to make what I would make for girls' night, that's not exactly what you were expecting."

I smiled at her. "No, no." I paused. "Well, I mean, sure, it's not exactly what I was thinking, but that's okay. I'm laughing because when I was pregnant with Wagner I couldn't eat anything — I mean, not *anything* — without getting sick. So my mom melted cheese on saltine crackers and put marshmallows on them and browned them in the oven. It sounded gross, but then they were all I could eat. These made me think of her."

I felt tears springing to my eyes again and decided either I had some serious PMS or I had officially, once and for all, lost my mind. Diana smiled. "That must be nice," she said. "To have all those memories with your mom."

Yup. Memories. I had a lot of those. "And then she left me when I needed her the very most." I laughed cruelly.

Diana cocked her head to the side. "Sister, you are *mad.*"

I was taken aback. "I'm not *mad.* The woman died, for heaven's sake. She didn't leave me on purpose."

She looked skeptical. "Well . . . Look, anger is a natural reaction to death. I was mad at my mom for a long time."

"So she died?" I asked.

Diana waved her hand, which I assumed was a yes. "But, Gray, you can't move past being angry if you can't admit that you are."

"I'm not mad!" I protested. "That's ridiculous." Who did this woman think she was? I didn't have to keep her around. "My mother was my best friend. Don't ever say that to me again."

Diana put her hands up in defense and

walked out of the room.

My mind was reeling. What right did she have to put something that awful on me? But, well . . . was she right? Was I *mad*? I mean, my poor mother had died of cancer. Who would be mad at that? But when I felt that familiar burning near my throat, I realized that maybe that's what I was. I was saying, "Oh my gosh, am I mad?" just as Trey breezed in.

"Why are we not dressed?" he demanded.

I suddenly felt very, very tired. I leaned my head all the way back until it touched the chair and I was looking at the ceiling. I didn't want to tell Trey about my potentially insane reaction to my mom's death, so instead I said, "Quinn."

"What?!" Trey screeched. "I'm away from your e-mail for ten minutes. Maybe nine. How did that little bitch sneak in there?"

Trey calling Quinn a bitch made a flash of fury run through me. She was a bitch. A huge one. But only *I* got to say that, blood being thicker than water and all that.

Before I could respond, Trey looked at the plate on my desk and said, "Well, good Lord, early heart disease isn't the answer to your problems."

"Hey!" Diana interjected, popping her head back in, startling me. "Those are the appetizers."

"The what?"

He gave me that look I knew all too well, the one that said, *Do I intervene here or let it go?* I gave him a look back that said to let it go.

"Okay," he said. "Get dressed, do your girls' night thing. I'm taking Diana out to dinner to formally educate her on the Gray Howard brand."

I stifled a laugh. Having someone to do your dirty work was the ultimate charm of a charmed life.

An hour later, my four best friends were drinking wine and lounging in a circle of low-slung beach chairs on the little stretch of sand that separated my grassy front yard from the expansive sound beyond. The sunset was my favorite deep pink, but no one was watching it. All eyes were on me. I supposed that in the midst of a divorce and Ritz crackers, this shouldn't have been a surprise. They hadn't seen me since the summer before, so now was their chance to gauge how far off the deep end I had fallen.

"Do you absolutely hate Brooke?" Mary Ellen was asking, well into her first bottle of champagne. "I mean, I hated Sarah so much after Eddie left me for her." Mary Ellen was a petite, pretty Florida transplant who literally wore only Lilly Pulitzer. She said the clothes fit her body and the prints fit her personality, so who could blame her?

"Of *course* I hate her," I said. "And I hate being that woman. I want to be the 'it was our marriage and he is the one to blame' woman, but I can't do it. I hate them almost equally. In fact, I might hate her even more, which is kind of unjustified."

My *I'm fine. It's fine. Life moves on* persona didn't apply to my best friends. I think that goes without saying.

Megan nearly spit out her wine. "She stole your husband, Gray. What do you mean, *unjustified*?"

"You can't 'steal' someone's husband, really. Can you?" countered Addie. Everyone glared at her. She was *the one* in the group. You know, the one who likes to play devil's advocate. You love her, but sometimes you just want to say: *SHUT. UP.*

Marcy picked up a jalapeño popper and, holding it up meaningfully, said, "Love bug, you need some serious sessions. I'm going to refer you to a colleague."

"I don't need sessions," I said, laughing. "Diana and I had a bit of miscommunication about the appetizer situation." I looked pointedly at Marcy, who looked like an absolute goddess in a flowy maxi dress cut almost to her belly button. She had the exact right willowy figure to pull it off. "I thought *you* were helping to steer her in the right direction."

"Ohhhhh," she said. "I see how you could have thought that. But, no. We were talking about her crazy ex-boyfriends."

Megan sighed, "Oh, thank God." An extraordinarily tall brunette, she had shocked us all by debuting her new hairstyle, the wavy curls that used to fall all the way down her back now chopped off close to her head. I honestly had not recognized her, but the look suited her. She added, "Don't get me wrong. Pigs in a blanket are delicious and it's great to get to eat them in public. It's just not really typical of you." She hiccupped, already on her third glass of wine. "I haven't had carbs in, like, a decade."

"I've been straight keto for six months now, but that Cheez Whiz and those Ritz crackers . . ." Addie said. Addie was the least appearance-oriented of us all, and certainly the most athletic. She was toned at any size, but she had complained for years about the weight she had gained when baby number three came two days before her fortieth birthday. She always looked great, and I was about to say so when Marcy asked: "When did we get too good for Cheez Whiz? I mean, really. Are we so fancy now that we can't enjoy a good microwaved appetizer every now and then?"

"Why do we punish ourselves like this?" Mary Ellen groaned.

I shrugged. "I know nothing is supposed to taste as good as thin feels, but" — I held up a whing-ding — "this tastes damn good."

My friends laughed, and Megan said, "Well, Gray, I guess even in the midst of the divorce carbs are magic. That's something, right? So maybe it could always be worse?"

I nodded.

"Yeah," Mary Ellen chimed in, raising her glass. "He could have left you for a dude."

I gestured to her and made a face. "Yeah. Is that worse?" I asked. "When your husband leaves you for a man? Or is it worse when he leaves you for a woman?" Mary Ellen was probably the only person in the world who could answer both of those questions from firsthand experience.

Marcy burst out laughing, while saying, "I'm so sorry. This shouldn't be funny at all."

Megan joined her laughter, and then, finally, Mary Ellen started laughing too.

Megan said, "How many people can honestly answer that?"

Mary Ellen rolled her eyes and shook her head. "I mean, I know." Then she raised her glass again. "Here's hoping third time's the charm."

"Hear! Hear!" I said. We all laughed again, and I turned to Marcy. "So, my love, have you told the girls?"

They all leaned in a little, excited for whatever piece of gossip was getting ready to come their way.

"Let's not make too big a thing of it," Marcy said. "Who knows if it will even happen?"

"It won't happen if you don't put it out there," Megan responded. She looked less ethereal with her cropped hair, but she still sounded it.

"Fine," Marcy sighed. "I am officially husband hunting."

Addie dropped her whing-ding. "Seriously? But you're our cool single friend."

"She's not wrong," I said. "I was kind of counting on you to be like my dating guru."

"You all need to hush," Mary Ellen chimed in. "If this is what will make Marcy happy, then we will be happy for her."

"But only if it means a wedding planning commission for you," Addie said with a totally straight face. More laughter as Mary Ellen threw a pig in a blanket at Addie. She missed, and we all squealed as an expectant seagull that had been waiting patiently on the end of the dock swooped down and carried it away.

When the laughter stopped, Megan turned to me and said, "So, seriously, a year in, does it feel different? I mean, can you move past it a little?" She paused, then whispered, "Do you miss your old life?"

I didn't really want to talk about it, but if you don't have friends to talk about this stuff with, to really bare your soul to, who do you have? "Well, y'all know I never wanted that monstrosity of a house anyway. Brooke and her twenty-eight-year-old cleavage can keep that."

It was true. When my husband had finally started making money, it was like he couldn't contain himself. He wanted the biggest house on the street, to take private jets on every vacation — while, of course, posting the photos, because how could you know something was good unless you could make your friends jealous? He wanted more and more and more, so I guess I should have seen it coming. Our pretty, normal-size home wasn't enough. Two nice cars weren't enough when you could have four. A big boat wasn't enough when you could have a bigger one. And your loving wife wasn't enough when you could have a younger one.

I hoped for Wagner's sake, and, in truth, for Brooke's, that a total life change would be enough for Greg to fill that giant hole that I couldn't. My thoughts flashed to Brooke again, and I started to feel sad for her. She would get swept up in it all as girls do when they're young. But in the end, she would forgo her own identity for that of a man who already had a past and a son — not to mention a poor track record with commitment.

Had I moved on? And then I said, "You know, I don't miss him. I don't even really miss the consistency of our life anymore. But until everything is settled, until our divorce is final, I think I will feel trapped by him." I still couldn't reconcile how someone you had loved so much could change so completely toward you so quickly. It took my breath away.

They all looked sympathetic. This wasn't our first divorce in this group.

Addie said, "I just can't believe he had the nerve to tell you he was leaving and then stay all those months like nothing had happened and then abandon you the day after your mom's funeral." She looked at me pointedly. "Gray, you win for worst divorce."

Mary Ellen nodded in agreement.

"Yay," I said with the least enthusiasm I could muster. They all laughed.

Those had been the worst six months of my life, but, in all honesty, having Greg stay, even under those horrible circumstances, was easier. I was with my mom as much as humanly possible, and I never had to worry about where Wagner would go or how to balance that. Looking back, it seems impossible, but in the moment, it felt necessary. I didn't have time to analyze what was going on or what would come in the next phase. I could only think of how to get to the next day.

I took another sip of wine as Marcy, I think realizing I didn't want to talk about this anymore as best friends do, said, "Speaking of winning . . . forget about the divorce. Tell them about the hottie."

I raised my eyebrows and glared at her.

Mary Ellen said, *"The hottie?"*

"Well . . ."

"Come on," Megan said. "I need details. Juicy, juicy details."

I smiled demurely, ignoring the flip-flop in my stomach when I thought of Andrew. It was ridiculous. He was a child, for heaven's sake. "Juicy is a wonderful, wonderful way to describe him."

"A rebound fling is exactly what you need," Marcy said.

"Marcy, I'm having one drink with him. I think *rebound* is a bit of an overstatement."

"Who is it?" Addie asked.

"No one," I said. "Just don't worry about it." Their fallen faces made me realize I had taken the fun down a notch, so I added, "Let's just say he's like one of those Abercrombie models — the ones we used to have taped up in our bedrooms when we were teenagers — come to life." None of us had known each other back then, but we had discussed the Abercrombie phenomenon at length.

"I just want you to win your divorce," Megan said.

I rolled my eyes. "You can't *win* your divorce."

"Oh, Greg is totally winning it right now." Freaking Addie. "He's prancing around town with the hot new fiancée."

"No, no, no," Mary Ellen said, "I totally disagree. I think Greg looks like an idiot and you look like you have some class."

"Trust me," Marcy said, "when word about Gray's first date post-breakup gets out, she will officially be winning."

Everyone laughed. I was eager to turn the conversation away from me, but Mary Ellen said, "By the way, Brad is furious about what Greg is trying to do to you with ClickMarket."

Brad was Mary Ellen's second ex-husband. Who'd left her. For Chad. "That's nice," I said.

"He and Chad want to help with the case in any way they can."

Now, *that* was nice. Brad and Chad had started one of the most high-powered corporate law firms in the state. "I would love their advice," I said. "I honestly don't think he even wants the company. We all know he hates to work. So now I just have to figure out what he does want."

Marcy stood up. "Just leave that part to me," she said. "Figuring out what people want and how to fix it is what being a therapist is all about."

"And I won't have to pay you!" I said enthusiastically.

"Well . . ." she said.

I threw my pillow at her and we all laughed. Then I said, seriously, "I love you, Marce, but this is one time when you can't really help me."

But then I realized I was wrong. They had all helped me. Only a few hours ago, I'd felt like my life was spiraling, dark, and empty. All it took was a few drinks, a few whingdings, and a few good friends to make me realize that, husband or no, ClickMarket or no, Diana was right: I still had everything I really needed.

Diana: Quick Study

The dinner with Trey had been a godsend. Even if I ate something simple and precooked from the grocery store, it'd still cost me five bucks. He took me to a real fancy restaurant and ordered all these appetizers and I ordered a salad and sandwich that I thought would keep okay, and I filled up on appetizers and saved most of my own food to store in the cooler in the back of the Impala. Food would be hard to come by over the weekend when I wasn't working, and the leftovers wouldn't be great, but they would keep on ice until Saturday at least.

After a few days, it gets pretty hard to hide stuff — like that you're living in your car. Lucky for me, I'd made friends with Billy down at the marina, and he let me shower there for free and didn't say anything. I didn't like to flatter myself, but I thought he might've had a crush on me. But maybe it was more that Billy knew what it was like to be down-and-out.

Trey did not. Trey wanted to talk to me about Gray's "brand" and how we were all a part of that. My brand was trailer trash, and I wasn't changing for nobody. I planned on telling Trey that right off, but then he ordered shrimp cocktail and calamari, and the butter was so good on the bread, and, well, I've got standards and I've got pride, but I've also got a good, heaping helping of common sense. Common sense says that you do whatever you can to keep the job where you get to eat most meals for free and make double what you'd get anywhere else. Although common sense also told me that I'd crossed a line with my new boss earlier. But I call them like I see them. And that girl was mad. The longer it took her to recognize that, the worse it would be for her.

I pushed that aside. "Trey, the men I know don't sip champagne and ask if the calamari can be breaded in rice flour," I teased.

Trey laughed. "The members of Gray's team that I know don't wear oversize T-shirts every single day," he retorted.

Well, yeah, I did. I've got a lot of self-confidence, but I will admit I felt a little out of place traipsing into the fancy restaurant wearing my huge Aardvark Pest Control T-shirt. It was from Harry's latest job that lasted about six weeks, controlling the roach population down here. People called them water bugs to sound fancy, like how people called these tiny hotel rooms condos. It might make you feel better, but it didn't change what they were.

"I wear these T-shirts for a good reason," I said.

Trey looked at me skeptically.

"They are a reminder. See, this one here is from Harry, who gambled away all my money. The one I wore yesterday, Bubba's Lawn and Limb, that was from Calvin, who I walked in on sleeping with our neighbor's twenty-year-old daughter. That NC State one was from Jimbo, who was real cute, but, damn, that man couldn't hold his liquor."

Trey was dying laughing. "So it's like self-defense. You won't make the same mistakes if you're wearing their shirts?"

"Hasn't worked out too well yet, though," I said. "But you . . ." I pointed at Trey. "I think I see your game, and I think you're pretty smart."

He raised his eyebrows at me and took a sip of his champagne. "Go on."

"I think you grew up good so you know about food and art and wine and stuff. And I think you're a Yankee so you wear your pants too tight and you slick your hair back. Those things are real. But I think you wanted to be Gray Howard's protégé, so you play up a few things like the fashion tips and the pop culture references so that you are her most favorite person to have around." I took another sip of champagne, knowing I was going to sleep good tonight, even in my car.

I'd figured out that if I could manage to stay away from the cops and keep my expenses to the very bare minimum — phone, a little gas, and a little food — for ten days, I could make enough to put down a deposit on a crappy apartment. The key was moving around a lot. One night I'd stay at the end of Gray's street, one night the parking lot over by the beach bars, which are always full all night on account of all the drunk people. It was pretty safe there because if you didn't stay too many nights in a row, nobody'd bother you — and if they did, you just pretended like you got drunk and passed out in your backseat. No harm, no foul. There was also this deserted place down by the old bridge, but I'll be real: it creeped me the hell out.

The weekend would be harder on not spending money but easier on finding good places to park and sleep. Four days down, six to go. I'd done way worse things than this. Way worse. At least, that's what I kept telling myself.

Trey winked at me but didn't acknowledge what I had said. "Gray has taken to you, Diana. There's no doubt about that." He paused. "Although I think you made her pretty mad tonight."

I cringed. I hadn't meant to, but I knew I had. I bit my lip, my heart pounding now. "Do you think she's going to fire me?"

He shrugged. "Nah. She loves people who stand up to her. She respects them." He gave me a pointed look. "But she loves them until she doesn't. You get me?"

"Noted."

Then, not looking the slightest bit uncomfortable, he said, "We just need to teach you about what she likes. What she's about. She can't Instagram girls' night photos of box wine. You know what I mean?"

I didn't, but I nodded anyway, ready for this to be over. "Well, you're the expert," I said.

"Which makes me indispensable," he added.

People underestimated this kid.

While we were finishing up, Robin texted to ask if I wanted to go out. I texted her back real quick: Dinner with the boss. Can't come.

The last thing I needed was to spend twenty dollars on drinks. That'd set me back a whole extra day. But Robin wasn't letting me off that easy.

Get your ass out here after.

My plan was to ignore her. But then, right as I was driving around trying to find a place to stay, my phone rang, and it was Janet saying, "Girl, why didn't you tell us you dumped Harry?"

"How'd you even know about that?"

"I saw him down at the store. Saddest damn thing you ever seen in your life. He's all weepy and pathetic." She paused. Maybe she was waiting for me to feel sad or something, but I wasn't. "All I know is that it's high time you got to finding yourself a man who can look after you."

One who could look after me . . . I'd been with a man who could look after me once. At least, I thought he could. I had been young then. Eighteen. And right pretty too. At least, that's what people always told me.

Frank was older, just graduating from college when I was graduating from high school. And that summer he'd come back home . . . well, that summer'd been the most magical of my life. Frank's momma, she'd said I was a quick study. I didn't know what *quick study* meant back then.

Frank was a little bit fancy compared to the other boys I'd dated. He had this '57

Thunderbird that he was fixing up and his daddy owned some auto parts stores. Frank was going places. I thought I was going with him. I reckon that I talked like Frank and dressed like Frank and acted like Frank because I didn't know who I was, same as why I act like Harry now. I guess when you grow up an orphan, you don't know who to be. You want everybody to like you, just hoping and praying that one of those foster families is going to stick, so you start acting as nice as you can, trying to be like whoever you're living with, hoping that maybe they'll forget you're even there, just let you stay so you don't have to go anywhere new where maybe the dad looks at you kind of funny when the mom isn't around or one of the bigger kids beats up on you and says you fell.

I used to swear up and down and sideways and around that when I was big enough I was going to have a family of my own. I was going to have a bunch of kids and a nice husband, and we were all going to love each other, and then I'd know what a family was all about. I'd have one of my own and they wouldn't ever leave me.

I thought it'd be with Frank. Hell, I knew it would. But Frank, he'd turned out to be like all the rest, worse even.

"Hello, earth to Di. You've missed two of our Thursday nights out in the last two months. You know how pissy Robin gets about that. You coming or not?"

Robin did get pissy. And that wasn't good for anybody.

"Oh, um," I stammered. "Yeah. Let me change my clothes, and I'll meet you out there."

"Where are you staying now that you and Harry split? Just give me the address of your new place, and I'll pick you up."

My new place. I hadn't told a single one of them about living in my car — or my new job, for that matter. Tonight would be as good a time as any. Maybe just the job. I couldn't stand always being the one down on her luck.

"That's all right. I might be a little late."

We were a ragtag group, these ladies and me. Janet had been married to Ray, her high school sweetheart, since the day after graduation. They seemed real happy together still. Two kids, hard workers, the kind of family that you dream about having one day. They had a nice little brick house in a subdivision outside of town. They'd earned it together and that made it perfect.

Then there was Robin, a big biker chick, always in leather. She'd been married to

Cal, then Chuck, and now she was married to Cal again. They'd fight and make up, fight and make up, but at the end of the day, they couldn't live without each other. I wouldn't want to be around a bunch of fighting all the time, but not being able to live without someone? That seemed pretty nice to me.

Frank crossed my mind when I thought about my girls and their men, but I pushed him away just as fast. Hell, I hadn't seen him in more than twenty years, kind of a long time to be pining away for some man who left you high and dry one day and probably hadn't given you another thought. I wondered where he was now, what kind of horse he'd hitched his wagon to.

Probably somebody like my friend Cheyenne. She was tall and thin and blond. She'd never smoked like the rest of us, so she didn't have those little lines starting to form around her lips. She had Kevin around her little finger, that was for sure. Married fifteen years, three kids, and he still looked at her like she was the Crown Jewels.

I sighed as I walked into the Beach Pub, already crowded and smelling of chicken wings and cigarettes. You couldn't technically smoke in bars anymore, but technically doesn't always pan out. Just like normal, Robin was in her leather jacket, Janet was in some sort of tight T-shirt she was too big to be wearing, and Cheyenne was in a crop top she was too old to be wearing — even though she looked damn good in it.

There was a big margarita waiting at my usual spot at the Beach Pub. The night was off to a good start. I could sip it real slow and not spend a penny.

"Your breakup special," Robin said with a wink.

Cheyenne stood up and hugged me. "I'm so sorry, baby. Why didn't you tell us? Why won't you ever let us help you?"

Why *wouldn't* I ever let them help me?

I waved her off. "Oh, Cheyenne, you know good as anyone I can take care of myself. Always have."

"But maybe we want to take care of you sometimes, Di. Like you take care of all of us all the time."

I did take care of them. Lord knows I did, but it wasn't with heavy stuff like this. I was always helping Cheyenne memorize lines for whatever local play she'd decided to try out for. She was pretty, but the woman could not memorize a line to save her life. And Janet and Ray were always working, so I picked their kids up from after-school care or took them to basketball or something. And Robin had got this wild hair to sell jam at the farmers market and sometimes I'd help her on Saturdays when I wasn't working.

But that's what foster care had taught me. To take care of other people but never, ever depend on them to take care of you. Because they wouldn't. In the end, no one would take care of you but you.

"Girl, where are you staying?" Janet chimed in.

This was the big moment. I had to tell them. Any one of my friends would take me in for a few days without a second thought. Of course they would. I almost said it, that I was staying in my car. But then Robin said, "Di, I respect the hell out of you. You never let this shit get you down. Not breakups, not job stuff. Nothing. You just keep rolling and you always land on your feet."

She was right. I always landed on my feet. A cat with nine lives. Maybe more. I might have nothing — not one thing in all this world — but I had these girls, and, what's more, I had their respect. And that meant more to me than hot water and a clean towel in the bathroom or getting dressed in front of a mirror. It meant more to me than sleeping in a real bed with sheets and covers and a pillow.

I didn't answer Janet. I just said, "I called and checked on Phillip today, and the nurse put him on the line. He talked a little to me." I could feel myself beaming. If Phillip was okay, I was okay.

"You're gonna get him out one day, girl," Cheyenne said. Once a cheerleader, always a cheerleader.

"Oh yeah," Janet said. "If anybody can do it, Di, it's you."

"Speaking of . . ." Cheyenne pulled a napkin out of her bag and handed it to me. There was a drawing on it.

"What's this?" I took a sip of margarita.

"Kevin drew this up for you. He's been saving all his scrap wood and metal and roofing for your beach shack. But then he got to thinking. . . . You know that hideous houseboat that washed up on the island across from the Cape Carolina docks that nobody's done anything about?"

"Yeah," I said, not quite following her.

"Well, he talked to the city, and they said if we could rehab it and you would pay the slip rent, you could keep it."

I was still confused.

"Your restaurant, Di," Robin said, filling in the blanks for me.

I picked up the napkin, staring at it with

my mouth open. "So what you're saying is that he'd take this side out, and this would be the window where people ordered?"

She nodded.

"Like right there on the dock?"

She smiled and nodded again. "And he said it'd be real easy to rig up everything you need for a commercial kitchen in there because there's already a regular kitchen, so the water and electric and everything are hooked up. It'll just need a few tweaks."

Tears sprang to my eyes. Not because I was so far away from ever achieving that dream, but because my girl and her man loved me enough to take my dream and make it their own. "It's not the best time right now," I started.

"It's okay, sweetie," Cheyenne said. "You know he'd do the work for free and get everything as cheap as he could. The city said it will be at least six months before they get it sent over to the salvage yard."

Six months might as well have been an eternity. But if I could work for Gray for three months before she went back home, maybe even stretch it out to four, and save every single penny, maybe, just maybe I could make it work.

I thought about that boat on the napkin again that night as I crawled into the backseat of the Impala in the parking lot of a bar across town that was full of Thursday night cars, most of which wouldn't be going nowhere until morning. I lay on my pillow, balling up a shirt and putting it over the seat belt buckle so it didn't dig into my side. In the morning, I'd drive over to the marina, take out my little duffel bag, take a shower, put on some clean clothes, and brush my teeth. I only had two pairs of underwear left, so I was planning on sneaking them into a load with Gray's stuff. Or if that didn't work, I'd do a load at the laundromat.

I won't lie. The fact that the car door didn't lock made it real hard for me to get settled. But I told myself that fear was a luxury for rich people. Fear is for people who can afford to change their circumstances.

I closed my eyes and felt my heart rate slowing down. I pretended that I was back in that apartment in the projects, all snuggled in the bed when Momma was there and she was acting right and Elizabeth and Charles and Phillip and me were all curled in with her like kittens. Even when he couldn't be around anybody else, Phillip could always snuggle up with Momma. I let myself be in that moment where I was that little girl and I was something like happy. I didn't know any better. I had my momma and I had my brothers and my sister, and that was all I needed.

As I felt myself start to doze off, it wasn't Momma's voice I heard in my head, as I sometimes did. Instead, it was Janet's.

If anybody can do it, Di, it's you.

CHAPTER 5

Gray: Moonshine

It was Friday already. *Friday* Friday. *The* Friday. The night when I was going on my first date in about a hundred years, my first date since my separation.

When I'd e-mailed one of my favorite fashion blogger friends about what to wear, she'd begged me to take selfies of my options to let her post on her blog as a part of her "Sexy CEOs at Every Size" series. Then she would let her readers vote in real time on Twitter via hashtag. I told her I would sooner die. Although a few hours later I realized that posting my foray into dating for her one million followers might have been less horrifying than having Marcy there to help.

"Marcy, stop it!" I scolded yet again. "I'm not hiking this dress up any farther. It is short enough as it is."

"I still say it looks better without the

Spanx," she said.

I stood back from the mirror and looked at my simple hot-pink dress with a bit of flair at the waist. I didn't look half bad.

Marcy was right; the Spanx didn't really matter. "But," I whispered, "they kind of make my ringworm not itch."

Marcy shook her head. "You are so gross. Where is he taking you, fungus fighter?"

I smirked and shrugged, slipping my feet into heeled sandals and tying them around my ankles. "He said somewhere that I'm guaranteed not to see anyone we know."

"If I was out with someone that hot, I'd want everyone to see," she said. "You should take him to Full Circle so that the whole town will be talking about how you're winning your divorce."

I rolled my eyes. "More like laugh at me for being such a pervy old lady."

Secretly, though, I did sort of wish that news that I was out with the tennis pro would get back to my ex. He could say it was pathetic or clichéd or whatever he wanted to, but, deep down, a taste of his own medicine would annoy the hell out of him.

"Hey," Marcy said, "what's Greg's schedule like?"

I rolled my eyes. "Well, let's see. When

I'm there to monitor him, he rolls in about ten, works for a half hour-ish, flirts with the interns for an hour or so, takes a long lunch, goes out on a 'call,' i.e., home to take a nap, and rolls back in around four fifty-seven to see if anyone wants to do happy hour."

Suddenly my mood had soured like ice cream left out in the sun. I didn't want to think about my husband or my divorce or his perky, coed fiancée. I just wanted to go out and have a good time.

"Why do you care?" I added.

Marcy shrugged. "Just wondering."

The doorbell rang, and I raised my eyebrows. "He's ten minutes early," I whispered.

She winked. "Just couldn't wait."

I casually strolled through the entrance hall, willing my heart to stop its pounding. Some of my nerves were because of Andrew, but most of them were because I hadn't been on a date in years. This was probably a good opportunity to dust off the cobwebs. There was no future here, so the stakes were very, very low.

When I opened the door, the first thing I noticed was that he had shaved. With his facial hair, he looked ruggedly sexy; but with a clean face, his big puppy-dog-brown eyes were even sweeter. And he looked younger . . . maybe a little too much younger.

Andrew handed me a bottle of champagne, leaned over to kiss my cheek, put his hands on my hips, and said, "You are beautiful. Seriously."

I wanted not to smile, but who doesn't want to hear that? I held up the champagne and said, "Thanks. I should put this in the fridge."

"I would have brought flowers," he said, "but this seemed like more fun."

"I totally agree," Marcy said, appearing from my bedroom. I cut my eyes at her, warning her without a word to behave herself. "Once you get this girl loosened up, she's a blast." She winked at Andrew, and I shook my head.

She walked by me where I was standing at the fridge and whispered, "I changed my mind about getting married. When you're done with him, can I please have him? Please, please?"

"Go. Home."

And with that, Marcy was out the door.

"So," I said. "Do you want a glass of this now?" I looked out the window at what was a perfect sunset. "It would be a shame to waste this amazing view — especially since my sunsets in this house are numbered."

"Wait, what do you mean, 'numbered'?" he asked with mild alarm, taking the bottle from me, grabbing a cloth off the stovetop, and popping it perfectly, letting it fizz over into the glasses without spilling a single drop.

"Because we're selling it in the divorce."

"You should keep it," he said.

I smiled. "I can't keep it. I have to buy a house for one and a half. This is a house for three."

Andrew clinked his glass with mine and said, "Here's to an amazing night with the most beautiful tennis mom in all the world."

I laughed. "I'm not sure if that's a compliment."

He looked taken aback. "Have you seen the tennis moms out there? I think you know that was a major compliment."

Andrew put his hand on my lower back, leaving chill bumps when he took it away, and I pretended to shade my eyes from the sun to hide my blush. *Come on. Pull yourself together.*

We sat down in the two Adirondack chairs facing the water, and I was very aware of Andrew's eyes on me.

"So here's the big question: Why on earth aren't you shacked up with some sexy sophomore this summer?" I asked.

He laughed and shrugged. "I'm kind of over it, I guess. I did the college thing, and I had a couple years off on the tennis circuit. Grad school is a new leaf for me." He paused and grinned at me. "I'm a serious, grown-up man now." Then he added, "Drunk, loud girls aren't my thing anymore."

I lifted my champagne flute. "Then this might have been a bad call. Champagne tends to up my volume."

Andrew ran his fingertips up my bare arm, where it was resting on the Adirondack chair. "I think I'm going to find you pretty irresistible at any volume."

I leaned my head back, closed my eyes, and smiled, the setting sun warm on my face. I wouldn't admit it to Marcy, but this was one fairly fabulous first date. I had expected to feel uncomfortable, but Andrew had a way about him. He was soft-spoken yet totally self-assured, and his confidence was infectious. No one wants to admit that her husband leaving her for a younger woman makes her feel insecure, but, come on, who wouldn't feel shaken?

I was afraid that being with Andrew would make me feel old. But instead it made me feel young — especially two hours later when we were barefoot on the sandy floor of the crowded Hook, Line, and Sinker, one of Cape Carolina's local bars, singing "Summer Nights" from *Grease* at the top of our lungs.

Andrew let out a loud whoop at the end, swinging the microphone over his head. The bar crowd joined in. He took my hand and kissed it, bowing dramatically at all the other drunk people singing along. I was laughing so hard as he dragged me back to the bar that I couldn't even cheer with him.

Andrew leaned down and rested his forehead on mine. "I really want to kiss you," he said, scrunching his nose in the most adorable way imaginable. I smiled, waiting for that kiss that I really wanted too, feeling my heart racing to the beat of "Get Low" blaring out of the karaoke machine. But then he pulled away.

"I'm not telling our kids that our first kiss was in Hook, Line, and Sinker. Not happening."

I swatted his arm. "We're not having kids, psycho. For heaven's sake, this is a one-time thing."

He handed me a cold beer dripping with condensation, then leaned over and grazed my ear with his lips. "Oh, we'll see about that."

As he pulled away, my eyes met his for a

second too long. Andrew grabbed my hand and pulled me through the crowd to the door. He looked down at my bare feet, handed me his beer, and scooped me up into his arms as he took off for the beach. I was laughing again, and, right before the shoreline, the moon illuminating the peaceful ocean, he tumbled dramatically, but softly enough that the landing didn't hurt either of us. The cool sand felt heavenly on my feet, which were sore from dancing in heels.

Andrew brushed back my hair, which was in a state of total disarray from the dancing, singing, and general sweat-inducing bar drinking. "You know what, pretty girl?"

I smiled. "What?"

"I like you."

I took a sip of my beer. "Maybe it's this talking" — I held up my bottle — "but I think I like you too."

With our faces only a couple of inches apart, Andrew leaned in and kissed me. I didn't even think, as I thought I would, *I'm kissing a twenty-six-year-old.* It just felt good to have a man, or, well, almost a man, as it were, wrap his arms around me.

I giggled, a sound that hadn't come out of my mouth in years, and he said, "See? Now, there's a first-kiss story for our kids. Beach.

Moonshine. Light breeze."

I rolled my eyes.

"So what do you want to do now?"

I shrugged. Then I leaned over and whispered in his ear, like he'd done to me a few minutes ago: "I want to win that karaoke contest."

Andrew's face became serious. "Oh, Gray. We're going to dominate. That booze cruise gift certificate is as good as ours."

We both laughed, and I had to admit that I hadn't had this much fun in quite some time. It gave me the slightest pang for my mother, a woman who always used to say that fun was the point of it all, that every woman wants to feel like her life is a great adventure. I'd always thought that adventurer gene must have skipped a generation, or that my sister got it all.

As Andrew took my hand again and led me up the beach, I realized that, at least for the moment, all of my reservations about Andrew and tonight and maybe even what my future held were gone. So I did what my mother would have done. I let go of his hand, ran up ahead, and did my best cartwheel. And I realized that, in the grandest of ironies, this year, the year I lost my mother, I might just have found a little bit of her too.

Diana: Mud on a Cow's Hind Parts

It was my first — and, God willing, only — weekend before I would get my apartment. I was tired from barely sleeping the last few nights and anxious about keeping it together all weekend, and my gratitude at coming to work for Gray had been replaced by the irritation that her life was moving forward and mine wasn't. It wasn't right. It wasn't fair. And I was so damn tired of being the one getting the short end of the stick.

I had splurged on a burger, fries, and a soda from the dollar menu, and I was sitting in my car finishing it up late. That's the secret — you have to wait as long as you can to eat because then you're still full in the morning, and you don't need breakfast. I'd learned that as a kid. During the week I got free breakfast and lunch at school, but after that it was every kid for herself at some of the foster houses. I think people outside the system assume someone's keeping track of whether or not kids are being fed, but that isn't always true. And sometimes it's the ones you don't suspect too. Like, the ones who can't keep house and seem kind of rude take the best care of you, and the ones that seem all perfect and holy leave you to starve while they're throwing a bunch of table scraps to the obese dog.

I climbed in the backseat and pulled some red polish out of my bag to get my toes looking presentable again when I saw a couple kids on the beach. It made me think of Frank and me back when I was young and things were good. I knew what they were feeling just by looking at them because I'd been there too. They're all madly in love, and they think they're going to be together forever. It takes you back and makes you feel warm and optimistic. But tonight I didn't feel anywhere near optimistic. I was pissed off at everyone, even the teenagers canoodling on the beach. Might have been the lack of nicotine. I couldn't really say.

Stupid kids, I thought. *Don't have one damn clue about the real world.* I watched that young buck moseying up the beach toward the lot where I was parked, his arm slung around the shoulders of some tiny girl in a dress so tight I could see her kidneys. I wanted to rewind time, find a good man, be young and in love. Or, more like, I wanted to rewind to the time when I *was* young and in love and have that same man I'd wanted deep in my heart for all these years. But since that wasn't ever going to happen, I just went on about my business of hating these damn loud kids interrupting my rest.

I was watching them pass by from the

backseat where I was lying, when that girl stopped. She smashed her darn face right up in my window, and then she gasped.

It took me until right then to notice that that wasn't a girl. It was Gray. Now my heart started racing. She would find out I was sleeping in my car. She'd fire me. Then I'd be back at square one, back to nowhere to go, looking for another job. I could feel the money I'd saved for my deposit floating away.

She opened the door like it was her car, slid into the front seat, and said, "Diana, what in the hell are you doing? Are you *sleeping* out here?"

I could tell she was kind of tipsy by the way the words came out real lazy.

"Well . . . um . . ." I didn't know what to say, but I was out of excuses. "I'm sure as hell not crammed in this backseat for my health."

She shook her head. "Nope. You're coming to my house."

I rolled my eyes. "I can't go to your house, Gray. We don't even know each other that well."

I wasn't sure why I was arguing. Going to her house sounded like the best thing I could think of, like jumping into the cool ocean when you've been sweating waiting outdoor tables all day in a hundred degrees and full sun.

"Oh, we don't?" she said, putting her hands on her hips. "We sure know each other well enough that you felt the need to say I was mad at my poor dead mother."

"Yeah," I said, feeling contrite. "I am sorry about that. I overstepped."

She nodded, but she didn't say I was wrong.

"Run along now, children. I need to get some sleep. And, again, I'm not coming to your house."

Gray leaned over between the seats real close to me. "You're right. Better to hang out in this deserted parking lot protected by a door that I'm assuming doesn't lock because I just opened it right up, and wait for God only knows who to get you, than to come spend the night in my guesthouse." She stopped, and when I didn't say nothing, she added, "With the running water and the pillows."

I sighed. The door didn't lock right, and someone *could* get me out here.

"But what about Trey?" I asked, my last feeble attempt to get out of this.

"Trey sleeps in the main house because he has to be near me at all times." She rolled her eyes. "I'm like his therapy dog or something."

"Who's Trey?" her friend asked as I felt myself coming around.

"He's a member of the brand," I said snarkily.

That cracked Gray up. "See how much fun we have?" she asked. Then she got serious. "If you aren't coming to my house, then we're all sleeping in your car tonight."

"Fun," the boy said.

I rolled my eyes. "You win, Gray. Is that what you want to hear?"

"It is always what I want to hear." She reached over and squeezed my hand. "Well, I think it's pretty clear that you're the only one who's fit to drive." As I started to get out, she slid out of the seat and pranced around to the other side of the car, moving the front seat forward without me telling her how and sliding into the back, that boy stuck on her like mud on a cow's hind parts the whole time. All sparkling and happy like she was, she didn't look a day over twenty-five. That was good, because that boy she was with, he had a baby face if I'd ever seen one.

I glanced in my rearview mirror at them all cuddled in my backseat. "Can I stay too?" I heard him whisper, sticking out his bottom lip.

"No!" she retorted. "Are you crazy, Andrew?"

"Please? Just to sleep?"

I rolled my eyes, because I knew that boy wasn't staying to sleep like I wasn't staying to play Pictionary.

"Hey," I said when they kissed. "This isn't Uber."

Gray laughed. "Oh, sorry, Diana."

I eyed her in the rearview. "Honey, that boy is way too young for you, and he's going to be gone before sunrise tomorrow."

She laughed. "Oh, don't I know it. But isn't he so adorable for tonight?"

He was.

"Hey," he said, "I'm sitting right here."

"Oh, lighten up, Di," she said. "We're just having a little fun."

Maybe it was because she was drunk, and maybe it was because I was mad and cigaretteless, but I realized that, me and Gray, we were talking to each other like we were family already. And when I pulled up in her driveway, I started feeling like, for the first time in a long time, maybe I had a place to go after all.

The next morning, it took me a minute to figure out where I was when I woke up. Not in the back of my car. Not in Harry's house. I stretched, feeling my limbs sink into the comfortable mattress, the sheets and covers feeling crisp and clean. I sighed and sank my head back into the pillows. This was heaven. Real, true heaven.

The sun was pouring through the crack in the white curtains that blocked out almost all the light. I glanced over at the clock and popped up. I couldn't believe I'd slept until damn near ten thirty. I hadn't slept that long since I was probably twenty. Hadn't ever had the chance, really, always working like I was.

And now I didn't know what to do. It was Saturday, so technically I wasn't supposed to work. So did I slink out of here and back to the car? Did I stay and work as a thank-you? I was scared and kind of embarrassed to see Gray after last night, but I decided to bite the bullet, face her head-on, and make myself useful.

I threw on a pair of shorts and a Quality Automotive T-shirt (Bobby: six kids, six moms, always getting pulled over and shaken down for unpaid child support on our dates, real winner), brushed my teeth and hair, and then walked down the steps, out the door, and over to Gray's back door. I started to put my key in, then realized the door was unlocked. Lord. I hoped she hadn't slept like that. But as I opened the fridge to make some breakfast, I could hear her and that boy laughing, so at least she had a man to protect her if someone came in.

I reorganized the fridge and found some good-looking bacon and eggs I had bought earlier in the week. Making breakfast would take my mind off that cigarette I wanted so bad.

"What are you doing here?" I heard a familiar voice ask.

"What are any of us doing here?" I responded.

Trey laughed. He was in a bathrobe and slippers, holding a laptop in one hand and a cup of coffee in the other.

"Do you ever quit working?" I asked.

He shrugged. "Do you?"

"Touché."

"So I guess the date went well?" Trey whispered.

"Sure seems like it."

I cut a perfect circle out of a piece of bread and was cracking the first egg, bacon sizzling away on the pan beside me, when I heard the door creak, and Gray came out of her room with her bathrobe on, smiling and giggly, that boy in nothing but his boxers trailing behind her. She stopped real quick when she saw me.

"Diana! What are you doing?"

"I figured you two might've worked up an appetite." I smirked.

Gray made a noise like she was shocked and said, "We did nothing of the sort! I am a lady."

Andrew half smiled. "Yes, ma'am, you are." Then he looked at me, as if I were Mom and they needed to explain themselves. "For real, I just passed out here."

"Please do not ever call me 'ma'am,' " Gray said. Then she whispered, "Maybe you should put some pants on."

Andrew shrugged like clothes were optional when you looked like him. She gasped.

"What?" I said.

"You're making egg on toast?"

I shrugged. "Yeah. What about it?"

"My mom used to make me egg on toast."

Then she got real quiet and walked inside her big pantry. I didn't know if I'd made her happy or sad, but either way I figured I had helped her have some real feelings about her mom. I heard some noise that I figured out was the Keurig once she came out a few minutes later with two steaming cups.

I finished plating the food, wiped my hands on my shorts, and said, "That's my cue to leave. Y'all have a good day. Thanks for putting me up and all." Then, in a loud mock whisper, I added, "You look like a damn fool carrying on with that kid."

"Hey!" Andrew said. "Throw me a bone here. I'm having a hard enough time as it is."

Marcy wandered in from the backyard, wearing Uggs, worn-out sleep shorts, and an oversize T-shirt. She added, "Yeah, come on, Diana. For God's sake, she had to sleep with Greg for a decade. She deserves a freakin' break."

Trey turned to me and said, "Where exactly do you think you're going?"

"I'm getting my new apartment today," I lied.

Gray raised her eyebrows questioningly at me. Then she said, "It's not like anyone stays in the guesthouse. Seems kind of dumb to waste your money on some apartment when you'll be coming over every day for the next few months. The summer is just starting," she added. "Why don't you stay?"

My instinct was to argue, but it's not like I could pretend I was doing great. She had seen me sleeping in my car. No way around that one.

"I did get you fired," she added.

I shook my head. I wanted to stay in that gorgeous guesthouse more than I could say, but I couldn't do it. It was too much, too soon. It felt wrong.

"How about we make a deal?" Gray said.

I wouldn't take her handout. But a deal? A deal I could do.

"I've been thinking about hiring a professional organizer to get all my closets and drawers and stuff straight. How about you help me with that in exchange for rent?"

I put my hand out to shake hers. "But it has to be in addition to my normal hours."

"Fine," she said.

I exaggerated a sigh and said, "Somebody's got to look after you. You're a damn mess."

"Preach it," Marcy said.

Gray laughed and backed up to where Andrew was sitting on the stool and rested against his leg. He slid his arm around her stomach. "No use wasting this gorgeous day," she said. "I vote we finish this up on the lawn."

I grabbed one of the plates and walked into the sunny living room, the rays warming the floors, making them look like fresh honey.

I breathed for the first time in a long time

without thinking about where I was going to go or work or eat. For a minute, for now, I had a place in this world. I couldn't believe it, but for the first time in a long time, I felt like I belonged.

Chapter 6

Gray: Strangers, Plural

Lying on my back on the grass, Andrew on one side, Marcy on the other, Diana in an Adirondack chair dozing, Trey sitting at the edge of the dock with his feet in the water, it finally hit me that I had gone on my first date in more than twelve years. I had kissed a boy who wasn't Greg and slept with my head on his chest. I had allowed a relative stranger to stay at my house. Looking over at Diana, I realized I had better make that strangers, plural.

But maybe this shouldn't have surprised me. I was a notoriously generous drunk. I made huge donations to charities, placed ridiculous bids on auction items, volunteered to help friends with projects I had no time for.

But sharing this house that I loved so much, this place where I felt calm and free and alive, was something I had always enjoyed no matter what frame of mind I was in. And maybe that's why it actually felt kind of right.

Yawning, I finally said what I had been thinking for hours. "I can't bear the thought of selling this house."

Andrew stroked my arm. "I wouldn't want to sell it either. This place is awesome."

Marcy sighed. "For the millionth time, Gray, don't sell it. Keep the place."

"I thought you had to sell it in the divorce," Andrew said.

Marcy laughed with a snort and said under her breath, "She could buy the whole damn street."

Andrew rolled over and rose up on his elbows, lifting his sunglasses to show me those gorgeous eyes. "Hot *and* rich. I knew it. You *are* the perfect sugar mama."

My mouth widened in surprise, and I slapped his arm as he laughed.

"I'm kidding, I'm kidding."

Diana chimed in, coming out of her doze at the perfect moment, "All kidding is at least ten percent truth." Then a moment later: "Why don't you keep the house, if you love it so much?"

I looked up into the sky, the clouds lazily floating by, sun warming this little patch of earth so perfectly. "I guess I thought it would be weird, you know? Like this was our dream house, and now that he's gone, the dream is gone." I sighed. "But I can still sort of see myself here at seventy years old, watching my grandkids run around in the yard, taking the boat across to the club. . . ."

Andrew leaned over and kissed me, his warm lips melting into mine.

"Get a room," Diana said under her breath.

It was one of those perfect early-summer mornings where the breeze is blowing enough to keep the heat down and the mosquitoes away and you're surrounded by people whose company you enjoy.

I was wondering when Andrew was going to leave so the rest of us could recap the night when he stood up and said, "Can I call you tomorrow?"

I patted his hand and looked from the sky to his face, where a five-o'clock shadow was forming, making him even more gorgeous, if that was possible. "You are so sweet, but you don't have to pretend this is more than a one-time thing."

"I'm not pretending, Gray. I can see this going somewhere."

"Yeah," Diana said under her breath. "To court for statutory rape."

Marcy laughed a little too long. I got up

and walked Andrew to the car as Trey called, "Bye, man."

I kissed Andrew softly by the door of his old Land Cruiser and said, "Thank you for last night. It was fun."

"It will be fun again," he said, leaning over and kissing that spot where my neck met my shoulder. "Much, much more fun." He winked at me.

"Look," I said, "you don't have to do this. I'm a grown-up. You don't have to pretend. It was a fun night. I'll see you at tennis when Wagner gets home."

"Okay, Gray," he said. "That's fine."

I didn't like how he said it, how the flirting was abruptly over. My heart started racing. Had I talked him into not seeing me again? Oh my gosh. Did I *want* to see him again?

He opened the door to the Land Cruiser and climbed inside. As he cranked it loudly, I said, "Or, I mean, you know . . . you could call me. If you want."

He smiled, closed the door, and rolled down the window, saying nothing. He waved as he pulled out of the driveway, and I realized that I wanted to see him again. I really, really did. And now I wasn't sure he would even call me.

Diana walked over to me on the driveway

and said quietly, "Look, Gray, are you positive about this guesthouse thing? Because if you've changed your mind . . ."

I hadn't been sure about it at all. In fact, I'd been the opposite of sure. But if I knew Sharon Marcus, Bill's wife, I knew that she had had this woman thoroughly vetted and background-checked. If my friends trusted Diana, I figured I could too. "I hate being all alone here, Diana," I said, then was shocked that I had opened up to her like that. I amended, "Then when Wagner gets home, if I need you to babysit him . . ."

"Or Andrew?"

We both laughed.

"You like him, don't you?" she asked.

I shrugged, but the butterflies in my stomach told me I did. I linked my arm with Diana's, and I could tell she was relieved by the way her muscles relaxed. I thought about the story she had told me about growing up in foster care. I wondered how many nights she hadn't known where she would lay her head. It nauseated me. And it made me really sure that my drunken, overgenerous offer had been the right one.

Late that night, Trey had gone to Raleigh for some meetings with clients, Marcy was on a date she had written off as boring before she'd even met him, Diana was in the guesthouse, and Andrew hadn't called or texted. No Wagner, no Greg, no friends, no distractions. Just me, alone at the end of the day, facing the reality that this was my life now.

I sat down at my vanity, studying my face. Had those lines on my forehead been there before? Hadn't my eyes been brighter? My skin suppler? Was this what divorce looked like on me?

Divorce.

I thought of my mom, of how her marriage was the biggest point of pride in her life, of how hard I had worked to hide the dissolution of mine during her last days. I felt a tear run down my cheek, but I brushed it away angrily. Whenever I had a quiet moment, I would almost always slide back into thoughts about how horrible the past year had been.

I opened the jewelry box on my vanity and slipped on my diamond eternity band and my three-stone engagement ring. I stared down at my hand, remembering the moments I had received each ring, how ecstatic I had been, how content. I never would have imagined that it wouldn't work out forever, that Greg and I weren't destined for happily ever after.

I closed the lid to my jewelry box and

pulled my sheets back. As I climbed in, the weight of the covers — and the rings — felt comforting and familiar. I closed my eyes and pretended that Greg was softly snoring beside me.

And I told myself that someday, somehow, I would learn to be happy again — whether a man was beside me in that bed or not.

Diana: Gold

When Gray confirmed that she wanted me living in her guesthouse, I almost couldn't believe it. My own Pinterest-worthy space on one of the most expensive streets in town, with plush bed linens and those real nice inside shutters on all the windows. It even had its own kitchen.

Plus, even though I gave Gray a hard time about what a disaster she was, she hardly had any laundry, and she didn't make that much of a mess. If she didn't work all the time, I wasn't sure she'd need me at all.

This morning I'd been over there and made her that green juice she liked and made her bed and folded the rest of Trey's wash, so it would be clean when he got back from Raleigh. By eight thirty, Gray had shooed me out the door and told me to get unpacked. "Just let me know if you need anything," she'd said.

I couldn't imagine needing anything besides what she'd already given me.

Before I left, I happened to glance down at Gray's left hand. I looked away quickly. She blushed. "Oh, um . . ."

"You don't have to explain anything to me. It's your ring. You should wear it if you want to." Even still, she took it off and put it back in her jewelry box. And I had the feeling that our girl Gray wasn't as "fine" as she led everyone to believe.

I didn't have too much stuff to unload, just the duffel bags I'd filled when I fled Harry's house. I sat down on the edge of the bed, feeling tired even though I'd slept nine hours the night before and woken up to a view of the water.

I got up and dumped out the first bag of my stuff on the bed. That's when I saw it. I'd wanted to get rid of it when things went down the way they did, but letting go of that locket was like letting go of the last piece of the life and the man that I thought I'd won for myself. I sat down again and rubbed the golden edges with my thumb. I didn't want to, but I had to. I opened that locket and stared at a picture of me, young and pretty, hair blowing in the wind, resting my head on Frank's shoulder. I wished I could see his whole face straight-on, but you couldn't because he was kissing my head. And, oh, that smile on my face . . . Well, I can tell you I've never felt that happy since. That's the God's honest truth.

Most of the time I was strong and brave, so when Frank popped up in my mind, I pushed him away. But today? Today I had a little bit of time. I could drink a cup of coffee and unpack my things — and my thoughts about Frank. Since it was my day, I didn't have to think about how it ended between us. I didn't have to break my own heart remembering what might have been. Instead, I could just focus on how good it was when we were together, how happy we were and how in love.

"You couldn't be more beautiful, Diana," Frank had said. "I swear it with everything I have, you couldn't be."

We were sitting in the sand on an early spring day in 1998, one of those days when it's warm enough to get outside in the fresh air and sunshine — but tomorrow there might be a blizzard. I was wearing my new jean shorts that my friend Robin swore made my butt look like Cindy Crawford's, and Frank had just got a brand-new camera. It was a fancy one, with an automatic timer and all that.

"I have to photograph you, Diana. Please

will you let me? I know you hate it, but please?"

See, I hadn't realized yet that, through the lens of someone who loves you, you can't help but look your most radiant. It's like the camera picks up on the energy of the person, and it starts to see you as beautiful as they do. It's magic, really.

"Oh, Frank," I had said, giggling. "Why on earth would you want to take a picture of me?"

Frank had wanted to be a photographer back then. He thought he was going to make his living capturing dolphins jumping in the water and waves crashing on the shore and the way a rose looks when it's about to bloom. Oh my goodness, I had thought he was the smartest, most artistic, most talented man in the whole entire universe. Frank saw the world through a different lens than I did, literally and figuratively. He had grown up in a stable, loving family. He'd never worried about where he would sleep or when he would eat next. He was free-spirited in a way that I knew I never could be, that my past simply couldn't allow. But I loved living vicariously through him, feeling how he felt even for just a moment.

He had jumped up, that camera in his

hand, and before I could even argue he was snapping away. I smiled and laughed and danced for the camera, but really for Frank, dipping my toes in the water and blowing him kisses. I don't know that I've ever been so carefree, before or since.

"The light is perfect," he was saying. "See how the sun is just beginning to set? It casts this gorgeous glow."

"No, you are perfect," I had said to him. To say I meant that with all my heart is an understatement. "Okay. Now let me get some of you."

Frank looked at me like maybe I was a little bit crazy, which, back then, I sort of was — especially about him.

"Look," he said, "I'm going to set the timer so we can get one together." When Frank did something, anything at all, he did it with his whole heart. His eagerness to learn everything about this new camera was symbolic of his zest for life. It was one of the things that had made me fall in love with him so hard and so fast.

I sat down dutifully, right at the base of the sand dune. "You better hurry up," I told him. "The sun is going to be all the way down in a few minutes."

I'd never seen the beach that secluded. It was like our own private island paradise. He ran and plopped down beside me. I laid my head on his shoulder, and he kissed me, and that's when that photo snapped, out of that joy. I didn't think that day could get any better, but Frank reached in his pocket and said, "I got something for you, Diana."

We were too young, and we didn't know each other well enough, but if it had been a diamond ring, I can assure you I would've said yes. I remember gasping and saying, "Frank, it's the most beautiful locket I've ever seen."

"For the most beautiful girl I've ever seen," he said, fastening the chain around my neck.

I kissed him, and when I looked up again, the sun had gone down. It was getting dark out there on that deserted beach, the waves crashing on the shore, the wind blowing just right. Me and Frank, we didn't have to say a word to know what was going to happen next. It was one of those perfect moments where you're young and in love and you know the person you're with is the person you're going to make love to for the rest of your life, not just on an old picnic blanket that night.

We laughed and carried on, and I can't even count how many times we said we loved each other. "I can't wait to marry you,

Diana," I can still hear Frank saying as I unbuttoned the blue Polo oxford he had tucked into his khaki shorts. "I can't wait to have you all to myself for the rest of my life, to have babies with you and our own little house. I'm going to treat you like gold. I'm going to make you the happiest woman in the world. . . ."

I wanted to leave it with that thought, so I started folding up my shirts and putting them in one of Gray's pretty drawers with the sweet-smelling shelf paper inside. I just wanted to remember him saying he was going to make me the happiest woman in the world. That day, at least, he held up his end of the bargain. That day was probably the happiest day of my life.

It's funny how sometimes what seems like a girl's happiest day can end up being the very worst one she'll ever have. And for a girl whose momma gave her away and left her out there to fend for herself, that's really saying something.

Chapter 7

Gray: A Promising Start

"Do you think I ruined it?" I was asking Marcy the following Tuesday as I spread my towel out on my lounge chair.

It was a little windy for the beach, but it was a glorious pool day — and yet there were only five or six people out here. I was feeling distracted and antsy over the Andrew situation, and I had decided to move Click-Market headquarters poolside, under a giant black-and-white-striped umbrella. Marcy, of course, had to come along because man hunting was always on the menu.

Diana had been standing in my bedroom folding a mountain of laundry — where did it all come from? — while we were making our plans, and I realized that, if I was going back to the site of last week's diving trauma, I needed all the reinforcements I could get.

"Absolutely not," she had said. "I won't do it."

"The laundry will be there when you get back," Marcy pointed out.

"Just come for lunch," I'd whined.

She shook her head.

"Remember your hairbrush?" I asked. "How that pretty hair didn't take away the bullies, but it made you feel like you could take them on?" She crossed her arms. "You told me that I had to find what made me brave. Well," I said. I pointed to her and then to Marcy.

Diana gave me that exasperated look that I was now so familiar with, as if she were the exhausted mother and I were the naughty, needy child. But then I knew I had won. She only gave me that look when she was relenting, which, honestly, was rarely.

"It's a low blow to use my own brilliant advice against me," she said.

I shrugged. "Then quit being so smart."

Now poolside, Marcy lowered her sunglasses. "Regular bikini. I assume this means you are fungus-free?"

I gave her a thumbs-up.

She raised her eyebrows. "Lucky Andrew."

"Oh my gosh," I said. "Do you think that's why he hasn't called me? Not the ringworm," I amended. "Because I didn't sleep with him?"

"No," she said as if the idea was ridiculous. "You've been on one date. I'm not saying he wouldn't have been thrilled, but I can assure you he wasn't expecting it."

I sighed and leaned back in my chair. "Good. I just don't know how any of this works."

She pulled her sunglasses up. "How it works is you do whatever makes you happy and don't do what doesn't."

"Really?"

Trey, who had made it back directly after his meeting in Raleigh, was spreading his towel on the other side of me, and Diana was getting an ice water at the bar.

"It's clear that you're an 'elder millennial,' " Trey chimed in. He grinned mischievously at me, and I stuck my tongue out at him. "You do you, girl. Those are the rules now."

"Lord," Diana said as she walked up. "I like you, Trey, but sometimes you lay it on a little thick."

I felt butterflies in my stomach again as I absentmindedly checked my phone for the millionth time since Andrew had pulled out of my driveway three days earlier. "That's what I'm saying. Not lucky Andrew. No Andrew. I finally decide I like him, and he has obviously decided he doesn't like me."

"You can only push a man so far," Diana

said. "If they don't think you like them, what are they supposed to do? Chase after you like a sad puppy?"

I smoothed out the wrinkles in my towel as Diana removed the T-shirt she had on over her bathing suit.

Trey was saying, "You're the older woman. You have the upper hand. You should call him if you want to see him."

That was technically true, I guessed, but somehow I felt like he had the upper hand, like the logical thing would be that since I was older and arguably less desirable, it was up to him to call me. Either way, I had made a big show of avoiding the tennis courts — despite the fact that Andrew spotting was 95 percent of the reason we were here.

"I think he's playing this brilliantly, actually," Marcy said. "Chasing you and then letting you miss him."

"Oh, yes!" Trey chimed in. "G, didn't you read Candace Bushnell's essay about cubbing? I think it was in *Vogue*. . . ."

"Or maybe *Bazaar,*" Marcy chimed in.

I sighed. "Okay. I'm taking the bait. What is cubbing?"

"It's reverse cougaring," Marcy said, and Diana burst out laughing. "You know, like when the younger man is coming on to you."

"Except that that essay was about like twenty-year-old men and fifty-year-old women," Trey said.

"Great," I said under my breath. "That makes me feel so much better."

"Hold up," Diana said. "Trey, you mean to tell me that you read *Vogue* and *Bazaar*?"

He shrugged. "I have to read all the magazines Gray reads because then when she says like, 'Trey, when we go to New York can you get us a reservation at that French restaurant they were talking about in *Vogue*?' then I know she really means the Moroccan restaurant in Chicago that she read about in *Elle*."

I didn't love how that made me sound, but he wasn't wrong. He was literally amazing.

"You aren't going to skin her and wear her, are you?" Diana asked.

Trey started to retort but then he stopped rubbing sunscreen on his shoulders, took my hand, and said, "You have *got* to be kidding me."

I looked up. Diana was in a faded one-piece that was starting to fray at the edges. But she was hot. I mean, *hot.* She was tall, probably five-eight, and had this gorgeous hourglass shape. "I'm sorry," I said. "You've been hiding *that* under those T-shirts? No, ma'am. No more."

She held up today's Root Cafe T-shirt. It looked innocent enough. "But, honey, you don't understand. Carl was the weirdest one yet. He had this foot fetish." Diana shuddered. "Let's just say it's in everyone's best interest if we leave it at that."

"Foot fetishes are more common than you would think," Marcy remarked. Then she added, "Diana, your boobs are amazing. Who did them?"

She rolled her eyes. "Yeah, I was sleeping in my car last week, but I've had my boobs done."

"I saw you in that Taylor Plastic Surgery T-shirt last week," Marcy retorted. "Don't lie to me."

Diana lay back on her chair as Trey whispered in my ear, "Do you think she's going to sue us for sexual harassment?"

"Probably," I said, thinking that that would just be one more thing to add to the shitstorm.

"That shirt was from Ken, the phlebotomist." She turned to Marcy. "When you find about a hundred vials of blood hidden in a man's laundry basket, you don't stick around to find out why they're there."

"Damn," I said. "You really have some stories, Di. I only have Greg stories. It's pretty boring." I felt a familiar anxiety grip my throat as I said his name.

"Yeah, but your Greg stories are worse than all my ex stories combined."

"Speaking of ex stories," Trey said, "you're never going to be telling ex stories about Andrew if you don't call him. Like I said, upper hand, sister."

Before I could retort, Marcy was calling, "Hi, Stafford," waving to a handsome man in the pool with three kids in Puddle Jumpers.

"Hi, Marcy. Hi, Gray," he replied.

"Hi, Stafford," I called sunnily. "I can't believe how big the kids have gotten!"

"I know," he said, "happens fast."

"So what did you hear about Stafford and Alice?" I whispered as soon as he was out of earshot.

"I heard that she had an affair."

I nodded. "Me too."

"But," Marcy said, "I heard she had an affair because he was a little more interested in his business partner than his wife."

"No!" Trey said. "I heard she left him" — he paused dramatically — "for her dealer."

"Oh, Lord," Diana said. "Oldest story in the book."

"Is it?" Trey responded.

I lowered my sunglasses to study Stafford

while he was throwing his three kids in the pool. "So, what do you think about him?"

"I don't know," Marcy said. "He's cute. He's nice. His kids are pretty. I could probably sport them around."

"So you don't mind the kids?"

She shrugged. "I mean, not really. I guess it's just one of those things. If I loved him enough, we'd work it out — and I could keep my figure."

I already knew Marcy didn't consider divorce a negative. In fact, she thought it was a plus. According to Marcy, a divorced man knew what commitment was all about. In her mind, a man's second marriage had a brighter future than his first. Statistics would disagree with Marcy, but once she got something in her head, that was it.

"Should you go talk to him, you think?" I asked.

"You should," Trey whispered.

"Y'all need to learn to mind your own damn business," Diana said.

Marcy reached into her bag and pulled out her sunscreen. She stood up confidently and rested her foot on the end of the lounge chair while languidly rubbing her leg. Stafford looked. And he kept looking.

"All right then. That's a promising start," I said.

I saw our summer friend Julian, notoriously single, notoriously hot, and partially out of the closet, walking through the gate. Marcy and I had felt relieved when he finally came out to us. Only days before his announcement a couple years ago, I had been saying, "I just want to know. I mean, if he is, we could vacation together and he could be my plus-one to events that Greg doesn't want to go to. If not, that's inappropriate."

"Exactly," Marcy had said. "And you know whether to keep him in the back of your mind as a possibility if Greg dies."

We had both burst out laughing.

"Okay," I said. "You get in the pool and chat Stafford up. I'll check in with Julian."

I waved, and he sauntered over. Eyes turned left and right because, believe you me, that man spent a lot of time in the gym. When his shirt was off, there was drool coming from every which direction. He leaned over and kissed me on the cheek. "Hi, gorgeous. You look as fabulous as I've ever seen you. How's the divorce treating you?"

"It's treating me pretty great," I half lied, eyeing Marcy as she laughed flirtatiously. Then I added my signature line: "It was a beautiful chapter in my life story, and now

I'm ready for a new one."

"Getting any action?"

Diana chuckled knowingly. I shot her a look. But Andrew did run through my mind.

"I heard that I'm-too-sexy-for-my-shirt Andrew has a thing for you," Julian said.

"How in the world did you hear that?" I was truly shocked.

"Well, let's see. . . ." He put his finger up to his chin. "Derrick overheard Brooke on the phone saying that someone at the club had asked you out, which obviously wasn't much to go on. But then Derrick was playing tennis later that afternoon and he saw Andrew smiling and texting, so he asked Tina who Andrew was dating and she said no one, but she wished he were texting her with that smile." That made us both laugh, as Tina was at least seventy. I motioned for him to continue. "So then Tina asked her daughter Margot if she knew who Andrew was dating, and when Margot asked her little cousin Roger, he said that he had seen Andrew at Hook, Line, and Sinker with one Ms. Gray Howard."

"Damn," Diana said.

"You should be in the FBI," I added.

Julian gasped. "So it is true! I want to eat whipped cream off his abs."

"So do I!" I said, laughing. "I'll keep you

posted."

"And that, my dear, is why we're summer soul mates."

"Speaking of soul mates," I whispered, glancing toward Marcy and Stafford, who were still chatting, "what's the deal with Stafford?"

"None of the rumors are true," he said. "Alice is trying to blackmail him." He paused dramatically. "From rehab."

"Hmm. Blackmail. Not a bad plan. What you got on Greg?"

We laughed again. "You have everything on Greg you'd ever need all on your own."

"And yet I'm losing this damn divorce." I finally turned and said, "Julian, I want to introduce you to Trey."

Julian pulled his sunglasses up onto his head as Trey stood up. "Oh my Lord, we finally meet in the flesh. All I have heard about from this one is Trey this and Trey that."

Trey laughed and held out his hand. "Nice to meet you," he said.

Julian looked at me, confused. "Wait. He's straight?"

I sighed. "Is this some sort of new cultural norm I've missed out on? Like I have to inform everyone now if someone is straight?"

"He wears his hair like that because he's a Yankee and says 'girl' because he's up Gray's butt," Diana said. "Now you're all caught up."

"And this is Diana," I said, laughing.

"And who is Diana?" Julian asked.

"Oh, um . . ." I didn't know what to say.

She interjected, "I'm her maid."

"She is my savior," I retorted.

A voice from behind me said, "Jesus, Gray. Are you so high-maintenance now that you have to take your maid with you to the pool?" I turned to see our "friend" Alexander (don't you dare call him Alex), who was cocky as hell and didn't care who he pissed off.

I could feel myself reddening with embarrassment. I glared at him. "We are all having a morning break, *Alex.*" I'd evened the score now.

"Maybe you could quit being so rude," Julian added.

Alexander just shrugged and continued to the bar, where he pulled out a stool and sat down.

I mouthed *I'm sorry* to Diana. She rolled her eyes. As Stafford turned to throw one of the kids in the water, Marcy looked at me and made a slicing motion with her finger across her throat.

"Really?" I said when she reached me a couple minutes later. "None of those rumors are true."

"He has *full custody,*" Marcy said as if she were saying, *"raging herpes."*

"Ugh," Julian said. "Nobody's got time for that."

"I thought you didn't care about the kids," I said.

"Yeah," she said. "Every other weekend I don't. But raising a one-, three-, and five-year-old on my own? Please."

"Agreed," Julian said. "Hey, what about Alex*ander*?"

"He brings his own wineglass to the bar," Marcy groaned.

"Ohhhh," Julian said. "I was under the impression that you were marrying for money. If you're looking for love, I have a few prospects in mind." Then he waved at a woman entering through the gate and was calling, "That bag!" as he walked away.

"He's too much," Marcy said. "But he really does mean well."

"Does he?" Diana asked.

We all laughed, and I felt myself relax. She didn't seem mad about the earlier slight.

The waiter came up, and I said, "We need to order lots of food."

"Oh, oh! Onion rings!" Trey said.

"And lots of rosé," Marcy added.

"Haven't you people ever heard of beer?" Diana asked.

"And evidently Diana will have some sort of beer," I said.

We were all smiling and happy. Yes, there was work to be done, but that's why God invented laptops. I missed my boy, so many thousands of miles away. But if I couldn't be with him, I realized, there was nowhere I would rather be right now than right here, lounging poolside, with my favorite people, all summer long.

Later that night, I tossed my phone on the outdoor couch beside me, finally giving up. Andrew wasn't going to call. He just wasn't. I had ruined my summer fling. I weighed my options. Did I call him? Did I casually run into him at the club tomorrow? Because there was no denying that I hadn't stopped thinking about him for a moment since he'd left my house. But I knew I wouldn't, because I had too much pride. Or maybe I was too afraid. What if he hadn't called because the divorced thing had finally sunk in? Or because I hadn't been pretty enough, or because I had cellulite on my thighs and he saw? Maybe he didn't think I was a good kisser.

Stop, I finally thought. *Enough.* I had always known that getting back on the horse would be hard. Maybe he hadn't called because he didn't want to, but maybe that had nothing to do with some shortfall of mine. The water was so dark and eerily still, only the moon's reflection giving away that it was water at all. The stars twinkled, and I sighed.

Before I could decide what to do, I heard the unmistakable putter of a small engine and saw the skiff it was propelling a few seconds later. As it pulled up to the dock, my heart leapt into my throat.

I wanted to run to him, but that would look too eager. So I held myself back, strolling down to the dock.

"Hi," I said casually. "Hi yourself," Andrew said, his back still to me as he leaned over to tie up the skiff. I watched his fingers as they wound the rope around the cleat. His hands were strong and practiced.

He stood up, wiping them on his wrinkled khaki shorts with a small grease stain on them.

Then he gave me that look . . . like he was the dying fire, and I was the kindling. I thought about being cool, but cool had gotten me these last few days of regret. I didn't want to regret anymore. Andrew took my face in his hands and kissed me with so much intention that I thought I might have melted into him, that my lips might not even be my own anymore. He smelled intoxicatingly of boat fuel and seawater, the back of his shirt damp from the humid night and sea spray.

"Hi, pretty girl," he said, putting my fingers, which were wrapped in his, to his lips.

"Hi," I whispered back, acutely aware of those dimples and of how completely like a teenager he made me feel. "You could come hang out on the porch if you want to."

"Really?" he said, feigning shock. "Mom and Dad won't mind?"

I smacked his arm with the back of my hand, feeling butterflies at the mere act of touching him. He must have felt them too because he kissed me again for what seemed like a very long time.

As we walked up to the house, the warm night air, still humid and sticky but with a refreshing hint of crispness, crept onto my skin. I grabbed a few pillows and a blanket from the basket on the porch and arranged them in the yard, then collected the bottle of wine I'd opened a few minutes earlier and two of the Lucite cups from the outdoor bar.

"So does this mean I'm welcome here?" Andrew asked.

I nodded and whispered, "I think it does." I almost added: *But only if you want to be.* But I stopped myself. If he didn't want to, he wouldn't be here.

"I know you're trying to keep this whole thing on the DL," Andrew said. "I just wanted you to know that I don't kiss and tell."

Then he leaned in and kissed me, and it occurred to me that I kind of wanted to tell everyone. I wrapped my arms around his tight torso, and for a minute I felt so safe in his embrace that I forgot to worry about everything in my life that had gone wrong.

"Julian knows," I said.

"Oh no," he groaned. "So the DL lasted twenty minutes."

"Less."

Andrew sat down, reclining into the pile of pillows, and put his arms out for me to lie on his chest.

"I just wanted you to know," he said, "that when I said that thing about you being the perfect sugar mama, I was only joking."

I placed my head in that sweet spot and said, "I know you were. I wasn't offended or anything."

"I'm really impressed," he said. "I mean,

you're so young."

I sat up, smiling. "One, thank you for saying I'm young. Two, are you fishing for advice?"

He laughed, putting his hands under his head, his elbows open wide. "No. Money isn't important to me. I'm only getting my MBA to please my dad."

Andrew was studying at the College of Charleston, and just thinking about the fact that he would be back in the same city as my sister in a couple months made me cringe.

"I want to play tennis forever, and I'm no Federer, so I'm never going to be rich. I don't want a big house or new cars or fancy stuff. I just want to be happy." He paused and added, "I love kids, and I love teaching them." Under his breath he said, "Plus there's this tennis mom I'm kind of into too."

I smiled. "I never saw all of my success coming, to be honest. I started a blog when I was in college, when blogs were the new thing, and I got a lot of followers really fast, and companies started to approach me about advertising their products."

"But that's not ClickMarket, right?"

I shook my head. "I got the idea to go back to them and ask for a percentage of the sales from my site instead of charging traditional ad fees. Most of them said yes, and the site kept growing, and as soon as I graduated I started hiring staff, and it grew more, and before I knew it I was this twenty-two-year-old making tons of money."

Andrew laughed. "A little Zuckerberg over here."

"It'll always be my first baby," I said.

"And Greg is trying to take it."

I thought back to the conversation I'd had with my lawyer earlier today. Basically, I was screwed. Greg wasn't just my husband. He worked for my company, if only just barely. He was probably going to win, and I had to face it.

I looked up at the sky, the stars twinkling so brightly. I noticed the moon illuminating the sandbar that was only visible at low tide, the spot where Greg had proposed to me. I had thought it was the most romantic thing on earth. He had said, "The water washes away this sand, but nothing on heaven or earth will ever wash away my love for you." It wasn't exactly accurate, but I thought it was so romantic.

"It wasn't easy," I told Andrew. "I built that business from nothing, on my own shoulders, when I was only a kid. I swear being young was one of the reasons it all fell into place. I didn't psych myself out of success, because I believed I was infallible."

The night Greg proposed, as we celebrated our engagement, I'd told him about the idea for ClickMarket. We knew it was going to be good, but we had expected the affiliate bubble to burst long before now.

I told Andrew all of that, and he said, "And now you're screwed. You and Greg are stuck together forever."

I laughed. "We're stuck together forever because of Wagner, so this is just one more piece of the pie." I looked at the sky again, marveling that nine years after that gloriously romantic night, I was back on the same beach with a different man discussing how it all went wrong.

"Well, damn. All I do is swing a racket all day."

"Being on the court is the same as being in the boardroom. Reading your opponent, learning to guess his or her next moves."

I lay back down on his chest, and he kissed my hair. "Like how I knew you were going to do that?" he whispered.

I laughed. "Exactly."

"I guess when you get down to it, tennis is a game of life."

"Of course it is," I said. "Oh, I used to

love figuring out how to get into people's heads."

"You're sure as hell in my head."

After those four long days of radio silence, his cheesy reassurance was a relief. Lying there, the cicadas and crickets singing their song, the one that reminded me of the freedom and innocence of childhood summers, I was happy that I was in his head. As much as I hated to admit it, he was in mine too, but I didn't say that. I didn't say anything.

Andrew shifted, and my pair of gold bangles, one with five intermittent rubies and one with five diamonds, clinked. Andrew lifted my arm. "What are these?" he asked.

I wore them all the time. I even showered in them. "They're for remembering," I said. I pushed up the top one with the rubies. "This one is for my mom." Then I pulled the second to meet it. "This one is for Wagner."

In the midst of my life falling apart, I'd been trying to focus on gratitude. And these bangles were a constant reminder of the good: *This night. Wagner. The years I had with my mom. The stars. This house. The way the grass feels under my feet.*

Andrew studied my face intently for a few

seconds. "You take such good care of everyone. Who takes care of you?"

He kissed me. And I added *Andrew* to the list.

Diana: That Wink

My favorite picture of me is one on my first day of sixth grade, and I'm standing there smiling and all optimistic. My new mom in foster care, she took that picture to make me feel special on the first day of school. Thinking back on it, she was always trying to make me feel special.

She was the first mom I had after my real mom, and she was the best. She was a nice mom. I mean, she had rules and stuff. We had to make our beds and clean up our rooms and set the table for dinner. But she checked my homework every night and snuggled up beside me on the couch to watch TV. Most important, she taught me how to cook. That was a real big deal to me. It was what started my dream of opening my own restaurant one day. Now that little napkin tucked in my back pocket with the drawing of that falling-apart boat was continuing it.

They say that people who lived through the Depression store stuff up because they've lived through something so traumatic they never want to do that again. It's the same with me. I'd lived through being totally alone, so instead of storing up stuff, I stored up skills. I needed to know how to cook and clean and do laundry, how to sew on buttons, mend tears, fix my own hair.

I only got to live with my first foster mom for two years before her husband got transferred away for work. I cried and begged and pleaded to go with them, but that wasn't in the cards. It was the second time I'd gotten left behind, but it was easier that time. I knew what to expect, and I knew how to take care of myself.

I think that's why taking care of Gray felt so right. I saw a little bit of my young abandoned self in her. And now, in just two more days, I was going to be taking care of Wagner too. I couldn't wait to meet the kid, but I was turned inside out about it too. Gray was acting like the queen was coming to visit. I'd never seen anyone so distracted. She'd be eating breakfast and then she'd pop up and say, "Wagner will need new bathing suits. I need to run to the surf shop."

And then she'd be working on her computer, and I'd hear her on her phone saying, "Trey, can you see if we can get tickets to that Cirque du Soleil show that's coming?"

And when I thought she was upstairs I'd see the car pulling out of the driveway because she just remembered that Wagner would want Rice Krispies Treats and she didn't have the stuff to make them. All in all, she was wearing me the hell out with her nervous energy. And he wasn't even back yet. I was terrified too, because Gray didn't have to say one word for me to realize that if Wagner didn't like me, I was out.

Finally I just sat her down and said, "Honey, you're his momma. No fancy Europe trip or shiny anything can change that."

"I know. I know that. But he's eight, and he's too young to have all his priorities straight. What if he loves Brooke? What if he has so much fun with Greg that he wants to live with him all the time?"

Poor Gray. All those things could happen. They could. And she wasn't wrong to be worried. But she didn't need to drive herself up the wall. "Look, honey, if I were you I'd just try to get real clear with Greg that none of that's going to happen. A solid arrangement in writing is insurance for him too, because Wagner could just as easily decide he wants to live with *you* all the time."

She glanced down at her phone and

smiled, and I knew that, just for a second anyway, she had forgotten all about Greg and Wagner and whose house he'd love more. I felt a pang in my gut, and at first I thought it was for me, for the love I had lost. But then I realized it was for Gray. Because she had a long road ahead of her. Dating and a divorce were hard, especially with a kid. Not that I knew firsthand, but I had seen it plenty. I felt like I had seen everything, really. And not all of it was pretty.

I had been to see Phillip that morning before I got to work. Gray was real flexible about my hours, especially on days I went to see Phillip. His new doctor and I had worked real hard these past few months with him on his medicines, cutting back a little here, adding a little there, switching an old medicine for something newer and better. And, I swear, a part of him was coming back to me. His color was better. There was a little light in his eyes. The only drawback was that he flinched now when I tried to touch his hand. But he didn't get mad. He was talking a tiny bit more. But the medicine was still enough to keep him from having those fits he had been prone to when something set him off. They didn't bother me so much, but I knew the home wouldn't —

couldn't — keep him there, so close to me, if he was violent. His condition wasn't where I wanted it, but I got the feeling he wouldn't be as good as he possibly could until I got him out. I was sure again now that I would. Someday. I smiled, thinking of the two of us rambling around in that boat, me cooking steamer pots and him helping me with simple kitchen tasks. He would be happy doing that work. I just knew he would.

It was Thursday again, and now that I had a place to live and a paycheck and a couple hundred dollars back in the bank, life was seeming better. It was summertime and the living was easy. I was meeting my girls for our regular night out, and as I eased myself into my normal seat at the Beach Pub, a big, salty margarita glass was waiting at my place. I sat down and said, "Thanks, y'all. You didn't need to order for me."

"We didn't," Janet whispered. Her eyes traveled across the bar, and mine followed. Sitting on one of the stools behind the rectangular bar was a man who looked vaguely familiar. Thick dark hair falling across his forehead; a neat button-down shirt, all clean and pressed, sleeves rolled up. I was about to be flattered that this man must've known who I was and bought me a drink even before I got there when my heart stopped. My eyes met his across the crowded room. I was too far away to be able to tell that they were that same navy blue they'd been all those years ago. But that wink? I'd have known that wink anywhere.

CHAPTER 8

Gray: First-Time Feeling

When it rains, it pours. Diana was trying to keep me calm, but how could I be calm? We'd lost two midsize clients to a competing affiliate firm in the past week, I was behind on a proposal for a new A-client I was trying to snag, and my boy was coming home. It had felt like the longest three weeks of my life, but it was almost over. That was the best news in the world. Knowing he would be back any minute was like anticipating the first day of spring after a long, freezing winter.

All I could think about was the books we would read together, the long days at the pool, the time on the beach, dinners out, having all his little friends over, making s'mores. I absolutely could not wait. I wanted to make this the best summer ever for him.

Andrew had texted me earlier: Dinner?

When I hadn't responded right away, he had added, Please?

I had seen him a couple more times after he showed up at my dock, and I was trying to tell myself that was enough. But in those quiet moments, all I wanted was more of him.

I had texted back: Crazy day at work and Wagner comes home day after tomorrow. Can I let you know tonight?

Sure. We could take the boat. Have a really special night. May have to be our last one for a while?

A question. I knew that Andrew wanted to ask me how everything was going to work when Wagner got back. I was totally positive that I wouldn't let Wagner know we were seeing each other. That was set in stone. But I wasn't sure about anything else. Would tonight be it for us? The thought made me sad, but I also thought that maybe that's the way it had to be.

That night, when Andrew rang the doorbell, I was dressed and ready for dinner.

He just smiled. "So you're taking me up on my offer?"

"Why not?" I shrugged. "I guess it's my boat, right?"

"Hell if I know," Andrew said.

He looked around. "No Trey?"

I shook my head. "He went back to Raleigh, so Wags and I could have a little time to ourselves."

We walked down the dock, and he stepped into the hull. Instead of taking my hand to help me, he put his hands on either side of my waist and lifted me. I squealed.

He eyed my shoes. "It didn't seem safe for you to climb in here with those heels on."

They were wedges. I sat on the bench seat right beside him. But when he turned the key, the engine cranked and promptly died.

In my life with Greg, that would have equaled pulling out a cell phone to call the mechanic and that our boat date was DOA.

"Oh well," I said. "I guess we can drive to dinner — or we can cook if you want to."

Andrew gave me a strange look and then turned his attention to the console. He stuck his head in, made some noise, and then walked to the back of the boat, where he did something near the engine. Returning, he turned the key once more — and, lo and behold, the thing cranked.

"Okay," he said.

"Wow. That was amazing," I said, snuggling up under his arm and kissing him. He ran his hand down my bare arm, and I moved closer.

"Not that amazing. The engine bulbs just

needed to be pumped. For a boat owner, you don't know much about boats, do you?"

Seeing him take charge like that made me see Andrew in a different way.

We'd been riding for a couple of minutes before I noticed the huge dark cloud looming just ahead of us. "Uh-oh," I said. "Think we should turn around?"

Andrew looked up and put his hand out just as the first crack of thunder broke and a few drops began to fall lightly from the sky. "It's probably only a summer shower," he said, "judging from the size of the cloud. Let's go back for a few minutes, and we'll try again later."

As he spoke, it was as if the sprinklers were turned on full blast and the bottom fell out of that cloud. "Oh no," I said, laughing over the roar of the engine and the beating of the rain on the windshield.

Andrew laughed too. "Note to self: get a T-top." He pulled me closer as the rain soaked us. "On the bright side," he said, "there's nothing more romantic than kissing the most beautiful woman you know with rain pouring down."

I smiled. "That *is* true."

A few minutes later, Andrew was docking the boat, running from the bow to the stern to tie it up, while I stood there uselessly, watching the rain drench my shoes. I took them off, and we ran through the grass, laughing as we finally made it through the front door.

Andrew paused and looked at me. He leaned in to kiss me like he was savoring it, like he was memorizing the moment. I realized that I was memorizing the moment too. He nuzzled my neck and, squatting down and reaching for the bottom of my dress, said, "We can't possibly go traipsing through your house in these soaking wet clothes."

I raised my arms over my head, suddenly acutely aware of my near-nakedness. I unbuttoned his shirt very slowly, my mind trying to catch up with my heart.

I was thankful that the lot jutted out into a bit of a peninsula. No one could see us.

I noticed Andrew glance behind me, and I turned to follow his eyes. My wedding photo, in a sterling silver frame, engraved with my monogram and the wedding date. I bit my lip and said, "Sorry."

"For what?" he asked.

"I should probably take that down now. I guess I was just so used to it —"

He shook his head slowly. "You shouldn't take it down."

"No?"

"No. Wagner needs to have that picture to remember that even though it's over, it *was* happy."

I smiled sadly. "Then why were you looking at it like that?"

Focusing on me with laser precision, Andrew leaned down and kissed me again. Then he whispered, "I was just thinking that if I could ever make you smile like that, I'd make sure I never let you stop."

I felt his lips moving down my cheek and my neck and my collarbone. "Andrew, I —" I heard myself start to say. But then his lips were on my ear, and he was whispering, "Everything is going to be fine, G," and whatever objections I was going to raise didn't seem to matter. I laughed as Andrew carried me up the stairs to my room. And I didn't think about how I hadn't done this in well over a year or how this was the bed I had made love to my husband in for all those years or whether my stomach looked flat. I didn't think about anything at all. I was lost in Andrew and the way he made me feel like none of that mattered now. He saw me, and I finally saw him too, for all the amazing things he really was. He was a man. He was an equal. And he didn't have to say a word for me to realize that he was all mine.

Later, happy and drowsy and lying on my freshly pressed sheets, I was astounded. I had done it. I had had sex for the first time in twelve years with someone who wasn't Greg. This feeling — freedom and happiness and fun — was what my life had been missing for more time than I would like to admit. Andrew and I lay in complete silence, lost in that sweet afterglow that I hadn't felt in so long I had honestly forgotten about it.

In the vulnerability of that moment I said, "I get why Greg left me." It just gurgled up out of my mouth, and I wanted to pull it back in as soon as it did. Why would I ruin tonight of all nights?

But Andrew just yawned, his hand trailing lazily up and down my back. "Greg is an idiot."

"I understand the feeling of first-time passion and not wanting it to end," I continued. "I understand the sweaty palms and beating heart and racing pulse he probably got with Brooke. I get wanting to have that all the time."

He rested his forehead on mine and whispered, "I get that feeling too."

I smiled. I couldn't help it. He kissed me so softly.

"That's kind of what it feels like when you win your first tennis match," he said, stroking my cheek with his finger. "You can't imagine anything ever feeling that good." He paused. "But then you go to practice every day. You drill and play and hit bucket after bucket of serves. You put in the time. And you win again. And again. And again. It still feels good, but you're used to it now. The butterflies are gone, but the joy remains. In so many ways, it's deeper, and it's sweeter because you worked so hard for it. You committed to it. And that feels even better." Here I was, complaining about losing that first-time feeling, and here he was, young and fresh and so incredibly wise. The butterflies end, but it's the love that's forming all along the way that really means something.

"Wow," I said. I looked into those brown eyes, and I felt more than I wanted to let myself feel. "How do you even know that? You're too young to understand the things you do."

He shrugged. "You know, Gray, everything in life is a metaphor for pretty much everything else. If you can get one area under control, the others come a lot easier." He winked at me.

I sighed, that glowy feeling seeping away, remembering that I had no area of my life under control. A familiar panic welled up in me as I realized that, despite what I had promised myself, I wasn't ready to let him go. But I didn't want anyone, not even adorable Andrew, to be in Wagner's life. I felt trapped.

"I don't know how to do this," I admitted.

"Do what?"

"I don't know how to be a single mother. I don't know how to date and have a son. I don't know how to balance all these things and it's not fair to you." Andrew put my fingers, which were wrapped around his, to his lips. It was one of the most endearing things he did.

"No one expects you to have it all figured out, G."

I laughed incredulously. "Yes, they do, Andrew. Of course they do."

He sat up and looked down at me. "Well, I don't."

It was next to nothing. And, yet, it was everything. The knot in my stomach uncoiled, just like that.

"How about this?" Andrew added. "What if we figure it out as we go along?"

He was right. One step at a time. He assured me so well. I panicked again as I realized that I was developing real feelings for him — and I knew I needed to break the intensity of the moment. So I jumped out of bed and raced to the kitchen, a blanket wrapped around me. I grabbed the whipped cream, a pint of Ben & Jerry's and two spoons, and raced back.

When he saw me, he said, "I can't imagine life ever, ever getting mundane with you."

I don't know if it was the words, Andrew, Ben, or Jerry, but I know for sure that, of all the nights in my life, that was one of the sweetest.

Diana: Trailer Trash Orphan

When I was developing the photos down at Meds and More, I realized right off that people only take pictures of the good times. But I say we'd all be a darn sight better off if we'd take pictures of the bad stuff too, so we wouldn't keep making the same mistakes over and over.

As I tried to pick up that margarita glass with my hands shaking, I wasn't sure if this moment would fall into the category of "take a picture so you can remember" or "take a picture so you'll learn your lesson once and for all." My mouth was so dry I couldn't talk.

"We couldn't believe it," Cheyenne whispered, as if Frank would be able to hear her across the crowded bar.

"Ain't seen hide nor hair of him since . . ." Robin trailed off.

She didn't have to finish that sentence. I knew better than anybody when the last time we saw him was.

"Di," Janet said softly, which was when I realized that I was staring into my margarita glass. "You okay?"

She reached over and touched my hand. Janet had been there with me that day, the only one who had the stomach for it, I guess. Cheyenne and Robin, they'd been there waiting when we got home, and every last one of them, they worked real hard to make sure I was okay. We were in it together, in a way. But in a much, much bigger way, I was the only one who had to live it over and over, and I was the only one who realized that maybe, in a situation like that, you can't ever truly be okay again.

And Frank? Well, Frank had got off pretty much scot-free. Frank had been wandering around all these years not knowing one damn thing I'd been going through. I couldn't help but wonder what he was doing here now. I felt pretty sure that he had some beautiful wife and a bunch of kids and a big house. His momma and daddy were probably real proud. He'd found himself a suitable woman, not a trailer trash orphan like me. It almost embarrassed me how fresh the wound felt, remembering his momma calling me that — and knowing she wasn't wrong.

I looked up at Janet long enough to say, "Oh yeah. You know me. I'm gonna be fine. Just surprised to see him here, is all."

It couldn't have been more than a couple of minutes that had passed, but it felt like it had been an hour, me sitting there frozen in my seat. "What are you going to do?" Robin asked.

I glanced over just in time to see Frank setting his money on the bar, getting up off the stool. Before I could answer, before I had time to think about it, I bolted right up out of my chair and, with the ladies calling after me, I was out that door, quick as a wink. It took me about until I got to my car to realize I'd left my purse on the table inside the Beach Pub. "Shit," I said under my breath.

"Diana," I heard that strong, deep voice say. Oh God, that voice. Even after all of it, after how he hurt me, after all the history we had together, that voice still made me weak in the knees. *Don't look at him,* I thought. *If you just don't look at him, he'll go away and it'll be like this never happened.*

Then I felt his hand on mine, that prickle

on my skin, the way his touch almost burned it felt so good. I exhaled slowly, trying not to remember it, the way it took my breath away when he held my hand, the way my heart told me he was the one I should be with forever.

"Was it all that bad that you had to run out of the bar like that?" Frank asked.

Then I made the worst mistake a girl can make. I looked at him. Straight in the eyes. Those deep, navy-blue eyes, the ones I thought I'd be looking into at the altar, the ones I thought our babies would have. I felt that familiar pang in my heart, that emptiness in my belly. *Our baby.*

My heart stood stock-still for a few seconds until I got the nerve to say, "You know, Frank? Yeah. It was that bad. In fact, it was worse than that bad."

His face fell. "But, Di, come on. My parents. And I was just a kid."

"You were just a kid?" I practically spat at him. "No, *I* was just a kid! You were old enough that you should've known better. You were old enough that you should've fought for me."

He nodded and swallowed hard. "I know, Di. I knew it then; I know it now. I've known it the whole time." He paused. "But, damn, Di. You were the one that left me. It took me a long time to figure out why, but back then, you broke my heart. I was devastated."

But I bet you still don't know why.

I shook my head. "I find that hard to believe, that you, smart as you are, couldn't figure out where I was." I tried to turn away from him, but he grabbed my hand. "Where have you been for twenty years, Frank? What have you been doing all this time that kept you from coming back before now if all that's really true?"

He stared at me and burst out, "My dad, D, he's gone."

And just like that, I was in the past, back in Frank's house, laughing on his porch while his daddy grilled hot dogs. I put my hand over my heart as my breath caught in my throat. I had loved Frank's daddy. He had loved me. I used to dream that I had a daddy out there who was just like him, that he would come find me one day.

"Frank," I said, his name tasting warm and familiar in my mouth, as if it hadn't been twenty-two years, as if no time had passed at all. "I am so sorry."

He shook his head. "For all these years, Diana, I haven't been able to move on. All I've dreamed about is you." He seemed sort of out of breath, and I found myself, as much as I didn't want to, reaching over to touch his arm, to steady him. "I just wanted you to be happy. I thought my staying away was the best thing, even if it meant that I would be miserable."

"So why now? Did you suddenly decide that you didn't care about me being happy?" I was trying to lighten the mood, but I could tell by his serious expression that that wasn't in the cards.

"No. I've known all this time that I'd never really be happy without you." He took my hand in his and said, "But it took me until now to realize that maybe this is how it is with true love, that it never goes away. And I thought that maybe you couldn't really be happy without me either."

Chapter 9

Gray: A Summer Thing

It had been three weeks. *Three weeks* of no Wagner. Three weeks since I had ruffled his shaggy blond hair or kissed his sweet, doughy cheeks — which were losing their doughiness by the minute, much to my chagrin — or pulled him into me for one of those great hugs where his entire body went slack. I was literally counting the minutes.

Sure, I wasn't thrilled about having to see Greg, but it was totally worth the trade-off. Despite being at odds, we were able to keep things civil around Wagner.

I'll just say, I gave myself most of the credit for that. My mom taught me to be the bigger person, to turn the other cheek. Some days it was harder than others to think about my husband — and, even more so, my son — with another woman, but I was tolerating it.

As I sat on the porch waiting for my boy

to get back to me, I automatically picked up my phone. When I realized what I was doing, my throat burned. Almost ten months later, ten months after she had died, I was picking up my phone to call my mother. I wanted to tell her how excited I was that Wagner was coming home. Would this feeling ever go away? Would it ever get easier?

My phone dinged, breaking me out of my unhappy thoughts. Andrew. I don't think I can make it a whole week. . . .

When I had decided that I couldn't fully let Andrew go despite my initial intentions, I'd mustered up the nerve to tell him I didn't want him around Wagner. Andrew had laughed, and, oh, the dimples. "Well, I'm around him all the time, G. I'm his badass, supercool tennis teacher."

My turn to laugh. And roll my eyes. "You know what I mean."

He nodded. "I've said it before and I'll say it again: you just need to relax, babe. We'll let it play out like it needs to."

I smiled in spite of myself, thinking about it. I had expected the tennis pro situation to be a one-day thing that maybe turned into a two-day thing. But, as Marcy sagely advised, why couldn't it be a summer thing?

I stood up and stretched, thinking, *How on earth did I get here?* I couldn't count the number of times I had thought that nothing would ever come between Greg and me. Nothing would break us up because we were as solid as couples came. Even on those days when our relationship wasn't thrilling, we had something deeper, a firm foundation that would help us weather any storm. Boy, had I been wrong.

Part of me hated him for abandoning me. The other part of me, the part that didn't mind having a tennis pro pining after her, texted Andrew back. Friday night I'm all yours.

He texted me back immediately. Great. I'll pick you up at 7.

I laughed. He was good for that, making me laugh. After the year I'd had, I needed to laugh. The thought must have softened me a bit, because I texted back: How about I call you tonight after Wagner goes to bed?

How about I drive over there and kiss you good night when Wagner goes to bed?

Greg's car appeared in the driveway. I think it must have been the sight of Brooke behind the wheel that made me type back: We'll see. . . .

Greg was having fun. Why shouldn't I?

But, really, this was nothing compared to the way my heart leapt as I ran at top speed down the four steps to the driveway and opened my arms for my little boy to fly into.

"Wags!"

"Mom!"

I kissed the top of his head. "I missed you so, so much. I can't even tell you. I want to hear about every detail of your trip."

He grinned up at me, his arms still around my waist. "Look. I lost a tooth!" He opened his mouth to reveal that the stubborn straggler in the bottom row had finally given up the ghost.

I gasped. "No way! Did the tooth fairy come?" I could totally see Greg pulling some crap about the tooth fairy only coming in the continental US or something.

So I was shocked when Wagner nodded enthusiastically and said, "She brought me twenty euros and wrote me a note with glitter and everything! Can you believe that?"

This was actually worse. Not only had the tooth fairy come, but now Brooke was besting me at the game.

"Wow!" I said.

"Am I taller?" He pulled away so I could inspect.

"I don't even recognize you!" I said.

"I need new shoes too. My feet have grown."

I nodded, and said, "We'll get some new ones this afternoon!"

"I'm going to unpack my stuff," Wagner said, whizzing by me into the house. The mushy time was over. On to logistics.

No doubt about it, he was his father's child. Greg and I had butted heads constantly because I was a total mess and he was a complete neat freak. Everything had to be organized at all times.

"Hi, Gray," Brooke said sunnily. I had never seen the woman not perfectly dressed like she was ready for a night out. Looking down at my workout clothes, I thought that maybe that's what had happened in my marriage. Maybe I had quit caring so much. But they were such cute workout clothes.

I tried to smile, hating her and her perky, never-breastfed boobs the whole time. Before I could ruminate further, I heard footsteps behind me in the driveway.

"You must be Greg."

Greg looked at me questioningly, then asked, "Who are you?"

Diana stuck out her hand to shake Greg's. "I'm the new Maria."

I burst out laughing and put my arm around her. "Greg, Brooke, this is Diana."

She gave Brooke a once-over that would have made anyone feel extremely self-conscious. "Geez," she said to me out of the corner of her mouth, "neither one of you can date someone age-appropriate."

"What?" Greg said.

I elbowed Diana. "Nothing. Thanks, guys, for bringing my boy back in one piece."

Greg squeezed Brooke's arm. "I'll be right there, hon."

She rolled her eyes and turned to go to the car, obviously irritated that she was being sent away. But this was what you signed up for when you set out to marry another woman's husband. I wanted to tell her thank you for making the tooth fairy so special, but the words got stuck in my mouth. Oh well. I was trying. For today, that was enough.

Greg looked at Diana, then back at me, and said, "I'm glad you found someone to help you, Gray. You deserve it."

I raised my eyebrows in surprise. Then he said, "Are you doing okay? I mean, I know this is hard for you."

"Yeah," I said, "not seeing Wagner was a nightmare, but I'm glad he had this opportunity."

He nodded. "Good. But I really meant with the whole Brooke thing."

I was feeling warm toward him for a half second until he said that. I thought Diana was going to choke beside me. I smiled tightly. "I'm a grown woman, Greg. I'm fine."

Diana chuckled. "I'd say she's more than fine."

Greg looked at her questioningly again. "Okay. Well, good. Because Brooke and I want to go on a trip this fall, and we really want to take Wagner —"

"Greg, you just got back. I am dying over here and have hardly been able to function for the last three weeks without him, so maybe we could talk about this —"

"Why don't you let me finish?"

I crossed my arms.

"What I was going to say is that Brooke and I want to take Wagner to Disney World for a week this fall, and we were thinking that maybe you could come too. I know you don't want to miss that."

I could feel my stomach turning over. I had had more than a year to get used to the Greg and Brooke situation. Things were better. I was feeling stronger. But a joint vacation? He couldn't be serious.

I didn't say anything, and Greg continued, "You were the one who was so big on us still doing things together as a family, on not having to have separate birthday parties and trying to keep Wagner's life as normal as possible. So why don't you come?"

"You're bringing Brooke," Diana chimed in. "Shouldn't Gray get to bring somebody too?"

"Diana," I said sharply, under my breath.

Greg looked amused. "What? You mean you?"

"Nope," Diana said, grinning broadly, "I most certainly do not." She paused. "Although I have always wanted to go to Disney World. . . ."

I grabbed her wrist and spun around, calling to Greg, "I'll think about it, okay?"

He just stood there, looking confused — and kind of pissed. And I have to admit that that made me happy.

"Are you crazy?" I said to Diana, laughing.

"What?" She shrugged. "I'm not going to let him stand there all holier-than-thou like you can't move on. Hell no. My girl's already found her the hottest, youngest piece of meat on the beach."

"I thought you thought he was too young for me. I thought you said it was inappropriate."

She stopped walking and shrugged again. "What the hell do I know? I'm forty and single."

That quick wit was one of my favorite things about Diana. What I loved the most about her, though, was how, already, she always, always had my back. No questions, no hesitations. She was Team Gray all the way. I hoped I was showing her that I was Team Diana too.

"I'm coming in to make dinner in a minute."

"It's Saturday, Diana. You don't have to. Get some rest."

She smiled. "I need to get to know that cute boy of yours. Now seems like as good a time as any. What's his favorite dinner?"

I could feel a lump in my throat, the burn that meant I was in danger of crying. "Fried chicken, macaroni and cheese, and butter beans."

Diana nodded slowly, registering the tears in my eyes. "Your momma's specialty, huh?"

I nodded. She acted like she was going to say something else, like she wanted to ask me something more. But instead, she said, "Okay. I'm going to the store. I'll throw in some of my best-in-the-world biscuits." Then she winked at me. "Then I'll butter 'em both up."

I smiled even though I still felt like I was going to rip at the seams to keep from crying. That's the thing people don't tell you about losing a parent, how many times a day you think about them, how many times you need their advice or wish they were there or want their fried chicken. Not somebody else's. Hers. Mom's.

I snapped myself out of it and walked to Wagner's room. He was mid-unpacking when I squeezed him to me. "Mom, come on," he said. "You're going to suffocate me."

That was okay. I felt the tears coming to my eyes, grateful for him again, thankful that while, yes, I had suffered a loss, it was a loss in the natural order of things. I was always going to lose my mom. It had happened earlier than I thought it would, but no matter what, my son was still here. My beating heart outside my body was standing here sorting his socks and his Nintendo Switch.

Our children are on loan, I could hear my mom saying. She knew all about that. There wasn't one single day that I didn't catch her in a moment, know that she was thinking about the brother I would never know.

I heard her talking on the phone one time to a friend of a friend who had lost a child. She said, "You will never, ever be the same. You will never be whole in the way that you once were, but you have others to live for. You're going to keep waking up. When you do, get out of bed. Do something he didn't get to do. Some days you won't want to, but while you're here you have to make the choice to live."

I used to wonder how my mom found the courage, later in life, when she and Dad weren't so strapped for cash, to travel with reckless abandon despite malaria warnings and terror threats or to take her morning run through the bad part of town.

Once I became a mother myself, I reasoned that, in losing her child, the worst that could happen to her already had. Her life meant less because a part of it had passed on before her. Or maybe that's just the pessimist in me, and the optimist in her would say that life is short and fleeting, and living full-throttle is the only way to go.

Either way, I felt like when she found out she was sick, she was relieved. She didn't have to put on her happy face anymore. She didn't have to get out of bed. She didn't have to pretend. She could just go meet my brother where he was. Quinn and I were furious when she refused treatment. Dad too. She said she knew that treatment would only make what could be a dignified death an undignified one.

"But what if it works really well for you?" I remember asking her, nearly hysterical. "What if there's a miracle?"

She smiled sadly and patted my hand.

"Honey, if there's going to be a miracle, it won't be because of any treatment."

In the last couple of weeks before she died, I was by her side almost all the time. One afternoon, I stood outside the door to her room, tears coming down my cheeks as I heard her laughing with an old friend.

"Are you scared?" I heard the friend ask.

"Oh, heavens no," Mom replied. "When you have lost a child, death comes as a relief."

I couldn't stay after that. It was childish, I knew, but I was furious. She had confirmed what I had thought all along. Instead of wanting to fight to stay with us, she was practically choosing to go. She had left me. And Wagner. She hadn't even tried to do anything to save herself. She didn't know it, but she had left us when we needed her the very most.

"Mom," Wagner said, breaking me out of my thoughts. I looked down. I was still squeezing him to me.

"Oh," I said, laughing. "Sorry, bud. I wanted to tell you that we have someone new staying with us. Her name is Diana, and you are going to love her."

He shrugged. "Okay."

"She's making fried chicken and macaroni and butter beans and biscuits for dinner."

He brightened. "Yes! I like her already."

"Hey," I said. "You doing okay?"

He nodded. "Yeah, Mom. I'm good."

"Is it weird? Being with Dad and Brooke?"

He shrugged. "Nah. Brooke's cool. Dad too."

In the land of eight-year-old boys, that was a pretty deep talk. I would take it.

"All right, cutie. You know Dad and I both love you more than anything in the world, right?"

He smiled. "I know, Mom." Then he said, "I'll be down as soon as I finish putting this stuff up," gesturing to postcards and trinkets he'd collected from the trip.

That meant: *Get the hell out of my room, old woman.*

I smiled. In the doorway, I turned to look at him another moment, my baby who was growing up so fast. That familiar fear, that terror at the thought of losing him, rushed through me. I thought of my mom again, of her joy over having another boy in the family, as though Wagner were going to be the reincarnated soul of my brother, Steven.

As I walked downstairs, I felt my phone buzz in my hand. Does Wagner by chance go to bed at six?

I smiled. And I realized that I was really looking forward to that good night kiss.

Diana: Cliché for a Reason

The way to a man's heart is through his stomach. It's a cliché because it's the truest damn thing of all time. Doesn't matter if he's five days or five years or a hundred and five years, a man will love you more if you can feed him well.

I knew that Wagner probably wasn't going to be all too thrilled about some strange woman taking up residence in his guest-house, so the importance of this dinner wasn't lost on me.

"Did Mom tell you that fried chicken is my favorite?" Wagner asked.

He startled me. I guess I hadn't expected him to walk right up without his mom and start chatting with me.

"She might have," I said.

"My grandma's fried chicken was the best in the whole world."

He was wrong, but I didn't want to get off on the wrong foot.

"Well," I said, "no chicken can replace your grandma's chicken. But sometimes when we can't have the real thing, some-thing kind of like it will do."

At that, my mind wandered to Frank. I'd sure as hell spent the better part of a lifetime convincing myself that whoever I was with at the time was as good or better.

As I looked down at today's TJ's Salvage Yard T-shirt, I remembered the time that TJ had left me at the bar without telling me because he'd won fifty bucks on a scratch-off and went down to the gas station to turn it in. He ran into his buddy Sammy, and they'd bought beer with the winnings, gotten drunk down by the pier, and forgotten all about me. I'd had to thumb home.

At the time, I was just looking to fill that huge, Frank-size hole in my heart with anyone and everyone. But I was old enough now that I'd accepted that some wounds just don't heal, never ever in your whole life. Same as Wagner was never going to taste chicken like his grandma's again, I'd never love like I'd loved Frank, no matter how many T-shirts I had to prove I'd tried. That love I had for Frank was infinite. Even when both of us were gone, it'd still be out there floating around in the universe. That part of me couldn't reason out why I had refused to answer his calls or see him since that night outside the Beach Pub.

But it boiled down to one thing, a thing I didn't like admitting: I was scared. When you've been nothing but left your whole life, it's what you come to expect. And with Frank, it wasn't just being scared of what could happen. It was being scared of what could happen *again.*

But I didn't say that to the kid, obviously.

"So, kind of like Brooke," Wagner said matter-of-factly.

"Kind of like Brooke what?" Gray asked, making her way into the kitchen, head wet from the shower.

Wagner shrugged. "Diana's chicken is kind of like how Brooke is the replacement for you."

I could tell it was taking all the strength in Gray's little body not to get persnickety about that, but she did a real good job hiding it.

"Sweetie," Gray said, "I don't know what you're talking about, but I don't think that's it at all. I'm me and Brooke's Brooke and Dad's Dad, and none of us are chicken. We've all made some choices this year that I'm sure have been tough on you."

He shook his head. "No, Mom, you don't get it. She's just like you. Sometimes she says stuff, and it's what you would say, and it's so weird. I don't get at all why Dad would want to marry her now. It's like being married to you, except she isn't as nice as you, and he's always having to give her something so she'll be happy." He paused. "And you haven't ever cared about presents and stuff unless they're from me."

Gray pursed her lips to suppress a smile, and I winked at her.

"Why don't we dive into dinner? I've been dying for some mac and cheese," Gray said.

"Oh yes, please," I chimed in. "It's already on the table."

I took Wagner by the shoulder and said, "Listen, I know your grandma's chicken is the best in the world, and I can't compete with that. But maybe you can give my biscuits a try and see if they're the best in the world?"

Wagner sat down and slathered butter on his biscuit, then a little bit of jam. I waited, holding my breath. This was a make-or-break moment, do or die. If he liked this biscuit, I was in. He'd hang with me in the kitchen while I was cooking or ask me to drive him to the pool. We'd be thick as thieves just like that. But if he didn't like it . . . if he didn't like it, then I was toast. Burnt toast.

Gray winked back at me like she knew all the stuff that was going on in my head. Wagner swallowed, wiped his mouth, and smiled. But was it a happy smile? Or a sarcastic smile like I wasn't nearly as good as I thought and he was going to prove it? He took a sip of water. I darn near thought the hands on the clock had stopped.

"Diana," he said, "you're right. That is the best biscuit I've ever had."

I breathed a sigh of relief and smiled triumphantly.

Wagner said, "Mom, Diana's cool. She can stay as long as she keeps cooking instead of you."

Man + stomach = love. All day, every day, every single time. If only every man in my life had been as easy as Wagner to hook with nothing more than my homemade biscuits.

Chapter 10

Gray: Zero Idea

The bad part about your almost ex-husband getting your eight-year-old a cell phone is that, well, he got your eight-year-old a cell phone. The good part is that an eight-year-old with a cell phone will Snapchat his mom pictures of himself and his friends all week so she can keep up with what he's doing.

Evidently, the ex-husband will do something similar.

Why in the world is Marcy at my office? Greg texted me Monday morning a couple weeks later as I was rushing around getting ready for my dad's visit.

I looked around. That was weird. Marcy hadn't come by for her usual coffee this morning. I have zero idea, I replied.

Sure, he typed back.

I was going to argue with him, but I didn't have the energy. I had done enough of that already.

On Saturday, I had been so excited when Greg brought Wagner back to me from Raleigh. As he came flying through the door that night, backpack on his back, I'd said, "Oh my gosh, I missed you so much!" We had been careful to make sure that he had two of everything, one at my house, one at his dad's, so the poor kid didn't feel like he was packing up and getting shifted around every week. Even still, he was always transporting stuff back and forth. He threw his arms around my neck, and I realized that I barely even had to stoop to kiss him on the cheek. I'd almost said, "Don't you ever leave me again!" but I caught myself. It was habit, but I had to be more careful.

"Hey, Mom," he'd said, "do you want to go play tennis with me next week?"

Andrew rushed into my mind, those luscious lips that I had kissed good-bye a million times not an hour ago. "I would love that, buddy!"

"Okay, great. Because Andrew bet me and Johnny ten bucks that we couldn't beat him in doubles no matter how sorry his partner."

Johnny and me. I decided to let it go. I gave him my best shocked and amused look. "So you chose me? Are you saying I'm not a good tennis player?"

"Not as good as me," he said, grinning

from ear to ear. I ruffled his shaggy hair, and he darted through the kitchen and up the stairs. *Not as good as I am,* I thought, mom mode fully reactivated.

"Well, hi," Greg said, leaning over to kiss my cheek, catching me off guard.

"Come on in," I said, closing the door behind him. "I miss the hell out of him, but boys need dads, right?"

He pulled out a bar stool and sat down, and I sat beside him. "Look, I know it's hard, but I appreciate it. I really do. I can't stand the thought of only getting him every other weekend. And I'll make sure to repay you for that when we're hammering out the . . ." He cleared his throat. ". . . details."

That did sound nicer than "settlement." I was about to make a snide remark, but then I realized that this was the best opportunity I was going to get to raise my voice about ClickMarket.

So I shot him my most ingratiating smile. "Funny you should mention that," I said. "Because I think the perfect trade would be that you quit trying to take half my company."

Greg started to stand up. "I thought we had agreed not to discuss this without our lawyers."

"Yeah, Greg," I said sarcastically. "We

agreed. But they're certainly not coming up with a solution anytime soon, so I thought perhaps we could try to have a civil conversation that didn't cost me five hundred dollars per hour."

I didn't sound super civil as I said it, but this was my major pain point, and Greg knew it.

He sat down again. "Fine. Let's talk. I helped you build that company. I've worked just as hard on it as you have."

The laugh that escaped my lips was cruel. "Are you kidding me? I have spent all day, every day, seven days a week working on that company since I was twenty years old." I paused and reiterated, "Twenty." Then I added for good measure, "I brought you into my carefully cultivated world, and you repaid me by cashing paychecks and screwing your secretary in your corner office!"

Civil was over.

His face darkened, and his voice was cold and callous as he said, "Who do you think was holding our family together while you were working seven days a week? Who do you think was taking care of our child? Who was doing your share of the work at home?"

I wasn't going to let him play the superdad card. He was far from it. "Maria! Whose salary *I* paid," I practically spat as Wagner came tearing into the kitchen. I could feel the fury in my chest. What Greg had said was kind of fair, and I knew that I had some responsibility for my divorce. But this was about my company, not my shortcomings as a wife and mother.

"Mom! Where's Diana?" Wagner asked, thankfully oblivious to what was going on. "I want to show her my new Wii game that Dad got me."

I cut my eyes at Greg, then said, "Diana's gone out, bud, but you can show me."

Greg leaned over to hug Wagner. "Love you, man."

"Love you, dude." Wagner gave his dad a fist bump.

Greg turned to me and whispered, "Maybe if you'd ever put me first, we wouldn't be here right now."

"Maybe if you had made yourself someone I wanted to put first, we wouldn't be here right now."

We were so good at this game, at cutting each other down to the smallest size.

"You amaze me, Gray," he said ruefully. "You really do." Once upon a time he had meant it earnestly. He had been in awe of my tenacity, of the way that I was able to achieve what he never could.

And I wondered how, if I had truly been

so amazing, I had ended up in this house alone.

Even now, two days after the fight, my blood boiled every time I thought of it. And, honestly, I was a little embarrassed by how cruel I had been. But why in the world was my best friend at my office — and, yes, still Greg's office too — in Raleigh? I texted her.

Greg's office?????

When she didn't answer, I texted Trey. Is M at ClickMarket?

Three dots appeared immediately. Investigating.

Diana was pulling something that smelled like what heaven must out of the oven and, before I could respond to Trey, I heard a soft rap at the back door. I shouldn't admit this, but I didn't know whether to feel excited or a little annoyed or something in between. I loved my dad so much. But ever since Mom had died, things were . . . awkward. She was the glue that held us together. It was sort of like when you were great friends with someone in a group but when you finally hung out solo, you had nothing to talk about. That was us. But we were trying. And sometimes trying was enough, right?

And he was an amazing dad. When I started my blog, my dad got on Facebook so that he could make a bunch of friends and share my posts every day. That's the kind of dad he was. He supported us in everything we did. And, truth be told, he had taught me everything I had ever known about business and hard work.

I hugged him and said, "Hey, Dad. Thanks for coming." After Mom had died, Dad couldn't bear to be alone in their house in Raleigh. He had bought a small condo over on the beach, about three rows back from the ocean. We were ten minutes apart, but we only saw each other a few times a month.

He nodded. I noticed he had put on a collared shirt with his jeans and flip-flops. It didn't matter to me what he wore, but I appreciated the effort. "How's it going, kiddo?"

I shrugged. "It's going."

If I had said that to Mom, she would have known that was an entry point, pushed me for more. But Dad didn't know that. If I said I was fine, I was fine.

"Greg and I just can't seem to reach an agreement about the company," I added as I waved him inside.

We sat down in the living room at the front of the house, which was rarely used, if ever.

"You know, baby girl, you're just not on

my level anymore. Your old dad doesn't even know how to tell you what to do."

This was what drove me insane. Yes, I had done well. I had worked my ass off for it, and I'd gotten a little lucky too. But he was always so dramatic about my success, as if I had purposely used it to drive us apart.

"Your mom and I, we were always just normal. We had what we needed. We had a few extras. We gave our girls a nice life —"

"You gave us a great life, Dad."

That was true. We hadn't had cable, so we'd read library books. We didn't belong to a pool, so we'd spent our summers running around the yard with the neighborhood kids. And my dad had been the one to swallow his pain, to hold it together, to love my mother with all his heart even when she was mired so deeply in her devastation that she couldn't get out of bed.

Even still, it annoyed me that we were here again. I was reassuring him when what I needed was for someone to tell me I'd be okay.

There was silence; then Dad said, "Well, that's why some couples stay together, I guess. It's not that they don't have problems; it's just easier than ending things." Before I had time to object, he said, "Where's that grandson of mine?"

I was thinking the exact same thing.

Dad sat at the head of the table for lunch with Wagner and me on either side.

"Diana," I said a little too enthusiastically as she brought the food to the table, "don't you want to join us? *Please?*" I had told her earlier I didn't like it when she served our food, but she'd said in the South, family lunches were supper and they were proper food with someone serving it, not some slapped-together sandwich.

She gave me a face like she'd sooner die and said, "Oh, can't. So much organizing to do in Wagner's room." That was actually impossible. Wagner's room resembled a well-curated museum.

"So, kiddo," Dad was saying to Wagner, "Mom tells me that you're quite the tennis pro."

Tennis pro. Andrew. Butterflies. Smiling too big. *Get yourself together, Gray.*

Wagner nodded enthusiastically, taking a sip of his milk. "I've played practically every day since the trip!"

"That's great, man," Dad said. "I can't wait to come watch you sometime."

We were settling in now, the awkwardness dissipating with each bite of food. What I really needed was a nice cold bottle of Sancerre. But Dad didn't drink at all, and I couldn't bear the brunt of his disapproval yet again today.

Wagner thought for a minute, chewing his last bite of corn. Diana's steamer-pot shrimp boil was his favorite thing to eat these days. "Well, I don't have a tennis court here, but I can show you my soccer moves!"

Dad and I raised our eyebrows at each other and smiled.

"Do you think you ought to wait until your food settles a minute?" I asked, always the cool mom.

"Nah," he said, running out the door, leaving it open and calling, "Okay. Now, don't take your eyes off me for a second!"

Dad smiled at me. "He seems like he's doing pretty good."

I nodded. "Yeah. He's adjusted really well. It's kind of shocking." I laughed. "I think he has adjusted better than I have."

"I wish your mother could see him," Dad said, and at that my eyes welled up with tears.

"Me too."

"You still think you did the right thing?" he asked.

"About what?"

"About hiding the divorce from your mother?"

I took a sip of water, giving myself a moment to digest his question. I had almost called off that Virgin Islands trip with Greg because we had just found out Mom had cancer. But she insisted. "Darling," she had said, "there's nothing you can do by sitting at doctors' appointments. It's only a few days."

I'd often regretted listening to her. Of course, we didn't know then how bad it was; we didn't know that she would be dead a few months later. It had only been a few days. But a four-day vacay seems like an eternity when you only had a few dozen days left. I remembered walking in her door the night I flew in from the islands and her immediately asking, "What's the matter?"

What was the matter was that my husband had told me he was leaving me and we had had to fight about it for three days after that, that he was still living in my house and working in my office. I had debated telling her, but I wanted her to die happy — whenever that might be — knowing that both of her girls were okay. So I didn't tell her that her older daughter was getting divorced and her younger one was marrying a religious fanatic who was better suited to an insane asylum than a pulpit. I still thought it was right to let her die in peace.

I smiled at Dad. "Yeah. I really do. Sometimes I wish I'd had her advice on the whole thing while she was still here, but it really was for the better. I didn't want her to worry."

Dad took a bite of his shrimp and smiled. "Can you imagine how hot she was when she got up there and realized what was going on?"

We both laughed. Mom didn't like to be kept out of the loop. I shrugged. "Yeah. She'll probably have an earful waiting for me."

Dad raised his eyebrow. "Or Greg. Let's hope he gets there first."

I smiled, and Wagner called from outside, "Pop, are you watching? Do you see me?"

Dad gave him his best thumbs-up. "So, what else? Are you doing okay besides the company and the fighting and all that?"

I shrugged. "Worse things have happened." I pointed out into the yard. "He's okay, I'm okay."

He nodded. "Are you dating anyone? After all that *Forbes* magazine business, you have to be careful. There are plenty of men out there looking to take advantage of a pretty, rich woman."

I smiled tightly. The "*Forbes* magazine business" was a nod in a "Companies to Watch" listicle. I had been thrilled that my name and my company had so much as graced the website, but it had panicked my dad. I guessed worrying about me was his right as a father. Even still, it took everything I had not to ask him how stupid he thought I was. But I didn't. Instead, I asked, "Are *you* dating anyone?"

He smiled sadly. "No. Never. Your mother was the love of my life." He shrugged.

I smiled, my heart warming again. I knew my father should be loved again too, but it was so very hard to think about someone replacing your parent in your other parent's life. I could only imagine how Wagner felt about it deep down. As he shouted, "Hey, Mom, watch this!" I said, "You know, Dad, you have to be careful. You might not be looking for love, but sometimes it sneaks up on you."

I was proud of how lunch with my dad had gone. It had started off rocky, but it ended well. I wanted that closeness with him. I wanted to be a united front. Mom was gone. Quinn was as good as gone. We needed each other now.

As I was putting the last of the dinner dishes in the dishwasher that night, Marcy walked through the unlocked back door.

"It's about damn time," I said. I was about

to put my wineglass in the dishwasher, but I thought better of it, filling it up again and pouring a glass for Marcy too.

"What?" she asked innocently.

I crossed my arms and leaned against the counter as she leaned over the island. "Don't play coy with me. Why were you at Greg's office?" I held her glass of wine to my chest and said, "You don't get this until you tell me the truth."

She laughed. "Okay, okay. You guys have been fighting about this long enough. I decided to take matters into my own hands."

I handed her the glass. "And?"

"And so I did."

I sighed. "Marcy, I know you love these long dramatic monologues, but could you cut to the chase?"

She smiled. "The bottom line is that after an hour or so of fancy therapizing, I finally got Greg to admit that, as you so wisely suspected, he doesn't even want your company. What he wants is to be out of your shadow and to do his own thing, but he's afraid of falling on his face and making a fool of himself."

"What do you mean, 'do his own thing'?"

She shrugged. "I don't know, Gray. Who cares? Start a strip club. Buy and sell used cars on the Internet. It makes no difference as long as he's out of your company."

That's when my mind started racing. I'll be honest: I couldn't imagine Greg running his own show. But that didn't mean he couldn't hire the right people and start a competing company. And I didn't know Brooke that well, but who knew what she was capable of? I remembered her sparkling résumé and how much she had impressed me during our interview. There was a good reason I'd hired her. I said all that, and Marcy responded, "He said, and I quote, 'I would never do this mind-numbing bullshit an hour longer than I had to.' "

I laughed. That was a relief. "So what does he want?"

She handed me a piece of paper. I opened it, saw the seven digits on it, and about spit out my wine. "That is insane. No. Absolutely not."

Marcy shrugged. "Look, I'm a therapist. We both know I'm not good with money. But I'm assuming this isn't close to as valuable as half your company, right?"

That was technically true. And I could get rid of him. I could be rid of Greg and not have to see him except at handoffs and not have to be annoyed every single moment that he had not only ruined our marriage but had taken half of what was rightfully mine. Mine, mine, mine. Yes, divorce drives grown adults back into toddlerhood.

"I love that you are suddenly negotiating my divorce. You have to teach me your tricks sometime, how you get into people's souls like that and figure out what they really want."

She scoffed. "I would never. I manipulate the hell out of you on the regular."

"I will give him half of this," I said. "Half of this should be enough for him to completely start over."

Marcy nodded. "I don't know that he'll take it. But I'll try."

I held up my glass. "Should we finish these on the porch?"

As Marcy followed me outside, she said, "Look. I'm getting you out of your marriage. In return, it would be fantastic if you could help me get into mine."

"Want me to see if Andrew has, like, a twenty-one-year-old friend for you?" We both laughed as we folded ourselves into the oversize cushioned chairs on the back porch.

"Keep the house," Marcy said. "I don't know what we'll do without this back porch."

I nodded. And I realized that I didn't know what I would do without a best friend like her.

Diana: Shine Again

One of the first things people do after a breakup is get rid of their pictures. Makes sense. But I had saved two. The one in the locket, and one of Frank and me standing outside his car. It wasn't a special day or a special occasion or anything like that. It was just me and him and his friend Ronnie. Ronnie had snapped a Polaroid of us. And we looked so happy. I pulled it out every now and then and thought, *This is all I want, to be this happy again.*

So, all I had been able to think about these past few days was Frank saying that he couldn't be happy without me — and my not being able to be happy without him. He was right. I couldn't be happy without him. Ever. None of the other many, many men in my life could take his place. Harry was the only one I'd managed to even somewhat settle down with for more than a couple of months.

But the scared little girl part of me had been avoiding Frank since I had seen him. Ignoring his texts, refusing to return his calls. His words — *I knew I'd never be happy without you* — ran through my mind over and over. But, well, I was in shock. And the ball was still in his court after all this time. If he wanted me, he knew where to find me.

When I pulled into the Beach Pub parking lot Thursday night, I recognized that car right off the bat, before I even saw Frank. That old, rusted-out T-bird was painted a perfect, glossy Carolina blue. Its fenders gleamed. I couldn't help but smile. He had done it. He had taken that beat-up car and made it shine again.

Frank was leaning against the side of the car, arms crossed, his hair lying just so across his forehead, looking so much like he did twenty years ago that I forgot for a minute we were forty and forty-four. And I think that's the danger — and the fun — of old loves, of past lives. When you haven't seen someone in twenty-two years, you have no frame of reference for each other as adults. You are, for a while anyway, thrust back to that period of time where you left off. I was still eighteen. Frank was still twenty-two. And in the moment of reconnection, you forget all the pain; you forget all the hurt. You remember the happy. You remember the good. I was trying to protect myself from that.

When I parked right beside him and got out of the car, I said, "You traded me for a chain of auto parts stores, Frank. How am I ever supposed to get over that?"

"Diana," he said soothingly, reaching his arms out to me. "I didn't trade you for a chain of auto parts stores. You know it was a lot more complicated than that."

I sniffed. "It didn't feel complicated. It felt like your mom called me a trailer trash orphan and threatened to take away the stores, and you caved like a barn loft holding too much hay."

He shook his head, and even though he didn't move, I could see that he was getting impatient. I studied his face. He had the same deep, dark tan and some lines on his forehead, a tiny bit of gray around his temples. He was even more handsome, if that was possible. The door of the bar swung open, and Robin came out hesitantly. The girls knew the battle I'd been fighting. I was sure Robin had been sent out to check on me.

"How you doing, Frank?"

He ventured a smile. "Oh, I been better, Robin. How about you?"

"I'm doing pretty good. You hanging around here for a while? Should we pull up a chair for you or grab our guns?"

"That depends on this one, I suppose." He gestured toward me.

Robin raised her eyebrows for about a half

second. "You okay, D?"

I nodded and she gave me a once-over to make sure I was telling the truth before she left.

"Look," Frank said, "let's go somewhere quiet where we can talk about this."

Suddenly it all came flooding back. The pain of leaving him, the nights I'd cried myself to sleep, the years I'd prayed he'd come back to me. Thinking every evening as I came home that maybe I'd see his car in my driveway, that maybe he'd finally come to his senses and tracked me down. But he never did. Twenty-two years, and he never came. And now he was here, begging for redemption. All I knew was I needed to get the hell away, just like I did all those years ago.

I opened my car door, slid in, and started the ignition in one smooth move. Well, as smooth as it can be when your battery only half charges and it sounds like a choking dog for a few seconds before it finally takes. Frank didn't try to stop me or ask where I was going. He just disappeared into his T-bird.

Tears welled up in my eyes as I took off across the bridge, trying to steady myself, trying to breathe. I banged my hand on the steering wheel. "I'm such an idiot," I yelled.

He had come back for me — what I'd waited for my whole life — and I had missed my chance. But that was me. No matter how old I got or how hard I tried or how much living I had in me, I was always going to run away from anybody trying to love me — anybody good, anyway. The possibility of losing it down the road was too much to bear.

About the time I pulled into Gray's driveway, I laid my head down on the steering wheel and started to cry. Nothing else to do. When I picked my head up, I screamed so loud I was surprised the neighbors didn't come out. Frank was standing there, face in my window.

"You got away from me once, Diana. It won't happen again without a fight."

I flung my door open. "Frank, I don't know why you don't get that I don't want you around anymore. Just get out of here." I took off toward the door of the guesthouse, him following right behind.

"That'd be a whole lot easier to believe if you weren't just crying about me in the car."

I opened the door, prepared to say something cutting, but he interrupted me: "You leave your house unlocked so any nutso off the street can walk right in?"

I looked at him pointedly, like, *Yup. And*

the nutso did walk right in.

"I can't do this again, Frank. I can't. I can't love you and trust you and fall for you and you disappoint me all over again." I tossed my purse on the tiny kitchen counter and sat down in one of the pair of club chairs.

"Diana," Frank said, crossing his arms and standing tall and strong right in front of me. "You're right, okay? I didn't want to lose those stores. But I would've figured out a way. I wasn't the one who left you. You left me. And I want to know why."

I crossed my arms, mimicking his action from a moment before. "I just knew that it was going to be too hard. I could see it that night, clear as day. I didn't want to spend my life with you taking your momma's side over mine. I didn't want to spend my life with us arguing over having to see them. . . ." I trailed off.

He was still staring down at me hard. "So you're telling me that that's it? That's why we never spoke again?"

I shrugged.

"You expect me to believe that, feisty as you are, you walked away because you were scared to stand up to my momma? I don't buy it."

I suddenly felt hard inside, like maybe he

deserved to feel what I had been feeling all this time, like maybe I didn't care about protecting him or his precious tender heart anymore. "I was pregnant, okay?"

That stopped him cold. His eyes got wide and his arms just fell down. "You mean to tell me I got a kid wandering around out there that I don't even know about?"

I looked at him like he was an idiot and shook my head the tiniest bit.

His eyes met mine, and I could feel the same pain flash through both of us at the same time. Like he was about to faint or something, Frank fell to his knees, his face in his hands.

"Look," I said, standing up, feeling like I couldn't breathe. "I've spent the last twenty-two years getting over this, so let's not make too big a thing —"

He wrapped his arms around my waist and rested his head on my stomach. "Oh, Diana," he whispered. "I'm sorry. So sorry. If I had known . . . things could have been so different."

He put his lips all along the expanse of that flat, tight emptiness. I could feel the heat running through me, muscle memory taking over, my body remembering how it was to have his lips on it, how his hands felt. It wasn't here. It wasn't now. It was then, and we were young and we were in love and we were the only two people in the world.

"Di, you are all I want in this life," he said. "You're the reason I never married. You're the reason I never told another woman except my momma that I loved her. You're the reason I have cried myself to sleep more nights than not. And when Daddy died, I knew that, no matter what happened, I had to try. I had to come back for you."

Maybe it was because I had missed him so much. Maybe it was because I was so vulnerable, at the lowest point in my life, and Frank was the only person who had ever really, truly taken care of me. Maybe it's because I just wanted to feel loved and cherished even for just a little bit.

But I kissed Frank. He held me in his arms like he'd never let me go. He lifted the white shirt with the lace trim that Gray had given me over my head and threw it on the floor beside him, and I thought briefly that if I'd had on one of my T-shirts I would have remembered. This never would have happened. And I thought about protesting, but, oh, those big navy eyes looking down at me, those powerful hands that took my face in them, the way he kissed me slow and deep and sweet, with a touch of whiskey on those lips.

"Frank," I whispered, wanting the heat of this moment to last forever. Wanting to rewind time, to tell Frank about the baby, to stand up to his momma, to be married with a family of our own. A tear seeped out of my closed eye, partially for the memories we'd lost and partly for all the ones we could still have.

"You're so beautiful, Diana," he whispered. "You're still so beautiful."

I unbuttoned his shirt slowly as he continued to kiss me. He said, "I'll never walk away from you again. I'll chase you to the ends of the earth."

My mind was swimming, lost in a collision of past and present, my body and mind struggling to remember what was then and what was now. In the swirling sea of all of it, in the heat and the passion and the relief, in the confusion surrounding his return, I could only make sense of one thing: this was the only man I had ever loved.

CHAPTER 11

Gray: Ready Position

If my life looked more like my Pinterest board, I'd be all set. I'd be a DIY queen (I've never done a DIY project in my life), have my house decorated to the nines for even the most secondary holidays (I can barely get my Christmas wreath up before December 15), and be able to bake a professional-looking wedding cake in an hour or less (I don't even need to clarify this one). But my smoothie recipes? My smoothie recipes I referenced religiously.

Diana looked a little sleepy in the kitchen this morning, making one of the aforementioned Pinterest smoothies. "It's Sunday," I said. "I don't think I can be clearer that you don't have to work every day."

She turned to me like I was dumb and said, "Maybe I want to see Wagner. And I'll work more if I want to. Get over it."

As Wagner walked into the kitchen, I said,

"Okay! Prepare to be dominated." I bounced up and down in mock ready position.

He rolled his eyes.

"Ah, there's the eight-year-old I know."

"I made you your favorite," Diana whispered to Wagner.

He brightened. "The one that tastes like apple pie?"

She smiled like she was so proud and nodded. She sipped from her own straw and handed me a glass, saying, "You too."

I took a sip, closed my eyes, and groaned. "Amazing."

Diana looked the same, but I sensed that something was up with her. Something was a bit different. She seemed . . . lighter somehow.

"Y'all get out of here," she said. "Don't want to keep the tennis pro waiting." She smiled at me slyly, and I tried not to laugh.

A few minutes later, I parked beside the row of tennis courts on the water. It was a hot day, but the breeze coming off the sound made it almost refreshing.

"Well, well, well," Andrew said as Wagner stepped out of the car. "Decided to take me up on my little wager, huh?"

"Yeah!" Wagner said. "Me and Johnny are going to wipe the court with you! Look who

I brought you to play with." He pointed at me and snickered.

Andrew winked at me. "You never know. Maybe I like playing with your mom. Maybe she's got moves you don't know about." I smirked, and he cleared his throat. "On the court."

Wagner looked at me like I was a hairball on the carpet and said, "Yeah, right. Good luck, dude." He took off running toward Johnny.

"Hey, guys, the old lady and I are going into my office to strategize a little bit."

They were already ignoring us. Andrew pulled me into the tiny house that served as his pro shop, and I could feel the chill bumps on my arms as they hit the air-conditioning. "Holy hell," he said, kissing me. "They might beat us because all I can think about is those legs in that skirt."

I smiled. "This was not my idea, just so you know."

He laughed and kissed my neck.

"You're so cute with the boys," I said. "Thanks for that. They need good role models."

Andrew looked at me and said, "I think I love you." Then his eyes got wide, and he put his hand over his mouth. "I'm really sorry. I didn't mean to say that out loud."

I stood stock-still as if maybe if I didn't move we could erase what had just happened.

Andrew filled the silence. "But I think I do. And I just can't stop."

The energy in the room changed in that instant, as I felt all the color drain from my face. My heart was racing as I turned and said, "Let's go play now, okay?" and flew out the door.

It had only been a couple of months. It was too soon. Too soon with Andrew. Too soon for someone else to tell me he loved me. Too soon for me to admit that he was more than a summer fling.

"All right, amateurs." Andrew pointed his racket at me. "I have the weakest player, and I'm going to play left-handed. I'm still going to destroy you!"

Wagner laughed. "Oh yeah? We'll see about that."

"And you know what?" Andrew said. "Forget the spin. You choose whether you want to serve or receive, give you even more of an advantage."

"Serve!" Wagner and Johnny said simultaneously.

They met in the middle of the court. Wagner was so happy.

"Which side you want?" Andrew asked me.

"I don't know, lefty. Which is best for you?"

He tried not to grin, but he did, just a little, and, oh my gosh, I wanted to wrap him up and kiss him all over right then and there. I motioned with my finger for him to come closer.

"I'm sorry, Gray," he said. "I really am. I know I shouldn't have said that, so let's not let it make things weird."

I nodded, and I thought about how Andrew had been so supportive on those nights away from Wagner when I'd been so sad, how he always said and did exactly the right thing. "Look. What I've always said about us being a summer fling and all that, that still stands."

"I know."

"So don't take this the wrong way." My face hardened, and I could see his fall. "But I think I might love you a little too."

He grinned, pointed his racket at me, and, backing toward his side, said, "I knew it, Gray Howard. I knew it was only a matter of time."

Even in that happy moment, it made me sad to realize that I knew it too. He was adorable. But this wasn't going anywhere. It was only a matter of time.

Diana: North

I couldn't figure out why I was trying to keep Frank out of the picture, why I'd told him I had to go to Gray's that morning when I knew she wasn't expecting me. It was like I woke up and everything I had dreamed of over the past twenty years had happened. It was exactly like I'd imagined it. Magical. Perfect. Hot. In a lot of ways, it was like no time had passed at all. Well, I mean, my boobs were a hell of a lot lower and my ass was kind of jiggly, but otherwise everything was the same.

As I was cleaning out the blender, I was mulling over what had me so panicked. All I'd thought about forever was him. I hated saying it even to myself, but Frank was the whole reason I never got married. Well, plus the fact that I had managed to attract every loser on the East Coast. I sprayed off the counter and took a real deep breath. It was time to go back. It was time to get that happiness I'd dreamed about all this time.

Frank was just sitting there at that cute kitchen table, and when I walked in, before I'd even got in the door good, he said, "Diana, we've spent too many years apart to play around like this now. I want our life together to start now. I want us to get to know each other again."

I wanted it too, but something in me needed just a little time to get my bearings, like I'd been thrust out in the middle of the ocean and was trying to figure which way was north. I went over to make the bed and began tidying up before I turned to look at him. "But what if you don't like the 'old' me?"

He smiled. "I don't see anyone old in this room."

I was spraying off the already clean countertops when Frank pulled me to him, the bottle and paper towels trapped between us. He kissed me, and, oh my Lord, how I had prayed for that kiss, how I had longed for it, pined for it, wished up and down for it to be mine again. I dropped that bottle to the floor and wrapped myself all around him. Frank hoisted me onto the counter, and I couldn't help but feel like we were making up for lost time.

"Hey," he whispered, "do we need to worry about, you know, protection?"

I shook my head, thinking that if he was worried about me getting pregnant today, maybe he should've thought about it a little bit last night too. "No," I said. "I can't get pregnant."

I was so caught up in the moment that I only thought about it for a second. That day Robin had sped down the road with me half hallucinating in the passenger seat, my fever was so high. I don't even really remember much, just that IV in my arm and finally starting to sweat the fever away and that doctor saying that I'd got some kind of infection, and I wouldn't ever have any kids of my own. It had messed me up, sure. But, way deep down, I'd felt kind of relieved. I mean, my momma, she'd left all us kids to fend for ourselves, just left us like the garbage on the back porch. At least I'd never be that kind of momma.

I felt my hands unbuttoning his pants as if by memory, and, somehow, now that Frank was here, now that Frank was back, none of that mattered anymore. I wanted to be cautious. I wanted to take it slow. I wanted not to make a mistake. But I had spent years waiting for this man.

What seemed like hours later, I was kissing Frank good-bye at the bottom of the steps. "Diana, please," he said, "I know you. Don't go back up there and get all in your own head and decide you're not sure. This is right. This is us. This is *it.* Just be sure, okay?"

I smiled. "Okay, Frank. I have to take a

breath to think about it all. I can't just rush into it again. I got my heart broke real bad last time."

He kissed me and rubbed his thumb across my cheek. "But last time I didn't know, Di. Last time we were kids. Last time we were making all our mistakes. I'm done with mistakes. I only want to make it right with us."

Butterflies and sighs. I didn't think of myself as one of those sappy women, but, damn. When a man talks to you like that, it's hard not to feel kind of sucked in. He opened the door and walked outside.

I heard Gray's voice say, "Oh, hi."

I walked out real quick to introduce them, but Frank was already shaking her hand. "I'm a friend of Diana's."

She winked at me and said, "I'm a friend of Diana's too. Nice to meet you."

"I'll call you later, Di," he said as he walked to his car.

Gray and I stood in the driveway looking at each other, but as soon as the ignition cranked, she said, "Oh my gosh. Are you kidding me? Who is *that*?"

"That," I said, "is the one who got away."

"Only now he's come back."

I nodded.

"So why are you not driving off into the

sunset with him?"

I just shrugged — but when I really examined my reasons, I had to admit that it had more than a little something to do with her.

CHAPTER 12

Gray: Pamphlets

The orange juice always gets lost in our fridge. I don't know why, but it's never up front when I need it. I was wondering how that could be, if it was a phenomenon like socks being eaten by the dryer, when I heard a tap at the back door. *Ugh,* I thought. Whoever it was could clearly see me through the glass door, so it wasn't like I could pretend I wasn't home.

I closed my eyes and crossed my fingers it was Marcy, even though I knew she wouldn't have knocked. Totally embarrassed that I was still in my bathrobe at, as the microwave informed me, 11:03 a.m., I turned slowly.

I felt my eyes widen in surprise at my visitor. It was a bit like looking in a mirror. Blond hair. Mole by her left eye. But that was where the similarities ended. I pinned on my most enthusiastic smile and opened the door. "Quinn! What on earth are you doing here?"

As she gave my attire a once-over, I leaned in to hug her. My sister. Formerly the most fun person I had ever known.

"Are you sick?" she asked, mock concern on her face.

"No." I tried to smile through gritted teeth. "Why would you say that?"

"Just wondering why you're still in your bathrobe at eleven in the morning." She forced a laugh. "I was in the neighborhood volunteering for the breakfast shift at the soup kitchen and thought I'd pop in."

I wanted to strangle her already. Instead of explaining myself, I said, "Oh, wow. That's so nice."

She looked around. "Where's Wagner?"

I rolled my eyes. "Brooke's family beach trip."

She pursed her lips. "So you obviously haven't thought any more about my advice from last time I saw you."

I evaded her question. "So, what brings you here?" Quinn lived in Charleston. "I wish I'd known you were visiting. We could have made plans."

But I was glad I hadn't known she was visiting, and I didn't want to make any plans. She brushed past me into the living room, setting herself pertly on the couch. I followed, rolling my eyes. She reached into her sensible black leather purse, and I remembered a time when my sister would have been carrying something neon, or maybe her glittery clutch because she was still out from the night before.

"I brought you some pamphlets," she said.

"Okay . . ." I felt like I was walking into a trap.

"On God's plan for marriage and how to save it from divorce."

And there it was. "Quinn, look. I've told you like a hundred times. I can't save my marriage. Greg didn't say, 'Hey, Gray, I cheated on you. I love you. Please forgive me.' " She stared at me blankly as I continued, "He said, 'I've found someone else. I'm leaving you.' There's no coming back from that. He's engaged to another woman. My marriage is over."

"Well, Pastor Elijah says —"

"I don't give two shits what Pastor Elijah says," I cut her off. "I'm tired of this same conversation. I'm getting divorced. You can accept that or not, but don't come into my house and tell me how to live my life."

She looked shocked, as though the f-word hadn't been the mainstay of her vocabulary two years ago. "You know what the Bible says about . . ." She paused and looked around and then whispered dramatically, "*. . . divorce.*"

I laughed ironically. "Yeah, Quinn. I got it. You've highlighted all the passages for me —"

At that moment, I heard, "Sorry I fell asleep, babe. You really know how to tucker a guy out."

It was like trying to stop a moving train. I couldn't see him; he couldn't see me. And his voice traveled. Before I could say anything, he was in the room. In his boxers. With those abs. And that tousled hair.

My sister looked at me as if I were the devil as Andrew said, "Oh, sorry. I didn't know you had company."

A moment later, I heard the back door open and Diana's voice saying, "Hi, Gray, I'm back. Hey, where is everybody?"

That's when my sister huffed, "I don't want to have to spend eternity without you, but I'm not sure Jesus himself can save your soul."

She picked up her bag and stormed out, brushing past Diana as I called, "Hey, Quinn, remember when you could do more blow than an entire fraternity house?" Then more loudly, "Oh, wait, remember when I was breastfeeding Wagner and had to leave in the middle of the night to bail you out of jail?" My "TWICE!" coincided with her door slam.

It might have been the first time that both Andrew and Diana had been rendered totally speechless. I sighed heavily, and Diana, who knew all about my sister and our past, hugged me. I wished she wouldn't have because it made me want to cry. Fighting with your husband is awful. But your sister? That's your flesh and blood, the person who has known you longer and better than anyone. I mean, it goes without saying that sisters fight. But this wasn't an argument, one of those we're-sisters-so-we'll-be-over-it-in-an-hour types of things. This was do or die.

"Ironically," I said, "the biggest fights Greg and I ever had were over her."

"Who was that?" Andrew said, sitting beside me where I had flopped down on the couch. I put my legs in his lap as Diana whispered to him, "Do you ever wear clothes?"

I actually smiled when he replied, "Don't act like you want me to." Then he squeezed my calf and said, "No, babe. For real?"

"That lovely creature is my sister. She was the wildest, craziest, most out-of-control person you've ever met. A little over the edge, but so fun and so vivacious."

Andrew grimaced. "So what happened?"

"Pastor Elijah." I rolled my eyes. "Do you think there's even a chance that's his real name?"

Quinn had met Pastor Elijah right after our mother's diagnosis. I don't know what took her to church; I guess a last-ditch attempt to pray that "terminal" out of Mom. But he had been utterly charmed by her, like the many, many men before him. And maybe he was looking for a soul to save, I don't know. My parents were so relieved. Their baby girl was finally growing up. She was finally making the right choices. She fell in love with him so hard and so fast, and, before you knew it, she had traded binge drinking for Bible study and sleeping with every man up and down the Crystal Coast for monogamy. We were all thrilled — at first.

I contented myself with knowing that my mom died thinking Quinn had found Jesus and the love of her life. But assuming she's looking down, she couldn't be happy that I was letting my sister carry on with this lunatic. And she'd just left me here to deal with it on my own.

"Trust me," I said. "No one is happier than I am that she found Jesus. But it's, like, in a weird way, you know?"

"What do you mean?" Diana asked.

"Like in a cultish, we-need-to-rescue-her-and-put-her-in-the-witness-protection-program sort of way." I stood up and started pacing. "I mean, she's just so damn judgmental all of a sudden. It's unbelievable. After all the times I picked her up at a stranger's house, all the nights I stayed up holding her hair . . . Like, I get that she has changed, and I'm so glad. But how do you forget so quickly that you weren't always perfect either?"

"Ohhhh," Andrew said. "So what you're saying is the nearly naked twenty-six-year-old emerging from your bedroom did not impress her?"

I smiled.

"But you know," he said, "I'm going to be twenty-seven soon. Do you think that would help?"

Diana gagged. "Little boy, go put some clothes on."

Andrew smiled that charming smile at her and said, "Yes, ma'am," and got up and wandered back to the bedroom.

Then Diana took my hand and sat us both down on the couch. "Look, honey, losing your momma, it's tough. I know. You won't ever get over that."

She paused. I knew I should feel grateful that I got to have my mom all the years I did, that she was there at the beginning of my marriage, that she helped me with Wagner when he was a baby. That she got to go to baseball games and grandparents' day and the school play.

Diana said, "Everybody handles loss in a different way. And it looks like maybe your sister's transformation was her response." She nodded toward the bedroom and said in a low voice, "I don't want to say it, but do you think that maybe Andrew is yours?"

If Diana had been my mom, I would have yelled at her then. I know I would have. I would've said, "You have no idea what I'm going through. He makes me happy, and I deserve a little bit of happy right now!"

I would have walked off and slammed the door, knowing she was right the whole time but not wanting to admit it. But Diana wasn't my mom. She probably wasn't going to take that kind of attitude from me, and, well, I needed her. So I just shrugged.

She wrapped her arms around me, and I rested my head on her shoulder.

"I've got this divorce hell going on, and my sister is a total wacko, and . . . I just don't even know who I am anymore."

She stroked my hair. "Honey, I've felt lost

a lot of times in my life, but do you know what I've learned?"

I sat up and wiped my eyes.

"You are always who you are. No matter what is going on around you. Your sister is crazy, and your mom is gone, and Greg is a nightmare, but you are still you, Gray. I swear that you are."

I wanted to feel as sure as she did, but I just didn't know. I was too sad and too overwhelmed to acknowledge her advice. "I've already lost my mom. Now I've lost my sister too."

"I wasn't anybody's momma," Diana said, "but I am somebody's sister. And I have a feeling that when your blood and your love run thick and deep, you can't ever really lose them. It sucks that she isn't here for you when you need her. But that doesn't mean that you can't still be there for her when this all blows up."

"You would have been such a good mom," I said. "The way you love on everybody, and all your good advice. And you make the best lemonade pie in the world."

I looked up to see a strange kind of sadness in her eyes, but she just kept stroking my hair. And it occurred to me that, as was abundantly clear from the woman sitting beside me, you didn't need to have a baby to be a mother.

Diana: The One Who Got Away

"You did it! I can tell!" Cheyenne was hollering, all of us sitting around the dining table in the guesthouse I'd finally gotten around to telling the girls about.

Robin nodded, her motorcycle jacket hanging over the back of the chair. "I knew it. I knew the minute I saw him that you was getting back together."

Cheyenne paused. "But don't let this get you off track from our boat restaurant."

I smiled just thinking about it. I had saved up enough money already for the first three months of slip rent. I needed enough for a used commercial stove and refrigerator and starting supplies, but if I didn't spend hardly a cent between now and Labor Day when Gray went back to Raleigh, I could probably swing it. Just barely. September wouldn't be the best time to open a restaurant at the beach, but it would give me a few months to get my feet wet before May rolled around and things got busy. "Don't you worry about that, Chey. I've been dreaming about my restaurant even longer than I've been dreaming about Frank."

Janet was leaned back in her chair, arms crossed over the muffin top rolling over the band of her jeans. I'd told her a hundred times if she would just wear jeans one size bigger, she wouldn't have all that mess hanging out. But did she listen? Nope.

She scowled. And I guessed she had every right to.

I was trying to pry the smile off my face. The Frank-induced, bathing-in-love-and-relief-and-memories smile. But, oh, hard as I tried, I just couldn't. Every time I got it off, it popped right on back up. But the absolute, pure joy alternated with hot, raging panic. I wasn't the kind of girl who got happy endings. Was it even possible that this could all work out for me now?

"What's up your craw?" Robin asked Janet.

She shook her head, that mean look still on her face. "Ain't nothing up my *craw,* Robin. I just don't know why we gotta be all excited and in love with Frank again. *Frank.* Am I the only one who remembers? I don't remember Frank being there. I don't remember him getting you hot water bottles or holding your hand or sleeping with you so you didn't wake up scared in the night." She shifted in her chair like she was done talking. But then she kept right on. "Was Frank there when you got that fever and was talking outta your head not making a lick o' sense? Was Frank there in the emergency room with all those tubes and IVs and antibiotics? 'Cause it seems to me like he wasn't around for none o' that. Seems like it was me. And Robin. And Cheyenne. So I'm sorry, *Robin.* Maybe *that's* what's up my craw."

We were all kind of stunned, but I don't know why. Janet always said whatever she thought right out. She just laid it out on the table, and if you didn't pick it up, then that was your own damn problem.

And I hated that she was right. I thought of Frank's face in the morning light, the way he whispered in my ear, the way he held me all night long, the way he took his time, memorizing every inch of me. I wanted it to be enough, but Janet wasn't wrong. Frank hadn't been there. And there wasn't a damn thing I could do to change that.

"Now look what you done," Cheyenne said. "I hadn't seen a smile like that on that girl's face in twenty-two years, and you wiped it right off."

Janet shook her head. "Fine. She can do whatever the hell she wants. I'm just reminding her how it all went down. That's all. And if she wants to do it anyway, then fine." Janet's scowl finally broke as she said, "I'll even wear one-a them hideous green bridesmaids' dresses with the puffy sleeves."

We all got a good laugh for a minute. When we stopped, I went to the fridge to get us a round of Mike's Hard Lemonade. People can say what they want. They can make jokes and make fun. But, hear this: there's nothing like a hard lemonade to quench your thirst on a hot day. Nothing.

I was handing them out when I heard footsteps and, "Hey, Lady Di, I'm going to —"

Gray stopped right in her tracks when she saw the girls sitting around the table.

"I am so sorry," she said. "I didn't know you had company. I'll just be . . ." She pointed toward the door.

"Don't be crazy," Cheyenne said in that high, peppy voice of hers. "You come sit that bony fanny down right now and have a lemonade with us."

Gray looked at me, and I smiled. "Oh yeah. These girls won't bite." Then I eyed Janet and pointed my bottle toward Cheyenne and Robin and said, "Well, these two won't."

Gray made a face like she was scared and sat down snuggling up close to me, far away from Janet.

Ten hard lemonades later we were laughing and carrying on like I don't know what.

We'd covered high school memories and hairdos, prom dates and birthing babies. But we'd skipped clear over Frank.

The laughter died down and Robin said, "So, for real, Di, what are you gonna do about Frank?"

Gray leaned away and made a face like she was amused and impressed. "Ah yes. The one who got away and came back. Do tell."

I shook my head and stood up, clearing the empty bottles. "No way. It's time to call it a . . ." I was going to say *night,* but, though our alcohol consumption would indicate otherwise, it was broad daylight. So I said, ". . . an afternoon."

"Frank," Cheyenne whispered to Gray as if I couldn't hear, "is the love of Diana's life."

"And he wants this one some sorta bad," Robin added.

Gray squealed and rubbed her hands together in delight. "Oh my goodness. So has there been a romantic reunion?"

"You'd know all about those, wouldn't you, Miss Gray?"

I was trying to change the subject, but she saw right through me. "What I have going on is a rebound, a summer fling. Yours is real love coming back to the light."

All of a sudden, I could hear, "Gray, where the hell are you?"

She opened the window and said, "Up here, Marce! We're talking all about Diana's hot rekindling with an old flame."

"Yesssss!" I heard Marcy say as she ran up the steps.

"We're talking about it up here so that no one can *hear* us," I said.

"Ohhhh," Gray whispered. "Sorry."

"Look," I said, "I'm down to my last six-pack of Mike's, so take it easy here."

Marcy was out of breath as she plopped down on the floor by the table. "Do tell," she said, taking a sip from the bottle I handed her. She looked at me confidentially. "I am a therapist, after all."

"Yeah," Janet said, "that's exactly who you need. She'll be on my side for sure."

I don't know if it was the drinks or the girls or what, but even though I wanted to resist telling the whole messy story to my employer, they wouldn't let me. She got all teared-up and hugged me and said she was so sorry. And it ended up all right. We tossed it all around, but, in the end, Marcy was judge and jury.

"I'm sorry," she said. "But, one, it's not fair to judge someone for something he did twenty-two years ago. Two, it's not fair to punish him for not acting the right way in a situation he knew nothing about. Three, he sounds so sweet, and if it doesn't work out, you had a good time this summer."

She stood up, took a little bow, and said, "Therapist out," as Cheyenne, Gray, and Robin clapped and Janet booed.

I hated being vulnerable. I hated letting my insecurity show. But I had to get it out. "What if he can't stand up for me and his momma wins again? What if he leaves me?"

It was Gray who took my hand. "Di, if you honestly don't think this is a good fit, then don't do it. Walk away. But if you want to give this thing a try, give it a try. Don't let fear hold you back." She smiled reassuringly at me. "If you try it and he breaks your heart, guess what?"

"What?"

"You still have all of us."

I bit my lip to keep the tears away. It was like a light bulb went off. Yeah. Things went bad — all the time. I'd always been okay. I'd be okay again. And I had these ladies to pick me back up if I fell. "You're right. I can spend my life wondering or I can spend my life living."

"Fine," Janet said. "You win. Give him another chance. But you be damn careful."

Gray lifted her bottle with the last sip

toward me and said, "Sounds to me, honey, like there's only one thing left to do."

"What's that?"

"Go and get your man."

Chapter 13

Gray: The Winner

"Remember that picture of Brooke with her in that sombrero drinking the fishbowl margarita?" I asked Marcy as we lay in the front yard, waiting for our lemonades to wear off so we could go paddleboarding.

She cracked up. "That was the worst thing I've ever seen. I mean, Greg is a total tool, but that is, like, seriously the worst." She sat up all of a sudden and said, "Hey, where's hottie with a body?"

"He had clinics this morning and then he's coming over."

Marcy leaned over me, her nose mere inches from mine. "Are you going to marry him?" she whispered. "I mean, seriously. Y'all are like all in love. If you get married for the second time before I get married for the first, I'm going to be super pissed."

"Marcy, you're making me jealous," I heard from behind me.

We all started cracking up as Andrew made his way toward where we were lying.

"Oh, oh, oh, it's my little stud muffin. I have miiiisssed you." I sat up and planted a big, wet kiss on him.

He backed away and made a face. "Babe, what have you been drinking?"

"Mike's Hard Lemonade," Marcy said through her giggles.

I pointed toward the guesthouse. "With Diana and her friends who have tolerances much, much greater than mine."

He nodded. "I can see that."

"Wait. Are you mad?"

"No!" He laughed. "In fact, I'm relieved. It's going to make you a lot easier to sway."

"Do I need to leave for this?" Marcy said, lying back down. "I mean, I'm not going to. But if I'm not supposed to be here, I'll try harder not to say stuff."

Andrew laughed. "It's fine. I might want you on my side." He took a deep breath. "Gray. I want you to come out with me on a proper date to a proper place, in public, where you will probably see people you know."

"No."

He laughed. "What? Why not? It's been weeks, and I'm ready to take this thing out on the open road."

Marcy started laughing.

"We can't be frolicking around town together," I said lazily, feeling myself starting to get tired.

He sighed. "So, what then? Am I supposed to sneak around in the shadows with you forever — well, I mean, forever until I go back to grad school in the fall? Is that the deal?"

I leaned forward and tried to charm my way out of the situation. "I kind of like sneaking around in the shadows with you."

He backed away. "I'm serious, Gray. Can't I at least meet your friends? I know they all know about me." He gave me that boyish grin that I found irresistible. *I bet his mom never punished him.* That thought horrified me. His poor mother. She would just die if she knew he was dating a thirty-four-year-old woman. It was probably a good thing that my mother was dead because she would have killed me. My resolve was strengthened.

Marcy interjected, "You know me. I'm the only friend who matters."

I pointed at Marcy and made a triumphant face. "See?"

But then he said, his irritation rising, "Are you embarrassed by me?"

Was I embarrassed by him? I looked him

over, closed one eye, looked him over again. Nope. Not one single bit of that adorableness was embarrassing.

I scooted in closer to him. "Sweetheart, I am not even close to embarrassed by you. You are a prize if ever there was one."

"Then what's the big deal?"

Marcy raised her eyebrows at me and mouthed, *You're going to marry him.*

"Look. I'm embarrassed of myself. I'm way too old to be gallivanting around with you when I have an eight-year-old and am in the middle of a divorce."

"I'm the one who pursued you and wouldn't take no for an answer," Andrew said.

I sighed. "Andrew, come on, this has to stop." But I think we both knew I had no intention of stopping anything.

"Why would we stop something so amazing?"

"Because it's a fun summer fling, but we've taken it too far."

He lifted his head from my shoulder. "I'm ready to not say that anymore. I don't want to hear it again." He paused. "It is going to be my birthday. I want to go out with you in public. Those are my terms."

I was about to say no, but he was serious. No Andrew coming over to keep me company when Wagner was gone. . . . No one making me laugh, wrapping his arms around my waist, telling me I was beautiful. . . . I wasn't ready for this bright spot to be over.

I smiled. "Okay. I agree to your terms." I shook his hand with my left one because it was easier to move, my bangles tinkling as our arms moved up and down.

"Yay!" Marcy cheered.

"But we are not telling Wagner."

Andrew nodded.

"So, what did you have in mind there, soldier of love?" Marcy asked Andrew.

"Oh, I have something in mind that would be perfect," I said.

"What's that?" Marcy asked.

"Hospital. Foundation."

We both laughed because we knew, without further explanation, that those two words translated to: *Beating. Greg.*

Andrew kissed me, and I felt like, out in public, in private, wherever he wanted me to be, I was the winner here no matter what.

Diana: Settled

Of all the photos I ever developed, the wedding ones were my favorites. The laughing, the kissing, the kids all gathered around the bride in their Sunday best. Every last one of those photos reminded me of Frank. In every Costa Rican sunset, there'd be his head and mine; in every handholding, before-the-priest moment, it was me and Frank.

Only it wasn't me and Frank, because we'd ruined that good a long time ago. He'd been texting me since that afternoon he left. I hadn't responded, not even one time, because I wasn't real sure what I wanted to do. But the girls, they got me thinking: here's a man I'd been holding on to in my heart for more than two decades, and this was my chance to see if all that had been worth it. I tried telling myself that it didn't matter if we ended up in those wedding photos. We just needed to see if, all these years later, it would work out in any form.

My old Impala was spitting down the road, and I started having some second thoughts. Frank had been the light I'd carried inside of me all these years, the person who, through it all, I believed was the one. If we did get back together and it didn't work out, I wouldn't have anything to hold on to anymore, nothing to get me through the dark days and nights when life feels like being too alone to even take.

My stomach was churning; I was exhausted from being up these past few nights trying to figure what was the right thing. I pulled into Meds and More where I used to work, and next thing I knew Mr. Joe was right there beside me, hugging my neck in the Tums aisle.

"We sure do miss you 'round here," he said, little wet eyes shining.

"I sure miss y'all too," I lied. Well, I mean, it wasn't really a lie. I did miss the people.

"I begged Bill to bring you back in. I overheard him telling this lady that comes in here all the time that he fired you on account of some cropping not being right and a lot of problems with the photos. But I told him that wasn't on account of you not being good at your job. That was on account of the machine and —"

I put my hand up to stop him, my mind racing. "Wait. So you mean Mr. Marcus told her it wasn't her fault I got fired?"

Mr. Joe, he looked kinda confused. "Well, I . . ." he stammered. Then he shrugged, all red-faced. "I don't really remember, Di. I didn't realize it was important."

I felt glued to my spot, my heart racing, but I couldn't tell exactly what I was feeling right yet. "Gray Howard? Eight-year-old son?"

He nodded. "Yup. That's the one."

I didn't say anything, caught somewhere between super pissed off and washed over with love. *I didn't need Gray's charity,* I huffed on the inside. *But, really,* that little voice said, *I kind of did, didn't I?* Was she trying to patronize me? Hiring me like that and telling me that she got me fired? And all this time, had she really known? Was she waiting to confront me about it? Did she know I had lied to her? Mr. Joe, he was chattering on and on and on, and I couldn't even hear him, all in my head like I was. I couldn't hear him, that is, until he said, red as I've ever seen a man, "I sure would like to take you out to dinner sometime."

Oh no. . . . Was he asking me on a date? Sweet Mr. Joe. I looked down at myself. If a man asks you out when you're wearing a stained, ripped Big Rock Fishing Tournament shirt from fifteen years ago, he really likes you. Gary, the owner of this shirt, had been the mate on the boat that won the Big Rock in 2005. He got $50,000 of the $1 million prize and went on a month-long bender in Vegas. Blew through every cent of that money and then came crawling back to me. Needless to say, I did not answer the door.

It was right about the time Mr. Joe asked me out that I decided to look at the bright side and assume that Gray had given me the job because she needed me and she was a nice girl. No harm, no foul. Just a little white lie. Lord knows I've told my share. And it was also right about that time, when I heard myself say, "Oh, Mr. Joe, that sure is nice, but I'm seeing someone," that I made up my mind about Frank too.

I put the Tums back, deciding I didn't need them, seeing as how me settling everything had settled my stomach.

As I pulled out of the parking lot, I knew I had to go talk to my brother. Instead of heading to Frank's, like I thought I was going to, I went to Cape Nursing. Phillip was really lucky because he didn't have a roommate right now. The girls at the home had moved the other bed out of his room, and I'd put in two chairs I'd found on the side of the road in Gray's neighborhood — I checked them for bedbugs before I took them — and I'd picked some flowers from Gray's yard and put them in a mason jar on the windowsill. The carpet was still old and stained and dirty, and the window unit was still real loud, but it made it look a little better in there.

The TV was on when I walked into Phillip's room, and he was staring at it, but he looked over at me. "Hi, buddy," I said. "Can I turn your TV off?"

"Okay," he said, as I hit the button on the remote.

I sat down in the other chair with the starfish cushions on it right beside him. "How you doing today?"

He didn't say anything, but he smiled at me, light behind those green eyes of his.

"You won't believe it," I said enthusiastically. I had gotten so good at having mostly one-sided conversations with him, at being as excited as I could manage to maybe give him a bright spot in his day. "I'm finally working on opening a restaurant. On a boat!"

"A boat," Phillip repeated.

I nodded. "You've met my friend Cheyenne. She comes by to see you sometimes. Her husband is helping me get it all fixed up, and I'm saving up some money to get it started. You'll work there when I get it open, right? Help me some?"

"Yeah," he said.

I wanted to hug him, but I didn't. I could see it clear as day. The two of us in my little boat restaurant, rambling around our new place together at night . . . with Frank. When I saw Phillip and me together in my head, Frank was there too. And that's what gave me the strength, I think.

As I pulled into Frank's driveway a few

minutes later, I thought about the first time he ever brought me here.

I felt sick to my stomach looking out onto the beach, remembering that right there on that dune, that's where we'd made that baby. At least, I think so. There was something so special about that night. I knew then that Frank and me, we'd be together forever. I turned to the house, but before I even got a chance to walk up the steps, I heard Frank's feet thudding down. When he turned the corner, I was standing right there on the bottom one, just waiting and smiling.

He put his hand on his chest, a little out of breath. "Di, you always did know how to get my heart racing."

He leaned in to kiss me, but I backed away.

That handsome face fell.

"Please, Di. Please don't be here giving me bad news. I can't take having you and then having to be without you again. Please."

"Frank, I'm so mad at you," I said. "Still. All these years later. You abandoned me just like the rest. Worse than the rest because you knew how hard it was for me to let anyone in. How can I ever trust you again?"

He took my hand, and I let him. "Di, it

isn't an excuse. I realize that it isn't. But I was twenty-two years old, and I wasn't just in danger of losing those stores. I was in danger of losing my family."

My ears perked.

"Look, like I said, it isn't an excuse, but my momma and daddy weren't taking away the stores; they were taking away themselves, our relationship. Everything. I loved you. I wanted you, and I see now that I made the wrong choice, but at the time I couldn't imagine my life without Christmases around the tree at the beach house and Easter lunch at Grandma's. It was too much. It was too big a choice. So I didn't choose. I just hid."

Now, I know for most women, that wouldn't be a good explanation. But for me, it couldn't have been better. Because I had never had a family. At least, not in the way I wanted to. And if I ever had, I wouldn't have let it go either. I'm damn sure about that. I was okay on my own. I was. But when you have a family and then you lose it, all you want forever is to get that back.

"I have never moved on past that day you walked away." He put my hand up to his heart. "I've carried you right here all these years. I love you, D. It's as simple and as complicated as that."

I could feel the panic rising in me that he couldn't ever really love me, that he was going to leave me, that if I let myself fall, even a little, it would be over, just like everything else. I couldn't bear it. "You don't even know who I am, Frank," I practically shouted, my voice suddenly shaking with fear and anger and passion. "You have no idea." I could feel myself trying to push him away; I was terrified that he would find out who I really was and leave me. I had to tell him now. He had to know the real me. It was easier for him to leave me now than later. "Two months ago, I had sixty bucks to my name. I was homeless. I was living in my car. I was washing my underwear in a sink at the marina." I was so worked up I had to pause to look away. "That isn't something new for me, Frank. I'm not some shiny, hopeful eighteen-year-old anymore. I've been through things that I could never even explain to you. Life has worn me down. Life has won."

He took my face in his hands. "I don't care where you've been or what you've done. I don't care about any of it, Diana."

"Your mom was right," I said, my voice still raised. "I'm a trailer trash orphan. That's all I'm ever going to be. I will never be good enough for you."

"Diana," Frank said quietly. He rubbed my arms, trying to soothe me. I was having trouble breathing. He bent down just a little so his face was even with mine. "She has always been shortsighted and she has always been wrong about you. You are more than enough for me. Hell, you are the *only* one for me."

I was calming down now. I was hearing him. And this huge part of me knew that he was right. We were meant to be. There was no other way to describe how it felt.

"I love you no matter what," he said. "I love you more than myself. I love you more than time."

There were tears in my eyes now, but I didn't want him to see so I looked away. All I could manage was, "What if it isn't as good as we think?"

"If what isn't?"

He sat down on the bottom step and patted beside him.

"Our life together," I said, sitting down, our hips touching. "What if it was all fun and games when we were kids, but now, as adults, it's just drudgery like everything else? I can't bear to ever be like that with you. You're the one I've always carried in my heart, that great love I held on to and compared to everyone else." I looked down at my polished toe peeking out of my sandal. "If that's gone, Frank, I don't think I can bear it."

He put his arm around me and pulled me in close to him, pushing my head against his strong chest. "We've spent the last two decades dreaming about our love. Let's spend all the rest of them living it." He looked down at me. "Okay?"

It was the perfect thing to say. It was the exact thing that all those nights I lay awake in bed alone or beside yet another wrong guy I had hoped and prayed to God that I would hear out of those very lips, lips I hadn't laid eyes on in so long that their memory was fading. Lips I couldn't quite see, but, if I closed my eyes, I could feel them on mine, just the same as it had always been. I felt that race in my heart and that ache in my stomach, the warning bell that told me to run. Could I be this happy? If I was this happy and it ended, would I ever be able to go back to living like normal again?

I don't know what gave me the strength. But I nodded. "Okay."

He kissed me long and hard, and I felt in that moment that everything in my life that had been tough — losing my mom, all them foster homes, losing Frank, losing my baby

— this moment was where all that got made up for. I might have been a forty-year-old princess. But I was going to have one hell of a happily ever after.

CHAPTER 14

Gray: Corporate Takeover

As I adjusted the collar buttons on Andrew's shirt, which he had paired with freshly pressed khaki shorts, I realized I was pretty sure that I'd never seen him in an oxford. It was sweet that he was dressing up for me to take him out in public for the first time.

"So why is this thing in the middle of the day?" he asked.

"I don't have the faintest idea," I said. "I am happy to say that I didn't have one thing to do with planning this soiree."

"It's because it's a fund-raiser," Marcy said. "And, theoretically, people drink less during the day and then the charity doesn't spend as much money on booze."

"Theoretically," Andrew said in a tone that implied they hadn't met us yet. We all laughed.

"Hello," I said. "Three for Howard."

The lady sitting at the table, wearing

glasses with a chain to keep them around her neck, said, "I see Howard for two."

Andrew put his arm around me. "That would be her idiot ex-husband."

He kissed me on the cheek, and Marcy added, "And his trampy new fiancée."

The woman looked shocked underneath her half-glasses and sort of stuttered, "Um . . . yes . . . I see Howard for three right here. Sorry I missed it before."

Andrew took my hand, and we walked into the party, surveying the scene.

"Oh, man," Marcy said. "These people just keep getting *older.*"

Andrew snickered behind his hand.

"Y'all need to behave, okay? I brought you both out in public under the condition of good behavior. You can shotgun beers at the Beach Pub later as a reward if you can keep it together now."

In his haughtiest voice, Andrew said, "Well, my love, in that case, I shall go rustle us up some chardonnay. Not too oaky. No, not on a day as warm as this."

Marcy and I giggled. As I watched Andrew walk away, I could feel eyes on me. I turned and did a double take.

He was tall, dark, and age-appropriate. He was handsome, but not ruggedly like Andrew. There was something that made him imperfectly attractive, like maybe his nose was a little bit too big for his face. He didn't have to say a word for every person in that room to know that he was powerful. He was in charge. He was a *man.*

"Oh my gosh," Marcy whispered to me. "Who is that guy?"

As if he had heard her, he turned. His eyes met mine for a moment too long, but it was as if I couldn't look away. He had me locked in his gaze. He winked and smiled and sauntered to the bar.

"You can't be serious?" Marcy said.

"What do you mean?" I asked breathlessly, using all the energy I had not to follow him.

She took a step back and turned toward me. "Do you see me?" she asked, running her hands down the length of her torso in a body-skimming dress with her tan, mile-long legs peeking out from underneath.

"You are stunning. If I were into women, I would be all over you."

"Awww, thanks, sweetie. So why was Mr. Corporate Takeover there giving you the stare-down and didn't even notice me?"

"I don't know what you're talking about," I lied.

"What did I miss?" Andrew said from behind me, making me jump.

He handed me a drink. I smiled, coming

back to earth, to this cutie-pie I was with.

"Oh, noth— there they are!" Marcy finished in a sharp whisper.

I looked toward the sign-in table to see Brooke gliding in, her long blond hair waving in the breeze, looking about as gorgeous as one could expect, on Greg's arm. He was smiling victoriously, as if he were signaling that he had won some sort of contest. You couldn't blame him, really. She was stunning, to say the least.

His smile vanished when he saw me. I waved and slipped my hand into Andrew's. It probably seemed like a ploy, but, in all honesty, I felt like I needed his support. It was the first time I had seen my almost ex-husband and his new fiancée out together, like, at an event. It wasn't that I wanted him back. But she was on his arm where I had been for so many years, and that was undeniably strange.

Brooke smiled at me. While she was chatting with the hostess, Greg beelined in my direction. "Hi, Greg," I said nonchalantly.

Andrew put his hand out and said, "Hi, I'm —"

Greg cut him off. "I know who you are." He peered at me. "Gray, could we have a moment, please?"

Andrew looked at me questioningly. I nodded and smiled at him, and he gave me a quick kiss on the lips and said, "It's time for a new beer. Can I get you one, man?" as he walked off.

Greg looked at him as if he were speaking Greek, which was not one of the five languages that Greg was fluent in.

"Are you serious, Gray? Bringing our son's tennis teacher to the party? Are you trying to make me jealous or something?"

I laughed and took a sip of my wine. "I'm definitely not trying to make you jealous. I tried to fend him off, but the man is *very* persistent."

"So you're telling me that this isn't a one-time thing."

I waved my hand. "No way. We've been together a couple of months now."

He looked at me in astonishment. "You have to be kidding me. What is he, twenty-five?"

I smiled into my glass, trying not to laugh at Andrew and Marcy making faces behind Greg's head, about twenty feet away. "Well, twenty-seven." I didn't want to, but I couldn't help it, so I said, "Wait. How old is Brooke again?"

"Twenty-eight," Greg said, his face getting sort of red. I knew I couldn't push him much further, and I loved that I could have this effect on him.

I made a face like she was on her deathbed. “Gosh, Greg. That’s kind of old.” I patted him on the shoulder and whispered in his ear, “Maybe try going a little younger with your next fiancée.”

He crossed his arms. “Oh, and just so you know, there’s no way I’m letting you off the hook for that piddly sum you offered me.”

I rolled my eyes. “That’s more money than most people make cumulatively in their lifetime. I think it’s very fair.”

“I’m glad you think that,” he whispered. “I don’t, and my lawyers don’t either.” He paused. “See you in court.”

That made my stomach turn, but I just smiled brightly and said, “Good move. After I testify, you’ll get nothing. I can’t wait!”

I was lying, but it felt good to say it anyway. Then I walked past him and bounded in what I hoped was a charming and adorable way toward my charming and adorable date.

“So how’d it go?” Marcy asked.

“Let’s just say that giving someone a taste of his own medicine has never felt so good,” I said. Andrew’s arm felt familiar and comforting as it slipped around my shoulders. But I had to admit that when I saw Mr. Corporate Takeover at the top of the steps, staring at me again, a shiver went down my spine.

Diana: Sink the Ship

Walking up the steps to Frank's house that day, all I could hear in my head was *trailer trash orphan* over and over. And Frank's momma, she wasn't wrong about me. Back then, I had been making crazy good money waitressing at the Island Grille, and I'd got me some nice clothes and rented one of them cute, tiny houses on the outskirts of Cape Carolina. But that didn't mean Frank's momma couldn't see right through me. I was, at my very core, a trailer trash orphan — or, more aptly, a project orphan, which was even worse.

Frank squeezed my hand and looked at me funny like he thought I was going to throw up or something. "She's not here, Diana. It's not like my momma's going to pop out of the paneling."

But, oh my Lord, she was everywhere. She'd sewn the curtains and decorated the bookshelves and found all them shells lining the coffee table. "We're being crazy, Frank. Nothing's changed. Your momma's still going to hate me."

He shrugged. "I'm almost forty-five years

old, Diana. I don't care what my momma thinks."

It was easy to say, standing there in her living room, in the family house she always knew she would pass down to Frank one day, that he didn't care. But he had to care. Or maybe that was just the fear talking. It was waiting in the wings, hiding in the background of every happy moment, asking, *What's going to sink the ship? What's going to go wrong this time?* I didn't consider myself a pessimist, but I couldn't wrap my mind around things being this good.

He led me into the tiny kitchen and poured a glass of wine and handed it to me. "You just need to relax," he whispered in my ear, kissing its lobe, then the nape of my neck, then my collarbone.

I took a sip, feeling soothed.

"I thought it was going to be just me, so I was going to throw a steak on the grill, but I'm happy to take my girl out if you'd rather."

I smiled. "I think dinner in sounds like just what the doctor ordered."

Cooking dinner with Frank felt easy, like we'd been doing it forever. He put the steaks on the grill, and I chopped the zucchini and onions and squash and tossed them in a little olive oil and threw them in a pan. He popped the bread in the oven, and I took the butter out of the foil. We carried our plates and wine to the tiny dining table on the corner of the porch. The house was small, modest, and nothing fancy. But the view of the ocean, waves crashing on the shore, was spectacular.

"Momma and Dad built them a new house over on Ocean Ridge right before he passed," Frank said. "So this one's all ours if we want it."

All ours. It wasn't lost on me. I smiled at him, the second glass of wine washing away my worries. He was right. He was a grown man. His mother didn't control him anymore.

"What about the stores?" I asked. "How can you live here and keep them all going?"

He chewed his steak and smiled. "I sold out of all of 'em but the Cape Carolina one."

I looked at him wide-eyed. That chain of stores was his family's pride and joy. They had something. Not just one but five stores that were real profitable. "Why'd you do that?"

He shrugged. "You see it, the chain stores — the real big ones — they're popping up on every corner. I knew I couldn't compete." He wiped his mouth and took a sip of wine. "Walgreens wanted my corner lot in Charlotte and paid me all kinds of money. And one of the auto parts giants bought the other three all in one deal." He shrugged. "It was kind of hard because it's family, but, I mean, I still got this one to tool around in — pun intended. Wasn't like I was ever going to make that kind of money out of the stores. Selling out was the right decision."

I got up to clear the plates. I rinsed them and put them in the dishwasher that his momma must've finally installed. *They aren't a fad,* I wanted to tell her again. Frank followed me.

I told myself that I didn't want to ruin our perfect night, taint it with the stain of our past. But it was true whether I said it out loud or not. And now was as good a time as any. "I thought I was punishing you," I said.

He cocked his head as I closed the dishwasher door. "When?"

"Having the abortion. I thought I was punishing you." I paused, picking up the dish towel on the sink. "When you said you were going to Charlotte no matter what, I felt so alone, like you didn't care about me. And that's why I disappeared that night to Cheyenne's. And you didn't come. I know you didn't know I was pregnant, but in my mind, you were abandoning me and your baby. I was trying to punish you. But I only punished myself."

It made no sense. I felt that now. In my mind, I had punished Frank for twenty-two years for something that was my fault. No, he didn't stand up for me the way I wanted him to. But I had left him. I hadn't told him about the baby. I had taken a piece of him away without even asking him. It hurt me to admit it, but I was the one to blame for so much of this.

"Can I be honest with you?" he asked.

I nodded.

"I'm angry that you didn't tell me. I'm trying to push it away because I'm trying to win you back and say all the right things, but, damn, Diana. That was my kid too."

My instinct was to argue with him, but I knew he was right. Maybe it was my choice, technically. But Frank and I had loved each other. That baby was his too. It wasn't a one-night stand; it wasn't a mistake. The mistake was on me. "You have every right to be mad," I said. "I thought about it a lot, Frank. I swear I did. But all it came back to was that I was eighteen, and I was going to be alone. I didn't believe that you would stand up for me, and even if you did, I didn't want to spend my life knowing that you only married me because I was pregnant. That wasn't the life I wanted." I could feel tears in my eyes as I said, "And I paid for it, Frank. I paid for it by never getting to be a mother."

Frank reached out his hand and pulled me into him. "I was too proud to come get you. I was too proud to beg." He shrugged. "What we lost hurts, but it doesn't hurt as much as the idea that we might never have a future together because of the mistakes of our past."

"We both made mistakes," I repeated, resting my head on his chest. I felt cleansed somehow, ready to really, truly move on.

He grinned down at me. "How about we take a walk on the beach? There's a dune down there that I'm quite fond of."

I thought about telling him, but what in the hell was the point of that? So he could feel all sick every time he had to look at that dune too? No. Some things you just keep to yourself, and it isn't lying so much as it is protecting. I was protecting him because I loved him. I had caused him enough pain.

As Frank led me by the hand toward the pitch-dark beach and onto the backside of that dune that nobody on earth could see unless they were at Frank's house, I realized that I'd follow that man anywhere.

So I decided to let it go. I'd make love to Frank on this dune for the second time. And this time I wouldn't get hurt. This time it wouldn't be hard. This time I could look out onto this beach and smile and think about the beautiful thing that had happened here. But, just like it had all those years ago, when the best day of my life had turned into the worst one, that damn dune kept on surprising me.

Chapter 15

Gray: Girlfriend

We had done it. We had made it through our first grown-up, in-public, real live outing. And we had survived. Hell, we had thrived.

"I think it's fair to say that I did something pretty great for you this afternoon. Right?" Andrew asked.

I smiled and kissed him lightly on the lips. "I think that's fair to say. And I know just how to repay you." I raised my eyebrows and pulled him in closer.

He smiled down at me. "Oh, I'm very aware of that. But I have a suggestion of my own."

I raised my eyebrows. "Yeah? What's that?"

"Well, we always stay at your house . . ."

I backed away. "Listen, babe, I adore you. But I'm not going to go stay with a bunch of twentysomething boys."

He laughed. "Is this how little you know

about me? I'm staying at my parents' house for the summer. It's big and beautiful and right on the beach."

It was a bad sign that I didn't even know where the kid lived. I'd give him that. But that was mainly because when I was with him on my weeks without Wagner, he was basically living with me.

"Okay. Are there dishes piled in the sink? Towels piled on the floor? Dirty underwear piled in the corner?"

He laughed. "(A) no. And, (b) if it weren't for Diana, you would have all that stuff at your house."

He wasn't wrong.

He kissed me. "I know the sound is beautiful, but I sure would love to spend a night with you falling asleep to the crash of the waves on the shore. We can take a midnight stroll on the beach. . . . The stars are beautiful, and it's very, very isolated. . . ."

I laughed, finally getting the picture. "Aha. So, you don't care about my staying at your house. You're looking for a little on-the-beach action."

He pulled me in suggestively. "Maybe the dunes? On the Cape?"

We both started laughing.

"It's a bucket list item."

I nodded. "Okay. I do owe you. But I'll

warn you, it's not as glamorous and romantic as it might seem. There's a lot of sand, and it gets in some pretty uncomfortable places."

He looked at me in faux astonishment. "Why, Miss Gray, how on earth would you know that?"

I winked at him and, in my most innocent voice, said, "Oh, I don't know. I've just heard."

He kissed me again and said, "Okay. So we have a deal?"

I smiled. "We have a deal."

He pulled away and jumped in the air, doing a little fist pump. "Yes! You are the most awesome girlfriend in the world."

Girlfriend. It was a weird realization. It was very strange to go from being someone's wife to being just a girlfriend again.

"Am I your girlfriend?" I asked teasingly.

"I'm not doing this with you tonight," Andrew said. He wrapped his arms around me. "Call it what you want, but I am all yours."

I didn't say it, but I was all his too.

Andrew's parents' house was big. And beautiful. And right on the beach. We sat on the built-in bench on the front deck, having a cocktail before dinner, watching the sunset. I snuggled up under his arm, and he kissed my head. "You know, Gray," he said, "this has been the best summer of my life." He winked. "I love you. I really mean that. And I know you want this to be a summer fling, but the idea of having to not be with you —"

I put my finger up to his lips. "Shhh. Let's just enjoy the sunset."

He nodded and looked back toward the water breaking and crashing to the shore just over the dunes, the sea oats waving in the wind.

"There's my little sweetie!" I heard from behind me.

I sat straight up and turned to see a polished, beautiful woman, probably in her late forties, a fact that was very well hidden by what I presumed was a good deal of Botox. She was wearing white jeans and a patterned silk tunic and looked like she belonged to this house perfectly. Andrew got up and wrapped her in a hug. "Hi, my little momma," he said.

My heart was racing through my chest and into my throat, and I felt momentarily like I might pass out. I was stunned to see this woman, yet Andrew didn't look surprised in the least. He had tricked me. I wanted to be mad — only he had to trick me, didn't he? Because I would never in a million years have agreed to meet his mother.

"There's my boy," another, deeper voice called as its owner, in crisp khaki pants and a blue-and-white-striped knit shirt, stepped onto the deck. He and his son hugged briefly. I stood up, my maxi dress flowing in the breeze, thankful that I hadn't worn the low-cut one I'd considered when getting dressed.

"Mom, Dad," Andrew said. "This is Gray."

If they were surprised to see me, they didn't let on. His mother took my hand and kissed my cheek. "We have heard so much about you," she said. "Please call me June."

Henry was next in line for a handshake and cheek kiss. They were so adorable. I turned and smiled pertly at Andrew. His wide grin told me that, yes indeed, he had been planning this, and, my oh my, he was so proud of himself. But a little heads-up would have been nice. They'd heard so much about me, but I didn't know exactly what that entailed. Did that mean they knew about the divorce? And Wagner? That I was substantially too old to be running around with their prize of a son?

"We won't be down next week, so we wanted to take Andrew to an early birthday dinner. Why don't we all go to the club and get to know each other a little better?" Henry asked.

"Oh, um," I stuttered, "I should probably be getting home."

That's all I needed, to walk into the Straits Club and have everyone call me Mrs. Howard.

Andrew took my hand and said, "No, Gray. You have to eat with us. You'll starve to death otherwise."

Everyone laughed, which made me realize that my lack of kitchen prowess was one of the things they had heard about.

"Oh yes, please," June added. "I've never gotten to show off a beautiful girlfriend of my son's at the Narrows Club. He never lets us meet anyone he dates."

He squeezed my hand and winked. Two things were fighting for position at the front of my mind. One, Narrows Club. Thank the Lord. It could still go badly. There could still be friends mentioning Wagner or Greg, but at least there wouldn't be any waitstaff calling me Mrs. Howard. Two, Andrew never let them meet anyone, and he was letting them meet me. My heart sank. I adored him, but standing on his parents' beautiful front deck I really faced how ridiculous this was. He was too young, and my life was too similar to his parents'. The entire thing was utterly absurd.

But I loved him. Ripping this Band-Aid off was going to hurt like hell. So I smiled and decided to wait until tomorrow. "Thank you so much," I said. "I think dinner at the Narrows Club sounds amazing."

I was going to drive separately, so I could have a word with Andrew, but June said, "Oh, no. I am a teetotaler, so you may as well let me. Then the three of you can have a little fun." She winked at me.

I slid into the backseat of her Mercedes sedan and gave Andrew the look I gave Wagner when he was misbehaving in public and I was going to give him a piece of my mind when we got home.

He avoided my glance and made small talk on the very short ride to dinner. But it wasn't long before we were sitting at the table, and June said, "So, where did you two meet?"

I smiled and Andrew squeezed my hand under the table again. "Actually," I said, "we met at the Straits Club."

"Oh," Henry said, "do your parents belong there?"

This was the only time I had ever been grateful that my mother was dead. "Actually, my mother passed away last year."

As expected, instead of them grilling me

about the Straits Club and how Andrew's girlfriend had her own membership, we got to talk cancer and "I'm sorries" and "that must be so hard for a girl your age."

A girl your age.

"So, were you two in school together?" Henry asked, as though he had read my mind.

Andrew started to speak, but I interrupted him. "Well, I'm not getting my master's like this smarty-pants, if that's what you're asking," I said, laughing lightly. *Because I got it twelve years ago.*

Andrew turned to me, a questioning look on his face. It was as if his eyes were saying, *It's not a big deal. Just tell them.* And under different circumstances, I would have. Andrew and I would have sat them down and we would have laid all the cards on the table. And their reaction might not have been great, but we would be the ones to decide how we proceeded. But I knew this was over. I couldn't bear to put them through it for nothing. Least of all Andrew. It wasn't fair to make him fight for me when I knew I wasn't willing to fight for him.

But June and Henry were so happy, sitting at dinner with their baby boy's girlfriend; they were positively glowing. I could almost hear June thinking that, with my mother gone, she would get to plan her dream wedding. Which she wouldn't. Because even if this did work out — which, I clearly saw now, it could not — it would be a wedding at the courthouse.

"Well . . ." June reached across the table and patted Andrew's hand. "We're very proud."

I smiled at her encouragingly. "Of course you are. Andrew is so talented. I'm sure he has always exceeded your expectations."

Mine too, I thought.

"Oh," June said, "he is marvelous, isn't he? Watching him play matches has been our favorite thing to do for years now. Have you seen him in action?"

I wanted to laugh. Yup. I had seen him in action. "I've only seen him at the club. But he is adorable with the kids. It's so heartwarming."

June looked at her son dreamily. "He is going to be a magnificent father one day."

I smiled at him. I wasn't mad anymore, just sad. "He sure will." I paused. "One day."

A cloud passed over his face.

Henry said, "So, Gray, what do you do?"

"I own an affiliate marketing company," I said.

June squeezed Henry's arm. "Maybe Gray can help you." She turned to me. "Henry's company, Sanford Properties, is looking for a social media consultant." She looked at him proudly. "The number-one commercial realtor in the Triangle this year."

I was thinking that that was not in the realm of what I did, but I said, "Congratulations. That is quite a feat."

"Thank you." He nodded humbly. "I'll make sure to put in a good word for you."

I smiled tightly. "Wow. That would be . . ." I stammered. "That would be just great."

Andrew piped in. "Gray won't need it. She's a total genius. She has a multimillion-dollar company and —"

I punched him lightly on the arm. "Andrew, honestly. That's enough."

"That is really something," June said.

"Yes," Henry chimed in. "Smart *and* beautiful. You should hang on to this one, son."

I felt that pang again.

"Oh, I plan to, Dad," Andrew said. Then he added, "You know what's the coolest thing about Gray?"

"What?" June asked.

"She has the most fantastic so—"

I kicked him and interjected, "Software. I patented a special software that makes affiliate marketing much easier."

June laughed. "That's wonderful, darling,

but I'd hardly say that's the coolest thing about her."

I waved my hand in the air and avoided Andrew's glance. "That's enough about me. Tell me about you two." I smiled. "Better yet, give me all the scoop on this one." I glanced in Andrew's direction.

By the time we got back in the car, I felt like I was going to be sick from the anxiety of not crushing these wonderful people's spirit by telling them that I was not at all who they thought. I also loved June and Henry. And that was unfathomably painful.

As we stepped out of the car in the driveway, I said, "Thank you so much again for a wonderful dinner. And son," I added for good measure. I was breaking up with him, but I still wanted his parents to think I was lovely.

June hugged me. Then she took both my hands in hers. "Darling, you are precious. I am so happy my son found you." I could feel tears glazing over my eyes. "He is in love with you," she said. "I can tell." I smiled and nodded. She took my hand and put it on her chest. "That boy is my whole heart," she said. "Please don't break his."

It took everything I had in me to not break down right there in the driveway. Andrew appeared and wrapped his arm around my shoulders. "Why don't you come in?"

"I can't," I said. "I need to get home."

He kissed me on the cheek and said, "I'm going to get Mom and Dad settled, and I'll come visit you later."

I nodded bravely and turned, barely reaching my car before the tears started streaming down my face. What had I been thinking? What was I doing? This was real. And then all I could think of was Wagner, my son who was sleeping under my roof fifteen days a month now. I couldn't control my sobs as I pulled out of the driveway and, instead of turning right over the bridge, kept going straight. It had taken me a couple of months, but I was tired of pretending. I heard June's voice in my ear: *That boy is my whole heart.* I knew where I needed to be.

Greg couldn't stand it when I cried. Tonight was no exception. I was relieved that Wagner was already in bed and that, when I pulled into the driveway, Greg was on the porch — sans Brooke.

He stood up quickly. "Gray, what's wrong?"

I don't know what it was about seeing June with Andrew, but it made me finally feel all of those things I'd been pushing away all this time. I wanted to do what was right for my son. I wanted to be that unselfish mother who realized that her son needed his father. But it struck me how little time I had left with him, how quickly he was going to be bringing girls home to meet me.

I shook my head.

Greg pulled me close to him and my head hit his shoulder. He rubbed my back and whispered, "What is it? You're scaring me."

"I can't do it, Greg," I said. "I want to, but I just can't."

"Can't do what?"

"I can't be away from my son every other week. It's too much. I know you want to see him too, but I can't stand it. I don't think I can live." Suddenly I didn't care about the company or the houses or the 401(k)s or any of that. I just wanted my son.

He pushed away from me. "But, Gray, we agreed on this. He needs a strong male influence. He needs his father too."

I nodded. "I know, and I'm not backing out of that. I just have to be with him during your weeks. I want to pick him up from school. I want to have dinner with him. I want to tuck him into bed."

"But Brooke —"

I felt my eyes widen. "But Brooke what? Carried him for nine months? Gave birth to him? Took him to the emergency room when that baseball split his eye open? Stayed up with him all night every time he had a fever?"

That got me, and I started crying again. Because what if he was sick, and I wasn't there? My sister was right. I should have fought. I should have done everything I could to save my marriage, for my son.

"Okay, okay, okay," Greg said. I could tell he was in that space where he would do absolutely anything to make the crying stop. "What do you need?"

If he was trying to dry the tears, it had worked. I hadn't even consciously thought of it when, "I want you to move. Here," flew out of my mouth.

But it was true. I wanted to stay here. I wanted to move full-time into the beautiful house that I had bought and planned and picked every last pansy for. I wanted to have coffee with Marcy every morning, not just the summer ones. I wanted to see Diana every day.

I could tell he was astonished, and I didn't want to fight. I was too sad. It was too hard. So I said, "Don't say anything now. Just think about it." I paused. "Where's Brooke?"

"Wine night or something."

I walked past him through the front door, up the seagrass-carpeted stairs, and into my son's bedroom at his dad's summer rental. Moonlight streamed through a crack in the curtains, illuminating his peaceful, sleeping face. I thought my heart would absolutely burst at the sight of him. I leaned over and kissed his cheek, breathing in his little boy scent, pulling his covers up tight around him.

I closed the bedroom door behind me, and Greg said, "He's amazing, isn't he?"

I nodded and looked him straight in the eye. "He is perfect. Move here. Please. For him," I said, as I walked down the steps. And I walked out the front door before he could protest.

Andrew was sitting on my front steps when I got home.

"Before you say anything," he called, scrambling to his feet as I was stepping out of the car, "I'm really sorry. I wasn't trying to ambush you, but I wanted them to meet you, and I knew you wouldn't do it otherwise."

I nodded, but I didn't say anything. I looked out over the yard, into the windows across the street, lights blazing, lost in my thoughts. I remembered the day we bought this house, how I couldn't believe it, how I had gotten this perfect life already. "I used to be scared I was going to die," I said.

Neither of us spoke for a few beats. But then he responded, "Because everything was so good?"

He knew me really, really well. "Yeah. I felt like, here I was, barely thirty, and I already had everything: the money, the kid, the husband, the beach house, the perfect life."

He nodded. "I get that. I do." He reached over for my hand, and I could feel my eyes filling up. "Because that's how I feel right now."

I leaned my head on his shoulder and wiped my tears. "You wanted your parents to meet me? Damn, Andrew. That perfect life has shattered in a million pieces all around me. I'm not some cute coed that they're going to be excited about their shiny son dating."

"But I was going to tell them all that. Why wouldn't you let me?"

I bit my lip and looked down at my shoe. "You know why," I whispered.

He pulled back and looked at me. "Gray, come on. Don't do this."

I shrugged, my eyes filling again. "Andrew, your mom. You're her perfect son. . . ." I couldn't help but think of my perfect son.

He turned toward me. "So, do you love me?"

I bit my lip again and turned to look out over the water. "It isn't that simple."

"But why isn't it?"

"Because you know it isn't, Andrew."

"But do you?"

I sighed. "Of course I do. You know I do. Do you think I want to do this? You have filled up that deep, dark, empty space where my son is gone every other week. You have made me feel beautiful and wanted when my husband tossed me out like yesterday's newspaper. Do you think I want that to be over?"

He stepped toward me and kissed me. "So don't let it," he whispered. "Let's just tell them. They loved you, and they won't care."

"They will care. They will think I'm preying on their son."

"Gray, I know you think you're fine, but for you to even think all those things shows me how badly all of this messed you up. You are *everything* that anyone could ever want. You're the only one who can't see that."

I smiled sadly, shaking my head. "It doesn't matter," I whispered.

I could see tears starting to form in his eyes, and I felt like the devil incarnate.

"I don't want to hurt you," I said.

"But you're breaking up with me anyway."

I nodded slowly.

He slapped his hand on the hood of my car. "Damn, Gray. I don't get why you would do this."

"Yes, you do," I said.

He hugged me, and I could feel his tears falling onto my bare shoulder.

"Hey," I said, lifting his head. "We might be breaking up, but I'm not the kind of woman who would deny a guy the chance to check something major off of his bucket list."

He wiped his eyes and brightened. "Really?"

I shrugged. "Yeah. I can't think of a better way to say good-bye."

"You can stop being my girlfriend, Gray. I don't have a choice in that." He paused and wiped his eyes. "But there's no way I'm letting you say good-bye."

Diana: A Secret

My life was finally back on track. Things with Frank were going great. We had had an amazing few weeks together. He'd even asked me to move in with him, and while a part of me wanted to, I knew it was too fast. I wasn't ready yet. I didn't think Gray was ready yet either.

When I'd show up in the morning, smiling and whistling, not even complaining about all the healthy stuff she made me cook, she'd give me a sideways smile and tease me. Then I'd laugh, and we'd talk, and I wasn't ready for all that to be over.

But this morning when I walked over from the guesthouse, she was in the kitchen looking like she hadn't slept all night. I knew she was having a real hard time being apart from Andrew, and even worse, with him gone she had all kinds of time to realize that her kid was somewhere else every other week.

She looked so pitiful. "What's the matter, honey?"

"Wagner has been throwing up all night, and it was so awful and so scary." She put crushed ice in a glass and popped the top of a Coke. "I've never been alone with him when he was sick." Gray shook her head. "I almost called Greg."

I put my arm around her. "Why didn't you call me?"

"I was going to," she said, "but you got here so early. You need to get out of here. I don't want you catching this."

I laughed. "Honey, I meant why didn't you call me last night to help?" I took the Coke and said, "I'll go up and check on him, then I'll come down and make him some tea and toast and go out and get some bananas for when he's feeling up to it."

"But, Di," she protested, "you'll get sick."

"Oh, Gray" — I winked — "I have an immune system of steel. I never get sick. Not ever."

She smiled weakly at me and said, "Okay." She sighed. "He's kept down Gatorade for about an hour now, so I think the tide might be turning."

"You go lie down and get some rest, and I'll get you if we need you."

She looked so grateful. I saw tears in her eyes. She hugged me and said, "I know you're going to leave me, and I don't know what I'm going to do."

I pulled away and squeezed her shoulders, looking in her eyes. "I'm not going to leave you."

Now I could see the tears really gathering, and she looked away and said, "Of course you will. You're in love. You're happy. I want that for you. I just miss you, and you aren't even gone."

With that, she turned around and walked down the hall, and I got the distinct feeling that whatever was going on inside that tired, pretty little head didn't have all that much to do with *me* leaving her.

Wagner managed a weak smile when he saw me walk in, carrying a Coke and saltines. I sat down on the bed beside him and rubbed my hand across his clammy forehead. "I heard it was a rough night, buddy."

He nodded. "Yeah. But I haven't barfed in a couple hours. I think I'm gonna be okay."

I smiled. "That's a relief."

"Do you think I'll be able to play tennis later?"

"I'm going to say no to that one."

His face fell. "Andrew really wanted me to play with him today. I think he wants a rematch after Johnny and I beat him and Mom so bad."

I nodded, and it made me feel sort of sad because I would have bet that locket I loved so much that Andrew wanted to see another member of Wagner's family even worse.

"Is my mom okay?"

I handed him the saltines and said, "Oh yeah. She's good. I just told her to go and get some sleep."

"Yeah," he said. "But, I mean, she seems sad, you know?"

I shrugged. "I think it's real hard for a momma to be away from her kid." I wondered after I said it if I shouldn't have. But, well, he was getting ready to be nine years old, and he wasn't stupid, and that's the God's honest truth of the whole thing.

"Yeah. All I kept thinking was that it would've been so awful if I got sick when I was with Dad, because I would've wanted my mom the whole time." He shrugged. "It's weird, right? Do you think my dad and Brooke are going to have another baby?"

I laughed. "Okay there. That's enough with the questions. I think that's for them to know and us to find out. You close those peepers. I'm going to go get some laundry done, but you holler if you need me. Deal?"

He sank back into his pillows sleepily, and I set the Coke on the nightstand. I pulled his covers up tight and kissed that sweet, clammy forehead. I thought about Frank. And Gray. And that baby I never had. And all I knew was that sometimes, in the most convoluted of ways, somebody up there looks down, smiles, and finally gives you all you really wanted this whole time: a family.

Chapter 16

Gray: Bare-Soul Truth

Poor Trey. Even he couldn't get me out of my funk. He was driving, singing show tunes at the top of his lungs, the stereo blasting. Ordinarily I would have joined him. But today I couldn't muster the energy.

"Come on, babe," he said. "Road trip to Charleston! Huge meeting with Glitter! What, what!"

I sighed. "I know. Why am I such a drag right now? I am literally the worst."

But Andrew was gone. It was my fault. I had pushed him away. He had texted me: I'm heading back to school. Can I come say good-bye?

And, bitch that I was, I had said, I don't think that's a good idea.

I mean, I was right. If he came to say good-bye, that would lead to a kiss good-bye, which might lead to other things, and any or all or none of it would make the heartbreak last even longer.

To top it off, I had been up all night two nights before with Wagner, stressed and panicked and terrified at how sick he was. Greg and I hadn't revisited the moving idea, and Wagner's school started in a couple of weeks. I had him enrolled in both Cape Carolina and Raleigh, but it was time to make a decision.

"You just need wine," Trey said sunnily. "And maybe a steak."

Now, that we could agree on. Every decadent bite and sip at Halls Chophouse that evening felt like an antidote as I was eating it.

Five hours later, as it was coming back up, I regretted the choice. Diana might have an immune system of steel, but I did not. Wagner's virus had hit me hard.

I don't think that's a good idea was running through my mind on a continuous loop. It's what always happens to me when I get sick like this. I have some phrase or song lyric or something equally annoying stuck in my head.

This is the worst feeling on earth. Well, good. That was at least something new. It kind of puts everything in perspective, having a throw-up virus. What you're going to say when you meet the client you're trying to bag, and the fact that you have to be nice to your husband's fiancée who you incredibly stupidly are trying to get to move to town with you, and whether you have completely ruined your own life all seem less important. Because all you can think about is how disgustingly horrible you feel. That's it. You just want to survive.

No one wants to be alone when they're sick like that, and you always want your mom. Always. Even when you know she's dead, you want her to appear to hold your hair back and put a cold washcloth on your forehead and bring you ginger ale and break the whole pieces of ice into little bits with a spoon.

But she wasn't going to come back. That was obvious. If she were, surely she would have done it by now. She would have come back to get my sister out of her horrible marriage. She would have come back to help me through my divorce. And, most of all, she would have come back to knock some sense into my head when I started dating Andrew.

Too exhausted to even get back to the bed, I curled up on my hotel room's bathroom floor, my head on one wadded-up towel, my body on another, alternating between freezing cold and unimaginably hot. And I thought about Andrew. If my mom wasn't going to come back, I just wanted Andrew. I knew he would rub my back no matter how disgusting I was and go to the store in the pitch-black dark to get me lemon-lime Gatorade.

It surprised me, lying on the floor, trying to catch a few minutes of sleep in between my bouts of sickness, that I felt like I could depend on Andrew. Because when the chips are down as low as they can be, when you're lying on the bathroom floor in the fetal position, there's a bare-soul, uncomplicated sort of truth about who it is that you are longing to have there beside you. I knew for sure that I had never wished for Greg like that.

Somewhere in there, I finally fell asleep, and, when my alarm sounded at eight thirty, all that remained was the feeling of exhaustion. But the nausea was gone, the vulnerability was gone, and the certainty that I was strong enough to get over a little summer fling — because that's all it was — was back.

I showered and dried my hair, applied my makeup, put on a sophisticated-yet-sassy white dress that was just businessy enough, and swallowed away the nerves of a pitch that I couldn't screw up just because I was tired and sad. I tried to ignore the awareness that Andrew was here, in Charleston, and that it was taking all the strength I had not to go find him.

While everyone else sipped gorgeous Bloody Marys with huge shrimp cocktails in the back garden at 82 Queen, I had ginger ale without a straw to save the turtles. The nausea was gone, but I certainly wasn't going to risk it. Trey was as effusive as ever, and I thought I was too, but who knew.

Heather Sinclair was saying, "We're extremely impressed with ClickMarket, but you know you have some competitors out there with lower percentage costs, and that's a holdup for us."

I knew what she was trying to do. I saw it all the time, and when I first started my business, sometimes I would cave to that pressure. But now I knew that all that did was end up hurting everyone involved. So I said, "Heather, I'll be honest with you. You've seen our rate sheet. You can come over to ClickMarket and choose a lower percentage bracket. But the influencers you are going to be working with are not going to be those fabulous micro-influencers with rabid followings and gorgeous branding. Creating those brands costs them money, and there is no way they are going to promote Glitter — as much as they all love you — for seven percent when they can promote Neiman Marcus for ten. They won't do it."

"But those other affiliate companies don't offer Neiman Marcus," Heather said.

Trey smiled at her. "Enough said."

We all laughed.

"Look," Heather continued, "I won't lie to you. Your site is the most user-friendly, and I see the benefits. I really do. But we're talking three percent of a massive amount of sales. That's significant."

I'd had spreadsheets made up of what we predicted Glitter's sales would be with ClickMarket over our main competitor, but I realized now that they didn't matter. I prided myself on being excellent at reading people, and my gut told me that all Heather wanted was to feel like she had made a deal, plain and simple. I could give her that.

I did some quick math in my head before I said, "Look, Heather, it's top secret, but we're rolling out an ad partner program next month that is going to blow your mind. All the best influencers with the most proven sales records. You're going to want to be a part of that. I'll give you a three-month exclusive during which I'll waive all my commission."

She raised her eyebrows. "Exclusive as in . . . ?"

I smiled. "Exclusive as in you will be our only client in the ad partner program for three months."

It was a big move, a huge thing to give her. But I knew it would be worth it. Every blogger in the country would be clamoring for a spot, and other competing companies would line up to sign up for the program once they knew Glitter was our first exclusive customer. It was genius, if I did say so myself.

I glanced at Trey. He looked impressed.

Heather smiled, and I knew I had won. "Ms. Howard, you have made me an offer I simply cannot refuse." She reached her hand out over the Bloody Marys, and I shook it.

"Trey will draw up the contract and get it over to you tonight."

We had already drawn up the contract. It didn't work 100 percent of the time, but it was the best way I knew of to put the deal out in the universe before we went in to negotiate it. And I had to admit that Trey was the best partner out there. He knew when to jump in, when to lighten the mood, when to be serious. I texted him under the table: You're getting a promotion.

He texted back: But I want to work with you. Duh.

We smiled at each other.

"Now that that unpleasantness is over," Heather said, "please tell me there's an exciting new man in your life."

I laughed, and I was so relieved to have sealed this deal that the laugh almost felt genuine. It almost didn't break my heart that I'd had a new man in my life and I had pushed him away. Almost.

When Heather left, Trey and I each breathed a huge sigh of relief. "Barfed all night and still pulled it out," he said. "So, about that promotion . . ."

"Oh, that was just something I said in the moment. Moment's over," I joked.

He elbowed me gently.

"No," I said. "New title. More money. All that jazz. I'll get you details, but you have been my go-to for years and you deserve it."

"But who will plan your cocktail parties? And make your matcha lattes the way you like them? And hide Quinn's e-mails? And put Greg on hold for egregious amounts of time to piss him off?"

I laughed. "Obviously you'll have to find and train your replacement."

He grinned. "Obviously."

He held his glass up and I clinked it with mine. "To moving up in every sense of the word," he said.

"Onward and upward," I responded.

And, for the first time in a long time, I meant it.

Diana: Warning Sign

For the past two days, I had been feeling confident. When I told Gray that I was meeting Frank's mother, she'd said, "Diana, you are a strong, beautiful, smart woman and you are deserving of everything wonderful that life has to offer. No one can take that away from you."

When I hadn't look convinced, she had motioned for me to follow her into her bedroom. She opened the jewelry box on her vanity and pressed a pair of pearl earrings into my palm. "These are my grandmother's," she said, "and they are lucky. I always wear them when I feel like I need some extra strength."

"But you have that big meeting with Glitter," I had protested.

Gray shook her head. "That's just a client, Diana. This is your life."

It had made me feel so warm inside, so strong. I had been a rock for Gray these past few months. Now I knew she was a rock for me too.

She had also cleaned out her closet and insisted that I take everything that fit. Some of the clothes still had the tags on them. "You could sell these," I protested.

"I could," she said. "But I will not let you see Frank's mother for the first time in twenty-two years wearing jean shorts and a T-shirt."

I couldn't really argue with that. I knew she was right, and I had been stressing about using part of my paycheck to buy something new. I needed that money to stock up on those little red-and-white-checked baskets I had dreamed of. Gray and I agreed on a pink dress that was fitted but not tight. It was elegant. And, better yet, it was free. I felt like the princess my momma always told me I would be.

Now that the day was here, I wasn't feeling quite so confident.

"I don't see why this is necessary," I said as I slid Gray's pearl through my ear and pushed the post onto the back.

Frank laughed. "Come on, Di. It won't be so bad."

I looked at him like he was totally nuts. "Not so bad? You sure about that?" *Trailer trash orphan* ran through my mind again. Yeah, it could be that damn bad, and Frank knew it as well as I did.

I felt my stomach churn. I leaned back on the bed and pulled on my other shoe. I put the back of my hand to my forehead. No fever, just nerves. "You know, Frank, I don't feel so great," I said.

He put his arm around me, pulled me close, and kissed my cheek. "Look," he said, "I've talked to her. I've told her that this is it. *You're* it. If she can't get along with you, then she won't have me."

I nodded and swallowed, my tongue feeling unusually thick in my mouth. "Okay," I whispered, unconvinced.

As I climbed in the front seat of his T-bird, a wave of nausea passed over me again.

I closed my eyes. "Frank," I said. "I'm serious. I really don't feel good."

He squeezed my hand. "Babe, it's just my mom. She's sixty-eight years old, for heaven's sake. She's not that scary anymore."

"Women get scarier as they get older," I said under my breath. Whatever. I had let her take Frank away from me once. I wouldn't do it again.

We pulled into the parking lot of the club, my head spinning. *Get it together,* I told myself.

Frank stepped out of the car, and I took a deep breath, trying to swallow away that queasy feeling. I took a sip of the water in my cup holder and scooted out of the T-bird as ladylike as I could muster in that pink dress that was too narrow at the bottom to really move right.

It was a gorgeous day, but the hot sun turned my stomach even more. I leaned over for a second, my hands on the car.

"Babe? You really don't feel good, do you?"

I shook my head. Then it hit me. Wagner's throw-up virus. Hadn't been sick in fifteen years, and today of all days . . . I was getting ready to tell Frank I needed to go home when I heard, "Yoo-hoo, Frank!" and saw his mother, wearing a pale-blue suit. I pinned on a fake smile.

"Well, hello, Diana," she said as we made our way down the stone path toward the dining patio. I knew already I couldn't eat anything. We were only a few steps away from the door, thank the Lord. Because, as I started to say hello to Frank's mom, I felt bile finally rise in the back of my throat. I beelined through the door and into the bathroom, thankful that I had spent quite a bit of time here this summer and had the place pretty well mapped out.

I wanted to be embarrassed and sad that I had ruined this day, but I felt so horrible that I couldn't be. Frank was waiting outside the door; mercifully, his mother was not.

He squeezed my shoulder. "Lose your lunch before you had it?"

I nodded. "Please take me home."

I didn't even care where his mother was. I was to that point where the sickness was all I could think about. Frank tucked me into bed and brought me a Sprite, but I knew I wouldn't be able to keep it down.

The next day, I was still getting sick sporadically. "Twenty-four-hour bug, my ass," I said, as Frank hoisted my weak dish towel of a body into the T-bird.

"You will go to the doctor today," he had insisted. "At the very least, you need some fluids and some Phenergan. This is ridiculous."

I had finally agreed because I was too miserable not to.

A few minutes later I was climbing up onto the doctor's table. Evidently this bug was spreading like wildfire, and they were making special arrangements to get patients seen quickly so they could go back home and vomit in private.

"I'm going to run a few quick tests," Dr. Gold said when he came in the room, looking exhausted and flustered. "I'm sure it's just this virus, but we need to be certain we aren't looking at a bigger culprit."

I dutifully followed him for testing, and was back in the exam room a few minutes later, lying on the crinkly white sheet. Frank kissed my hand and said, "You're the bravest woman I know. Do you know that?"

I smiled weakly and heard my phone ding. I motioned for Frank to see who it was. He laughed. "Gray sure does feel bad about how sick you are."

"It is her fault," I mumbled. But I didn't mean it. How many times had she told me to stay out of that house? Stubborn old mule, I was.

A soft rap on the door immediately preceded Dr. Gold flying back into the room. He sat down on a stool with his clipboard and said, "Well, Diana, it is definitely something bigger than a virus."

I sat up, alarmed. "What do you mean? Do I have E. coli or something? A parasite?"

He shook his head gravely, and my heart sank. It was cancer. I had stomach cancer. I had finally gotten Frank back after all these years. I was finally living the life I had always dreamed of, and now I was going to die.

"Kids," he said, "you're having a baby."

My head spun to look at Frank. I know I looked shocked. He, on the other hand, looked like how I imagined him to on the day he got that check for his land.

"Oh my Lord," he said.

"Dr. Gold, you know I can't get pregnant."

He shrugged. "Evidently you can."

"Dr. Gold," I said. "I'm forty years old."

"Indeed you are," he said, "which is why we're going to need to monitor you extra closely to make sure this pregnancy goes well. We'll need to go ahead and get some initial blood work. . . ."

He was still talking, but I couldn't even hear him. *Pregnant.* I didn't know how to feel. After twenty years of knowing I would never be a mother, of knowing this would never happen for me, it seemed impossible, like the obvious truth wouldn't set in.

Frank hugged and kissed me and said, "I think we've finally got it right, babe."

We walked out into the parking lot, and I put together the first coherent words since I'd heard the news: "They ought to put some sort of warning sign on that sand dune."

Chapter 17

Gray: Bitter Divorcée Territory

The bar at the Spectator was utter perfection. Trey had invited me out with some friends of his who lived in Charleston, but I wanted to get some rest. I was feeling up to eating and drinking again, so I decided to pop down to the hotel bar and grab a cocktail. I felt terribly guilty because Diana had texted that she had been struck down by the throw-up bug too. This one was intense. I hoped Trey didn't get it — or Heather, for that matter.

When I glanced down to see We need to talk pop up on my phone later, I assumed it was from Andrew. My heart felt a little heavy, but then I saw it was from my sister. This was her turf, but surely she didn't know I was here. I'd done a couple of Instagram posts, but, as one could imagine, Pastor Elijah didn't allow social media.

I flicked my phone across the bar. I caught

the bartender's eye and said, "Yeah. I'm definitely going to need another."

"So, rough day?" I heard a voice beside me say.

I laughed. "Oh, you know, just family drama."

I turned to look at the man the voice was attached to. He looked vaguely familiar, but I couldn't quite place him. Super handsome, but maybe his nose was a little too — oh my gosh! It was Mr. Corporate Takeover.

"I know you," he said. He took a sip of his beer, smiling, and said, "From that boring party at the beach. I couldn't take my eyes off of you."

I shrugged. "Oh yeah?" I asked coyly, as if I hadn't noticed.

"Price," he said.

"Gray."

He raised his eyebrow. "As in *Fifty Shades*?"

"Sometimes," I said seriously.

We both laughed.

The bartender handed me a glass, and Price said, "Add that one to my tab."

I smiled. "Well, thank you, sir."

I could feel myself getting kind of nervous. If he was buying my drink, then that meant he kind of liked me. And if he kind of liked me, then this might be kind of a date. "What are you doing here?" I asked.

"Drinking. Same as you."

I smirked, and he smiled at me. "No, I actually have an investment property here — I live between Raleigh and Cape Carolina, but I come down here a couple weeks a year to check on it."

"That's awesome," I said.

He nodded. "Yeah. But don't be impressed. I've lost money on every real estate venture I've ever pursued except this one. I guess I was bound to get lucky eventually."

We both laughed, and I realized that my first impression of Price might have been wrong. I'd thought he might be a little cocky, but he was charmingly self-deprecating.

"So, what's your story?" I asked, sounding so much cooler than I felt and mentally patting myself on the back for it.

He shrugged. "You know . . ." From his tone and facial expression, I was expecting something like: "Investment banker, divorced, three kids." Instead, he said, "Virgo, enjoys long hikes up mountain streams, the jackass who makes the bagger at the grocery give him paper instead of plastic."

I laughed so hard I nearly spit out my drink. He stayed serious. "What?" Then he grinned, displaying a row of teeth that weren't perfect, yet somehow managed to be perfect for his face.

"Your turn," he said.

"Okay." I paused. "Libra, thwarted tap dancer, carries her own reusable bags to the grocery to pretend she's green but then doesn't recycle her glass bottles."

He gasped in mock shock and pretended to get down from the stool. "If you don't recycle, then I'm out of here."

We both laughed, and I felt those nervous butterflies.

"Have you eaten?" Price asked.

"Do you mean ever or tonight?" I smiled.

"Okay, smarty-pants."

We laughed again. I wanted the ease of this, the lack of intensity, to continue.

As if the universe had heard me and thwarted my plans, my phone buzzed three times in quick succession. "I'm so sorry," I said. "But I just have to make sure this isn't my son." I smirked, reaching for my phone. "My soon-to-be ex-husband got him an iPhone. He's eight."

Oh no. I cringed. *I just crossed over into "bitter divorcée" territory. Reel it in, Gray.*

But Price laughed. "Ah yes. Classic divorced dad move. I bought my son a PlayStation *and* a Wii."

I laughed, relieved that I hadn't killed the

mood. But then I felt the blood drain from my face as I read the texts. "Oh my gosh," I said, reaching for my purse, then realizing I couldn't drive. So I looked at this total stranger and asked, "How many drinks have you had?"

He shrugged, lifting his glass. "Like, three sips?"

I smiled. "So, this is a bit of a strange request since we have only known each other for five minutes, but could you take me to pick up my sister?"

"Sure thing," he said, reaching for his wallet and dropping a twenty on the bar. "Where is she?"

I rolled my eyes as I said, "Jail."

Diana: A Cockamamie Kidney Bean

I just kept staring at it, that little photo in the frame. It looked like a cockamamie kidney bean with some growths coming out the sides. But it was *our* kidney bean, our first photo of what I trusted would become a full-size baby.

It's amazing how finding out you're pregnant and not dying of some rare strain of E. coli makes you feel a hair better right off the bat. And then, when you start having a panic attack that, holy hell, you're forty and pregnant and not married and is this guy going to stick with you this time? Well, then you start feeling right sick again.

I had gone straight home to take a good nap, and I really did feel a smidge better. Frank, he lay in bed with me, but I don't think he slept because when I went to sleep he was staring at me, and when I woke up he was still staring at me.

"Have I got some sort of zit or something?"

He laughed. "No. You're just beautiful. You're always beautiful, but now you're even more beautiful. You're giving me a baby, Diana. A *baby.* Can you believe that?"

I had forgotten for about a half second that I was even pregnant, it was so new. But, no, I couldn't believe it. And it scared me to death. Because what if it didn't take and I lost the baby? I had promised myself I wouldn't read about all the risks of having a baby at forty. But I knew they were real.

"May I take you to dinner tonight?" he asked, smiling. "To celebrate?"

Good Lord, he was so handsome. I hoped the baby looked just like him. I nodded, feeling like I might actually be able to eat something, and I said so.

"But, Frank?"

"Yeah?"

"Can I show you something first?"

Cheyenne's husband, Kevin, and I had been down to the docks a few days earlier and spent hours on that boat. And, let me tell you, it was a dump. But that didn't matter. We were going to tear everything out. All I needed was a simple kitchen and a big window on the dock side where people could come up and order their steamer pots for lunch. I had decided on a simple menu, no options: shrimp, sausage, vegetables, corn, and potatoes over rice cooked in my secret, special blend of spices. We'd serve from 11:30 a.m. until 2 p.m. That was perfect.

And now that I knew about the baby, I realized this was the best way to do it, because I could work a little, have my dream, but still be there for my kid. The only thing I couldn't figure out was how I was still going to help Gray every day. And I dreaded telling her.

Frank kissed my lips and squeezed me to him a little tighter. "Babe, I'd go anywhere with you."

I hauled my tired bones out of bed and got myself in the shower. It felt so good, that steamy water running down my skin. I looked at my tummy. I was only nine weeks now — pretty long not to know you were knocked up, but not that long in the scheme of things — and I couldn't imagine what it was going to look like to have my tummy all protruding and full of baby, kicking and flipping about. What a miracle, all of it.

"Hey, babe," Frank said, turning on the sink and slathering shaving cream on his face.

"Yeah."

"I don't want to upset you or anything. But do you think that this . . . ?" He trailed off.

"Do I think this what?"

"Nothing."

I peeked my head out from around the curtain. "Well, you have to say it now."

"Do you think that maybe this is the same baby?"

I pulled my head back in. All that hot water was running down my face, and I thought tears might be mixed in too, but it was all so warm and steamy in there that I couldn't be sure.

I felt a cold blast of air on my behind and turned to see Frank peeking through the shower curtain. "See," he said, "now I've gone and upset you. We're supposed to be celebrating. Just forget I said anything."

I shook my head. "No. I really think you're right. I don't know why stuff happens or how, but I feel like this is that same baby that we were always supposed to have, and it has some real big purpose in this world to go through all this mess to get here."

Frank grinned at me and puckered. I leaned forward and kissed him.

"Is there room for two in there?" he asked.

I threw my dry washcloth at him and said, "Let me shower in peace, you crazy man."

An hour later, we were walking down the dock in downtown Cape Carolina, looking at all the sailboats on the moorings in the harbor and the yachts docked beside them.

The sun was setting all orange and fire and lipstick kiss, and the wind was blowing just right. Kids were licking ice cream cones and musicians were playing on the deck of the Pier House. I leaned into Frank's chest, him smelling of fresh aftershave and testosterone. He wrapped his arm around my bare shoulders and kissed my hair. I took in a real deep breath. I had grown up feeling like nobody wanted me, like everyone wished I were dead. But standing here, right now, I felt like I was wanted after all, like here was a man who saw past all that, who made me feel like I had a place in this world. And that was beside him.

Then we stopped at my wreck. Now that I was going to show it to Frank, I saw it through different eyes. I saw that it was falling apart and run-down and, well, belonged at the salvage yard. But it was going to give me my dream. "This is what I wanted to show you," I said.

Frank looked around. "What?"

"This boat. Kevin's going to help me, and I'm going to redo it and start a little lunch spot with my steamer pots."

Frank looked shocked, but he recovered quickly. "Oh, babe, that's awesome." He pulled out his phone. "I'll get Steve down here. He's been restoring boats forever and —"

I put my hand gently on his. "Frank, this is something that I have to do on my own."

I still didn't know exactly how I was going to get the money together. But I was going to. And I wanted that to be all on my own, not because Frank gave me a handout. I could tell he wanted to protest, but he just nodded.

"Think we ought to get going?" I asked, feeling a low rumble in my stomach that meant, if I didn't eat soon, the nausea was coming.

Frank, he stopped and turned to me. He kissed me quickly and then, before I even knew what was happening, he got down on his knee in front of me. I was so surprised I didn't even throw up on him.

I got chill bumps all over my arms. I couldn't count the number of times I'd dreamed about this moment, of Frank being down on one knee, of him asking me to be his wife. And now, in front of the boat that represented the future I was moving into, I couldn't imagine anything being better.

"Diana, I love you."

I wanted to say I loved him too, but my throat was so clogged with tears I couldn't talk. But my heart was about to bust wide open with joy and love for this man I'd held there for all those years.

"All I've wanted since the minute I laid eyes on you was to be with you for the rest of my life. I don't want to screw it up again. I don't want to run away again. I just want to love you until my last breath. Please, Diana, from the bottom of my heart. Please marry me."

He put this pretty, shiny diamond on my shaking hand. He stood up and we kissed, and I didn't even know what to do, but I started to realize that all these people, they were standing around looking at us, and a few even clapped. One walked up and said, "You're going to be the most beautiful bride."

It was like time stood still and flew by

right at the same time. I couldn't even comprehend that this was happening. This was real. It wasn't a dream. He had asked me to marry him. I was going to be Frank's wife. I was going to have Frank's baby. He was going to be all mine. They both were. I just stared down at the pretty ring he'd put on my finger, one of them antique-looking ones with a bigger diamond in the middle and a couple of smaller ones on the sides. Oh, it was beautiful. We were walking again toward Full Circle, where we were having dinner, and Frank stopped.

"Babe," he said. "Do you know you haven't said yes yet?"

I laughed. "Oh." I turned and smiled and kissed him. I felt that familiar fear that maybe this was too good to be true, that this could all be taken away, that it could be over as quickly as it started. But my girls had said, and I knew it too, that living in fear wasn't a life. "Yes, Frank. Yes, I'll marry you. I'll marry you and have your baby and love you with all I've got until the second I die. The rest of my life isn't enough for how much love I've got to lay on you."

He laughed and kissed me again. "Well, then, I'd say that pretty much sums it up."

I couldn't believe it. A couple of months ago, I was homeless, single, jobless, and utterly alone in the world. And now, I was engaged, pregnant, and had family coming out my ears. It was such a huge reminder that, even when the chips are down, life can change in an instant.

Chapter 18

Gray: The Kool-Aid

"So is your sister in jail often?" Price asked as we stepped into his car.

"Used to be," I said under my breath.

"What?"

"She used to get in trouble kind of a lot, and then she found this man who I swear is a cult leader, drank the Kool-Aid, and runs around tossing pamphlets in everyone's faces."

"Pamphlets, huh?"

I pulled the visor down and checked my lip gloss in the mirror, though I'm not sure why. Maybe in case I needed to sweet-talk someone to get my sister out of the slammer. It wouldn't be the first time. "Yeah, you know, like on abstinence before marriage, even though she slept with everyone on the Eastern Seaboard before this transformation. Pamphlets about how I'm going to hell because I'm getting divorced. You know, light reading like that."

I was trying to be cool and a little snarky, but inside I was reeling. What in the hell had my sister done? Was she okay? Was this Elijah-related? Did I need a lawyer for her? Yeah, she'd done me wrong, but Diana was right. It didn't matter what she did. I was her big sister, and it was my job to pick up the pieces, whatever they might be.

I laughed in spite of my nerves, and Price joined me. "So, this is impressive, right? I mean, I'm sure you're just dying to take me out now."

"Actually," he said, "this is the most fun I've had in a while."

"That is sad," I said, checking my phone again. "Let's talk about something else. Let's pretend that we are driving to, say, a movie, not to pick my sister up from jail."

"Great," he said. "So, do you prefer Charmin or Angel Soft?"

"What?"

He glanced over at me and grinned. "These are the important questions. I lived with a woman for fifteen years who liked Angel Soft. So every day for fifteen years I had to wipe my ass with a toilet paper I hated. It's just toilet paper, but, damn. I'm not going back to that."

I laughed. "Who the hell likes Angel Soft?

Charmin all day, baby. But I do switch it up between ultra soft and ultra strong, you know, just to keep things interesting."

Price stopped at a red light and looked at me, wide-eyed in amazement. "Me too. I mean, sometimes you need softness and sometimes you need strength."

"Paper towels?" I asked.

"Ninety percent Bounty, ten percent Viva."

"Oh my gosh," I said. "Me too."

"Christmas or Fourth of July?" he asked.

We looked at each other and simultaneously said, "Christmas."

"Cats or dogs?" I asked.

"Neither," he said definitively. "I've spent years cleaning up after kids; I don't need one more thing in the mix."

"Preach."

He pulled into the parking lot of the Charleston Police Department. My stomach gripped as I noticed rows of police cars all in a straight line. Price put the car in park. "Let's go get that sister of yours."

"Is it bad that I can't wait to rub this in her face?"

"Sounds to me like she has it coming."

"Hello," I said sunnily as soon as we entered, walking up to the desk. "I'm here to pick up my sister, Quinn Taylor."

The woman nodded, nonplussed.

"What's she in for anyway?"

The woman smirked. "Stabbing someone."

"What?" Now my heart was racing. I hadn't imagined she was in for something *serious.* I looked at Price. "I swear, it's normally stuff like public drunkenness or skinny-dipping or possession or something. She's not like a *criminal* criminal."

"Oh yeah," Price said. "Doesn't sound like it." He looked at me skeptically.

A few minutes later, Quinn appeared, looking contrite. I didn't even know what to say to her, but she spoke first. "Thank you so much, Gray. Seriously, from the bottom of my heart, thank you."

She looked at Price and then back at me, and I could tell she was about to say something, but she refrained. I squeezed the top of her arm and pulled her into the corner. "Stabbing, Quinn? Seriously? What in the hell is wrong with you? Where did Sister Mary Quinn go?"

"It was self-defense," she said. "Turns out Elijah wasn't exactly who I thought he was."

"They never are, honey," Price chimed in. "They never are."

"Oh," I said. "Price, this is my sister, Quinn. Quinn, Price. We met tonight, and he brought me here to bail you out of jail."

"Yikes," she said. "So, not the first impression you were hoping for." Then she added under her breath, knowing full well he could hear her, "He's kind of handsome."

As we walked out the door, I said, "Oh, wait. No pamphlets? No lecture on how I should be at Greg's singing him love songs? No indictments on what the devil is going to do with me, jailbait?"

She shook her head. "I said I'm sorry, okay? The past few weeks have been . . . eye-opening."

It was crazy. It was as if my sister, the girl I had grown up with, was back. I was caught in this middle ground between horrified and relieved. Honestly, I would rather bail her out of jail than have her completely brainwashed. It was sad that this was an improvement. What had happened to my sister? And was she really back for good?

Price opened my door and said, behind his hand but so Quinn could hear him, "Sounds like the Kool-Aid wore off."

"Is Elijah, like, okay?" I asked hesitantly.

"Oh, I hope not," Quinn said.

I turned to look at her in awe as Price pulled out of the parking lot.

"I just stabbed his arm, Gray. Geez. And, like I said, it was in self-defense. He's fine.

He probably needs, like, three stitches." I heard her add under her breath: "Little bitch."

I closed my eyes and shook my head. It did seem like the Kool-Aid had worn off. Six months ago, if I had said "bitch," I would have gotten a pamphlet.

"So . . ." I was waiting for details.

"I just don't want to talk about it, Gray," she said. "Later. Not now."

I was going to press her, but I heard the tears in her voice.

Price must have too, because he said, "So, Quinn. Charmin or Angel Soft?"

"Oh, Cottonelle, obviously."

Price and I both said, "Boooooo."

Then he looked at me, smiled, and said, "You know something, Gray, felon sister and all, I think you and I might be meant to be."

"You know what, Price? I think you might be right."

Diana: A Very Nice Man

I walked into Gray's that morning feeling a little nervous. "Good morning, my love," she practically sang.

I smiled. I was happy that she seemed so much happier today. She handed me a cup of coffee and sat down at the kitchen island.

"Wow," I said, sitting on the stool beside her. "Impressive. Looks like you've learned to make coffee in the real coffee pot like a big girl."

She laughed like that was the funniest thing she'd ever heard. "Actually, my sister stayed over, and she got up this morning and made it before she went on her run."

"Your *sister*?"

She nodded. "Yeah. Seems like the allure of Elijah wore off. I've never been happier to have to bail my sister out of jail. I think she's back."

She smiled again, and she was so glowing that I knew this was more than happiness over her sister. "Well, well, well," I said. "Did somebody get a little action?"

She laughed lightly. "No action. But I met a very nice man."

"A man?" I raised my eyebrows.

She laughed again. "Yes. A *man.* A forty-year-old, perfect-for-me man."

"Well," I said, "that sounds grand. I can't wait to meet him." I paused and added, "I may have a little news of my own."

I put my hand casually on hers.

She squealed. "No way! Oh my gosh, Diana. You're getting married!" She smiled and hugged me. "I'm so, so happy for you. This is amazing — and that ring. Oh my gosh. Is that a family heirloom?"

I nodded. "The best part is that Frank's momma is going to have a stroke that he gave her momma's ring to me."

"When are you getting married? How did he propose?" She squealed again. "Tell me absolutely everything."

"Well," I said, tapping my fingers on the countertop. "That isn't my only news." I cleared my throat.

Gray's face fell. "Oh no. You're moving away. You're moving far, far away, and we're never going to see you again."

"We love it down here. We're staying put. It's just that . . ." I bit my lip. "Remember that throw-up virus I had?"

A voice behind me said, "Oh my gosh. You're pregnant."

I turned to see Marcy, ponytail swinging.

Gray gasped. "Pregnant! You're *pregnant*?"

"I know. Forty years old, supposedly sterile, and pregnant."

Gray leaned over and hugged me as best she could without making the stool topple over. She was grinning. "I probably shouldn't say this, but, well, it seems meant to be, doesn't it?"

"And, Gray —" I said, swallowing hard.

"Don't say you're moving out for real. I know you already spend half your time at

Frank's, but I can't hear you say it."

I was moving out, of course. I had to. I was marrying him. I was having his baby. I still couldn't believe it. I nodded and kissed her cheek. It was all real Southern and respectable.

That night, getting ready for a redo date with Frank's mom, I asked, "So, do you think I'll do better this time?" I slipped on the same pearl earrings I'd worn to our last lunch attempt, still feeling nauseated, but happy that at least now I knew why. Gray was right. These things *were* lucky.

"Well," he said, grinning from ear to ear, "at least if you vomit on her this time, she'll be kind of happy because she's getting a grandchild."

"Do you think she'll be happy?"

Frank shrugged. "I don't know if that woman's ever been happy a day in her life."

He kissed me. Then he leaned down and kissed my belly, a new habit he had, a new habit I kind of liked. He looked into my eyes and said, "Diana, I didn't think I could love you any more. But, wow. This is the best surprise of my entire life. You, this baby. It's like it's all coming together, everything I've wished and prayed for, everything I ever thought possible."

I kissed him again, despite my nausea.

"Oh, Frank."

My phone rang, and I wasn't going to answer it, but I saw it was my brother. "Hi, Charles."

"Hi, Di."

"What's going on?"

"I wanted to see if I could come visit next week. I need a beach fix."

"Of course! The boys too?" I stood up and started pacing around, realizing that I couldn't invite my family to come stay at Gray's. But now I had Frank's. It made me smile.

"No. Just me."

"Come stay with Frank and me!"

He cleared his throat. "That's part of the reason I'm coming."

"Oh?"

"Frank called."

I was surprised at first, but I guess it made sense. Charles was the one who'd introduced me to Frank, after all. Charles and Frank had worked together on a fishing boat one summer. Well, *the* summer. It had been only a few months, but I had so many memories from that time it could have been a decade.

"And, D, I was skeptical," Charles continued, "but I think he's serious. I just wanted to see you two with my own eyes, make sure he's going to take care of you right this time."

"I think he is." I debated whether I should wait to tell him in person or just say it now. But I didn't have all that many people to tell, and I couldn't contain myself, so I said, "Charles, we're getting married."

He hooted. "Well, hot damn!"

I laughed. "I know."

"I knew he was going to do it, but I didn't know it was going to be so soon. Now I really can't wait to see you." He paused. "And, Di, I've got a surprise for you."

"You know, Charles, I might have a surprise of my own."

What a happy, happy time.

An hour later, almost to Frank's momma's house, I wondered if love was enough. The mere idea of having to spend the next however many years with his momma was about enough to do any woman in.

As we pulled up to the imposing cedar-shake house, of a size and scope that seemed more like New England than North Carolina, it was like Frank could feel my nerves. "It's going to be fine, you know," he said. "We've talked about it. She knows we're together, and she knows there's nothing she can do about it."

I nodded. "But the wedding and the baby

might be more than she bargained for."

Frank walked through the front door calling, "Mom! You here?"

"Yes, darling, I'm here." She strolled into the entryway, the white of her suit popping against the wood of the walls and floors.

"Hi, Mrs. Harrington," I said, in what I hoped was a sophisticated way. One look from that woman took me from a confident and independent forty-year-old back to that scared eighteen-year-old I'd been.

I could feel anticipation welling in me as she leaned over to give me the smallest hug you can even imagine. How would we tell her? And when?

Then Frank just blurted out, "You're not going to be the only Mrs. Harrington soon, Mom. Diana and I are getting married."

He smiled and put his arm around me and looked as happy as could be. I felt myself go whiter than that suit or those giant pearls around her neck. Just decided to dive right in, I guess.

Mrs. Harrington turned and led us to the living room. Oh, that view. Water and sand in all directions. I wouldn't hate living here when she kicked the —

Mrs. Harrington interrupted my thoughts. "That's fine. I've made peace with this whole thing."

I raised my eyebrows at Frank. That's when my nerves finally began to subside.

"Mom, we've loved each other for twenty-two years. We don't want to wait."

"I'm too old to run," I agreed. I winked at Frank. "Pretty soon I'll be too fat too."

She gasped in shock. "You aren't saying . . . ?"

Frank filled in: "Diana is carrying your grandchild."

"Good Lord." She put her hand on her forehead like she was going to keel over right there from the mere thought of it. She smirked at me. "So this is how you roped him into it? You got pregnant."

Looking around her pretty living room with all her things, I kind of quit being scared of Mrs. Harrington. Instead, I felt right sorry for her. So I smiled and said, "Yup. That's exactly right. I just knew that at forty I'd get pregnant, no sweat, and trap your son right into marriage. And it worked too. Lucky me!"

Frank squeezed my shoulder and looked at his mom. "Diana didn't rope me into anything. I tracked her down, and I wasn't letting her run away from me again. I've loved her for more than twenty years, and I'm too old not to live my life and be happy."

She shook her head. "It keeps getting

worse. Well, you need to go get married right now before people start talking."

Frank and I both laughed.

"Mom," he said, "with all due respect, I'm not sure that us being unwed is the most shocking part of this." He added, "Just think, Mom. You can buy bootees and tiny pajamas."

It softened her a touch, and I about fell plumb out of my chair when she said, "Well, I have always wanted a grandchild." She looked at Frank. "Darling, could you please go in the kitchen and get us all some iced tea?"

Frank looked at me questioningly, and I nodded my approval. Frank had my back now. That was all I needed to know.

When he was gone, she said, "Diana, I'm going to be honest with you. You weren't what I wanted for my son —"

"But —" I protested.

She put her hand up. "Let me finish." She started again: "You weren't what I wanted for my son back then. But you have been between us for all this time. I saw you in every one of Frank's far-off glances, in every quiet moment." Tears were forming in her eyes. "I thought he was better off without you, but the only thing pushing him away from you did was keep him from ever marrying, from ever having children, from ever having all the things I thought I was giving him by breaking you two up."

I could feel the tears in my eyes now too. "Can I be honest with you?"

She nodded.

"I have spent twenty-two years feeling unworthy of your son, unworthy of his love. But, Mrs. Harrington, Frank and I have both realized that we aren't whole without each other."

A tear rolled down her cheek now, and she whispered. "After Frank Senior died, I realized that life is short. You two both deserve to be happy. I might not be perfect, Diana, but I will never stand in the way of my son's joy again."

I swear, she looked something right near happy. But it was only for a second. As Frank walked back in with a tray of iced teas, she sat up straight, composed herself, and said, "Have you two set a date? We need to start thinking about flowers —"

"We don't need all that," I interrupted. "I think we're going to get married somewhere simple by ourselves."

"Yeah," Frank said. He turned to me. "We need to figure out where."

I smiled, so surprised and happy at how this day had gone, so relieved that, after all of it, I might just get another momma out of Mrs. Harrington. Family was all that mattered now. Family was everything. And I realized that when it came to our wedding, I wasn't clueless about where it should be after all. In fact, I knew just the place.

Chapter 19

Gray: Happily Ever After, the Sequel

If I thought I was good at social media, once I started following Brooke, I realized I was wrong. That made sense, because she had six more of her teen years to use it. I figure that, by the time Wagner grows up, kids will be born knowing how to make their YouTube videos go viral. It will be a biological adaptation like opposable thumbs. Brooke had started a blog to document her ever-fascinating life, and, much to my surprise, she had jumped on my idea for her and Greg to move down here as soon as he had pitched it. She loved the idea so much, in fact, that she had asked me to go house hunting with her.

Before we left, Diana had sat me down and said, "Look, Gray. I know you don't want to be friends with Brooke. But if you want to win the fight with Greg, she's your best shot at getting what you want." I had sighed and rolled my eyes. But I always do what Diana says.

We had spent sixteen hours — yes, sixteen — over two days looking at every house on the market. Either they weren't close enough to the water or they were too big, too small, didn't have an office for Greg, didn't have a nursery for their future baby (*gag*), needed too much work, didn't need any work . . .

Until we looked at the house next door. As in, next door to *me.* It was a cedar-shake, four-bedroom, four-bath house built in the late 1950s. It had tons of character, a chef's kitchen, and a view that was almost as good as mine. The bathrooms hadn't been redone to Brooke's specifications, but that was good because it gave her a project.

"Gray!" she had squealed. "It is perfect, perfect, perfect! Don't you think?" We were sitting on the back porch, from which you could just make out my back porch. The exhausted realtor had claimed she had a call, but, really, I think she needed a power nap in the car.

"It is a good house," I agreed.

"Gray," Brooke said seriously. I could tell an abrupt subject change was coming. "Can I talk to you?"

"We've been talking for two days," I said

with only the tiniest hint of snark.

She laughed and looked down at her hands. "No, I just . . ." She trailed off and then looked back up at me. "I want to apologize to you. I've never really done it, and I want to now."

I was shocked. I looked back at her, but I didn't say anything.

"I didn't think about you," she continued. "I swear I didn't. It was just like you and Wagner were this inanimate roadblock between what I wanted — Greg — and where I was. And I didn't care about your family or the consequences or anything." She looked into my eyes as she said, "I was wrong. And if you don't want me next door, I understand."

This was my moment. I had the golden opportunity to talk her out of buying this house. But, again, sixteen hours. *Sixteen* hours. Don't ever underestimate that woman. She knew what she was doing. It kind of made me like her.

And I didn't even try to talk her out of it. I just grinned and said what I was thinking: "Now Wagner will be right next door on my off weeks!" There was something seriously wrong with me. But that was true about Wagner.

Now Brooke had a great excuse to walk

the short distance between our two houses pretty much every day and ask for advice on her foray into the Internet. Truth be told, she was gaining followers so rapidly I thought I might need some advice from her. She usually brought some sort of fresh-squeezed cocktail, which made it tolerable.

Otherwise, life was getting back to some semblance of normal. Well, as normal as it can be with your ex-husband and his almost new wife living beside you and your kid going to a new school with new friends and sharing custody and your sister taking up what might be permanent residence in your house. It had been a few weeks since I'd seen Price, but we had talked daily, and he'd finally convinced me to go out with him.

"What in the hell are you waiting for anyway?" Diana had asked me. "Your boobs to fall all the way to the floor?"

"Yeah," Marcy said. "He's cute. Get in the game." She paused, looking totally dejected. "And see if he has any friends. I'm not doing so hot on my finding-a-husband quest."

I looked at her in amazement. "Marcy, I had everyone in town trying to find you a man and then you started hooking up with the hot lifeguard."

"I know," she pouted. "But you just looked

like you were having so much fun with Andrew."

Fun, I thought. *And now I am alone.*

I smiled at Diana, still a bit shocked to see her with that tiny protruding belly of hers. "Speaking of marriage," I said, "you waiting for the delivery room to tie the knot?"

In all honesty, selfishly, I wanted her to go ahead and get married before she got big enough that Wagner noticed. I wasn't thrilled about having to explain to my kid that the whole "you fall in love and get married and have a baby" thing didn't necessarily happen in that order. I was trying to hold on to his rapidly retreating innocence as long as possible.

"I wanted to talk to you about that," she said.

"If you're wanting her to be a bridesmaid and wear a hideous dress," Marcy said, "I'll be in the front row."

"No, no. No hideous dresses. It's just . . ." She paused.

"Oh my gosh!" I said, not even realizing that I was interrupting. "You should get married here! In the yard or on the porch or whatever."

She smiled. "Great minds," she said. "That's what I was going to ask. We won't be a whole lot of trouble. We're not inviting anyone. Just us and the preacher."

"Well, and me," Marcy said. "I'm obviously coming. It will save the awkwardness of my hanging out the window with my binoculars."

"I'm coming too," I said. "I'm a little hurt you aren't inviting me, but it doesn't matter because I'm coming anyway."

Diana shook her head. "I don't want all that."

But I wanted it for her, I realized. "Just picture it," I said. "A tent set up overlooking the water, a beautiful cross of flowers in between you and Frank, the sun dancing on the water, a quartet playing as you walk down the aisle. . . ."

Now Marcy chimed in: "Rows of gold chairs with flowers on them and flowers on the tables and flowers everywhere —"

"Hey," I said, "flowers are my thing. You know that."

Marcy shrugged. "Well, fine. Get there faster."

"Peonies and hydrangeas and bells of Ireland."

"Sushi and prime rib and those little lamb chop lollipops."

This was when I would bring it home. "And a vintage black-and-white-checked dance floor, with you in the arms of the man you have loved for your entire life." It actually brought tears to my eyes. Marcy and I were *good.*

"Damn it!" Diana said. "Guess that means I'll have to invite Frank's mom. . . ."

"Oh, we'll make short work of her," Marcy said.

Diana smiled. "She's actually kind of come around. I think it's going to be okay." Diana sat down and sighed. "Now I'm exhausted. I didn't want any of that."

I smiled at her. Diana had gotten her happy ending. It made me hopeful for tonight with Price. It had been long and convoluted, but maybe I'd get my happy ending too. Well, maybe more like my happy ending mulligan.

My phone rang, breaking me out of my thoughts. Andrew. Damn. It was as if he sensed I was thinking about another man. I wasn't going to answer. But it was Andrew, precious Andrew. I couldn't help myself. "Hello," I said, walking out of the kitchen.

"Hi, beautiful."

I smiled. He was so very adorable. "How are you?"

"I'm okay," he said. "But I'm missing you."

I didn't say anything. But I was missing

him too.

"Look how good I've been," he said. "I've left you alone. I've dated. But all I can think about is that whoever I'm with isn't you."

I sighed. I wanted to agree with him. I wanted to give in and say, *Forget about what I said. Let's be together.*

But nothing had changed. He was still too young for me. It still wasn't going to work out long-term. There was no reason to drag it out.

"Andrew, look." I bit my lip. I couldn't bear to hurt him, but this would make it easier, right? It was for his own good. "It was a fun summer, but it's over. Move on."

"But, Gray —"

"Andrew, I'm serious. It's probably best if we don't talk anymore."

It was like ripping out fresh stitches.

"Fine," he said, his voice cold. "But I want you to hear me when I say this. I'm out, Gray. For good. And let me tell you right now that you are going to look back, and you're going to wish that you hadn't brushed me off so easily. Yeah, I'm young, but I want to be very clear about something: No one — and I do mean no one — is ever going to love you like I do. No one is ever going to take care of you like I do." He was so angry and so hurt that it shifted something in me. Maybe I hadn't taken him seriously enough when I'd had him. "I was willing to fight for you, Gray. I was willing to give you time to get over your hesitations. But it's very clear to me now that I never meant anything to you. So, good-bye. For real. I hope you find what you're looking for, because it sure as hell isn't me."

And with that, he hung up — and I felt awful. I walked back to the kitchen, sat down on the stool, and put my head in my hands.

"What?" Marcy asked.

"I just broke up with Andrew. Again." I paused. "And he was, like, super pissed." My heart was still racing from our exchange — and also with the fear that maybe I had done the wrong thing.

"Yikes," Marcy said. "The good news is, you'll be bringing Price home tonight to ease your pain."

"I will not," I protested.

"Will not what?" The back door slammed. Ah, Quinn. My pretty-much-back-to-normal sister.

I'd never seen anything quite like it, the way she bounced back. I mean, she didn't bounce all the way back. She was like a normal human now. She wasn't snorting lines off my bathroom counter, but she also wasn't pushing pamphlets. She seemed to have found some middle ground.

"So," Diana said. "I hear you've crossed back over from the dark side."

"Ha-ha," Quinn said, opening the fridge. She grabbed a can of whipped cream and sprayed it into her mouth.

"Quinn, honestly."

"What do you have all that whipped cream for anyway?" she asked.

Marcy laughed, and Diana looked at me pointedly. Simultaneously, they said, "Andrew."

I felt my face redden. "Marcy, I shared that with you in the confidence of best friends."

"Oh, puhleeze," Diana said, "do you think I was born yesterday?" She sashayed across the room, wiggled her eyebrows at me, and said, "Do you think I haven't had my share of whipped cream?"

"Ooh la la," Marcy said. "Pregnant lady's a little saucy."

"So," Diana said as Quinn hoisted herself onto the counter, firmly planting her rear end on my marble, "do we need to get you in the witness protection program or something?"

I was going to miss that wit of hers. Frank had been by and asked me to let her go. I liked Frank, I did, and I wanted the best for Diana. But if she wasn't ready to let go of her job, I sure wasn't going to push her out. Plus, I couldn't even think about not seeing her every day. I never would have imagined it from that day we met at Meds and More, but I felt like, in some weird way, we were always meant to find each other.

Quinn shrugged. "Nah. I think stabbing Elijah scared him pretty good." She sprayed her whipped cream can again. "I mean, I know the Bible says women should be subservient to their husbands, but, damn. I have limits, you know?"

She still hadn't told me exactly what happened that night, and I wasn't totally sure I wanted to know.

Marcy opened the fridge and popped the top on a can of sparkling water. She leaned over the counter, her impossibly long, tan legs peeking out of her frayed jean shorts. "So how, pray tell, did you decult?" She took a sip. "I mean, purely for therapy research purposes, of course." She winked at me.

"It's so weird. It's like, all of a sudden, I realized that this man was a nutjob. Like, I don't doubt he loved me or anything, but I just saw him really clearly for who he was. And he wasn't good." She shrugged. "I'm still glad he got me in church and everything. But I realized that the Jesus I was getting to know would have wanted more for me than a man trying to tell me what to do every second."

"And the stabbing was because . . . ?" Marcy prodded.

"I came home from the store and was getting ready to cook the spatchcock chicken Elijah had requested for dinner that night, and I walked in the bathroom and all my makeup was gone."

She had all of our attention. "Just as I was cutting the whole chicken apart, Elijah came in, and I asked him where all my stuff was, and he said he threw it out, and he was super pissed because he found birth control pills in my makeup bag. Of course, I got pissed because he'd thrown out about five hundred dollars' worth of Trish McEvoy and three months of birth control. And then he started getting all mad and crazy-eyed, so I stabbed him in the arm with a pair of scissors to keep him from getting closer." I'm pretty sure my mouth was hanging open. "In fairness, I warned him that I would."

She told the story in a tone that would lead you to believe she was saying, *One day I was walking to the mailbox, and I saw a butterfly.*

Marcy twirled her finger by her head, signifying that my sister was cra-zy. Diana cocked her head, peered at Quinn, and said, "Remind me never to ask you to babysit."

"Quinn," I said. "For goodness' sake. You stabbed the man with scissors?"

She rolled her eyes and hopped down off the counter. "It was three stitches, Gray, and it was self-defense. He's fine."

"Anyway . . ." Diana said, "maybe instead of talking about *Breaking Amish* over here, we could talk a little bit about my wedding plans."

And we did. All afternoon long. We talked about music and flowers and tents, and Diana hadn't thought she wanted a wedding, but you could tell by the flash in her eyes that the more we planned and the more ideas we had, the more she was in love with the thought of celebrating in this very magical way.

And, as excited as I was about my date that night, I couldn't lie to myself about the fact that when I pictured myself in Diana's shoes, I couldn't really see Price standing at the other end of the aisle.

When Pinterest was first introduced and Greg and I were trying to grow our platform for ClickMarket, we used to have a weekly competition. We'd each pick five pins and bet which one would get the most likes and re-pins that week. Loser had to buy the entire staff drinks on Friday night.

Having drinks that night with Price, I remembered that, like those long-ago competitions with Greg, I had bet Marcy that I wouldn't bring Price home. After laughing through two-thirds of dinner, I thought this might be a bet I was willing to lose. There was something totally magnetic about Price, and it was like everyone around him was attracted to it. It wasn't unadulterated good looks. It was something more than that.

He was perfect for me, and it had taken only a few hours to figure that out. We could get married and blend our families and be totally happy together — except for one thing: Andrew's harsh words had shaken me. But I guessed this was what the aftermath of a breakup was like.

Price was saying, "I have this work trip in Valle Crucis next week, and I'd love it if you could get away and come with me."

I smiled. "September is the perfect time in the mountains."

He nodded. "Gorgeous weather. Not too hot, not too cold."

"Don't you think it's sort of early to go

away together? I mean, I have practically no dating experience, but aren't there rules about these kinds of things?"

He took a sip of his wine and grinned. "Oh, you mean because we haven't slept together yet?" He winked. "I was planning on remedying that tonight."

I laughed. "Oh, you were, were you? But see, here's the thing. I know about the three-date rule, and this is most definitely only our second by my calculations."

He leaned over and took my hand. "But, see, here's the thing. Drinks and jail count as . . ." He picked up my hand and put up one of my fingers, then another, then kissed them.

Swoon. "Well then, I can't argue with that."

He looked shocked. "That worked? Where's the waitress? Let's get out of here!"

I smacked him lightly on the arm. "No, it did not work. Where is this trip?"

"The Mast Farm Inn in Valle Crucis. Maybe in one of those private cabins."

I made my most delighted face. "I'll have to check with Greg to make sure it works for Wagner's schedule, but, sir, I kindly accept your invitation, if you don't think it's a little much to go away with a woman you've met twice."

He nodded and said seriously, "Who has a violent criminal as a sister."

We both laughed, but it crossed my mind that he wasn't totally wrong. She *had* stabbed someone. With scissors.

Price took another sip of wine and said, "Gray, you're beautiful. How anyone could let you go, I'll never know. Truly, you're all I can think about."

And just like that, happily ever after, the sequel, was under way.

Diana: An Institution

I didn't know if Gray was trying to punish me or help me, but it was very clear that she was avoiding the guesthouse. I'd seen her pull in and out of the driveway three or four different times, and she hadn't come to check on me once. Oh, I'd get her back for this.

"This one?" Trey asked, holding up a Sanitary Fish Market T-shirt.

I could feel my mouth gaping. "Now, you listen here. The Sanitary is an institution."

He dropped the T-shirt into a garbage bag. "It has cigarette holes in it."

"Well, yeah. I had to put my cigarette out on Larry one night when —"

"No. Done," Trey said. "Do you hear yourself? These aren't happy memories to cherish. We should burn these things in a fire so no other unsuspecting person gets harmed by their negative energy."

I crossed my arms and sat down on the couch across from the closet, pouting. To his credit, Trey had hung in there with me for fourteen T-shirts so far. He'd only let me keep the last one, and that was because I convinced him that the girls and me had actually gone to a Wilson Phillips concert and that had nothing to do with some guy.

Trey turned to me. "Diana, I don't think I can," then he sang: " 'hold on for one more day.' "

We both laughed, but then he got serious. "There's no room for your horrible past in your fabulous new future."

Then he pulled out a J-B Weld T-shirt, and I almost forgot I was pregnant. But I remembered in the nick of time and didn't throw myself on it. Instead, I grabbed one sleeve and Trey was holding the other. "I won't let this one go!" I shouted.

"Oh, yes you will," he groaned.

We looked like we were playing some kind of tug-of-war, Trey trying to get the shirt in the bag and me trying to save it.

Frank's voice calling, "What in the world is going on here?" broke us out of our feud. We both dropped the shirt like it was on fire and said, "Nothing!" right at the same time.

Frank walked over and picked up the shirt. "Man, I haven't seen this in forever."

Trey ran his hand through his hair. "Fine. That one you can keep."

I smiled victoriously.

"Trey is helping me pack," I said.

"Is he?" Frank asked.

I glared at Trey, and he glared right back at me. Frank picked up a box and turned around, and Trey whispered, "You'll thank me one day, crazy lady."

Trey picked up another box as Gray finally made her appearance at the top of the stairs; he scooted by her, saying, "She's all yours. I'm exhausted."

Gray laughed and sat down beside me. "So, it's really happening, huh?"

I nodded. "Gray, I can't tell you what these last few months —"

She put her hand up. "It's too much for me today, Di. I can't handle it."

"In that case, can I ask you something?"

She nodded.

"Well, Kevin is almost finished with the construction on the Barnacle." That was what we had decided to name my new restaurant, because it sort of looked like it was growing on the dock.

"Di! Why didn't you tell me? That's amazing." She looked genuinely thrilled.

"I'm good on everything up until now, but I need just a few thousand dollars to finish with the kitchen outfit and permitting and all that."

"Anything you need, Di."

It had taken a lot for me to ask her, but I just knew that Gray would support me. "Well, five thousand would really put me where I need to be."

"I'll write you a check right now."

"No!" I interjected before she could move. "You don't understand. I'm asking you for a loan. I want to write it up with a schedule for interest and payments and all of that."

She shook her head. "Absolutely not. I owe you so much, D. I wouldn't be here without you. Let this be my wedding gift to you."

She tried to stand up, and I put my hand on her arm to stop her. I looked her in the eye and said, "Please, Gray. I need one thing in the world that is all my own, that no one can ever take away from me. I wouldn't let Frank give me the money, and I won't let you do it either. If you won't do this my way, then I'll have to figure something else out."

She smiled. I knew she would understand.

"I can't think of anything better, Diana. I am seriously so proud of you, and I will be your first customer on opening day." She paused, and I knew there was more that she wanted to say. "What will I do without you?"

"Geez, I don't know." I'd been training my replacement, and she was not up to my standards, to say the least. "Harriet can't clean a glass shower door to save her life. I keep showing her over and over. Bar Keepers Friend, sponge, rinse, glass spray, wipe dry, but her shower doors just don't look like mine."

"No one will ever replace you, Diana. Ever."

I knew she didn't want to talk about it, so I didn't say it. But no one could ever replace Gray either.

Chapter 20

Gray: That Bullet

I'd followed the Mast Farm Inn on Twitter for years, so I knew already that it was the perfect place for an impromptu getaway. I'd pictured Price and me holding hands driving through the mountains, taking a leisurely road trip. When we parked at the airport, needless to say, I realized that picture wasn't going to develop.

My hand-holding visions were instantly replaced by those of us plummeting out of the sky and onto the highway.

"You're kidding, right?" I asked as Price walked up to a tiny four-seater plane.

"No, I am not kidding." He tipped a fake hat. "Best pilot on the East Coast. This will be my second flight." He grinned.

I started to walk away, and he laughed. "Come on, Gray, I do this twice a week. And the plane has an emergency parachute."

I hadn't wanted to come on this trip at all once I found out that Brooke and Greg were going to the British Virgin Islands for their wedding planning trip. I had said to Diana, "Really? Who goes away to 'plan' their wedding? And the BVIs? Couldn't they have picked somewhere a little more original, like, not where we went on our second honeymoon?"

She had just rolled her eyes. "If you're trying to get out of your own trip, it isn't going to work. You've given up just about enough for Greg."

Quinn, who had her head in the fridge, said, "Come on, Gray. I'm here. I'll keep Wagner."

Diana and I had shared a terrified look, and she mouthed: *I'll stay here the whole time.*

I had nodded. Ever since, she and Wagner had been plotting every time I came in the room. I was pretty sure it was just about how they were going to make pizza, but still. He loved her, and she loved him. Wagner and I were both going to take it really hard when Diana left for good.

Now, on the tarmac, Price was saying, "Wait. How much do you weigh? I need to make sure we can still take off."

"Ha-ha."

We landed an hour later in one piece, and it sure beat the pants off of the seven-hour drive.

A car awaited us at the airport, and we arrived at the Mast Farm to lunch. Wine and the first course, soup made from vegetables from the farm, were already waiting for us.

"Wow," I said. "This is great. So, what kind of work do you have to do tomorrow?"

"Let's see. I thought I'd start the day with a stack of pancakes and fresh sausage here, then take a long hike with my favorite girl." He winked at me.

I nodded. "Your job sounds pretty great. Where do I apply?"

"Did I say this was a work trip?"

"You did."

"Ohhhh. I guess I should have specified that it was more of a 'work on getting Gray to fall in love with me' sort of trip than an actual 'things for the office' trip."

I laughed. He looked me in the eye, and I said, "Well, I'd say so far, so good."

"So do you think we should just bite the bullet?"

I looked at him inquisitively. "What bullet would that be?"

"Families. Sad stories. Yada yada yada."

"Oh . . . that bullet." That was a bullet I was hoping to avoid for a little longer, pretend it was just us hanging out like we were fifteen and this was all fun.

"You first," I said.

"Okay. CliffsNotes?"

I swallowed a sip of wine and said, "Definitely."

He took a deep breath. Here we go. "Exwife, Kate. Went back to get her master's. She found a love of Italian literature, and I found her in the back of her Suburban with her Italian literature professor."

"Ew."

"You have no idea. Those Italian men . . ." He cocked his head and squinted as if trying to erase a memory. "Anyway . . . Anna, twelve. Adorable. Perfect. Slept through the night at four weeks old. Never needs anyone to check her homework. Jackson, ten. Athletic. Disorganized. Slept through the night . . . well, we're still waiting. Thinks his floor is a depository for sweaty soccer socks."

I was laughing so hard I thought I might choke. But my stomach turned over at the mere thought of attempting to mishmash a bunch of families together.

He smiled. "It's your turn. I told you my sad story."

I sighed. "Fine. Greg traded in his Suburban with the TVs in the headrests" — I pointed at myself — "for a Maserati with the top down."

Price nodded.

"Wagner. About to turn nine. The love of my life. I only technically have him every other week, but I made my ex move next door so I can see him every day no matter whose week it is." It sounded better when I framed it like that instead of that I had somehow gotten swindled into it by Brooke.

"You want more?"

I shrugged. "I'm not opposed to it, but I'm not married to it either." I paused. "Wait. More time or more babies?"

He laughed. "Babies."

"Oh, okay. Do you want more babies?"

"I think the world is made for even numbers. Four children seems right."

That was funny. Marcy always said the world was made for even numbers too.

The rest of the day passed just as gloriously, hiking in the mountains and perusing Blowing Rock's charming downtown.

The one chink in the armor? A harmless-seeming beep from my cell phone. One little beep. Or maybe it wasn't the beep so much as what it signified. I'm sorry about last week. I meant what I said, but I shouldn't have gotten so mad at you. I really do hope you find what you're looking for.

My heart sank.

"What's up?" Price asked.

"Nothing," I said casually.

I was all ready for our dinner, hair fixed, makeup on, and dressed. Price, with his mussed hair and goofy grin, had just woken up from a nap.

I kissed him, trying to erase that text message from my brain. "Hey," I said, "I'm going to go for a quick walk around the property while you get spiffy for dinner."

He wrapped his arms around me and nuzzled my neck. "Don't you want to just order room service?"

"You have been so excited about this tasting menu," I said. "I'm not going to let you miss that."

"What I'm excited about is you. I don't care a thing about what I eat."

I shrugged. "Shame to waste this dress?"

He nodded. "Oh yes."

I smiled and kissed him. He was so damn cute. But I felt like something was missing. And I felt like I needed some air. "Perfect."

I *did* need to call and check on Wagner. Afterward, I sat down on a bench by the small farm, rubbing my arms against the chilly night air. In a cabin over there was a man I couldn't have even dreamed up, he was so right for me. So why did I feel so conflicted? I watched the sun as it made its descent, so gloriously beautiful that it blocked out the confusion in my head.

My mother never missed a sunset. She loved them all. I sighed. She would have known what to do in this situation. I closed my eyes and tried to imagine what she would have told me. She would have loved Price. He was son-in-law material.

But this was ultimately my decision; I was on my own now. Andrew's *I hope you find what you're looking for* kept running through my mind.

Half an hour later, Price ordered the Mast Farm's finest champagne, and I couldn't help but be taken with him, not because he could order fine champagne, but because he was this walking billboard for *don't take yourself too seriously* and *seize the day.* He had come to me when I needed to be reminded of both.

"Let's order for each other," he said.

"What?"

"Let's order for each other, so we'll try something new. Okay?"

I smiled. "Yeah, sure. Sounds fun."

That was what I meant. He made me laugh; he gave me butterflies — and all I could think about was Andrew. I thought about how Andrew would catch my eye and wink when we were across a crowded room, how, when he was near me, he always had a hand or an arm on me, how he always got me a glass of water before bed and set his alarm for ten minutes earlier than he had to get up so that we could have those first few minutes of the day to just be together. He made me feel protected and, what's more, totally adored. And I let myself consider, for the first time without batting the thought away, that maybe Andrew and I were something more than just a summer fling.

Price was laughing, and I sighed. "We really are perfect for each other, aren't we, Price?"

I could see his face fall as he said, "Why do I get the feeling that this isn't going to end with 'Let's go back home, sign a prenup and make an "ours" baby'?"

I laughed. "An 'ours' baby?"

He shrugged. "Yeah. You know, like *Yours, Mine and Ours.*"

"I'm entirely too young to understand that cultural reference."

"Oh . . . okay," he said sarcastically. "So, what's the deal? Why is our match-made-in-heaven going to hell?" He grinned, but there was a sort of sadness behind it.

I shook my head and looked down at the

table. "It's so stupid," I said under my breath.

He sat up straighter. "Is it my table manners? Because I've had complaints before, but I can work on it." He put his elbow on the table and reached for his wineglass, winking at me.

I smiled. "No. It isn't your table manners — although they are atrocious. It's just that I dated this kid this summer —"

He put his hand up. "Wait. Kid?"

"Yeah. Kid. He's twenty-six years old. Well, I guess twenty-seven now. It was supposed to be a summer fling, my fun rebound after Greg before I got back in the saddle for real again. Only . . ."

"Only it turned out to be more than a summer fling."

I nodded. Then I said out loud what I wouldn't let myself admit all this time. "If I'm honest with myself, I think I'm in love with him."

"That's great, Gray. Love is kind of the endgame, right?" Price wiped his mouth and smiled. "I mean, it sucks for me because I'm in love with you, but I'm a big boy."

I rolled my eyes. "You are not in love with me." I paused. "I haven't told you the worst part yet."

"What's the worst part?"

"His job."

He grinned again. "Ooooh. Let me guess. Bartender?"

I shook my head.

"Male stripper."

I gave him a *get serious* look.

"Okay. I give up."

"Tennis pro."

I thought wine was going to fly right out of his nose.

"Oh no, Gray. That is the worst. Cougar divorcée sleeping with the twentysomething tennis pro."

I held my head in mock shame. "I know." Then I looked up at him and smiled. "It's a cliché for a reason." Then I brightened. "Wait! I have the perfect person for you to go out with."

"Who?"

"My best friend. She's the most gorgeous person I've ever seen in real life, she has never been married, she has no kids, she's younger than I am."

He raised his eyebrows. "Good Lord. I should hope she's younger than *you.*" Price was well aware of my almost-thirty-five panic.

We both laughed. I almost decided to take it back. I mean, here was a man who was exactly everything I thought I wanted. And

I was going to give him away? But this was my best friend. She was light and fun and free, he was light and fun and free, and they both thought the world subsisted on even numbers.

"Her name is Marcy," I said.

"So why isn't gorgeous, childless Marcy married?"

I shrugged. "She has always been pretty wild, but she's ready to settle down now."

He nodded. "What does she do?"

"She's a therapist," I whispered.

"No," he said emphatically. "No, no, no."

I laughed. "At least go out with her. She's not like that. She doesn't analyze you or anything."

He sighed. "I knew I should have taken you to Nantucket. But I was afraid it was too far away, and you would say no."

I laughed. "You're so adorable."

"But not as adorable as Andrew."

I shrugged. Andrew was pretty damn adorable. "Well, on the bright side, I may be Gray, but, trust me, Marcy is way more *Fifty Shades.*"

Price took my hand across the table and squeezed it. "In all seriousness, I hope you find your happiness. I only hate that we couldn't give this thing a real shot."

"I just know that ten years from now, we'd

be in Martha's Vineyard with our beautiful blended family, and I'd be smiling and kissing you, but on the inside, I'd be thinking about him."

He nodded. "Then I wish you well."

We sat there for a second, and I was happy that the waiter came and broke our silence. This was the problem with breaking up with someone when you were on a trip together that wasn't ending for another day. We ordered for each other, and he said, "Well, on the bright side, I do have one night to change your mind."

I lifted my glass. "Here's to that!"

The next morning, as Price opened the door of his Cirrus for me, I did a gut check. This was what I wanted, right? He was perfect husband material. But I had married husband material, and now I was divorced. If I ever got married again, I knew that being in love was entirely more important.

Price slid into the pilot's seat of the tiny cockpit and leaned over, cupped my chin in his hand, and kissed me tenderly. I have to admit that, feeling his lips on mine, butterflies welled up in my stomach.

"I think you're amazing," he said. "But I know when to say good-bye. No one wants to be second choice."

I shook my head. "It isn't like that, Price. It's just —"

"No," he said, "I get it completely. I'm happy for you. I'm just sad for me."

I was afraid that the flight home might be like the one I had taken not all that long ago with Greg. But it wasn't. Price and I sat in companionable silence, and I realized that, even though I wanted to, I just didn't feel that spark with him. We were two compatible people. We were great friends, and maybe this time around that's what I should have been looking for. But I realized I still believed I deserved someone who looked at me with that fresh enthusiasm that could only come from new, young (or, in my case, young-ish) love; I still wanted to be with a man who could make me feel like I was ten thousand feet in the air.

As we pulled into my driveway a few hours later, I said, "Why don't you come in for a drink?"

He hesitated, and I added, "I'm sure that Marcy is in there waiting to hear all about our weekend."

Price put his hand on my back and led me up the stairs, and I wasn't surprised at all to see Marcy, hair in a ponytail, tube socks up her ankles, legs stretched on my couch, reading a magazine.

She popped up when she heard the doorknob turn. "Oh, sorry," she said. "I just came over to borrow this month's *Vogue.*" She winked at me.

"Marcy, this is Price," I said. "Price, Marcy."

She gave him her most engaging smile.

"Marcy, I was telling Price all about you over dinner last night," I said.

"Yeah," he added. "And besides the whole therapist thing, you sound pretty great." He grinned.

Marcy's look turned to one of confusion as she glanced from Price to me. "Excuse us," she said, pasting on a smile, and dragged me into the kitchen.

"Wait," she whispered. "Are you *giving* him to me?"

I laughed. "He's a man, not a scarf, Marcy. I can't give him to you."

She peeked through the doorway and whispered, "He is an Hermès scarf of a man." She paused. "So what's the no-go with you two?" Before I could answer, Marcy peeked around the corner at Price again. "Damn, he's hot. What is it about him?"

"You can't quite define it, right? Because he's not all that classically handsome."

"Exactly," she said. "You're nuts."

"He's perfect," I said. "The perfect man, perfect husband material."

She shrugged. "So again I ask, why . . ." She trailed off. "Oh. Andrew. This is about Andrew." She did a little dance and said in a singsong whisper, "You love him, you want to have his babies, you want to eat whipped cream off of him when you're an old lady!"

I rolled my eyes. "Okay. That's enough. Why don't you go out there and act charming to your new potential husband? Men like him don't come around often."

"Are you going to have babies with him?" she whispered.

I smiled.

"Oh my gosh, you are. I was right. You love him, and you're going to marry him, and you're going to have hot, tan, tennis-playing babies." She put her hand in the air. "Up top, sister. I have a feeling this is going to be a very good year for both of us."

I sat down on one of the barstools after I kissed Price's cheek and told Marcy goodbye.

And I thought of Andrew. Part of me wanted to run to him right now, wanted to tell him I had changed my mind. But delayed gratification was the definition of adulthood, right? He was so cute. He was just a kid. He wasn't that great on paper.

But in my heart, Andrew was absolutely perfect.

Diana: A Perfect Day

As the warm air was starting to get chilly — and I was starting to get less nauseated — I couldn't stop staring at my protruding belly.

"Hey, babe?" Frank called from downstairs. I was supposed to be eating breakfast with him.

"Yeah."

"Do you want me to be here when your brother gets here?"

My brother. My Frank. What a perfect, perfect day. "Of course I do! He'll love to see you."

I heard footsteps up the stairs, and it wasn't long before Frank was behind me, kissing my neck, his hands rubbing my bare belly. "Damn, pregnant looks good on you," he said. "Are we going to tell him?"

I smiled and nodded. "Thirteen weeks, and all is well. I might not start telling random people yet, but I think it's fine to tell him." Frank knew how worried I was about this pregnancy. I knew the pregnancy was at higher risk for complications, that there was a higher chance that something could be wrong with the baby, that I was at a greater risk for a laundry list of problems and even death. But I couldn't dwell on that. I had to move forward.

I had already told Phillip at our visit the week before, and he had smiled so big and even put his hand on my belly. Every time I thought of it, I burst into tears. He understood.

It was like Frank was inside my head when he said, "Do you want to see if we can find somewhere else for Phillip?"

"Where, like here?"

He shook his head and sat down on the end of our bed. "Babe, look. I don't want to focus on this, but you are in the middle of a high-risk pregnancy. And you know how hard a change like that will be on Phillip, how much it will disrupt him. . . ."

I wanted to argue, but I knew more than anyone that he was right.

"Maybe we should start by trying to find a place where we can get him more personalized care," Frank said.

I shook my head. "I don't want to move him more than we need to. I want his next move to be permanent."

I slid an empire-waist dress over my head. I couldn't wait to look full-on pregnant.

"Okay, then. Yeah. You're right. We'll do everything we can from where he is now, and then when the time is right, we'll move him in here with us."

I smiled. "Really?"

He nodded. "Of course. He's your brother."

I kissed Frank right as the doorbell rang. "He's here! He's here!"

Throwing open the door, I hugged Charles so tight I hardly even noticed the woman standing right behind him on the front porch. I was getting ready to blurt out all about the baby, and I was kind of irritated that he had brought someone with him so I couldn't. I pulled away and smiled at the woman. Her face seemed familiar. I was about to introduce myself when she said, "Diana."

Her voice came rushing back, and I swear I lost my mind for a minute. "No!" I screamed. I slammed the front door and walked out the back.

"Diana," Frank called. I heard the front door open, but it didn't matter. I was getting the hell out of there. As I bolted out the back and down the steps into the detached garage, I realized I didn't have any car keys. And surely they were in the house by now, so it wasn't like I could go back. But Gray's was only a couple miles away, so I started walking. I expected them to come after me, but they didn't. I tried not to, but

I couldn't help but think about all those other times I'd been alone before — and worry that nothing much had changed.

Chapter 21

Gray: The Car Crash

I hadn't spoken to Andrew since the day I had told him it was over between us for the second time. And I knew that, before I confessed to him how I was feeling now, I had one more thing to do, something that terrified me to my core: I had to talk to his mother.

I could see her rear end pointing up toward the sky from her trunk before I saw her face. She looked shocked when she turned and my car was in the driveway. I waved, and she laughed.

"Hi, June," I said, opening the door, figuring it was safe since Andrew's car was nowhere to be found.

"Well, hi there, darling. What brings you here?"

I got out of the car and lifted my sunglasses so that we could see eye to eye. "I'm sorry I didn't call. I just wanted to talk to you for a minute, but if this isn't a good time I can —" I pointed back to the car.

"Don't be silly." She winked at me. "You can help me carry up my groceries."

"I don't want to put you in a weird spot," I said, as we climbed the stairs to the front door.

She paused and fumbled for her keys in her purse. "Well, I asked you not to break his heart, darling, and, without a doubt, you did."

I sighed, following her through the door. "I know. But I did it then to make it easier. I didn't want to drag things out, prolong them, because I knew that, realistically, this wasn't going to work out. I mean, he's just a kid, and I'm not exactly who a parent would dream about their star of a son marrying." I paused and added, "I didn't want you to think that I was latching on to your son because I was desperate or something."

She laughed heartily. Opening the fridge, she pulled out a bottle of white wine and retrieved a corkscrew from a drawer. "I think we're probably going to need a little of this." As she poured, she said, "I am not going to patronize you, Gray. I have . . ." She paused. "Concerns."

She walked toward the back deck, and I followed her. She looked around as she sat down and said, "You're a mother, so I feel that you understand where I am coming from and won't take offense when I say that, no, you are not who I envisioned for my son."

I knew that. Even still, it stung.

"Well, that's not true," she said. "Under different circumstances, you are precisely what I envisioned for my son."

"But we aren't under those circumstances," I agreed. "I've been married, I have a child, and I am barreling toward my thirty-fifth birthday."

She bit her lip. "We raised him to be a steadfast man. We raised him to follow his heart."

I nodded. "That's very, very clear." I turned and looked out over the ocean.

"He has always been so focused. He has dated a lot, but whenever I asked him if it was serious he would say, 'When I find her, I'll know.' "

My heart was racing.

"When he told us all about you and Wagner, I asked him if he was sure it was worth it, knowing that, in the end, it might not work out, knowing that even if it did work out he would be taking on quite a lot." She paused and looked out over the ocean, then back at me. "And he said, 'Mom, I know.' "

I smiled and closed my eyes, shaking my head. "That is so sweet — but, June, we don't have to get ahead of ourselves."

"I think you know my boy is very strong-willed."

"Oh, he is that," I said, thinking of that first day I saw him at the tennis court. I shrugged. "He is special, June. He is so wonderful, and I wanted to talk to you, mom to mom. You want what's best for your son, and I want what's best for mine, so I respect that. I —"

She interrupted. "Are you asking for my son's hand, dear?"

I laughed. "No. Not exactly. I just . . ." I paused. "I've been thinking about all the reasons that our relationship couldn't work, all the reasons it was wrong. But being apart has made me realize that, right or not, I only want to be with Andrew." My eyes filled with tears. "I tried to push it away, and I've tried to fight it, but if it's okay with you, I'd like to at least give it a fair shot. And if it isn't, no one understands better than I do."

She smiled sympathetically. "I might not fully understand it, but I would never keep my son from true love."

"Okay —" I started to say.

But June interrupted me again. "I have to ask you something. And it's none of my business." She paused, then waved her hand. "Oh, never mind."

I laughed. "Well, you have to ask me now!"

She swallowed hard and whispered, "Do you want more children?"

That was much easier than what I had been expecting. "I certainly want more if it works out that way."

"Like I said, it's none of my —"

We both turned to look as we heard a girl's laughter, followed by a, "Mom!"

I could see the car crash before it happened, and there wasn't anything I could do about it. I couldn't be mad, because I had pushed him away.

But when he walked onto that deck holding the hand of a beautiful blond girl, who probably wasn't a minute over twenty-one, it took my breath away.

"Hi," I said brightly, taking a sip of my wine so that I would have something to do with my hands and mouth. I set down my glass, patted June's hand, and turned to Andrew and said, "Just catching up with your mom, but I need to be going now."

"Gray, I . . ." Andrew looked at me, and then the girl, whose hand he had abruptly dropped.

"Thanks, June. I always love seeing you."

I bolted through the house and out the

front door. I probably should have cried, but I laughed instead. Because the world was as it was supposed to be.

I decided that I wouldn't cry. I would take some deep breaths instead. I drove slowly, calming myself, realizing that my life wasn't over. He was a wonderful man, but there would be others. And if there weren't? Well, then that would be fine too. The past was in the past, and I had to move on. I thought about stopping by Greg's to see Wagner for a minute, but I decided that a glass of wine might be more appropriate right now. Hell, maybe even a cigarette.

Diana was leaning on the kitchen counter, cup of coffee — decaf, I'm sure — in hand when I tore through the back door. She handed me a cup too. I kissed her on the cheek.

"Gray, I . . ."

Her face was white. My first thought was the baby. This was Diana's biggest fear. But nothing could have prepared me for what she said next.

Diana: The Ends of the Earth

I'd always wished that I'd got to go to my momma's funeral, that I could have thrown a handful of earth on her grave, and then I wouldn't've had any lingering questions.

But I guess there was a good reason I hadn't gone: she hadn't had a funeral.

"What's wrong?" Gray asked, out of breath. "Are you okay?"

Before I could answer, Charles tore in through the back door, into Gray's kitchen. "Diana, I wasn't trying to spring her on you."

"Then what the hell were you trying to do, Charles? Did you think I'd laugh and squeal and hug her neck? She's dead, Charles," I screamed. "Dead!"

Gray was white as a sheet. "Who's dead?"

"No one," Charles said. "No one is dead. Everything is fine."

They looked at each other like they thought it would be nice to introduce themselves but knowing this maybe wasn't the time.

"Should I leave?" Gray asked.

I said, "No," as Charles said, "Yes."

I could feel myself getting kind of hysterical, and it was like all those years were just flooding back to me. The getting left, the being alone, Charles trying to raise us, all those hellacious foster families, Charles trying to get me again, that not happening. The only way I could make it right in my mind, the only way I could move on even a little, was telling myself that my momma was dead, and she couldn't help it, and if she could have, she'd have traveled to the ends of the earth for me. She couldn't be alive. She just couldn't.

Gray was trying to calm me down, but I couldn't even hear what she was saying. She pulled me into the living room and sat me down on the couch and rubbed my back in these long, slow, even strokes. I guess it must've worked, because I caught my breath, and I was still crying hard, but I could hear again.

"Diana," Charles said. "I wasn't trying to upset you. Let me explain."

"Diana," Gray whispered. "You have to calm down. It isn't good for the baby."

"The baby?" Charles asked.

Shit.

"I'm so sorry," she said, covering her mouth. "But, seriously. This is bigger than that. You have to calm down."

"What baby?" Charles asked.

Gray, she got up, and she said, "Look, I don't know who you are, but you're upsetting Diana. Yes, she's pregnant. I'm sorry you found out that way, but I think it's best that you go now. Being this upset is dangerous for her."

She led him to the door, and I felt torn. Because, on the one side, I wanted my brother. I wanted him here to comfort me. On the other side, he'd brought *her* back into my life with no warning, no preparation at all, and I wasn't ready for that. So that part of me was pissed. Did he really think I was going to be *happy* to see her? I've never understood men, and I never will.

Gray closed the door behind Charles, and my mind was spinning, and the room was spinning, and she helped me lie down on the couch. She sat on the floor beside me and said, "You don't have to talk about it unless you want to. Okay?"

"Okay," I said.

"I can get Marcy if that would help."

I was starting to see clearly again, the room coming back into focus, my mind getting right. And I knew I didn't need therapy. I just needed a friend. As good a one as I'd ever had in my whole life was sitting right beside me all wide-eyed.

"My mom," I said. "I opened the door and my brother Charles was there with this woman, and she said my name, and I realized it was my mom."

"And you thought she was dead?"

I put my hand up over my eyes. "Yes." I threw both hands up in the air. "I don't know what I thought. I mean, yeah, I had to think she was dead. Because if she was dead, she couldn't help it. It wasn't like she could control her death. If she'd died, she hadn't meant to abandon us. But she's not dead, and that's so much worse."

Gray nodded. "I get that. I totally get that." She paused. "That would have to be the worst feeling in the world, for the one person who is supposed to love you more than herself to abandon you like that. But maybe she had a reason, you know?" I heard her voice catch in her throat as she said, "Maybe she just couldn't help it."

I realized that a little part of this wasn't about my momma. It was about Gray's. Her mom dying, and her thinking her mom wanted to die. In some small way, even though, I'll be honest, it seemed a hell of a lot better than what happened to me, she felt like her momma'd abandoned her. It explained a lot about her, really.

I was calmer now. Nothing had changed, had it? I still had Frank. I still had this baby. I knew my momma was alive, but, hell, way deep down hadn't I known that all along? It was going to be okay. I had a family now. Nothing was going to change. Feeling right better and feeling that need I always got to protect the girl sitting on the floor beside me, I patted her hand and said, "Honey, maybe your momma just couldn't help it either." I paused. "And Charles," I continued. "I mean, he's my brother. Shouldn't he have known better than this?"

Gray shook her head. "I have crazy-ass Quinn as a sister. Trust me, I can relate."

"And you just forgave her for all her crap? Just like that?"

She scrunched her nose, and I could tell she was debating what she would say. "Well . . ." She shrugged. "She's my sister, Di."

I sighed. Damn it. I hated when she was right. He was my brother. Even if I wanted to be mad at him, it felt biologically impossible. He had fought for me his entire life. I knew, deep down, that he meant well. But I wasn't ready to move forward. Not yet.

"What are you going to do?" she whispered.

"I don't know," I said honestly.

"I'm here," she said.

"I know."

For now, that was enough.

Chapter 22

Gray: Leaving

What almost-thirty-five-year-old woman in her right mind blames her dead brother for taking her mother away from her? I knew it was insane; I knew it was irrational. But I knew now that it was true. Diana had been right. I was mad at my mother. I felt like she had just left me here to sort out all these problems.

When I put it in perspective, my mom dying when I was already a mom, after she had loved me and raised me and brought me up day in and day out forever, that wasn't leaving me. Leaving was when you did something like Diana's mom. Leaving was when you left your kids there by themselves to rot. But, as I'd told Diana earlier, she must have had a reason.

I felt my stomach clench, and I closed my eyes and took three deep breaths. Wagner was fine. Wagner was going to be fine. Nothing was going to happen to my son. I wondered if this was every mother's most common fear, if every mother pictured her child being ripped away from her, or if this was my fear because of my brother.

Everything is fine. Well, everything except Andrew. And it was all my fault. I had pushed him away. I had let him go. I deserved what I was getting now. Even worse, I had let Price, a man I could have really loved and made a life with, go too. What the hell was wrong with me? Was this what divorce did to women, made them terminally insane and bad with men?

Even still, I knew that what Diana was going through was so much worse than all of that put together. My problems were temporary. Hers was something that had haunted her for a lifetime and, no matter the outcome, would continue to. I had come outside because she'd asked for some time alone and, even though I was more of the smothering kind, I let her have that.

I knew as well as anyone who had grown up coming to this little part of the coast that warm September air didn't equal warm water, but I couldn't shake this overwhelming need to go for a swim. I almost wanted the cold, the pins-and-needles burning, the shock of it all pulling the breath right out of my lungs. It was the closest thing to a lobotomy that I knew of.

I slipped on my smallest bikini and checked out the now pointless progress of all those squats I'd been doing. Walking across the yard into the setting sun, I dropped my towel on the dock and dove in. It was like that day in the British Virgin Islands, the day when Greg told me he didn't love me anymore, all over again.

The tears I'd been pushing away finally came. I could see Diana watching me from the glass French doors of the living room. I composed myself because I didn't want her to know that I was upset, especially because if anyone had a right to be upset, it was her.

But she knew anyway. She opened the door and came out. "What's wrong?"

"What do you mean?"

"You know, the late afternoon swim in freezing-ass water is not necessarily your normal behavior."

I shrugged, walking up the sand until I was about waist-deep. "I'm just worried about you." That was true.

She looked at me sideways. "I know, and thank you. But what?"

"I think you're having a real problem right now. I'm not going to bore you with my absurdly trivial one."

I smiled at her expanding belly. She looked so cute it almost made me want to do it again. *Via in vitro,* I thought, *because I am going to be alone forever.* Wagner had turned out pretty good. Maybe I could have some of Greg's sperm. . . . I shook my head. Now I really was going off the rails.

"Yeah," Diana said, "but I think your trivial problem might help take my mind off my real one."

I wrung my hair out, my bangles tinkling on my wrist, and said, "I was too late."

"Whoa!" I heard his voice before I could see him. "Is that Bo Derek?"

"Maybe you weren't too late after all." Diana winked at me, then turned and walked back into the house.

I managed a small smile. "Andrew, I'm sorry. I know I put you in a bad spot. Please go back to your girlfriend."

He pulled his shirt over his head. "Good Lord," he said as he waded into the cold water, clutching his arms and shivering. Then he wrapped his arms around me. "Sorry. There's no way I'll survive this temperature without a little body heat." He looked at me earnestly. "The girl is not a girlfriend. She was a date to an oyster roast that my parents insisted I go to."

I nodded. "So, do you like her?"

He shrugged. "Do you like me?"

I started to answer, but he put his finger over my lips. "Wait. I need to talk for a minute."

I nodded.

"I have two job offers on the table right now for after graduation, one at the Straits Club and one at the Lowcountry Club."

"Well, I —" I said through his finger.

"I'm not finished." He grinned at me. "Obviously, the Lowcountry Club is sort of my dream job, and I can stay in Charleston with my friends."

My eyes locked on his, and I found myself searching his face as if it were for the first time.

"But I've already accepted the one at the Straits Club, making way less money. Would you like to know why?"

I smiled, his finger still on my lips, and nodded.

"Because I love you, and I want to see if we can make this thing work despite your very stupid reservations about it. Would that be okay with you?" He finally dropped his hand.

I nodded again. "I shouldn't have underestimated you, Andrew. And I do see you. I see how extraordinary you are, and I promise I will never take you for granted again. I am ready to put you first, to try this for real, to give you what you deserve and what you want."

"Gray?"

"What?"

He took my hand in his, and we walked toward the shore.

"Do you know what I want more than anything?"

I shook my head and smiled.

"To take this relationship out on dry land."

Diana: Come Hell or High Water

I couldn't avoid Charles and Momma forever. But I wasn't going back to Frank's house until I was good and sure the coast was clear. I wasn't sure how I was going to know the coast was clear, so I sat in the guesthouse that used to be mine, and I waited — and sort of half-heartedly tried to straighten up some of the mess that was Quinn. Lord. It must've been genetic.

I wasn't real clear on what I was even waiting for. Just waiting, I guess, like an old preacher for the deliverance day. When a pair of lights shone through the darkness and onto the driveway, I felt that deep, internal sigh, like maybe I was finally getting saved too.

He got out of the car, all tall and strong, and I'd been sitting in here blaming him just a little, though Lord knows it wasn't his fault. I guess the part of me that had been really scared that he wasn't coming was so relieved that when he walked through the door I ran to him and he held me tight. He hadn't left me. I wasn't alone.

Neither of us said anything for a long time, just letting that love sink in, letting it wash over us and cleanse us deep into even our very worst parts.

When Frank spoke, I wished he hadn't, because I didn't want to think about it. I didn't want to have to care about her. I wanted to be with him and our baby. We would have our own little family. Only, way deep down, even I knew that wasn't how this stuff works.

"She's an addict," Frank said.

"Who?"

"Your mom."

"Okay," I said, my voice noncommittal but my blood running cold. "Sure. That's fine. Whatever. I don't really care. I've been twenty-nine years without a momma, and I don't need one now."

"But it doesn't change the fact that your mother has been fighting this disease for your entire life." He took a deep breath and said, very calmly, "I don't want you to be upset, but she got into some trouble and was in jail. That's why she never came home."

I was pissed because I could feel myself starting to care just a little bit, not even really as her daughter but more as like an innocent bystander who was finding this story interesting. "So how's she out now?"

"Well, that's the tough part." He bit his lip. "She was only in jail for five years, but then it took her a few years to get the right help, and then she figured y'all wouldn't even want her back."

I felt it again, that thing that I was trying to distance myself from — hot and intense and piercing — pure, unadulterated anger.

He just kept on yammering. "She started looking for you a few months ago. For all of you. She just happened to find Charles first. She's doing really well now. She's been clean for almost ten years."

I could still feel it, that bubbling anger, mixed with probably the worst pain of my life. Well, maybe not as bad as when she left, but pretty bad all the same. My mother had been out of jail since the time I was sixteen years old, and she never even cared enough to look for me. And *now* she wanted us back? *I don't think so.* But I wasn't going to cry over any of it. Nope. So I yawned. "You know, Frank, she was dead this morning. She'll be dead again in a few years. I don't really have the energy for all this. I don't need a mom now. Don't want her either."

He didn't say anything, but I could tell he didn't approve. And I got that. Because I'd seen people I'd really loved go through that shit, and I knew they couldn't help it. I knew it wasn't their fault. But when it's your own mother, it feels different. Frank didn't understand. He hadn't lived through the mess I'd lived through.

I swore inside, like this little baby could hear me, that it didn't matter what happened, come hell or high water or something we didn't even know about yet, I'd do everything in my power to never leave it. Frank and I had been debating our wedding date, whether we should take a long time and plan a big wedding or put the pedal to the metal and do it as soon as possible. It all seemed really clear now.

"Frank," I said, "can we get married now?"

"Darling," he said, "I thought you'd never ask."

"I can't wait for you to see him," I said to

Frank for about the millionth time.

He squeezed my hand. "Me too, babe."

I walked up to the window where I normally checked in.

"Hello there, Miss Diana," Karen said. "You've got that glow. When's that baby coming?"

"Thanks," I said, looking down at my ever-expanding belly. I looked at Frank, and you would have thought his son had just pitched the winning game of the World Series for how tickled he was over all of it.

"You here to get the rest of Phillip's things?" she added.

I cocked my head to the side. "The rest of his things? What do you mean?"

Karen furrowed her brow. "Well, it says right here that somebody checked him out."

I felt myself starting to panic, my breath getting short. "What do you mean, somebody checked him out?" I could hear my voice getting louder and sterner.

She looked real worried. "I wasn't here, but it says that somebody checked him out. All his discharge paperwork's been filled out."

I looked at Frank and could see my panic mirrored in his eyes. "I'm sure there's an explanation, babe," he said. "Let's calm down."

Sure. Right. An explanation. "Charles," I said. "Charles got him."

Frank took my hands in his. "I'm sure he did. Let's try not to get so worked up. This has been a very stressful couple of weeks for you, and we need to remember what's important here, okay?"

I was pretty damn tired of everyone treating me like some sort of terminal cancer patient. I was pregnant. People were pregnant all day, every day without everyone all up in their grille about it.

I marched back to the car, Frank following right behind. I slid into his convertible and was barely in the seat before I had my hand on the phone and was dialing Charles.

"Hello," he answered. He sounded miffed. But I was thinking that if anybody should be miffed, it was me. Springing *her* on me like that. What was he thinking?

"I went to see Phillip, and he is gone." I was trying not to get hysterical again.

"Yeah," he said. "I got him."

"Well, thanks for telling me," I said, "the one who actually goes and sees him all the time." My voice was strained. "Did it occur to you that maybe I would be worried when I went to see my brother and he was gone? Did you think about that, *Charles*?"

"Geez, Diana. Chill out. Just come over

to the beach. I rented a house for me and the kids and Lanna, and I thought I'd bring Phillip too."

"That's all well and good, Charles, but in case you didn't remember, our brother has autism. New environments are very hard for him. Change makes him anxious."

"I know, Di. His doctor and I talked all about it."

That fired me up good, Charles acting like him and Phillip's doctor were just best friends when he'd met him maybe twice. "So what's your plan then? Just checking him out for the week and dumping him back in there?"

He sighed. "Why don't you come on over here, please."

I told Frank the address.

I crossed my arms, still huffing. "Just takes him away like I wasn't even going to know. I should have been there to talk him through it. I should have been able to warn him. He probably doesn't even know who Charles is. He's probably terrified."

I knew Charles only had Phillip's best interest at heart, but I was the one who had been there day in and day out. It was hard to let go of the control.

All of that floated away when we drove up to a plain yellow house, and Charles and

Phillip were sitting in rockers on the porch, just like old times, just like regular brothers and nothing had changed.

Maybe it was all the pregnancy hormones, but I could feel my eyes filling up right off. I didn't even think he'd seen me, but as soon as I got to the top step, Phillip said, "Diana," and then I started crying for real. There was something about seeing him living his life like he should have been all this time that killed me — and made me the happiest I'd ever been at the same time. He stood up, and I wanted to hug him so bad, but I knew I couldn't; I knew it would make him agitated. This moment was too perfect for that.

"Phillip." I said it quiet like I couldn't believe it was really him. I reached up real slow and so careful and held his cheeks in my hands. He didn't even flinch too bad. "Phillip, you're here."

"Yeah," he said, giving me that goofy grin of his that I loved so much. "Diana, you always come and see me. I love you. You're the best sister." He said it in his slow, stilted way, but to me it was music.

And I was all crying and a wreck again because I hadn't seen my brother out in the real world in so long.

He was rubbing his fingers together, and I

knew I was making him nervous, so I pulled myself together. "I love when you come see me," he said.

I looked at Charles, and he looked at me, and it was one of those moments that I think can only happen between siblings or lovers or best friends. We just looked at each other, and in that look was the happiness that our brother was back and doing good and the sadness for all the years we'd lost.

"We met with a new doctor a couple days ago," Charles said, standing up, "and she's got him on something that's really helped his anger and outbursts, something that helps him with being scared of people touching him, and another drug that's even helping the way his hands do. And they're getting him into occupational therapy, and there's a bunch of stuff we can do to help with his talking and stuff." He shrugged. "I mean, he can't take care of himself or nothing, but as long as he's got somebody to help him out, this might work."

Now I was confused. A new doctor. Occupational therapy. "Are you taking him back with you to Asheville?"

"Actually —" Charles started.

I heard the glass door swing open before I saw it. And there she was, that sorry excuse for a mother. She made me sick, even having to look at her. Her cheeks were sort of saggy and sallow, deep lines around her eyes and mouth. Her eyes, they looked tired but also hopeful all at once, world-weary like she'd seen too much for one life. Her hair was dark like mine with gray at the roots, tucked behind ears that stuck out a little too far. She was my same height but thin. I mean, I'm thin when I'm not pregnant, but she was too thin.

"Phillip is going to come live with me," she said. She hugged him sideways, and he laid his head on hers like she'd never left him, like she didn't disappear, like she didn't just throw him out to the wolves or the social service people, and I wasn't sure which one was worse. I was shocked. Absolutely shocked. Normally that much physical contact would be a trigger for Phillip. But I guessed even all these years later, she was his momma. She was still the only one who could really comfort him.

"Oh yeah. That's a great idea," I said as sarcastically as I could manage, grateful that Phillip didn't catch on to sarcasm. "Who do you think you are?" I could feel myself getting worked up again, but before I was all the way down that steamed-up road, Phillip in his simple, stilted way said, "Diana, this is our mom. She takes good care of us, remember?"

I felt those tears coming again, and I did remember. I did. That's why it was so hard. I remembered laughing with her. I remembered having fun with her. I remembered building pillow and blanket forts that nobody cared if we cleaned up and turning cardboard boxes into spaceships and sitting around that pitiful cast-off Christmas tree feeling happy together, feeling like a family. We didn't have a daddy, but we didn't need one. Momma, she maybe couldn't keep food on the table for us all the time, but she loved us.

"Diana," Mom said softly, "I know you're angry, and I know you're hurt, and being left alone as a child is the most unspeakable thing. I never in a million years would have left you on purpose. I went out of my mind, but I've cleaned myself up. It was a battle every single day, but every time I wanted to go back to that life of drugs and drinking and emptiness, I thought about you. I did it for you, for all of you. It has taken me until now to be totally sure that I will never go back to where I was again, to even hope that maybe I could be a part of your lives. I know I don't deserve it, but . . ." Her voice broke.

I guess, if I really got to thinking about it, I started to feel sorry for her then. A little

— not much. Because I already loved this baby so much. And I knew, way deep in my heart, even all this time later, that my momma, she loved us something fierce. But I didn't care about her excuses or nothing else. I was done with her.

I glared at Charles. "When this all goes down the tubes and she forgets to feed Phillip for three days, you just call me instead of dumping him back in that institution. You hear?" And I guess really what was going on inside me was fear. A whole lot of fear. Taking care of Phillip the way he needed and deserved to be taken care of was going to be a full-time job. Could Momma handle that?

Frank put his arm around my shoulders, and it was like I could hear him saying, *Calm down.*

I turned to walk away again, but Phillip said, in that childlike way of his that was so innocent and so profound, "Diana, our mom loves you. Don't you love her too?"

The tears were spilling over on my cheeks now. I loved her so much that I couldn't bear to have her back. The only way for me to deal with the pain of losing her the first time was to think that she was dead.

I thought about Gray and what she wouldn't give if she'd thought her mom was dead and she came back. Maybe if I could just be a little more like Charles or a little more like Phillip, a little more forgiving and a little simpler, maybe I could just let myself be happy and maybe we could be a family, all of us.

I didn't really want to, but it was like something outside me made me start walking right then, and I kept walking until I was back in the arms of my momma, and I was crying, and she was crying, and Charles was looking like his pig just won Best in Show at the fair. Everybody was happy, so I figured there wasn't much else to do but be happy too.

For a minute, I was that little girl again, the little girl whose momma left her, that eleven-year-old clinging to anybody who would even think about loving her or trying to fill up that huge, gaping hole that her momma leaving had put there. Frank coming back had helped, and that baby being in there had helped. But now my momma was here. She was back. It might have been twenty-nine years too late, but if this year had taught me something, it was that, in reality, it was never too late for anything.

Gray: Wicked Spin Serve

My strategic growth team on my old website (i.e. two of my college roommates and some guy that sold Greg weed) used to study *Baby Center* and *What to Expect When You're Expecting* when we were planning our marketing. They were masters of getting people to sign up for an email list and stick with it long-term, and in studying them, trying to gain some insight from their massive success, I'd read a whole lot of their articles.

Today, I wished I still had my App because, in my eight years of parenting, I'd rarely been this nervous. I needed some guidance.

I'd gone over and over and over it in my head. Andrew thought that maybe he should come too. But I knew this was something that should come from your mom. It didn't matter that Wagner loved Andrew, that he thought he was cool and enjoyed playing tennis with him. No one wants his mom to date anyone new. That's normal. But I rationalized that when he was all grown up with a family of his own, he would appreciate that I had found my own life and didn't spend every waking minute trying to control his. So, really, I could convince myself, I was doing this for him.

But when he walked through the back door, I lost my nerve. Completely. "Hi, cutie pie!" I hugged him and planted a big kiss on his cheek.

He rolled his eyes and said, "M-o-o-om."

I was so embarrassing. I know. I was also so tired because I had stayed up all night worrying about my son's reaction to his mother dating — and not just dating anyone, dating the hunky tennis pro. He walked to the fridge and pulled out a bottle of water and took a sip.

"So," I said. "What do you want for lunch?"

He looked around. "Where's Diana?"

"She's off planning her wedding." This was a good way to procrastinate. I could talk about Diana. "She's getting married here," I said, "on our front lawn. Isn't that so fun?"

He shrugged. "Yeah. That will be really cool. Hey, can we go out to eat or something?"

I gave him my most offended look. "You don't want me to whip up something delicious for you?"

"Sorry, Mom. I'm going to go play tennis with Johnny later, and food poisoning will really throw me off my game." He grinned, and I ran my fingers through that sweet head of blond hair, remembering how white it had gotten in the summers when he was a baby. But he wasn't a baby now. He was growing up, and he was going to figure out what was going on if I didn't tell him.

I picked my bag up off the floor and said, "Sure, bud. Where would you like to go?"

"I know it's kind of far, but can we go to Beaufort Grocery?"

Perfect. Fifteen whole minutes in the car to discuss the Andrew situation. I couldn't chicken out or else it would seem sort of strange when he came to Disney World with us. Only, after we got in the car and had talked about Wagner's week and the tests he had and who he wanted to invite to his birthday party, we were at the restaurant. *You can't talk about this stuff in a restaurant.*

After about the third bite of my overflowing cobb salad, I realized that if I didn't get this off my chest I was going to be too sick to eat.

"Buddy," I said, wiping my mouth, "I need to tell you something, and I want you to know that you are allowed to feel however you want about this, and we can talk about it and we will figure everything out. Okay?"

He looked at me like I had grown a unicorn horn and said, "Okay."

I took a deep breath. "I'm dating Andrew."

He looked confused for a minute. Then he lit up. "Andrew from the Straits Club?"

I nodded enthusiastically.

"Mom, that's awesome! Now he can teach me that wicked spin serve!" He took a bite of his sandwich and said, with his mouth full, "Johnny is going to be so jealous. Do you think you'll get married? I mean, he'd be the coolest step-dad ever!"

I raised my eyebrows. This really wasn't how I saw this conversation going. I wanted to be thrilled, but I felt like somehow that was the wrong reaction. "I don't know, buddy. There's a long way between dating and marriage. We're just enjoying each other's company for now."

He nodded. "Okay. Hey!" He brightened. "If you get married, do you think we could get our own ball machine?"

Seriously? "I don't know, sweetie. We'll see. Do you have any concerns or anything? Do you have any questions? Anything you want to talk about?"

He nodded, and I braced myself.

"Yeah. When's Diana going to be back?"

So that was it. A night of sleep that I would never get back and all that worry for absolutely nothing. He couldn't have cared less. I didn't know if it was because he was eight, and he didn't really get it, if it was because he liked Andrew so much, or if it was because my screw-up of an ex had paved the way, but, whatever the reason my son was so laid-back about my dating, I was eternally, unendingly grateful.

For about an hour. Then I called Marcy. "He didn't care," I said.

"He's an eight-year-old boy," she replied. "It will come to him little by little. He'll have questions. You'll be there. I'll be there." Then her voice took on an undeniable glee when she said, "Andrew will be there!"

We both laughed. Andrew would be there. He absolutely would. And for the first time in a long time — maybe ever — that didn't make me feel conflicted. Not even a little.

Chapter 23

Gray: The Very Best Year of Your Life

It was the day I had been dreading. Only, as the sun came up and the water gleamed outside the window and Andrew was beside me, I realized that maybe it wasn't going to be as bad as I thought.

Diana came by early and handed me a cake. "Before you get all sassy, I am still perfectly capable of making cake. I'm pregnant, not on my deathbed." She winked at me. Then she paused, her face changing. "This is bad timing," she said, "but can we forget it's your birthday for five minutes?"

I crossed my arms. "I'm trying to."

"I lied to you."

I could feel my heart racing. Diana had become one of my best friends in the world. More than that. She had become my protective big sister, the mother figure I had needed so desperately.

"Bill Marcus didn't fire me because of you."

Ohhhhh. I put on my most confident face and could feel myself blinking really fast. "Well, I'm disappointed that you felt you needed to lie to me, but I'm ready to move forward."

She studied my face. "Oh. So you did know."

"I have no idea what you're talking about."

She nodded. "Okay, so that's how you're going to play it?"

"It is indeed."

"Thank you, Gray. I'm grateful. Truly."

I could feel myself welling up, mostly because *I* felt grateful. She'd made me feel like I had somebody again, like I had a person to count on no matter what, to turn to with anything. But I didn't have to say it because I knew she knew. And now I knew I could trust her. I knew I could get what I had been thinking off my chest. "Di, you were right," I said.

She smiled. "Aren't I always?" She paused. "But why now?"

"I was so mad at my mom."

She nodded.

"I felt so abandoned by her. But you changed all that for me. You made me see that my mom wasn't choosing to leave me.

That's just how it ended up. You and your mom made me see that I had to move forward from those feelings, even if it was hard."

And it was true. "Well, good. That's something, right?" She got up and hugged me.

"You have helped my heart so much," I said.

"Okay," she said. "Enough. Birthday back on! Am I the first to tell you happy birthday?"

A scantily-clad-as-usual Andrew entered the room and said, "Oh, believe you me, Diana, I made sure this one had a very pleasant entrance into her thirty-fifth year."

I grinned at him. I wanted to tell him that I was actually beginning my thirty-sixth year, but that made me feel even older, so I let it go.

Diana said, "Gross," but I could tell she was amused.

The back door flung open and Price, Marcy, and Quinn trailed in with three bottles of champagne, singing, "Happy birthday to you . . ."

And, as a familiar figure came in on their heels, I squealed, "Trey!"

I leaned over on Andrew, who wrapped me up and planted a kiss on me. "Is this happening?" I asked.

"Oh, it's happening," he said. "But if it makes you feel any better, I think your ass is tighter now than it was at thirty-four."

"That would make *me* feel better," Marcy said.

Quinn popped a cork and said, "Yay for thirty-five-year-old asses!"

"Guys," I said, "I love y'all. But it's eight a.m. Could you come back at, like, noon?"

Price looked at me like I had lost my mind. "You'll need to be well lubricated by noon to ensure that the thirty-five depression doesn't set in." He handed me a glass of champagne and gave Andrew the up-and-down. "Jesus," he said. "I think I'm pretty much the most amazing thing ever, so to say *I'm* in a deep depression right now isn't an understatement."

I looked at him, confused.

"You left me for that?"

I examined Andrew's perfectly defined abs and muscular arms, precious dimples, and that gorgeous face. Damn, he was hot. It never got old. "It's not only because he looks like a model," I said seriously.

"Yeah," Andrew said, yawning. "She loves me for my brilliant mind."

We all had glasses. Quinn raised hers and said, "To my sister, the most beautiful thirty-five-year-old I've ever known."

We clinked glasses and drank. Well, Diana didn't drink.

"To my best friend," Marcy said. I braced myself for something raunchy or inappropriate, so it surprised me when she said, "Who is positively timeless."

Diana raised her eyebrows at me, also surprised.

Price raised his glass. "To Gray, who put me in my place by dumping me for Mr. Universe."

We all laughed. "Don't forget he's a professional athlete too," Marcy said.

"Thanks, babe. That really helps ease the sting."

Trey raised his glass. "To the woman who has taught me everything I know."

I put my hand on my heart. "I didn't," I said.

He shook his head. "You did."

Diana said, "Okay, I guess it's me." She sighed, tears welling up in her eyes. "To Gray, who took a woman off the street and gave her her life back. I'll never forget it."

I could feel the tears in my eyes too. I hugged her. "Diana, I didn't give you your life back. You did that all on your own." I wiped her tears and said, "And, truth be told, I feel like you're the one who gave me my life back."

"Couldn't talk you out of dating a damn teenager," she said.

"Hey," Andrew said.

I walked back over to Andrew, and he said, "Mine is simple. To Gray, the woman who was meant for me. May you look back on this as the very best year of your life."

"Hear! Hear!" Marcy shouted.

Eight sixteen. One glass of champagne down. Several batches of tears. Thirty-fifth birthday right on track.

I had the joyous pleasure of being treated to a lovely lunch by my precious son, my darling boyfriend . . . and my estranged husband and his fiancée. This was the new normal.

Late that afternoon, Andrew said, "You want to go over to the beach and go for a walk?"

I nodded. "Sure. I'm thirty-five now. Need to be getting those steps in."

A few minutes later, I was slipping my shoes off and putting my toes in the sand. Andrew and I walked for a while in silence. I'm generally not much of a reflector, but it seemed like a good time to reflect, with the waves crashing on the shore. My first thirty-five years had been good to me. College. An amazing company. A first marriage that had been pretty good. The best kid on earth. Andrew swooping into my life. *Next thirty-five,* I said to myself, *you have a lot to live up to.*

Interrupting my thoughts, Andrew said, "Well, my love, I've made peace with the fact that I'm never sleeping with a woman in her early thirties again."

I punched him lightly on the arm. "I'm grateful, you know. Like, on the one hand, I'm so grateful that I'm here, and I'm happy and alive and at this point in my life." I could feel my breath catching in my throat as I said, "You know, my brother didn't get this chance. So I'm thankful for every day." I paused. "But still, it's like the end of my youth or something."

"Yeah," he said. "I get it."

He stopped walking and looked at me, squinting from the setting sun in his face. He kissed me. "Gray, I'm going to love you until you're one hundred and fifteen. I swear I am."

I wanted to argue with him, but why? It was my birthday, and it felt nice.

He brushed the hair out of my face and kissed me again, lightly this time, so sweetly it almost brought tears to my eyes. "Do you want to marry me?" he asked. "I mean, I know you don't want to get married now.

But ever?"

Looking at him with the last light of the day glowing on his face, I thought I did. But did I? Really? I wasn't sure I wanted anyone to be that much a part of Wagner's life. I wasn't sure that I wanted to put myself in a position to be that close to someone again. So I said, very truthfully, "I don't know. Maybe one day?"

He nodded and winked at me. "Girl, I got nothin' but time."

We both laughed.

He sat down on the sand and patted for me to sit down beside him. "I knew from the first minute I saw you at the tennis court that I was going to be with you for the rest of my life. It was just this moment, and I knew that you were it for me." He grinned at me. "And you haven't made it easy, Gray. But I swore in that moment that I would do anything I had to do, that I would fight for you."

I leaned my head on his shoulder, the waves crashing to the shore making me feel so content. He handed me a rectangular box. Not a tiny one, thank God.

I smiled delightedly. "And what is this?"

"Just a little something," he said.

I tore into the paper, and when I opened it, there was a key with a gold circle around it. I picked up the bracelet first. It was a gold bangle that matched my others, with the most beautiful white opals, my birthstone, instead of diamonds or rubies.

I gasped. "How did you . . . ?"

"Let's just say I had to go pay Greg a visit to find out who made your other ones, and if you've ever questioned my love for you, there's no need to continue to do so." He paused and helped me slide the bracelet on my wrist. "I thought it might help you remember that you have to take care of yourself sometimes too."

I kissed him. "It is perfect. I've never loved anything more."

Then I raised my eyebrow and held up the key.

"You know those condos on the beach beside the Straits Club?" I nodded. "I bought us one."

I didn't want to ruin the moment, but there was no way I was going to move in with him.

"I just thought," he continued, "that with Greg and Brooke right next door, you might need a break sometimes. This way, you'll have a place to go when you need to escape." I didn't say anything, so he kept talking. "I hope that you'll marry me one day, and I figured we would live at your house, but in the meantime . . .”

I smiled at him. “There has never been a more thoughtful man. I love that you did this for me. It’s incredible.” Then I looked at him questioningly. “Are you growing pot in your basement?”

He laughed. “Let’s just say that I’ve been winning tournaments since I was eleven. My dad finally helped me invest some of my winnings.” He paused. “Speaking of, can we go to my parents’? They want to tell you happy birthday.”

I laughed at his enthusiasm. “Of course.” We were only a few houses away.

As I walked up the steps, feeling my way as the sun had all but set, I realized that the house looked dark. “I don’t think they’re home, sweetie.”

“Well, let’s just check.”

We were still holding hands as he opened the door and flicked on the lights.

It took me a minute to register that everyone I loved in the whole world was standing in that room shouting, “Surprise!” at me.

Wagner came running from the crowd, and I kissed him. He and Andrew high-fived. “Good work, little man,” Andrew said.

“Yeah, Mom,” Wagner said. “I was in charge of getting all the lights off and making everyone be quiet. Were you surprised?”

I looked at Andrew. "I have to say that everything about the last few hours has been a gigantic surprise. Yes."

June came over and gave her son a huge hug and kiss, and Henry did the same for me. June held both of my cheeks in her hands as she said, "I told you he loved you."

I eyed Price as he shook Andrew's hand. "You got yourself a good one here," Price said. He stood up very straight and added, "You know when she leaves *me* for you, she's in love."

We all laughed, and Price said in a shout-whisper to Marcy, "I can't say it enough: I wish he had been a little shorter or a little less good-looking."

I kissed my dad — and his new "companion," as he called her. Mary had brought him a casserole, and that was that. I took a deep breath and told myself that I was a big girl and that I wanted him to be happy. But my subconscious still whispered *hussy* when I looked her way.

She took my hand in both of hers and kissed my cheek. "Happy birthday, dear," she said. She smelled like Thymes Goldleaf. I loved that scent and had decided that it would most certainly be my fragrance of choice in my grandmother years.

I smiled tightly. "Thank you."

She patted my hand and said, "I just want you to know that I think your dad is a fine man, but my Timmy was the love of my life, my one husband, same as your mother was for your father."

I could feel my eyes welling, and I felt a little guilty for thinking she was a hussy.

"I know you're a grown woman," Mary said, "but I think even a grown woman needs to know that another woman is not trying to replace her mother — or be the new woman in her father's life."

I put my hand up. "You don't have to —"

She smiled warmly. "But I do, dear. I do."

And, well, she was right. I did feel better after that.

I would talk to them all that night. Dad and Quinn, Diana and Frank, Mary Ellen, Megan, and the rest of the girls. But as I kissed Andrew, to the delight of the onlooking surprisers, I realized that something my mom had told me all those years ago was true: it doesn't have to look perfect to be perfect for you.

Probably the best part of the whole night was when my dad came up and whispered in my ear, "How did my little girl get to be thirty-five?" I squeezed his hand, and I knew that things between us might not ever be like they were between my mom and me.

But we were trying. We were figuring it out. And, with family, I believe with my whole heart that that's what counts.

Despite my shock at the party, it was actually Greg who gave me the biggest surprise of the night. "I have a gift for you," he said, interrupting Dad. He put an envelope in my hand. I raised my eyebrow.

"I've accepted the terms of the settlement that, weirdly, Marcy negotiated."

I gasped. "No! Are you serious? Don't toy with me, Greg."

He laughed. "I'm not. And I signed your damn noncompete." He cleared his throat. "Brooke and I talked about it, and she helped me see that you're right. It's your company. You deserve it. I still want my money and—"

I shocked him silent by throwing my arms around him. It was like a million pounds had flown off my shoulders. No court date. No fighting. We could be finished. We could move on. "As a husband, you really sucked, but as an almost ex-husband, you're pretty great."

He was saying, "Um, thanks, I guess. . . ." as I turned to go tell Andrew.

Later that night, so late that it was actually early the next morning, Marcy, Quinn, Diana, and I were sitting in my kitchen.

"You want a snack?" I asked.

"Yeah," Diana said. "Always."

"But since we're getting a little" — Marcy dropped her voice and whispered, "older," then grinned at me — "maybe we could make it something healthy." I opened the sparse fridge, almost excited about taking Wagner to the grocery store the next day to fill it up. I was officially turning over a new cooking leaf. I took out a couple of apples and a jar of peanut butter.

"I can cut the apples," Quinn said.

"No!" we all responded at once.

She rolled her eyes. "Y'all have to relax about that. It's not like I'd stab *you.*"

Marcy examined the diamond on her left hand. As I'd suspected, she and Price had realized they were soul mates in short order. "So, should we have a double wedding?" she asked.

I laughed. "I'm not getting married, if you'll remember."

"Just a matter of time." She grinned.

I shook my head. I had told Andrew on the beach that I wasn't sure if I wanted to get married again. But with my past finally feeling like it might be in the past, I had to admit that it was a more tempting thought. "You are such a dork."

"You know," Diana said, "it might be real

good for you to marry Andrew now. He's young. He isn't set in his ways."

"Uh-oh," Quinn said. "Is Frank a little set in his?"

Diana rolled her eyes. "Well, you know, he has to have everything a certain way." She paused and smiled. "But he is still the love of my life."

I felt a familiar sadness that I couldn't name as I began to chop the apples, admiring the three bangles on my wrist. And then it hit me. "Wait. So when are you moving?" I asked.

"Moving?" Quinn asked. "I'm going to live in your guesthouse forever."

"Obviously," Diana said under her breath.

"Not you, Quinn. I've accepted that you're going to be living with me until we're ninety." I paused. "P.S. You're taking over Trey's old position at ClickMarket."

Quinn groaned, and I said, "It's happening. Embrace it, sister." Then I said, "Marcy, I meant you. Won't you be moving to Raleigh with Price?"

She shook her head and opened the jar, dunking a spoon into the peanut butter. "Hell no. My parents are so excited I'm finally getting married that they gave us the house as a wedding gift."

I raised my eyebrows. "No way! So we still

get to be neighbors?"

"Of course!"

We both squealed, and I handed her an apple slice.

"Shouldn't the pregnant woman get the food first?" Diana asked.

We each picked up an apple slice, touched them together as if we were toasting, and crunched.

"I knew all you needed was to find a man," Marcy said. She paused. "But maybe I was wrong about that."

"You were?"

"Yeah. I think you needed to find *the* man."

"You think I found that?"

"Do you?"

I just smiled. Because with best friends, as with true loves, there are some questions that don't need to be answered out loud.

It had been the scariest year of my life, no doubt about it. But I smiled anyway, looking at the three women who had defined these past few months for me. They had helped me in more ways than I could say. They had helped me move forward into my future. And I believed Marcy, Diana, and Quinn had moved forward into theirs too. We had given that to each other.

I thought back to two years ago, to a time

when I thought my spreadsheets could keep me safe and my color-coded calendar could give me the life I had always wanted. I knew now that, when it came to happiness, there were certain things you simply could not plan.

And I realized that sometimes when you're speeding through thin air, the brakes worn out and the engine shot, maybe it feels like you're falling. But, in reality, that's when you're learning to fly.

Diana: Exactly Where You Started

If somebody'd told me that Frank's mother would be the one zipping me into my dress that afternoon, I never would have believed it. But once she got on board, she got on board big. She was the one who'd bought me my wedding gown. My girls were kind of ill about that, but it was gorgeous. Plus I didn't care one thing about the dress.

I realized pretty quick that night that I didn't care about the rest of it either, not all the people and the tents and the flowers. I didn't care that the food was the finest money could buy. I didn't care if Frank carried me over the threshold of a single-wide and made love to me for the rest of my life on a pallet on the floor.

There will never be a moment that means

as much to me as when he stood there, tears running down his face, and promised to love and cherish me for the rest of his life. I had waited for that day for what seemed like an eternity. And there it was. All those people, they may have been watching us, but up there, in that moment, it was like it was just the two of us.

Maybe my baby would be born, and I'd realize that that moment was even better, but it was going to be a close call. Because if it weren't for this man and this love that we had shared for so very long, there wouldn't be a baby in the first place. That baby would know every day that its momma and daddy loved each other to the ends of the earth.

I never got that, never saw it. I was okay with it that my own momma was sitting in a chair in the fourth row listening to me pour my heart out to the man of my dreams. But mostly because she got Phillip set up with her in a nice new apartment on the outskirts of town that Frank, man that he was, furnished. She was taking really good care of him. It was the one single thing she could have done to open a door between us, that could make me be a part of her life. Because I knew for damn sure I would be there every single day for my brother, so that he had everything he needed and, way more than that, that we were giving him every advantage so he could live the bright life he was capable of having. Because there was so much underneath the surface, so much more. I saw that already. That part of me was grateful that our momma came back, that she was spending every hour she wasn't at work with Phillip, teaching him, bringing out the man we knew was inside.

Then it was my favorite part, where I slipped that plain gold band onto that beautiful finger and said, "With this ring, as a token of my love and affection, I thee wed."

And I do. I do with all my heart.

He kissed me, and then he did the cutest thing a man had ever done at a wedding: he leaned down and kissed my belly. Everyone laughed and clapped, and I felt mascara running all down my face, and I didn't care what Frank's momma said. Because that was the happiest I'd ever been in my whole life. And, damn it, I deserved it.

We walked back down the aisle, and I realized that I didn't even hardly notice the sun sparkling over the perfect water. Me and Frank, we could've got married inside one of them Pods Greg and Brooke had all over the yard while they were redoing that house next door.

They gave us a minute alone with each other before the photographer and the bridesmaids and everybody started running after us.

Frank wrapped me up in his arms and planted one on me like it might be the last. *But really,* I thought, *it's just the first.*

"There has never been a more beautiful bride," he said.

"Even though I'm all fat and pregnant?" I grinned at him. I was fishing for a compliment even though I'd never felt better.

"Diana Harrington, I am so in love with you that I can't even see anybody else."

I smiled. "Thank you," I said. "Thank you for all of this, for giving a poor girl this fancy day."

He kissed me. "Hey, Diana, I got a secret to tell you."

"What?"

"You aren't a poor girl anymore."

I guessed that was true, and I thought maybe it would feel weird, but it didn't take me long to figure out that me and Frank, we were as good as the same person now. It was only money, and that way he looked at me, I knew he'd give me anything I could ever imagine for the rest of my life. Good thing for him that the only thing I wanted was him.

Mary Ellen, Gray's party-planner friend who she'd hired as our wedding gift, came flitting in. "Okay, kids. People are gathered for your first dance."

Frank grinned. "You know, I don't think I can wait any longer."

Mary Ellen looked from Frank to me and said, "Well, I'm assuming you don't mean to consummate the marriage." She chuckled nervously.

"No," he said. "I've just got to know what this baby is."

He grabbed my hand and took off toward the stage where the band was playing. The singer stopped abruptly and handed the groom the microphone. "Thanks, everybody, for being here," Frank said. "I can tell you right now that this is the best day of my entire life. I have loved this woman for as long as I can remember, and it feels like today, right now, all my dreams are coming true." Everybody whistled and hollered. "Now, I think it's pretty clear that Diana and I don't care a whole lot about the proper order of things." He pointed at my belly, and everybody laughed. "We know we should be doing a dance or something right now, but we've waited too long to find out what this baby is, and we are as ready as can be. So what do you say we have us some cake?"

Everybody clapped, and there was this rush of bodies over to that beautiful, towering wedding cake that held a big secret we were dying to know.

"Are you sure you're ready?" I asked.

"Are you?"

I nodded. "Definitely."

Frank took the knife, held his hand over mine, and we cut right into that cake. As we slipped the slice out, I saw pink right away. "It's a girl!" I shouted.

Everyone applauded, and Frank kissed me. "I hope she's just like her momma," he said.

We fed each other and kissed again. All these people were standing around us. And the band was playing and the wine was flowing and the laughter was nearly deafening. But I realized that, even amidst the hustle and bustle and craziness of a wedding, Frank looked at me like I was the only woman in the world.

As Frank and I ran out the door, birdseed flying, I waited until we were past everybody and then I threw my bouquet high in the air. Not so somebody'd catch it. Just to celebrate. It felt like a victory; we'd done it. The wedding was over. Life could begin.

What I didn't know was that Gray, she was running behind me to tell me good-bye. And she caught the darn thing. We both doubled over, our arms around each other, a big puddle of laughter. "I told you I'm not ready to get married," she said between her gasps for breath. "Can't you just let it go?" It was the perfect end to a perfect night.

We'd decided to take our honeymoon in a few weeks because tomorrow was one of the other biggest days of my life. The Barnacle was opening — just for family and friends. But it was happening. It was starting. Momma was going to bring Phillip down, and he and I had practiced how he'd fix the baskets and then I'd hand them out the window. I was going to have something that was all mine, and I was going to be with Phillip again every day, just like I'd always dreamed.

There was no fancy trip Frank and I could have taken that could ever be that good. So Frank drove us back to our house, to that same place where we had spent so much time together as kids. As we walked down to the beach, down to our sand dune, Frank said, "Diana, it took some time, but, damn, babe. We made it, didn't we?"

He didn't mean because he'd just bought

me a new car or my diamond was pretty flashy or we had a nice house on the beach. He meant because we had this right-now moment with this beautiful baby girl in my belly and the two of us together and all this love. And we had this beach with its millions of grains of sand, and in the scheme of it, we were so small. So very, very small. Feeling small, that didn't hurt me like it used to. Instead, it made me feel blessed.

I reached over and took his hand, the one that was outstretched to me, that had been outstretched to me for more time than I liked to think about if I would have just reached over and taken it. "We have, sweetie. We've made it."

I'd had to be brave sometimes, and I'd had to be strong. My life, it hadn't been easy, and that was the God's honest truth. But right then, I realized that if I'd had it easy, I would never have known how good it could be. I would've taken all this for granted.

This same sand dune. This pink sunset. This gentle breeze. This loving man. We're always trying to move forward and keep going and make progress toward the next thing. But sitting on this dune, I realized that maybe I'd been wrong about all that. If this life — this simple, beautiful life — had taught me anything, it's this:

Sometimes we get right where we need to be by ending up exactly where we started.

ACKNOWLEDGMENTS

So much of *Feels Like Falling* is about true friendship, about family, the ones we're born with but, maybe even more so, the ones we choose. So I think, first, I have to thank my family. My husband and son, my two Wills, are the ones who make it possible for me to live my dream every single day — and, in all honesty, are my biggest one come true. My parents, Beth and Paul Woodson, are beside me every step of the way and always have been, helping me, encouraging me, and teaching me to never accept less than my very best. The older I get the more I learn what a rare gift that is. This is the first year I don't get to thank my grandfather, Joe Rutledge, but I think my grandmother, Ola, gets an even bigger thanks this year for always, always being a living example of how we carry on. One of her favorite sayings is, "This too shall pass," but I have a feeling losing my grandfather is the one thing that, for her, will never pass. And the lesson in that is an even greater one, one I am so grateful to have seen my entire life.

My author family, my Tall Poppy tribe, Mary Alice Monroe, Patti Callahan Henry, Kristina McMorris, Julie Cantrell, Heather Webb, Liz Fenton, Lisa Steinke, and Courtney Walsh: you teach me, you help me, you lift me up and you keep me going. Whoever said writing was a lonely profession has never met you!

Lauren McKenna, Elisabeth Weed, and Kathie Bennett, you are my triple pillars, and I simply cannot imagine my life, much less my work, without any of you. Lauren, thank you for being so convicted that Gray and Diana were the right next step and for working so hard to make sure that the story was the best it could be. Kathie, you exhaust me, and I love you for it. You have given me so much of what I had always imagined this life to be. And Elisabeth, your advice and guidance are invaluable. I couldn't be luckier to have you in my corner.

Olivia Blaustein, what a great first year we've had together! I can't wait to see what happens next.

Tamara Welch, I am convinced you can read my mind. And thank goodness. I couldn't do any of this without you.

Jen Bergstrom, thank you for being a champion for my work and for the incredible opportunities that you have given me. Michelle Podberezniak, I think you're a genius, the most organized human on earth, and you are so cool under pressure. Thank you for the millions of things you do that I know about and the millions more that I don't know about! Same goes for you, Maggie Loughran. You're amazing, and I'm so grateful for all you do.

To the BookSparks team, a big thank-you for taking a wish list and bringing it to life and for always thinking outside the box.

I absolutely would not be here without my fabulous, generous friends I have met through my blog, *Design Chic,* who have opened their homes, their shops, and their corners of the internet to my books and me. I am so grateful to each and every one of you. There are too many to name, but a special heaping helping of love to: Cynthia James Matrullo and Carolyn James McDonough from *The Buzz* and Diane James Home, Kathie Perdue from *Good Life of Design,* Tina Yaraghi from *The Enchanted Home,* Patty Day from *Patty's Epiphanies,* Katie Clooney from *Preppy Empty Nester,* Lisa Mende of *Lisa Mende Design,* Danielle Driscoll from *Finding Silver Pennies,* Debra

Phillips from Scentimental Gardens, Patricia van Essche from PVE Designs, Marty Oravetz from *A Stroll Thru Life,* Lucy Williams of Lucy Williams Interiors, Leslie Sinclair of Segreto Designs, Shelley Molineux from *Calypso in the Country,* Cindy Hattersley from *Cindy Hattersley Design,* Carrie Waller from *Dream Green DIY,* Kim Montero from *Exquisitely Unremarkable,* Lidy Baars from French Garden House, Lissy Parker from *Lissy Parker,* Cindy Barganier from Cindy Barganier Interiors, Celia Becker of *After Orange County,* Elizabeth Moles from *Pinecones and Acorns,* Nancy Powell from Powell Brower Home, Kelly Bernier from Kelly Bernier Designs, Rhoda Vickers Hendrix from *Southern Hospitality,* Teresa Hatfield from *Splendid Sass,* Karolyn Stephenson from *Town and Country Home,* Luciane from *Home Bunch,* Shelley Westerman from *Crazy Wonderful,* Laura Janning of Duke Manor Farm, Vel Baricuatro-Criste from *Life and Home at 2102,* René Zieg from *Cottage and Vine,* Shannon Aycock from *Pop of Pippi,* Addie Wemyss from *A Daily Dose of Class,* artist Kendall Boggs, Sandy Grodsky from *You May Be Wandering,* artist Jeanne McKay Hartmann, Michelle Black White of *Black,*

White and Kuhl, Darrielle Tennenbaum from *DD's Cottage,* Meredith Lewis, Rachel Sansing from *Rachel Emily Blog,* and Emily Lex from *Jones Design Company.*

I am so grateful for you, Stephanie Gray, and all your support both through The Book Lover Book Club and Porter Marketing Co. You're so talented! Grace Atwood, thank you for supporting my books for years through the Stripe and now, thank-you to Grace and Becca Freeman for allowing me to be a part of the *Bad on Paper Podcast Live.* I loved getting to share a stage with you! Ashley Bellman from NBC New York, you are proof that reading brings people together in extraordinary ways. Thank you for your kindness and generosity.

I am eternally grateful to the bloggers, reporters, reviewers, and book angels in my life. Andrea Katz, thanks for being a listening ear and fantastic support system since the very beginning. Susan Peterson and everyone in Sue's Reading Neighborhood, thanks for all you do and have done from day one! Kristy Barrett, Tonni Callan, and everyone at A Novel Bee, I love y'all and am so grateful for your book buzz. Bloom, our fantastic Tall Poppy Writer Facebook Group, is the best, smartest group of cheerleaders and book fans I know. Deirdre Parker Smith, Susan Roberts, Linda Brinson, Linda Zagon, Nicole McManus, Susan Schleicher, Megan Wessell, Monica Ramirez, Kristin Thorvaldsen, Bethany Clark, Meagan Briggs, Melody Hawkins, Kate Vocke, Heather Finley, Marlene Engel, Charlotte Lynn, Jessica Porter, Jaymi Couch, Erin Bass, Kinah Lindsay, Beth Ann Chiles, Amy Sullivan, Mary Ann Miller, Jessica Padula, Judith Collins, Reeca Elliott, Donna Cimorelli, Amber Shemanski, Kaylie Orlan, Amy Jones, Sarah Slusher, Kate Tilton, Jennifer Clayton, Kristin Jones, Jennifer Vida, Margie Durham, Anne Mendez, Mary Hundley, Jamie Rosenblit, Stephanie Burns, and Katie Taylor: I can't thank you enough for taking the time to review my books and share them with your readers.

And to my real life best friends: Kate McDermott, Drew Beall, Kate Denierio, Millie Warren, Lee Taylor, Leeanne Walker, Jennifer Amundsen, Haley Hall, Jessica Wilder, and Margaret Scott, thanks for teaching me the power of friendship, of how long it can last, of how real it can be, and of how it feels to have people in your life who have your back no matter what. Y'all are my family, and I couldn't love you more.

All the love to the booksellers out there who hand readers copies of my books, the librarians who recommend them, and the bookstore owners who have the passion to create havens for authors and readers alike.

Speaking of readers, thank you to mine. Someone asked me recently what I value most in a friend. My answer was that they show up when it counts. (And even when it doesn't!) Thank you for showing up for this, my sixth novel, and the ones that came before. People who read really are the best people.

ABOUT THE AUTHOR

Kristy Woodson Harvey is the bestselling author of six novels, including *The Southern Side of Paradise, Slightly South of Simple,* and *Feels Like Falling.* A Phi Beta Kappa, summa cum laude graduate of the University of North Carolina at Chapel Hill's school of journalism, her writing has appeared in numerous online and print publications including *Southern Living, Traditional Home, USA TODAY, Domino,* and *O. Henry Magazine.* Kristy is the winner of the Lucy Bramlette Patterson Award for Excellence in Creative Writing and a finalist for the Southern Book Prize. Her work has been optioned for film, and her books have received numerous accolades including *Southern Living*'s Most Anticipated Beach Reads, *Parade*'s Big Fiction Reads, and *Entertainment Weekly*'s Spring Reading Picks. She blogs with her mom Beth Woodson on

Design Chic, and loves connecting with fans on KristyWoodsonHarvey.com. She lives on the North Carolina coast with her husband and son where she is working on her next novel.

The employees of Thorndike Press hope you have enjoyed this Large Print book. All our Thorndike, Wheeler, and Kennebec Large Print titles are designed for easy reading, and all our books are made to last. Other Thorndike Press Large Print books are available at your library, through selected bookstores, or directly from us.

For information about titles, please call:
(800) 223-1244

or visit our website at:
gale.com/thorndike

To share your comments, please write:
Publisher
Thorndike Press
10 Water St., Suite 310
Waterville, ME 04901